1805200410

ABOUT THE BOOK

When the fog clears one December morning in Essex, the body of a teenage girl is discovered lying face down in a field.

The victim, Lily Monteith, was murdered in a peculiar and unique way — so unique that it could have only happened to her. As a result, the case quickly lands on DS Tomek Bowen's desk who, while trying to juggle his newfound life as a single parent to a thirteen-year-old daughter, must unearth the deadly sequence of events and bring the truth to light.

But as soon as the investigation begins, Tomek discovers Lily's death may be linked to a killing spree that has lain dormant for many years — with no one ever being brought to justice for it.

And, if that's the case, he fears another killing spree, this time years in the making, is yet to come.

JOIN THE VIP CLUB

Your FREE book is waiting for you

Available when you join the VIP Club below

Get your FREE copy of the prequel to the DS Tomek Bowen series now at jackprobynbooks.com when you join my VIP email club.

CHAPTER ONE

There was something in the air tonight. A rawness, an electrifying tingle that rippled through John Burrows Park. As though, when the clock had passed midnight, everything had reset. The street lights surrounding the park had flickered on and off and now gained a new lease of life. Even the wind seemed to bring with it new energy. More assertive, powerful, headed in a particular direction rather than a random bout of movement, clearing the clouds and bringing into view the myriad constellations of blinking lights overhead.

There was something in the air tonight, all right.

And in particular the smell.

The smell of horny teenagers doused in litres of perfume and cologne, the smell of alcohol lacing their breath. The smell of desperation, indecision, desire.

And soon to be the smell of death.

He was watching them from afar, from the other side of the park, shrouded by a canopy of low-hanging trees on a bench. Their screams and shouts were audible from here, the sounds rolling over the undulating field, carried by the determined wind. Their every word tingled his body.

But one in particular.

Hers.

The loudest, liveliest.

She was wearing next to nothing. A skimpy little black skirt with a white crop top. A brave yet naïve choice in this weather. The temperature had dropped below zero and a thin layer of frost was beginning to settle on the grass and park bench. He fought to hide his breath from fogging in front of him, lest he be spotted. But in hindsight it was a pointless endeavour; they were too busy enjoying themselves, too busy getting drunk as kids their age were wont to do, for them to even give him a blind bit of notice.

Still, it didn't hurt to be careful.

He checked his watch. Nearly 1 a.m. With any luck they would be leaving soon having succumbed to the elements and been forced to seek refuge, shelter in some warmer place.

Timing was key. Timing was perhaps the most important part of tonight. Too soon and he risked being spotted. Too late and he risked losing her, losing his one chance to get this right entirely. Like Goldilocks, he had to time it to perfection.

As he waited, he closed his eyes and let the electricity in the air radiate through his body and tingle his senses.

It had been a while. So long. Too long, in fact. A part of him had almost forgotten what it was like. The hunger, the sensation, the euphoria.

But it had been a necessary evil, the wait. Everything had to be prepared meticulously. Groundwork needed to be laid. Steps needed to be traced. Every corner of his story needed to be accounted for.

Tonight was the night he was going to kill. And he needed to make sure he could get away with it.

Time passed as it always did: slowly, especially when waiting for something to happen. Watched pot, and all that. It was a little after 1:30 a.m. when the group decided they'd had enough of the cold. As he watched them shuffle towards the edge of the park, he lumbered off the bench and trailed behind them, masked by the darkness. Their cheers and laughter continued to bounce off the houses that surrounded the park. Shortly after, the group headed along a narrow path that led onto the main road.

He knew he didn't have long for this next part, so he hurried the hundred-metre distance to the alleyway a little farther down and raced to his car. Jumping in, he ignited the engine, dimmed the headlights and then switched on the heaters. Full blast. In his absence, the chill of the night had choked the car and encased it in a thin layer of frost.

Similar to what he had planned for her tonight.

He gripped the steering wheel, massaging it with his gloved fingers. Latex, the colour black to match the steering column and his coat. Not wanting to waste any more time, he pulled out from behind the parked car and started towards the group. By the time he drove past them, standing at the mouth of the other alleyway, they were still talking, huddled together, protecting themselves from the cold.

Not yet. Too soon.

He would have to wait and come back, linger in the background a little longer, somewhere he could watch without being seen. The same way he had done for the past few days. He'd been watching her for a while, monitoring her movements, witnessing her go out with her friends the same way she had done tonight. But each time there'd been a problem, a distraction. She'd never been on her own, always with someone, always connected at the hip to her friend or that boy who appeared to be infatuated with her. Tonight was proving to be no different. With the exception that he could feel it in the air. Something different.

He rolled down his car window and listened. The voices were distant and he was only able to catch the end of the conversation.

'You gonna be all right getting home?' one of the boys asked Lily.

'I'll be fine. I'll walk. I only live round the corner,' she said with an air of defiance about her that he admired.

He waited a few minutes for the group to disappear in the other direction and for her to come towards him. Once she'd passed him on the other side of the road, he started the engine, massaging the thick rubber of the steering wheel. Then he turned in the road and caught up with her two corners later.

Sensible girl, he thought, sticking to the main roads, staying in the light, making herself as visible as possible. He slowed the car down and pulled over beside her, wheels turning, car coasting. He lowered the window and leant across as much as he could, keeping one eye on the road and the other on her short skirt.

'Lily? Is that you? Lily, are you all right?'

Her reaction was immediate – and exactly as he'd expected. At first, she had jumped at the sound of her name but hadn't looked at him, didn't dare look at him. Then she'd kept her head down, eyes focused on the pavement in front of her, her hand shielding her bag and pulling it closer to her body. But as she began to realise the voice was friend not foe, she'd relaxed, lowered her hand, and turned.

'You shouldn't be walking around here at this time of night,' he told her. 'There are strangers and weirdos about.'

Yes, yes there were. Except they weren't always on the pavement; some of them preferred a car as their mode of transport.

'Are you calling me a weirdo then?' she said, a hint of playfulness in her voice.

'Don't start putting words in my mouth.' He brought the car to a steady stop, surveyed his surroundings and then continued, 'Come on, I'll give you a lift. You shouldn't be out here on your own. It's a jungle out here.'

'And there are creepy-crawlies all over the place.'

You bet.

Lily slipped down the kerb and hopped into the car, bottom first. As she swivelled herself in, her skirt rode up her thigh, and he forced himself not to look.

There would be plenty of time for that later if he needed it.

'What are you doing around here at this time of night?' Lily asked after he'd pulled away.

He turned to her, eyebrows knitted together. 'I could ask you the same thing. And I could even ask why you smell of alcohol.'

Her face flushed the colour of her lipstick, an expression that made her look five years younger.

'Fair point,' she conceded.

'If you must know,' he replied, 'I was visiting my mother. She's in hospital. I only get to see her at this time of night, otherwise, I won't get to see her at all.'

'I'm so sorry,' she said. 'Is she okay?'

'Not really, but it's all right. It is what it is. I've come to terms with it.'

They drove the rest of the journey in silence. That was until they reached the cul-de-sac where Lily lived. Instead of turning into her road, he continued ahead, manoeuvring his way around the parked cars.

'We just missed my road,' she said, turning her head to look back.

He remained silent, eyes focused on the street. His hand deftly moved to the control panel on the side of his door and locked the car.

'Where are we going?' Lily asked. The fear and anxiety were obvious in her voice. Just the way he liked it. 'Where are you taking me?'

'Detour.'

'Where?'

'A little place I know.'

'What place?'

She was asking too many questions. He didn't want questions. Didn't like them.

It was time for her to shut up now. He slammed on the brakes, grabbed her seatbelt clip to keep it in place and to stop her from undoing it, and then punched her in the throat. As she gagged and gasped for air, he reached into his bag in the backseat and pulled out a thin latex glove. Black, similar to the ones on his hands. Then, keeping one hand over her mouth, pinning her head against the headrest, he began to stretch the glove over her face, all the way to the back of her head.

She thrashed violently, her nails swinging in his direction, but each time they missed. And then she began to realise what was happening to her.

What *would* happen to her.

The last thing she did before he knocked her out was scream until her lungs had almost burst.

CHAPTER TWO

‘Can I get this?’
    ‘No.’
‘But it’ll—’
‘No.’
She turned to face him as her last resort. The puppy-dog eyes.
‘Still no.’
‘But I think it’ll look nice!’
‘I think a Ferrari would look nice, but you don’t see me buying one.’
‘Only because you can’t afford it.’
Tomek ignored the jibe and sighed heavily. Then he reached out his hand for the object in hers and hesitated. A look of excitement and anticipation blossomed on her face.
‘Oh my God, *really*?’ she said, unable to contain herself.
Without saying anything, Tomek took the Christmas decoration from her and placed it back on the shelf with all the other Christmas trees that had been designed to look like marijuana leaves. Beside it was an assortment of juvenile and immature Christmas decorations that Tomek admired and saw the funny side of, but would never admit to: a figure of Father Christmas bent over flashing his arse; of

Jesus smoking a spliff, offering the Peace sign to passers-by; and a black Santa playing basketball.

Christmas for him was as much a waste of time as all the other holidays. Valentines, Halloween, Easter. Though he came from a devoutly religious Polish family, he wasn't the only one to veer away from the societal and cultural expectations his parents, namely his mother, had placed on him. His older brother Dawid, since becoming a dad and creating a family of his own, had moved away from the religious aspect and more towards the capitalist one. Whereas Tomek was neither. It wasn't because he didn't believe in it or because he didn't like the idea of receiving gifts every year. It was because, historically, he'd never been able to enjoy the Christmas season for what it was. He knew that it was a time for family, for laughter, for togetherness. But when he'd lived alone for so long, and been shut out from the family invitations to his parents' dinner every year, it was a little difficult to get excited about it.

There was nothing worse than someone from the opposite end of the spectrum. Someone who was Christmas-crazy. Someone who started listening to George Michael and Mariah Carey months before it was socially acceptable. Someone who obsessed over the non-existent Christmas decorations in his flat.

'You don't have to be such a...' Kasia thought of the kindest word possible. 'You don't have to be such a *bag of poop* about it.'

'I'm not.' He looked down at the trolley in front of them and the several bags of shopping in his hands. 'Don't you think we've got enough?'

He'd already dropped a couple of hundred quid on a brand-new box of tinsel; a ginormous box of forty different-coloured baubles; a wreath that looked like it would be better suited in a bird's nest high up in the trees somewhere; over ten metres of flashing lights that he would be the one tasked with putting his life at risk to drape over the windows outside the top of the house no doubt; and a brand-new Christmas tree that he instantly regretted purchasing. Foolishly, he'd lied and told Kasia that he bought a fresh one every year to save the world from plastic-waste, but then she'd reminded him that killing live trees was harmful to the environment and that a plastic one was reusable and more sustainable. He had argued that not purchasing one in the first place, and even not buying *any* of it, was the greatest step they could have taken towards sustainability, but he'd lost that battle, and so the plastic tree had found its way into his arms, along with the extra few kilos added to his carbon footprint.

'You can never have enough, Dad,' she replied. 'Mum and I used to go all-out. We'd have Christmas-themed everything: gingerbread houses, picture frames, chocolate tins. We'd cover the house in tinsel and stick snowmen and reindeer cut-outs to the windows. We even had a giant Santa out the front in the garden, with fake snow all over the grass.'

Yeah, and your mum probably had the drug money to pay for it all.

Whereas he didn't. He had his measly sergeant's wage that was rapidly depleting – what with the recent home move, feeding his daughter, paying for school clothes, and all the other expenses that came with having a child you knew nothing about.

'I think we've got enough for now...' he told her as he ushered the trolley away from the wall of decorations and made his way to the cash desk.

'You're such a Scrooge.'

'That's unfair,' he replied, wondering if she knew the whole story of Dickens' tale. 'At least I've *spent* money. This is the most decorations I've had in about twenty years.'

'You must have been such a sad little man,' she said. If she knew the damage those words could have done to someone other than him, she didn't show it. There was no wry smile, no hint of sarcasm. Fortunately for her, he was thick-skinned and had received much worse in his time – from kids much younger.

They came to a stop at the end of the queue which had already grown to a ridiculous length in the short time since he'd last looked.

'I'm more than willing to take it all back if you want?'

She placed a concerned hand on his arm. 'No. Please, no. We can't have Christmas without a Christmas tree or the decorations.'

'Then I suggest—'

He'd lost Kasia's attention. Something had distracted her. A festive-themed plant, possibly. Or a fire poker covered in tinsel. He didn't know. It all looked like the same shit to him. But whatever it was had captivated her. Without saying anything she hurried away to a table, reached for something and then brought it back triumphantly, like a cat who'd just brought back a rat for its owner. Tomek looked down and saw a ceramic plate that had been stencilled with a garish illustration of Santa climbing down a chimney.

'What the fuck is that?' he said, his voice rising a few octaves.

'Don't they look so cute?'

'No. They're the sort of thing you end up buying and giving away to charity because you've finally come to your senses and realised how stupid the decision was to buy them in the first place.'

The perplexed look on her face told him she had no idea what he was talking about.

'Fair enough,' he said. 'That's a specific example, but they're still horrible. And we're *not* getting them.'

'But we *need* Christmas plates!'

'No. We *need* air. We *need* food. We *need* water. We don't *need* these. Besides, we're only going to use them once a year.'

'Exactly. Special occasions. At least they'll get used. And if they get used then they won't end up in some charity shop like you said.'

Tomek opened his mouth to respond but couldn't. She'd got him. Used his own words against him. He couldn't fault her for that. Nor, as it turned out, could the woman standing in front of them in the queue.

'I think she's got a point,' the woman said, inserting herself into their private conversation. 'They do look really nice. And they go with the rest of the things you've bought.'

'Great. Thank you for your unwanted input.'

Tomek rapidly became aware that he couldn't shout at this nosy bitch in front of Kasia, so instead he would just have to keep it to passive aggressive smiles and an even more aggressively passive look on his face.

'You're welcome,' she said with a grin, and as she returned to whatever she was doing in the queue, she gave Kasia a sly wink.

'I saw that...' Tomek whispered to his daughter.

'So... Can we? Can we get them?'

Tomek sighed deeply. He'd lost the battle, one battle of many. But he wouldn't lose the war. Actually, no. Who was he kidding? Of course he would. She had him wrapped around her little finger and she wasn't letting him go.

Not anytime soon, at least.

Shortly after they paid for their bits, they left John Lewis and started back towards the car on the other side of Chelmsford High Street. Outside, the sky had turned a darker shade of slate, and a light rainfall had begun to trickle. He'd only been to the area for shopping a few times in the past, and it was all fairly new to him. But Kasia knew exactly where to go and what to do, even though she'd never been there before. It was as though she had an innate sense of direction that pointed her towards her favourite shops, like a bloodhound capable of sniffing out the smell of H&M and Primark from half a mile away.

As they sauntered towards the car, bracing themselves against the cold, Tomek surveyed his surroundings. Observing the middle-aged woman on her own with bags from the various chains, rushing to the next one, he wondered what was inside, what she'd spent her money on. What treats her relatives would be ungrateful for. Whether they were the right things or not.

That reminded Tomek about something.

'What do you want for Christmas?' he asked, coming to the sudden realisation that he'd maybe left it a little late. A few weeks to go... he'd be all right, wouldn't he?

'What do you mean?'

'For Christmas. Presents. You know... you get them at this time of year... What do you want?'

She offered him a confused frown, as though she'd just eaten a sour sweet and was trying to save face. 'You want me to, like, give you a list or something?'

'Ideally, yeah...'

'But... That's not... That's not how you do Christmas.'

'Yes, it is. You tell me what you want. I buy it. You receive it. You're happy. I'm happy. Everyone's a winner.'

'But where's the fun in that? Where's the surprise?'

'This isn't Secret Santa, Kasia. If I'd wanted to get you a shitty gift you're gonna throw away after five minutes, I'd have bought you some more plates. I'd rather buy you something you want, rather than guess. I'm not very good at guessing. I need to be *told*. You need to give me a list.'

She considered for a moment, scratching beneath her eye.

'What about some AirPods?' she asked as they crossed a small bridge over the River Chelmer that ran through the town.

'No. Definitely not. Do you know how expensive they are? And you're only going to lose them at school. Think again.'

'So I can't get anything I want then, can I?'

'I never said that. I said give me a list, and I'll get what I can from it—'

'But you didn't say that bit either.'

She'd got him again. Used his own words against him. She was becoming too clever for her own good. And he would have to think hard about what he said around her in future.

They arrived at the car. Tomek dropped the bags and Christmas tree onto the ground and unlocked the car.

'Well, I'm telling you now, give me the list of things you want and I'll get what I can, and I'll make it so that you won't know which ones I get you... *There's* your surprise.'

AS SOON AS they got home, before they even considered anything like what they were going to have for dinner, Kasia insisted that they spend the rest of the evening turning the flat upside down and transforming it into a cheaper, smaller (but by no means less tacky) version of Santa's Grotto. It took them a total of two hours. And in that time they'd managed to assemble the tree and equip it with all the tinsel, baubles, lights, and other unnecessary decorations he'd purchased. They'd also placed a wreath, complete with glittery balls and plastic leaves that fell off every time Tomek breathed, onto the front door to the flat. Tomek had been insistent on not placing it on the outside front door because he'd said that it was a beacon for criminals and thieves, signalling that there were expensive gifts and a lot of money somewhere in the flat. Neither were true for him at the moment, but he didn't particularly want anyone thinking they could come into his home whenever they pleased.

The biggest and toughest task that had befallen them as they'd redecorated the flat, was making space for the Christmas tree itself. The six-foot tall behemoth, which Tomek thought was larger than any Christmas tree needed to be, and was certainly larger than *they* needed it to be, required at least four square metres of space in a room that was barely large enough for both of them (even though they'd just upscaled from an even smaller property), it meant all the furniture needed moving. When Tomek had originally bought the flat a few weeks before, he hadn't factored an artificial plant into his limited interior designing capabilities. Now, after everything had been moved, the room looked considerably smaller, and the feng shui of the place was all off-kilter. Not that he believed in any of that type of stuff, he just used the words to make her feel guilty about having to move it all about.

'Now my neck's going to hurt when I'm watching the TV,' he told her. 'And my neck's not made for that sort of angle.'

'I don't think anyone's is—'

'And it's going to make my back pain even worse.'

'You didn't have it two minutes ago.'

Tomek ignored her and instead massaged the area of his lower back that he'd felt twang as he'd lifted the tree into place.

'Why are you being so Scroogey?' she complained.

'I'm not. I'm sorry. I was just joking. My back'll be fine.' He massaged it a little harder to alleviate the pain. 'Are you happy with it?'

'Yes.'

'Then so am I.'

To celebrate, Tomek ordered a pizza from their local takeaway. A pepperoni for him, full of flavour and delectable saturated fats. And a boring four cheese for her, without the gluten, without the flair, and without any of the fun. Their usual pizza takeaway place, the only one they ever used, was familiar with Kasia's nut allergies, and so made the joyless pizza especially for her. At a premium, of course. Away from all the other ingredients that may contain nuts, as much as possible.

As they sat in the living room that now lacked any sort of feng shui, Tomek switched on the television and tuned in to a nature documentary. David Attenborough was teaching them about the animals of the African Savanna. Lions, hyenas and all other manner of beasts prowled along the desert, hunting, stalking and killing.

Until the screen turned to an image of a herd of docile buffalo, minding their own business, grazing on the grass and mud along an oasis.

'Do you think you could fight a cow?' Kasia asked, surprising him. He turned to face her. She'd finished her slice of pizza and was staring at him intently, a look of seriousness on her face.

'I think you're going to have to ask me that again. I don't think I heard you properly...' he replied, as he slowly dropped his half-eaten slice back onto the plate.

'A cow. Do you think you could fight one?'

Turns out he'd heard her absolutely fine the first time.

'What sort of question is that?'

'Well, when we were at the farm the other day on our school trip, Billy Turpin squared up to one of the cows and raised his fists to it. Miss Wells had to pull him away.'

So many questions. So many things he wanted to say, comments he wanted to make.

He'd totally forgotten that she'd gone to the farm for one of her geography school trips. Though he did remember seeing the letter for it and thinking that they were a bit old to be seeing cows and goats and chickens in secondary school. That it was something more suited for those in primary school. Evidently not. And evidently, Billy Turpin didn't look out of place there.

'Billy Turpin sounds like a bit of an idiot,' he replied.

She looked visibly offended. 'He reckons he could fight one and knock it out.'

Tomek shook his head, trying to grasp the conversation. 'Fighting a cow and knocking it out are two separate things. Anyone can *fight* a cow, but that doesn't necessarily mean they'll win. And it certainly doesn't mean they'll knock it out.'

'But could *you* do it?'

'I've never thought about it. I can honestly say the thought has never crossed my mind.'

And he was worried because, now that it had, he wouldn't be able to think of anything other than a cow on the receiving end of his fist.

'What did Miss Wells say?' Tomek asked.

Kasia shrugged, as though she'd suddenly lost interest in the conversation. 'She called Billy stupid.'

'Well, she's got that right. Billy sounds like a bit of a tit. Stay away from Billy.'

Kasia fell silent, her gaze falling to the carpet just before the television stand. She crossed her legs on the sofa and placed both hands in the gap between her legs.

'Well, actually...' she began, unable to meet his eye. Hesitation laced her words. 'I was going to ask you...'

Uh-oh. Tomek could sense where this was going. The B word. Boys. In particular, *a* boy. A singular boy who she considered to be a cut above the rest. A boy who thought he could fight a fucking cow.

'Would Billy be able to come over one afternoon after school?' she said shyly. Once the words were out, her body tensed even more and she remained frozen on the sofa. 'Just to watch some TV or something...'

Or something. Tomek knew exactly what that *something* was. It was happening right in front of him on the television screen. Two wild beasts mating, the male lion mounting and preparing himself to inseminate the lioness.

Just to watch TV or something...

His imagination ran wild as paranoia and overprotectiveness set in.

'I'll have to think about it...' he said. 'But I'm not keen on the idea of the two of you being at home on your own. I don't need to tell you about the birds and the bees, do I?'

'Ew, Dad! No, gross! I'm thirteen! Billy's just a friend. He's a boy... *friend*,' she explained, placing extra emphasis on the word *friend* to remove any further doubt he may have had. 'Besides, we already know all that from school. They've been teaching us that for years. Please don't tell me how babies are made.'

'If you two are just friends, then you shouldn't need to worry about me telling you how that sort of stuff works.'

To that, she had no response. And that made him even more concerned.

'I don't want Billy coming over,' he told her. 'Your evenings are busy enough with your Polish lessons and your homework. I don't want him distracting you any more than he probably already is in your classes... or at the farm.'

CHAPTER THREE

As he'd suspected, the question hadn't left his head. The stupid, idiotic and frankly infuriating question. Could he fight a cow? Of course he couldn't. He knew he couldn't. It was ridiculous to think so. The animal outweighed him ten to one. And out-powered him at an even higher ratio. But he was more agile... more nimble. He had the advantage of two legs over four.

Still, it was a fucking ridiculous thing to lose sleep over.

And yet the thought wouldn't leave him. So much so that when he got to Southend CID Headquarters the following morning, he felt like it warranted further discussion. A wider conversation with adults, those who possessed more logic and intelligence than a thirteen-year-old pubescent boy.

He'd been sitting at his desk for over an hour, working his way through the leftovers of yesterday's work, when he'd finally summoned the courage.

'Sean...' Tomek began, suddenly experiencing the same insecurity and fear Kasia had shown the night before when she'd asked him the question.

'Yes, mate,' DS Campbell replied.

'Got a question for you...'

Sean stopped what he was doing and turned to face Tomek. In the past couple of days, they'd had a re-jig of the seating plan in the office, and now they were only separated from one another by a desk. It was nice to be so near to his closest friend; it made for a more conducive and productive work environment. The only downside was the inane and constant chatter. Like being in the school classroom, sitting at the back, disrupting the rest of the class.

'This sounds important,' Sean said.

'It's not,' Tomek replied. 'Honestly. It's fucking stupid, is what it is.'

Sean grunted and leant forward. 'You really know how to sell it, mate. You've got me on the edge of my seat.'

Tomek wished he hadn't; DC Rachel Hamilton and DC Nadia Chakrabarti behind Sean had turned to face him as well, wedging themselves into their discussion.

He breathed in deeply before asking the question.

'Do you think you could fight a cow?'

There was a brief moment, a fraction of a second of absolute silence, the calm before the storm, right before the room erupted into a cacophony of laughter.

'That is possibly the best question I think I've ever been asked,' Sean said after he'd managed to control his laughter.

'And I hope your response is as good as the question,' Nadia said, weighing in.

Sean knitted his fingers together, stretched his arms, and clicked his knuckles in one fluid movement. 'I think I could...' he said. '*Easy.*'

'Easy?'

'Yeah,' he said with a shrug. 'I get that they're big n'all, but they're not very fast. And if I got some time to train, I reckon I could do it in a couple of punches.'

The girls laughed.

'Of course you do,' said DC Hamilton. 'You men and your fucking egos.'

Sean wagged his finger in the air. 'Ego's got nothing to do with it. What it all boils down to is preparation, training, and a decent right hook.' Sean's face dropped as though a thought had instantly occurred to him. 'Question: does the cow get to train?'

'What?' Tomek hadn't expected a counter question, a question that would lead them further down the rabbit hole of cow-punching.

'Does the cow get to train for the fight as well?'

'I have no fucking idea. How am I supposed to know?

'You're the one who asked the question, mate.'

Tomek scratched the side of his head. 'Erm. I guess so. Yeah. I mean, that's only fair.'

'Well, in that case, no. No chance. Cow wins every day of the week.' Then Sean turned to Nadia and Rachel, who were sitting on the opposite side of their bank of desks, and said, 'Told you, ego's got nothing to do with it. It's all about logic and whether you back yourself.'

'And in this instance, you clearly don't back yourself,' Nadia said, as she bounced on the suspension of her desk chair with one hand on her baby bump.

'Not if the cow has the same training as me. I'm not stupid.'

'Clearly,' she said sardonically. Then she turned to Tomek. 'What other stupid questions have you got going on inside your head?'

It was then that Tomek felt compelled to tell them the story behind the question. He couldn't have them thinking he spent most of his free time fantasising about getting into scraps with livestock. None of them, however, seemed to believe him and remained convinced that the question was his own.

'You can't keep using Kasia as an excuse for things anymore, Tomek,' Nadia told him.

'I'm not!' he protested. 'She even asked me if she could have a boy come over after school. The same boy that asked the stupid fucking cow question in the first place.'

'Wow,' Nadia said. 'She's bringing boys over already, is she? I thought you had at least another year or two before that started happening.'

'Before *what* started happening?'

Nadia's face warmed. Then she made two ovals with her thumbs and forefingers and began prodding them together, making kissing sounds as she did so.

'Shut up,' he said, shaking his head profusely. 'It's not happening. Nothing's happening. Because she's not allowed to have him over. She's not allowed to have anyone over. There, it's decided.'

'Don't you trust her?' Rachel asked, her voice soft and quiet as though she were personifying the voice of reason.

'It's not her I have a problem with,' he replied. 'It's Billy-the-cow-fighting-hero-Turpin that I have the problem with. Anyone who thinks they can fight a cow shouldn't be anywhere near my daughter... Including you, Sean.'

The man threw his hands into the air in dismay. 'Why've you gotta bring me into the conversation like that?'

Before Tomek was able to explain himself, he noticed DC Martin Brown hovering on the edge of the conversation, a note in his hand. Martin had joined the team only a few weeks prior. Transferred from Colchester, Essex Police's Headquarters, with the team's newest inspector, Victoria Orange. Since his arrival, Tomek had spent little time getting to know the man. He seldom joined them on their evenings at the pub after a shift, nor did he engage in many of their office discussions.

'Sir,' he began after waiting patiently for Tomek's attention.

'Morning, Martin.'

'Here's a question for you, Martin—' Sean started.

Tomek shot his friend a look that ordered him to stop talking, which Sean swiftly did.

Then he turned his attention to the man with long hair tied in a ponytail and a beard that Tomek was more than envious of.

'Yes, Martin. How can I help?'

'I've just had a call from control, sarge. A body's been found in John Burrows Park in Hadleigh.'

CHAPTER FOUR

December sixteenth. Just over a week to go till Christmas. What was supposed to be a happy, festive and enjoyable period had now become a nightmare for one family.

John Burrows Park was situated a few hundred yards from the A127, the road that linked Southend to Rayleigh and beyond. On one side of the field was a set of tennis and basketball courts, and on the other was a row of football pitches, the white lines of which had faded over the years. In the summer, the park and, in particular, the tennis courts were filled with children from the local schools coming to chill, chat and play some sport. Now, however, in the blistering cold of winter, the park had emptied, and the knots of friends had been replaced with piles of fallen leaves on the grass.

The body had been found on the northwest side of the park, on the opposite side to the courts. Slumped in the bushes, limbs resting at various angles. A ghostly shade of white beneath the grey clouds overhead. Rain had lashed at the face for so long that very little make-up remained on the girl's face. She was wearing a short black skirt and a small white crop top that wouldn't have been warm enough even for summer. Her hair was tied in a ponytail, her nails had been painted the colour of the grass, and lying beside her was a small clutch bag that looked barely large enough for a mobile phone. A thin blanket of frost that glistened in the mid-morning light surrounded her as if protecting her.

At first, it appeared to Tomek that she had fallen, collapsed, and struggled to get herself to her feet until she'd eventually succumbed to whatever had killed her. There was nothing to suggest foul play, nothing to suggest that she'd been attacked. Except for the rouged cheeks and the slightly swollen neck. But even that could be the onset of bloating in the decomposition process.

It was a while before Tomek truly began to appreciate the scene for what it was: a girl, of similar age and build to his daughter, lying dead in a field. Ever since Kasia had come into his life less than three months ago, he'd found himself starting to react and behave differently to certain things, see certain situations in a different light. Crime scenes were a perfect example of that. Especially when the victim was a teenage girl.

To distract him from his thoughts, he turned to Rachel.

'Say something, please,' he said to her.

'About what?'

'Anything... So long as it isn't about cows. I've had enough of that conversation for one day.'

Mercifully, before they were about to dive straight into an awkward silence as Rachel thought of something interesting to say, Lorna Dean, the Home Office pathologist, shuffled towards them. Behind her, a team of Scenes of Crime Officers were in the process of setting up the tent that would be erected over the body. Beyond, on the outskirts of the park, was a group of uniformed police officers, setting up the outer cordon with the help of white-and-blue police tape.

'Lovely morning for it,' Lorna said excitedly.

Tomek had always found her to be overly jovial about her job as if she got some sort of kick out of dissecting dead bodies all day every day. He couldn't have done the job himself, and he admitted it required a particular sort of desensitised person in the first place, but she was something else. She was numb to all sense of decorum and respect.

'At least it got me out of having to do my morning run,' she continued.

Now there was a thought. Tomek couldn't remember the last time he'd been for a morning run. He used to go every morning, rain or shine, without fail. Ten kilometres along the seafront and towards the end of Southend Pier. But now that his priorities and responsibilities had changed, it had fallen to the bottom of the list. And, now that he thought about it, he realised he wasn't missing it too much. The job, and looking after Kasia, were doing their best to keep him healthy and distract him from gorging on the snacks and treats he would have usually found himself eating in the evening. However, there was another part of him that missed it. Missed it greatly, in fact. The endorphins after the run, the refreshing wind battering his face, waking him up. The way it let him clear his head and process the events of the day before. Let him see things in a different light.

Like every time he saw a dead teenage girl he was reminded of his daughter.

Something, he didn't know what – intuition, perhaps, but it was something prescient and deeply worrying – told him that he would be seeing more situations like this. Constant reminders of Kasia. It wasn't every morning that a teenage girl was found almost half naked in a park. But something told him this wouldn't be the last.

'What we saying then, Lorna?' Tomek asked in order to help silence the thoughts.

'Well, she's dead. I know that much.'

'Great. Off to a good start. Anything else?'

'From what I've been able to see so far, no. It doesn't look like there's any evidence of sexual assault; she's still fully dressed and her underwear's still on, though, judging from the swollen neck and hives on her face, I'd say she's had some sort of allergic reaction to something.'

'An allergic reaction?'

'Yeah. You never had one?'

Tomek shook his head. 'Never. Think I was blessed in that way. Though I don't like mosquito bites.'

23

Both women looked at him, faces blank.

'Nobody particularly likes mosquito bites, Tomek,' Rachel said sternly.

'I mean, I don't get on well with them. They seem to swell to the size of one of those flying saucer sweets you used to get as a kid—'

'With the sherbet in?'

'Yeah.'

'I remember those. The outside tasted like paper and the inside was just filled with sherbet. I don't know who ever thought they were a good idea.'

'I don't know why we ever ate them. They tasted egg.'

They both looked at him blankly again, though he couldn't think why.

'Did you just use the word "egg" to describe something bad?' Rachel asked.

There it was.

'Yeah. If something's not very nice, it's *egg*.'

Rachel shook her head derisively. 'Does Kasia know you use that word?'

'What difference does that make?'

'I think she has a right to know. If I found out my dad was using that word to describe things completely unrelated to it, I'd probably want to disown him.'

Tomek smirked sarcastically. 'Good one. But don't you think we should get back to the matter at hand?'

'You're the one who distracted us with your stupid word choice.'

Tomek ignored her and shuffled a little closer to the body in his scene of crime suit. The heavy rainfall that had started to descend bounced off the material. Before he looked down at the body, he looked skyward and wondered what the conditions had been during her death, whether it had been clear or rainy. Whether it had made any difference to the way she'd died.

As he moved closer, he crouched down and inspected her face. No more than fourteen, fifteen. Maybe sixteen at a push. Young yet mature. Pretty, but not showy about it. Quietly understated. Her whole life ahead of her.

It was then that he did something he hadn't done in a while.

He started to talk to her.

'What happened to you, eh?' he whispered to himself, keeping his voice low lest Rachel and Lorna hear. 'How did this happen? Did someone do this to you?'

Of course there was no answer. There was never any answer. And he always hoped there wouldn't be because otherwise, he'd be on the receiving end of a heart attack, but it helped him deal with the scene, to process it. And, he also liked to think that it helped them pass into whatever life or existence they were going to. A comforting bridge that connected them from one side to the other.

It also allowed his mind to start thinking about the circumstances surrounding the person's fate. As though he was there, watching it happen from afar. Seeing it happen in real time.

And this time was no different. He imagined a group of them. Maybe six, seven. A group large enough for there to be a lot of chatter and screaming. Maybe some alcohol thrown in. A combination of boys and girls. All similar ages. Perhaps from the same school. Drinking and socialising out of hours when they weren't supposed to, when their parents wanted them home.

And perhaps she'd gone home with the rest of them. Bumped into someone she knew. Or someone she didn't. And found herself in this state.

Or perhaps she'd stayed while the rest of her friends had gone home. Stayed with a boy that she wasn't supposed to be seen with. It was taboo for them to be together. Someone she hadn't wanted the rest of the group to know about. She'd stayed, and so had he. One thing had led to another, and then...

The girl's face was immediately replaced with Kasia's, and he was no longer able to look at her, no longer able to think about what had happened, *how* it had happened.

He pulled away and turned to his colleagues.

'Do we know her name?' he asked them.

Lorna shook her head, then called for a SOCO to come over. Shortly after, a tall figure, dressed from head to toe in white, appeared, slightly wheezy and out of breath.

'Can we have a look inside her clutch bag?' Tomek asked. 'I'd like to see if there's any identification on her.'

It took the man longer to bend down than it did for him to move to the other side of the body. As he lowered himself onto the grass, Tomek could hear the noise of his knees creaking over the sound of the wind whistling past the material protecting his ears. A moment later, the man pulled the clutch bag from beneath the victim's arm and opened it with the delicate precision of a surgeon. Then he reached inside and removed a mobile phone. The screen immediately illuminated and an image of the girl, sitting with a friend on the beach somewhere, smiling ebulliently up at the front-facing camera, appeared. The photo was recent, summertime unless Tomek had missed a sunny spell at the beginning of winter. Holding the phone delicately in his hand, he swiped up, but it required a password. He should have known. He'd made the mistake of thinking he could get into Kasia's phone whenever she'd passed it to him several times. Each time she snatched the device from him and entered the code herself. One of these days he'd find out what it was.

He didn't notice it at first, but when he looked away from the screen, he saw the SOCO's hand hovering in front of his face. Holding a school bus pass. With the victim's name and date of birth beside it.

Lily Monteith.

Aged fifteen.

CHAPTER FIVE

The last person Tomek expected to open the door in front of him was DC Anna Kaczmarek. But then again, she was the team's family liaison officer, and it was her job to reach out to the families of the deceased and bridge the gap between information and misinformation. It was an important role. One that sometimes proved pivotal in the capture of a villain. More likely than not, the cases they dealt with were related to the family in some way, and she was an expert at blending herself into the background, so much so that you hardly knew she was there. Listening in, noting down relatives' behaviours, reactions, arguments and disagreements. Sometimes the family of the deceased treated her like one of their own and admitted something incriminating in her presence, or they inadvertently gave something away that proved vital to the case. She was the snake in the grass, reporting everything back to Tomek and the team.

She was good at her job, yes. But he hadn't been expecting her to be as good as this, turning up at Lily Monteith's house before he'd even had a chance to speak with her.

'*Cześć*,' he said to her as she swung the door open.

'*Dzień dobry*, Tomek,' Anna replied.

He stepped into the house. 'How the bloody hell did you get here before me? You and Rachel direct messaging each other or something?'

'She thought it would be a good idea for me to be kept up to date.'

That was a yes, then.

'I'm impressed,' he said. 'How long have you two been working so closely with each other?'

She didn't reply, just offered him an embarrassed shrug of the shoulders.

'Next thing you know you'll both be coming after my job...'

This time Anna chuckled, which unnerved him. The prospect of being kicked out of his position by those beneath him while he was trying to fight for the position above was unsettling to him. He didn't like the idea of finding himself in the middle of a promotion sandwich. Even less so when it was with colleagues he admired greatly and considered some of his closest friends. Anna, in particular. He'd known her for the third-longest time (after Sean and Nick), and because they were both from Poland they shared a unique bond.

'They're in the living room,' Anna told him with a flick of the head.

Tomek gave a quick glance down the hallway and spotted the room she was referring to.

'How're they doing?'

'Same as always.'

'Triple-D?'

Anna nodded.

Ah, the Triple-D. A term coined by Tomek when he'd been sitting in the office one time trying to think of the words to describe the emotions a particular family were feeling. He had known the words, of course he had, it was just in that moment, in that moment with all the eyes of his colleagues watching him, he'd struggled to recall them. At first, the phrase had landed horribly, and he hadn't seen a future for it, but now that Anna had remembered it, he considered the possibility of bringing it back, like a has-been music group bringing back their careers from the dead because they were all skint and in desperate need of an influx of cash.

The Triple-D.

Distraught.

Devastated.

Distressed.

Tomek imagined they were usually the same emotions the aforementioned bands felt before they made the decision to announce their reunion tour.

With maybe a hint of disgust thrown in there too.

He made his way into the living room, careful to open the door cautiously, and poked his head around. Sitting there on the sofa in the middle of the living room, wrapped in each other's arms, were Mr and Mrs Monteith.

Mr Monteith was a broad man, with thick, wide shoulders that seemed to echo life as a former rugby player. And the beer belly that bulged the front of his shirt proved it.

Mrs Monteith, on the other hand, was the opposite in every way. Skinny, small, slight. Triple-S. Yet there was a ferocity behind her eyes, and the way she sat upright suggested to Tomek she was anything but the pushover her stature seemed to imply.

'Mr and Mrs Monteith, I'm Detective Sergeant Tomek Bowen. I work with Anna in the Major Investigation Team. I'm so sorry for your loss. Myself and the team will do everything we can to find out what happened to your daughter.'

Mrs Monteith reached out a hand for Tomek. He took it. Her palms were wet, either slicked with tears or sweat, and her grip was strong, as strong as he imagined her husband's to be.

'Thank you, Detective,' she said. 'Thank you for coming down. This should never have happened to our little girl.'

Tomek gave her hand a gentle squeeze before perching himself on the edge of the sofa opposite. At that point, Anna arrived with a glass of water for Tomek and sat at his side.

'Has my colleague explained the process to you?' Tomek asked.

Both parents nodded their heads solemnly, clinging onto one another even tighter than before.

'Do you have any questions associated with what my colleague has discussed?'

This time they shook their heads, and Mrs Monteith began breaking down into her husband's chest.

The first sign of the Triple-D.

'Very well then.' Tomek placed both palms on his knees and inhaled deeply. 'My role is to unfortunately ask some of the uncomfortable questions. If there are any you don't feel ready to answer, or there is something you don't feel like you can explain to me, then that's what Anna is here for. You can tell her anything.'

Anna smiled at him, as if to say, "Thank you for that introduction, Tomek", and then she turned to the grieving parents. Without being asked, she reached into her bag and produced a packet of Kleenex tissues, and handed them to Mrs Monteith. The woman thanked her then dabbed delicately beneath her eyes, looking skyward as she did so, revealing the whites that were no longer white at all and had been commandeered by an army of red snakes.

'Would you be able to tell me what your daughter was doing last night?' Tomek asked after Mrs Monteith had finished wiping away her tears.

'She... she was out with friends,' Mr Monteith said, his voice as deep as Tomek expected. 'A sort of house party but not a house party. A gathering, she called it. Round a friend's house – a kid called Marcus. Just a couple of friends from school, chatting, talking. You know how it is.'

'What time was she due home?'

'She wasn't. She told us she was going to stay round Gabby's afterwards.'

'Gabby?'

'Her best friend from playschool. They go everywhere together, do everything together.'

Tomek knew what that was like. It was the same for Kasia and her friend Sylvia. Kasia was always talking about her, always meeting up with her before and after school. It was nice, good that she had such a close friend so soon after arriving in the area.

'Do you know the names of the other people she was with?'

Lily Monteith's parents considered a moment, then shook their heads. 'Only a few. Marcus, Brett and Thomas. But I'm told there were going to be a few others there. Friends of friends. They've all met up before.'

Tomek nodded thoughtfully.

The images in his head were beginning to change. Perhaps Lily and the group hadn't been out in the park after all. Perhaps they'd all gone round to Marcus's house and then something had happened to her on the way to Gabby's house. But why had she been alone if she was staying at her friend's house?

'Have you heard from Gabby at all?' Tomek asked.

'Only her mum,' Mr Monteith replied. 'To tell her the news. Gabby's fine. And she doesn't know anything about what happened to Lily.'

Tomek would have to see about that. It still didn't explain why Lily and Gabby had been separated if they were both supposed to be returning to Gabby's parents' house for the evening. Perhaps they'd had an argument. Perhaps it had been over one of the boys.

'Did Lily have a boyfriend at all?' Tomek asked. He was about to navigate himself into awkward and uncomfortable territory – for everyone in the room, but mostly Mr and Mrs Monteith – and so he needed to be careful with his choice of words. Something he wasn't all that great at.

'Not that we know of,' Lily's mum responded.

'Any boys that she may have been talking to? Messaging online?'

They looked at one another before shaking their heads.

'Anyone she's gone to meet?'

Another shake of the heads.

'Has she ever had a boyfriend in the past? Someone who may have got jealous over her at all?'

'There was someone when she was thirteen, but that was never serious; never serious enough for them to be considered boyfriend-girlfriend.' Mr Monteith shuffled uncomfortably on the sofa, as though the topic of conversation made him nervous. The thought of a boy being with his daughter.

Tomek had felt the same way after his and Kasia's discussion the night before.

Billy the fucking Cow Fighter.

'I presume the relationship ended a long time ago...' he said.

'They were only together a couple of months. Then he found she had a latex allergy and decided to split.'

'A latex allergy... At thirteen...' Tomek whispered to himself. And then it made sense why the boyfriend had left her.

Latex. Condoms.

Sex.

Thirteen years old.

That did nothing to allay the concerns in his head about Billy the Cow Fighter.

Keen to move the conversation on, Tomek asked Lily's parents for a profile of her character, her personality. What type of kid she was, what she was like in school, and at home. And, as he'd expected, they sang her praises. As any parent would. As he would have done himself. Lily was a hard-working, caring girl who spent the right amount of time between them, school and her friends. Her favourite lessons were geography, maths, and Spanish. And on the weekends she went to her local swimming club where she was a keen swimmer. She was never late to school, she had loads of friends, was well behaved and well mannered. In their eyes, she was perfect and without fault. She wouldn't have hurt a fly nor would she have disturbed a bees' nest for fun.

These were all things Tomek had expected to hear. But it was what Mr and Mrs Monteith neglected to mention that caught his attention.

The fact that she'd never drunk alcohol. That she'd never had a sleepover anywhere other than Gabby's house. That she had never snuck out of the house or stayed out later than she should have. That she had never tried cigarettes or drugs.

Perhaps these were all things that they were oblivious to, or perhaps they were aware of them and they just didn't want Tomek to think badly of their daughter. Either way, he doubted the true Lily Monteith was the saint her parents purported her to be.

Because he knew from experience that he hadn't been an angel at that age either. That he had experienced similar things himself. Which made it harder to punish Kasia and restrain her from experiencing them for herself.

Call for Tomek.

Yeah?

The pot called. Something about a kettle...

As he left them to their grieving, a process that would be overseen by Anna and another of the junior detective constables she worked closely with, Tomek thanked them for their time and headed to the front door. As he placed one hand on the handle, he turned to face Mr Monteith, who'd accompanied him on his way out.

'You wouldn't happen to know Gabby's address, would you?' he asked. 'I think she might have a few answers for us – for *you*.'

CHAPTER SIX

G abby Longhouse was every bit as obnoxious as he expected her to be, though for her sake he put it down to heredity, an unfortunate personality trait she'd inherited from both parents.

While they'd professed to being upset about Lily's death and had spent several minutes assuring him that they were, in fact, grieving, it was an emotion that hadn't made its way onto their faces, nor had it filtered into their voices.

He thought it was more likely that the cockapoo he'd passed on the drive down to the Longhouses was more cut up about the death of Lily Monteith.

Even Gabby's first words to him – 'I'm not under arrest, am I?' – concerned him. If that was her attitude straight off the bat, then what would her attitude be when he asked her the questions?

'Not unless you've done something wrong,' he replied. Usually he would have altered his speech for someone her age, spoken in a softer, gentler tone. But not for Gabby Longhouse. Not for any of the Longhouses.

'I wanted to ask you a few questions about where you were last night and what you were up to.'

They moved into the living room, Tomek and the Longhouse family. Just as he was about to seat himself on the sofa, Gabby turned to her parents and asked that they leave the room. After putting up a fuss, they eventually conceded and shut the door behind them, not before reminding her that if she needed them at any moment, they were on the other side of the door.

Tomek didn't think it would be long before they were pressing their ears against it with the assistance of some drinks glasses.

'Tell me about what happened last night.'

As soon as he got himself comfortable, Tomek dived straight in. It took her a while to find a spot for her to feel comfortable. She looked nervous, reserved, as though there was something she wanted to tell him but was too afraid to. She had just lost her best friend, after all. Maybe he should cut her some slack.

'There were ten of us. Me, Lily, Marcus, Theo, Brett, Thomas, Liam, Henry, Callum and James.'

Tomek made a note of the names immediately, leaving a line between each one for any further details he might find useful.

'We were supposed to go round Marcus's originally, but then his parents had to cancel their plans. So we all went to the park instead.'

'Which one?'

'John Burrows.'

Tomek didn't say anything. Waited for her to continue.

'We... we took a little bit of drink from Marcus's house with us to the park, and we spent most of the evening drinking and chilling in the field.'

'Just the ten of you?'

'Yes.'

'And what were the plans after that?'

'I was *supposed* to go home to Lily's once we'd finished.'

Tomek stopped, hesitated, looked into her eyes. The lie was as obvious on her face as it was in her voice.

'Don't lie to me,' he said. 'Lily's parents told us that she was coming home to yours after the party. So where were you really supposed to end up?'

Gabby dropped her gaze and began playing with her hands. 'I... We... We were going to stay over at Marcus's house after the party originally. But because his parents were there we had to scrap that plan. Then Henry invited us over to his house.'

'Who?'

'Henry.'

'I know that. But who did he invite?'

'Me, Lily, and Theo.'

'Why just you four?'

'Because... because we're all really close friends.'

'And is anything going on between any of you?'

Slowly, as if answering his question, in one movement, Gabby turned to face the kitchen door, checked that it was shut and that her parents hadn't miraculously manifested on the other side without opening it, and then turned back to face him.

He lowered his voice. 'You can tell me. I won't tell them if I don't have to.'

That seemed to settle her nerves slightly. 'Well... Theo and I are going out. And Lily and Henry are... well, well... they're sort of in a situationship, if you know what I mean.'

He didn't. And he all of a sudden felt very old. Out of touch with the younger generation, the generation that his daughter was currently growing up in.

Mindful not to swear in front of her – *at* her – he instead said, 'I'm sorry but you're going to need to explain that one to me.'

'What? A situationship?'

'Yes. I have no idea what that is.'

'Well, you know... It's a situationship.'

Tomek chewed his bottom lip in frustration. He couldn't stand it when people used the same word they were trying to define in the definition. That wasn't quite how it worked.

'What does a situationship mean?' he asked again.

'You know. When they're not quite together-together. They're just... seeing each other.'

'From across the street, the classroom, where? What do you mean? You can be honest with me. You can say things as they are. I'm an adult. I've heard it all, and worse, before.'

It didn't take long for Gabby to feel comfortable to say the word, though she did tilt forward slightly and whisper it to him, lest her eavesdropping parents hear and come barging through.

'They're having sex but they're not together. You know... they're like friends with benefits.'

Now there was a phrase he knew, a phrase he recognised. Friends with benefits. He'd had a few himself, but not when he'd been that age. Not as young as fifteen. He'd gone to an all-boys school and hadn't met the opposite sex until he was in his college years.

But *fifteen*...

And then that number changed to thirteen. Kasia. Billy the Cow Fighter.

Is that what they were? In a situationship? Is that why she wanted him to come round?

Well, he certainly wouldn't allow that now, not when he knew what he did about what the kids nowadays were getting up to. No way. No, sir. No sex in his home for the next six years at the very least. Himself included.

'How long had this been going on between them?' Tomek asked, determined to get the conversation and his thoughts back on track.

'A couple of weeks,' she replied, continuing to play with her fingernails. 'They proper like each other though. I think they would have got together in a couple of months if things hadn't happened the way they did.'

'What things?'

The answer hit him as soon as he'd said it. If Lily Monteith hadn't died the night before. If she hadn't been found in the middle of a field, then she and Henry would have upgraded their relationship from situationship to boyfriend and girlfriend.

Tomek made a note to speak with Henry after this interview.

After he'd finished writing the young boy's name in his book, he moved the conversation along to the events of the night before. Gabby explained that they'd been drinking. That they'd left the park just before two in the morning, that they'd been invited back to

Henry's house. Gabby had said yes, while Lily had surprised her and said no.

'I wasn't expecting her to say it,' Gabby continued. 'I thought she'd have been well up for it, but all of a sudden she'd decided to back out.'

Tomek nodded, pensive. 'Do you know why that might be? Had she given any indication throughout the night that something was wrong, that she wanted to go home or was perhaps meeting someone else?'

Gabby considered for a while. Playing with her hands, looking down at her lap. In that moment she looked several years younger than her age. More her real age than the person she tried to portray to the outside world. Even though he'd never met her before, he felt like this was the real Gabby Longhouse. The quiet, reserved, considerate Gabby Longhouse that didn't have overbearing and obnoxious parents breathing down her neck.

'I... I don't know if I should tell you this,' she began, her voice faltering.

'If it's important, then you probably should.'

'There were... We were... Theo had managed to get some weed, so we were going to smoke it back at Henry's place. I've done it before with Theo loads of times, but I guess Lily wasn't expecting it, so she removed herself from the situation and said she would walk home; she only lived round the corner so I thought she'd be fine.'

Removed herself from the situation and walked straight into her death.

'Did anyone walk with her? Anyone see where she went?'

Gabby dropped her gaze into her lap. She was unable to bring herself to look at him.

'No,' she replied slowly. 'She went one way. The rest of us went the other.'

They went one way, while Lily Monteith went towards her death.

CHAPTER SEVEN

'I didn't think you'd've had time to fit this one into your schedule,' Tomek said.

He watched as Lorna whizzed from one side of the room to the other, carrying in one hand a scalpel and a pen in the other.

'Death waits for no one,' she said, then realised it didn't make any sense and corrected herself. 'The cadaver I had lined up for early afternoon didn't take as long as I thought it would, so I've managed to squeeze our teenage girl in.'

'Generous of you.'

It wasn't often that Tomek was called to the mortuary to oversee a post-mortem – he usually handed that task off to one of the detective constables in the team – but on the phone, Lorna had sounded concerned. There was something she needed him to see and it couldn't be done over the phone.

The gown strapped around his neck was beginning to chafe and irritate his soft, sensitive skin, and he was itching to get it off. It had been a long time since he'd last worn one, and an even longer time since he'd wanted to. But needs must. He couldn't complain. It was better than the alternative – being the one on the table, his chest split in half and his skin folded over his rib cage.

'How have things been going so far?' Lorna asked him as she finished the last of her preparations.

'Busy, but not productive in the slightest,' Tomek replied.

After his interview with Gabby Longhouse, Tomek had paid an impromptu visit to Henry Swallow's house in Benfleet. The teenager had been home at the time, with his parents and younger sister. There, he'd explained to Tomek his version of events which matched those that Gabby had told him. Weed and friends with benefits, included. As such, Tomek had given them his details, told them to contact him if they could think of anything further they thought was important and then left them to their Saturday afternoon; a Saturday afternoon that would forever be remembered as one of their worst.

'Hopefully what I'm about to tell you will shift the dynamic then,' Lorna replied.

Tomek was all ears. He placed his hands in his pockets and carefully made his way over to the table where Lily Monteith lay flat on her back, shining under the fluorescent light.

Without saying anything, Lorna turned away from him and reached for a small metal tray on the other side of the table. Resting upon it, glistening beneath the bright light, were two objects. Both looked like pigskin that had shrivelled and dried up. Except they were of different colours: one black, one white. Lorna picked them up in each hand as though they were dirty laundry, and Tomek immediately recognised them for what they were.

'At first, I didn't find a single thing wrong with her,' Lorna began. 'Yes, she'd been drinking, the remains of that were still in her stomach, along with her pizza for dinner the night before. There were no signs of puncture wounds, nothing to suggest she'd been strangled... nothing. Until I got to her oesophagus.'

Lorna placed the items back on the tray and handed it across to Tomek. He looked down at them, eyes wide.

'Until I found these...' she said.

'Are they what I think they are?'

'I'd be surprised if you guessed correctly.'

Tomek looked at her unimpressed.

Smiling, in an attempt to disarm him, she pointed to the item on the left. 'The condom was the first thing to go down her throat, right down, like all the way down. Then the latex glove.'

'And why wouldn't I know what either of those things are?'

Lorna turned coy, sheepish. Afraid to say what she'd really meant. 'Nothing. Sorry. I didn't mean to offend you.'

'You haven't offended me yet because you haven't said anything.'

'Well, it's just... you know. The condom... because of Kasia. Unless the one you used thirteen years ago broke. And the gloves because... well, I never had you down as an avid cleaner.'

Tomek thrust the tray back to her. She took it and set it down on the table.

'Okay, now I'm offended,' he said.

'Are you really?'

'Can you blame me?'

'I guess not.'

'Good. Well, you owe me one for that now. I don't know what for, or when I'm going to cash it in, but you owe me one. Deal?'

Lorna's face seemed to brighten a little at the prospect that their relationship wasn't completely dead in the water thanks to her stupid and offensive comments.

'Deal,' she said.

'Good. Now tell me more about this condom and glove.'

'Well,' she began, 'one of them is to stop the transmission of sexual diseases and any unwanted pregnancies.'

This time, Tomek pretended to be angry, but he was unable to stop the smirk from showing on his face.

'Anyway,' Lorna began again. 'As I was saying. The condom was shoved down her throat first. A hell of a long way down. And I suspect our killer would have had to use some sort of apparatus to get it down there.'

'Like what? A stick?'

Lorna shook her head. 'A stick would've been sharp and, if he'd done it while she was conscious, then I would have seen some scratch marks or abrasions on the inside of her throat, but there was nothing. Instead, it was soft.'

Please don't say like a baby's bottom.

'Like a baby's bottom.'

Tomek grimaced at the phrase and wished he hadn't heard it. Not only was it cringy, it also wasn't the best time or place to use it. Although, having said that, he couldn't think of any occasions where it was appropriate.

'So the killer used something soft to lodge the condom in her throat?' Tomek asked.

Lorna nodded. 'Possibly his fist.'

'But wouldn't that have snapped her jaw?'

'Not if he had a small hand.'

Tomek considered for a moment. Tried to conjure an image of the scene as it had taken place, as the assailant had grabbed her from the side of the street, dragged her back into the park and then proceeded to shove the latex down her throat. Someone big enough to control and overpower Lily Monteith, yet small enough to shove their hand down her throat.

Or worse.

Something softer.

He shuddered at the thought.

'What about the glove?' Tomek asked. 'Was that used to get the condom down there in the first place?'

Lorna shrugged and held the glove closer to the light. 'Difficult to say. We won't know that until the lab results come back.'

Tomek nodded and took a step back, surveying the young girl's body in front of him. It was trim and supple for her age. Her skin was smooth and covered in a thin line of freckles along her left thigh leading up to her waist.

As he surveyed the freckles, he asked, 'Did the condom have anything else to do with her death?'

'In what way?' Lorna asked.

'I'm talking sexual assault.'

'No. Like I said earlier, no signs of that at all. And, more interestingly, she's still a virgin.'

Still a virgin? Tomek considered what that meant. That someone, somewhere along the line was lying about the situationship. Someone had been inflating the reality of what they got up to. Whether it was Henry, lying to seem bigger and more of an adult in front of his friends; or whether it was Lily herself telling Gabby that they'd had sex out of peer pressure or to seem older, more mature than she was.

'So she was attacked, possibly pinned to the ground and then she had that shoved down her throat?'

Lorna nodded glumly. 'That's my professional opinion,' she replied. 'Though I think it's worth noting that she didn't die from the foreign objects down her gullet.'

'It was the anaphylaxis?' Tomek said, as though unsure of himself.

He had always admired that word. The way it sounded. Ana-phy-lax-is. Funny to say, funny to hear. Except not in these circumstances. Not in many, whichever way you looked at it, to be honest.

'Yes. She was severely allergic. Fatally, even.' Lorna moved round to the end of the table and stopped beside Lily's head. She placed a delicate hand on the sides of the girl's cheeks and then opened her jaw first.

'I found what I think might have been trace samples of latex on her skin and in her hair, though we won't know for certain until the results are back, which suggests to me that something was placed over her head. Something made from latex. From there she had an allergic reaction. At first, she would have struggled to breathe, her throat would have closed up, and then her heart would have started to slow down as she slipped into anaphylactic shock. She would have needed urgent medical attention, and if there was none coming, then it wouldn't have taken long for her organs and heart to collapse.'

'And it wouldn't have been helped by the foreign objects in her throat.'

'Naturally.'

Tomek turned away from her and his eyes fell on the freckles again. Six of them in a row. Like stars in a constellation. He tried once again to imagine what had happened to her. *How* it had happened. And each scenario that played in his head was as grisly as the last.

It then became clear to him that whoever had killed Lily Monteith had targeted her for a reason. They had known about her allergies. They had known that she was susceptible to anaphylaxis.

And that meant it was someone who knew her intimately.

CHAPTER EIGHT

Less than an hour later, Tomek found himself in Victoria Orange's office. Today the new detective inspector was wearing her platform shoes that sounded like drums banging with every step, and a smart blouse tucked into her chino trousers. She had tied her hair back and applied a thin layer of make-up to her face. No matter the occasion, Tomek always thought she looked the part and led the line from the front in that respect. Appearance wasn't something he ever gave any second thought to – stick a pair of trousers on, a white shirt if he was feeling studious, or a checked one if he was feeling relaxed, and be done with it – but her arrival into the team had made him see the importance of looking professional. Especially if he wanted to lead investigations as an inspector one day. If you wanted their respect it came down to two things, people's impression of you and your ability to do the job. There were no politicians or lawyers or doctors dressed in jumpers with *Star Wars* logos on them and jeans that hadn't been washed in weeks. And there was a reason for it.

'I've spoken with Nick, and he's explained to me your aspirations for a promotion to Inspector,' she said. 'As a result of that discussion, we've decided to let you have control of this operation.'

'Really?'

'Really-really.'

Tomek beamed. The first time in a very long time since he'd last been given the opportunity to prove himself. Especially since his return from suspension. Even before then he'd struggled to apply himself, struggled to prove his worth, struggled to find the motivation. For a long while he'd felt like his career had been stagnating, floating hopelessly in the pond.

Now, with Lily Monteith and the suspicious events surrounding her death, perhaps that might begin to change.

'Thank you, ma'am,' Tomek said, unable to wipe the grin off his face. 'I really appreciate the opportunity.'

Though the smile was short-lived.

'I will want to have oversight of the operation,' she said, cleaning it from his face almost instantly. 'You'll report to me on a weekly basis, maybe more if the situation requires it, and then from there we'll set out objectives and priorities.'

'So it'll be like you telling me what to do, and then me doing it, and then we all pretend that I'm the one in charge?'

Victoria's back stiffened slightly and she looked down at her notes. 'No, Tomek,' she said, firm but fair. 'I think you may have misunderstood me. You will have operational oversight of this case, and I will offer my guidance where applicable. I don't want to step on anyone's toes, but if I need to then I will have the final say.'

Tomek folded his arms across his chest and steadied his breathing. He admitted that it made sense; he just didn't like it. Ever since Victoria's arrival at Southend CID, he hadn't been able to shake this perception of her, that she was out to get him, the one that had been tarnished by her predecessor, Tony Hunt. Or Hunt the Cunt as Tomek had called him. The two of them hadn't always seen eye to eye, butting heads and causing arguments in the middle of briefings, and he didn't want to have the same type of relationship with her. Not if he could help it.

'I understand,' he told her calmly. 'Thank you for clarifying. I'm looking forward to seeing what we can do together.'

'As am I. And I guess a good place to begin would be with what you know so far.'

And so Tomek told her. About the suspected events leading up to Lily Monteith's death. About the park, the drinking, the weed, Henry and the lies about their relationship, the journey home that had been brought to an abrupt stop. Lastly, he'd explained to her the way the teenager had been killed.

'Latex?'

'She was allergic. Ana-phy-lax-is,' he said, enunciating each syllable with every part of his mouth. 'The condom was first in her mouth, then the glove. Although Lorna suspects there may have been another glove used to smother her face and hair. However, we won't know until we get the lab results.'

Victoria nodded thoughtfully and eased back into her chair slightly. A withdrawn expression played on her face as she rocked back and forth.

'What are you thinking?' she asked him.

'Generally, or…?'

'About the case, stupid,' she replied. 'Which means I know you're not thinking about fighting any cows.'

Tomek flushed red. 'You heard about that, did you?'

'Everyone did, Tomek. I think it's going to feature in our newsletter. Or maybe I'll ask it at my reading group.'

'You're part of a reading group?'

'Funnily enough, I *do* have a life outside these four walls.'

Intrigued, Tomek placed one leg over the other and began massaging his chin.

'What are you reading at the moment? *Fifty Shades*?'

Victoria rolled her eyes. 'No. For fuck's sake. We're not all sex-deprived women in our forties. Though there are a *lot* of those in the group. You should hear some of them talk, Jesus! But—'

'When do you meet? I might come down and introduce myself to some of these—'

'Shut up,' she told him. 'Don't be such a pig. Besides, when was the last time you picked up a book?'

'Just this morning actually,' he said, feeling proud of himself. 'One of Kasia's. *Midsummer Night's Dream*. Shakespeare.'

'Yes, I'm familiar with who wrote it, thanks. But that doesn't count. You didn't read it, did you?'

He wagged his finger in the air. 'That wasn't the question. If you'd asked the last time I *read* a book, then we'd have to go back a few months, maybe even a year.'

'You should do it more often. It's good for the soul.'

'So is drinking green tea and spending more time in the woods or the countryside, but you don't see me doing that. Anyway, doesn't the concept of reading seem utterly fucking bizarre to you?'

From the look on her face, she was choosing not to answer the question.

'I mean, think about it. You're just staring at dead pieces of tree, with little black markings on them, hallucinating. Doesn't that just...?' Tomek made an explosion gesture that came out of the sides of his head.

In response, Victoria simply stared at him, blown away by his idiocy.

'I'm really tempted to bring you along now. First the cow fighting, now this. They would tear you to absolute pieces.'

'Like women do to strippers on hen dos? Or at Magic Mike concerts? Savages, some of them.'

The wry grin on his face was too much for her, and she moved the conversation back onto the topic of Lily Monteith.

'Tell me what you're thinking,' she finished.

'Aside from a group of sexually deprived women in their forties, I'm thinking that it's strange, very strange indeed. I've never had anything like this come across my desk before. Death by ana-phy-lax-is. Especially when it seems to be, targeted.'

'You think whoever killed her knew her?'

Tomek shrugged. 'Impossible not to. Otherwise how else would they have known about her allergy?'

'They might have found it in her hospital records.'

And if that was the case, then that might mean there were more to come.

'Possibly,' Tomek replied. 'But I need to look at the different angles. Whether anyone held any grudges against her, any ex-boyfriends that wanted to get back at her, even though I doubt the fifteen-year-old had anything to do with it. Maybe it was someone she'd pissed off on the playground. Someone large enough to over-power her but small enough to get their hand down her throat. And I don't think Henry or any of the other boys in the group are respon-sible because they all headed home. The team have spoken with them and they've all got solid alibis for the time she died. My gut tells me someone knew she was out and waited for their chance, and last night they got lucky.'

As she listened, Victoria nodded thoughtfully. 'Have you consid-ered the possibility that she was maybe going to meet someone else last night, someone older than her, someone she might have been speaking with online?'

Tomek hadn't up till that point. And if she wanted to play it like that, a competitive tally of valid arguments and lines of enquiry, then he was ready to unleash his ace card.

'If it's all right with you,' he started, 'I wanted to spend some time looking into previous cases.'

'Cases of what? Dead teenage girls?'

'Cases of death by ana-phy-lax-is.'

Any excuse to use that word.

He continued. 'It just seems so bizarre to me, so unique, that a part of me wonders if it's *too* unique, too bizarre. Something that might have previously slipped under the radar at some point.'

Victoria pondered. Ran her finger over her lips.

'I don't want you spending too much time on it. It's just—'

Before she could finish her sentence, a knock came at the door and startled them both. Victoria called for the person on the other side to enter, and a moment later DC Martin Brown stepped into the room.

'Sorry to interrupt,' the man said, his breathing heavy. 'But, Tomek, I have that list for you.'

'Right on time,' Tomek said as he twisted in his seat to look up at Martin. 'We didn't plan this. Honest.' He reached out a hand and took the document from the constable before turning back to face Victoria.

'What's that?' she asked, eyes widening, eyebrows rising.

'A list of all the deaths in the Southend and Castle Point borough, for girls aged ten to twenty-four, in the past six months, where the cause of death has either been attributed to ana-phy-lax-is or the victim has suffered from ana-phy-lax-is.'

'So you went ahead and did it anyway?'

'Looks like it.'

'Then why ask for my approval?'

Tomek shrugged. 'I took a punt. You miss a hundred per cent of the chances you don't take.'

And this was a chance he was going to make absolutely certain he didn't miss.

CHAPTER NINE

That evening, Tomek walked the short distance from his car to the front door with a marked spring in his step. And it had absolutely nothing to do with the spirit of Christmas. If anything, it was in spite of it. There was no escaping the constant reminder of what was only a few weeks away: the radio was playing the same recycled classics on repeat; Christmas lights and decorations hung from the street lamps along the Southend road; along his street a number of the houses and flats had placed multi-coloured festive lights in the windows, making them look like they were taking part in an eighties disco. And if that wasn't bad enough, then there was one neighbour, one of the many he hadn't bothered to acknowledge with a curt nod yet, that had kitted out their front garden with a giant inflatable snowman that blew smoke in your face every time you walked past it. Besides it being a giant waste of money to buy the bastard thing in the first place, Tomek was sorely tempted to walk past it several times to ensure the owners a) ran out of smoke and had the added expense of buying replacement cartridges, and b) suffered the electrical cost of running such an exorbitant and over-the-top piece of furniture at all hours of the day.

But he was in a good mood tonight. His *bah humbug!* behaviour would have to wait for another day.

As he entered the front door, two voices echoed from the living room at the top of the small flight of steps. Voices speaking Polish.

'*Latem lubię... podróżować z rodzicami... do Anglii.*'

'Very good,' came the response from Phillip Balham, Kasia's Polish tutor. Since she was a quarter Polish, she had considered it important to learn the language of her heritage (with a few helpful and pressing hints from Tomek), and so he had happily found the best Polish tutor in the area to teach her at least twice a week, with the option of a third day if neither of them were busy. So far they were on their third lesson, but it was clear to see she was already making strides in the right direction. Polish was a notoriously difficult language to learn, and even he was the first to admit that if he hadn't been born there, and if he hadn't grown up speaking, writing and listening to it from birth, then he wouldn't have come anywhere near it. As a result, he was immensely proud of her for taking the plunge. Now it was just up to them both to ensure she maintained it.

'You're a professional already,' Tomek noted as he entered the living room. He found them both sitting at the dining table, hunched over a series of books and resources.

'I'll be better than you soon,' Kasia said as she climbed out of the chair and raced over to give him a hug.

'Of that, I have no doubt,' he replied, massaging her back. Then he made his way over to Phillip and shook the man's hand.

'How's she getting on?'

'Much improved since last week,' he told Tomek. 'I might even suspect that she's been practising on the side.'

'I should bloody well hope so,' Tomek said. 'Amount it's costing.'

'I, er—' Phillip started, but Tomek placed a hand on his shoulder.

'I'm joking, mate. You've gotta earn a wage, pay your rent some-how. I've got her practising nearly every day. Weekends she gets off. Though if she's blitzing through this, I might get her learning some-thing else while she's at it. How many languages did you say you could speak?'

A look of pride rolled over Phillip's face and stayed there. Tomek could hardly blame him when he heard the number.

'Seven,' he said with all the indication of someone who knew they were intelligent and wasn't afraid to admit it. 'I'm what you might call a polyglot.'

'A poly-what?'

'Polyglot.'

'Just repeating the word isn't going to make me understand it any better, I'm afraid. What is a polyglot?'

'A polyglot is someone who can speak several languages. Typically more than three.'

'But you can speak seven, so that must make you a super-polyglot—'

'A hyperpolyglot,' Kasia corrected.

Tomek turned to her and saw her mobile phone in hand, the Google search she'd just conducted in the blink of an eye already on the screen.

'A hyperpolyglot,' she said, reading from her device, 'is someone who can speak at least six languages, according to the Association of Hyperpolyglots.'

'Wow. There's an *association*,' Tomek remarked. 'So you must be in high demand then?'

'You'd think, but sadly no. I also have to work nights at the casino in Southend as a croupier.' He paused. 'Besides, for a lot of those types of translation jobs, you have to be accredited and have qualifications.'

'Speaking in different languages for your application isn't enough?'

'I wish. And, don't get me wrong, it's great that they've got an association, but it's all a bit incestuous.'

'Like Mensa. Or the Masons?'

'Almost. But not nearly as exciting or secretive.' Phillip removed his glasses from his face and cleaned them using his shirt. 'Besides, a lot of the languages I speak are largely the same. So I don't think it counts.'

'Oh, yeah?'

'Well, English is the obvious one. But if you can speak English, then you can pick up German as they're not too dissimilar. And if you can speak German, then you can speak Polish and a lot of the other Eastern European languages as their dialects all sound the same. And if you can speak Spanish, then Portuguese and Italian are virtually identical. The only odd one out is French, which funnily enough is the last one I learnt.'

'Put you off learning any more, did it?'

Phillip chuckled and placed his hand on his chest as he did so. 'I can see why you might say that,' he replied. 'I just fancied pausing for a while. But I did have one child I was tutoring ask me why he was learning French because he thought the French didn't exist.'

'Be careful who you say that around,' Kasia said, jumping into the conversation. 'If they hear you across the water they might start rioting.'

Tomek looked at her for a moment in stunned silence, stunned that she'd come up with such a joke at her age. He was impressed. Then he turned his attention back to Phillip and started counting the languages on his fingers. 'So we've got English, Spanish, Portuguese, Italian, French, German, Polish.'

'Fluently, yes. The rest I can pick up phrases and words, but wouldn't be able to converse with a native much. Although I did recently come back from a trip to Recife where they spoke a dialect of Portuguese I'd never come across before, so that was interesting!'

It sounded it, but as Tomek checked his watch, he realised he didn't have time to be standing in the living room discussing foreign languages. He had a murder to solve, and he wasn't going to do so in Phillip's or Kasia's company. So he excused himself, thanked Phillip for coming over (which Phillip duly reminded him was only because he was being paid to do so), and then entered his bedroom.

They had moved into their new place only a couple of weeks before, and evidence of the move was still everywhere to be seen. Cardboard boxes piled in the corner, filled with old clothes he needed to take down to the local charity shop. Items of furniture that had been removed from their cardboard protectors but were still to be put in their final resting place. And lastly, there were the outfits that had been worn, used, and placed in various hiding spots about the place. The room was a tip, but he didn't mind. He was used to it.

The only clear sections of the room, however, were the windowsill and his desk. A small section of clarity, tidiness, and the only part of the room that didn't look as though a fourteen-year-old boy who'd just discovered microwaveable meals and video games had been living in it.

Resting atop the windowsill were some of his prized possessions. The ones that, in the event of a house fire, he would rescue before anything else, before his laptop, before his phone, before anything (the only exception being the coat his brother had worn on the night that he'd died; that he would never leave behind). He adored his bonsai trees and plants almost as much as he did Kasia, though it was a close contest, and Kasia had only recently nipped them to the finish line. He had owned them for decades, cared for them almost every day, and trimmed, pruned, and nurtured them for longer than he cared to admit. He'd also given them names, but he didn't like to admit that either and was only prepared to share that information, that closely guarded secret, with people he truly trusted. When he was working on them, perfecting their shape and bending their branches into place, he always found himself in a place of Zen, a place of calm, of reflection. Just him and his trees, him and his plants. The outside world – the outside world that he was looking at right now; the street below, with the cars and the street lights – was all a blur to him.

Just him and his trees. Him and his thoughts.

'Evening, gents,' he said as he seated himself at his desk.

Big Ken the Weeping Fig.

Dudley the Dracaena.

Gandhi the Peace Lily.

The Lads.

'And Lady,' he added, nodding to Freya the Swiss Cheese plant.

Owing to the size of the one that had previously lived in the living room of their old flat, Tomek had been forced to purchase a smaller one so that it would fit into his bedroom, and he lamented that decision every day. There was very little room for him to spread out across the surface and oftentimes he frequently found himself on the bed, sitting cross-legged looking at his notes, chewing on his pen, the same as he caught Kasia doing.

They weren't frequent, but he liked to think there were signs that she was definitely his daughter (aside from the obvious DNA test), and that was one of them.

Tonight, he'd brought home with him his laptop and a small folder. The bare bones of the case. The facts they knew to be true. The rest was in a note application on his desktop. But the most important piece of evidence he'd brought home was the information DC Martin Brown had given him.

The man had surprised him. He had joined the team at the same time as Victoria, but unlike her, he had found himself grounded in the team much faster. Tomek supposed it was easy to do so when you were one of the lowest ranked: you came in, did what you were tasked with doing, earned your respect, then went home. Martin didn't have the same sort of operational and logistical pressures that the detective inspector did. In fact, none of them did. Except for Tomek. It had only been a few hours, but he was now beginning to feel an omniscient presence over his shoulders. Watching him. Judging his every thought, his every decision. Like the voice inside his head criticising everything he did.

Pushing that thought to the back of his mind, Tomek turned his attention to the document that confirmed that there had been no anaphylaxis-related deaths in the Southend or Castle Point boroughs in the last six months. However, when Tomek had asked to widen the net for deaths in the last two years, Martin, in true *Blue Peter* style, had pulled out another document from his pile and handed it to Tomek.

'Here's one I prepared earlier, sarge,' Martin had told him, standing smugly in the doorway.

'Good stuff, Martin. Keep it up. We'll make a young Tomek Bowen out of you in no time.'

'That's the last thing the world needs,' Victoria had interrupted.

To which Tomek had instructed Martin to ignore her, said that there was nothing wrong with being Tomek Bowen, and then sent him on his way.

As he looked at the document in front of him now, he was reminded of the feelings he'd felt as he'd uttered the words: Two years ago a young schoolgirl, aged seventeen, died inside the concert hall at the Cliffs Pavilion. She and her friend had gone to the concert together. A combination of ecstasy, ibuprofen and paracetamol was found in her system. Cause of death was declared as a drug overdose, but anaphylaxis was said to have had a significant impact. She was extremely allergic to ibuprofen.

Pride, optimism, and a renewed sense of determination; that his hunch had been right, that his intuition had led him on to something possibly much larger than Lily Monteith's death, flowed through him.

The only problem now, however, was that his discovery indicated something else. Something larger. A potential serial killer, targeting victims via their allergies. First the concert, now Lily Monteith. Two years apart.

And if there was one thing he knew about serial killers, it was that the time between their kills, the time they needed to satiate their desires, grew shorter with every kill.

If that was the case, then he worried there might be more bodies to come.

Sooner rather than later.

CHAPTER TEN

Tomek had got very little sleep. He'd spent most of the evening reviewing the witness statements and the reports into Mandy Butler's death. And as the night had worn on, he'd become increasingly convinced that there was something to it, some method in his madness. Rather, the killer's madness.

Mandy Butler had been seventeen when she'd died, on the brink of adulthood. She'd gone to an Example concert with her friend and never come home. She'd taken a concoction of drugs and her body had collapsed as a result. To the unsuspecting officer looking into the case, it would have seemed like a normal case of a drug overdose, an unfortunate and devastating case of drug overdose, by all accounts. But now that Tomek had discovered the link between them – ana-phy-lax-is – a deeper suspicion grew within him. Yes, the link was tenuous. As far as he'd been able to make out, the girls didn't know each other, they hadn't gone to the same school, and yet they'd died as a result of their allergy. Anaphylactic deaths were extremely rare in the UK, with only a few deaths being attributed to the fatal allergic reaction every year. But for two girls of similar age to have died under similar circumstances in a short space of time, in the same area, that was more than a coincidence.

And it was a thought that had sent the alarm bells ringing.

So much so that, before he'd ventured into the office that morning, Tomek had called ahead to speak with Mandy Butler's parents. But as he'd soon found out, it was just the one.

'Mandy's father passed away six months after Mandy did,' Jennifer Butler explained as she led him into her office. She worked for a local architect's firm in Leigh, which meant the drive had been brief.

'I'm sorry to hear that,' Tomek replied as he sat down.

'It's been tough, but I'm finally getting myself together from it.'

Tomek could only imagine. Losing a daughter and a husband, akin to a lung and a heart, within six months of each other. Dreadful.

'I like to keep myself busy here,' she said. 'Helps take my mind off things. And it's better than going to an empty home every night.'

Tomek smiled thoughtfully and nodded. The office was plain, with all the usual fixtures and furnishings of an architect's office: a desk, computer, and photos of recent designs hanging from the wall. Everything in there was minimalist, straight-edged and screamed of design.

'Done anything I might have seen?' Tomek asked as he pointed at one of the pictures on the wall.

She turned to look at it. 'Probably not. We do a lot of internal designs for office spaces, as well as the occasional structural design of buildings. Unless you've been to the business park up in Colchester, I can't imagine you'll have seen any of our stuff.'

Tomek admitted that he hadn't. But if he was in the area, then he would pop in and have a look. Once they'd completed the platitudes and got the introductions out of the way, Tomek was keen to find out as much as he could about Mandy's death. There was only so much he could learn from a police report.

'Take as much time as you need.'

'Can I ask why you want to know?'

Tomek admired the question and respected her greatly for it. There was no point in her reliving the worst experience of her life without reason.

'You won't be aware of this yet, but yesterday morning a young girl was found murdered in a field, under similar circumstances to your daughter.'

'Similar how?'

'I suspect she was killed by her allergy.'

'Hmm.'

And then he lost her. She turned her attention away from him and stared at the keyboard in front of her as if willing the keys to type out the story inside her head.

'She was going out with her friend to a concert. She was seventeen. It was her first ever. Example. She'd loved him ever since she was a child. I thought about going with her, of me and her dad just standing in the back of the hall, but that wasn't cool, that wasn't the right thing to do. She wanted to be alone, without either of us cramping her style. Freedom, she called it. So we decided to release the chains and let her go.'

A lump caught in her throat and she swallowed it down. It was a few moments before she continued again.

'We got the call shortly before the concert finished. My husband was due to pick them up, so he was already there. I came down separately and by the time I'd arrived, they'd cleared the concert hall and stopped the music. She'd collapsed in the middle of the crowd, but it was too late for the paramedics to do anything. The coroner's report said that she'd died from a drug overdose. But, but I didn't believe it. Couldn't. Wouldn't. There was ibuprofen in the drugs they found in her system. Why? Perhaps I didn't want to think my daughter would be so foolish as to take drugs after we'd both explained the dangers and consequences of it so many times to her.'

As she spoke, Jennifer's gaze bored deeper and deeper into the keyboard.

'For a long time, I wanted to think that she'd been spiked. That someone had put something in her drink deliberately. But after Elsie's witness statement saying that someone had come up to them and offered the drugs, I knew it wasn't possible. My daughter had bought drugs. She'd seen them, paid for them, and consumed them. For an even longer time, I battled with wanting to know why, or how, wanting to know what had possessed her, but I was never going to get any answers. That all changed when I heard from Nisha.'

Bingo. The real reason he'd come to see her. A little nugget of information like this.

As part of his research last night, Tomek had discovered several news articles in the local paper with interviews from Jennifer Butler, where she'd berated the police for their handling of the case, how quickly they'd been to dismiss it as an overdose. She had gone on record as saying that the police hadn't cared about Mandy's death, just the same as they hadn't cared for all the other times it had happened. When he'd read that, Tomek had struggled to find out what she'd meant. And he was hoping now she was about to tell him.

'Who's Nisha?'

'Someone I met online.'

Tomek pulled out his pen and notepad and made a note. 'Could you be more specific?'

Still keeping her gaze fixated on the computer keyboard, Jennifer continued, 'She reached out to me on Facebook a couple days after everything had happened. I didn't have time to reply to her until after the funeral. It was all so quick, all so busy...' She paused as she pulled herself from her thoughts. 'She'd contacted me saying that her daughter had gone through something similar. Like Mandy, she'd been to a concert and had been offered something, and like Mandy, she'd taken it. And, just like Mandy, she'd had a strong reaction to them and had collapsed. Except this time the paramedics arrived in time to administer the shot that would save her life.' Jennifer lifted her head and met Tomek's eyes for the first time. Her unrelenting glare unsettled him slightly. 'The funny thing is, it wasn't the first time it had happened.'

Tomek remained silent as he waited for her to finish.

'Nisha had spoken with several other mums, all coming together on Facebook, to discuss what had happened to their daughters. Five of us in total. All with daughters of similar age. Fifteen to seventeen. Some of them went to the same school, while others had never heard of each other. But there was something that linked them all. They'd all been given drugs that had been spiked with ibuprofen and parac-etamol, and each and every one of them had nearly died at a concert at the Cliffs Pavilion. It was all too similar for us to ignore.'

'Did you go to the police with that information?'

Tomek tried to recall if he'd ever seen or heard anything about Mandy Butler and the five other girls who had been drugged at the Cliffs Pavilion two years ago, but he drew a blank.

'We took it to the highest level we could find, but he didn't want to hear it.'

'Who?'

'We took it to the chief inspector.'

Nick.

Nasty by name, nasty by nature.

'And when he didn't follow up with anything, we took it to the *Southend Echo*.'

This time Tomek tried to recall if he'd come across the news article she was referring to, if it had appeared in his investigations last night, but nothing. He must have missed it.

'I still have a copy of it at home,' Jennifer said, her focus entirely on Tomek now.

'What about an online one?'

'Of course.'

It took her less than a minute to find the article she was referring to. Tomek shuffled round to the other side of the desk to get a better view. A few inches separated them. At the top of the screen was the red banner of the *Essex Live* logo. Beneath it was the article's title with an image of the Cliffs Pavilion off to the side.

Beneath that was the name of the journalist who'd reported on the case.

Ever since Jennifer had first mentioned it, a name had immedi-ately appeared in his mind. And now it had just been confirmed.

CHAPTER ELEVEN

There was no perfect time to sit inside Morgana's Café on Hadleigh High Street. Their all-you-can-eat full English breakfast buffet ran from the hours of seven to eleven, and after that, they continued their lesser version which consisted of everything else inside a full English, minus the bits nobody wanted: tomatoes, black pudding and mushroom. It was a decadent feast for all ages, and it was all ages that stepped through their doors. In the hour that Tomek had been waiting there, drinking painfully slowly from his cup of tea, trying to make it last as long he could before he faced the decision of ordering food with his next round, he'd counted no fewer than seventy people setting foot inside the restaurant, eager and happy to shell out the tenner it cost for the buffet. Men and women of all ages and all sizes. Some were regulars, who knew the owner Morgana by name (though it didn't take a genius to work out who she was), while others had mentioned they'd heard about the place from friends. The second group were the type of people to leave Google Reviews about everywhere they went: some good, some bad, some rather unpleasant, and actually think that people read them and paid attention to them.

The smell of grease, fat and oil was thick and musty in the air, and had permeated through the furniture; every time he moved, he caught an extra whiff of the pungent aroma. But he didn't mind. This was what a quintessentially British café was like. The smell, the sounds of sizzling fat and shouting in the open kitchen at the back, the cheap ingredients, the even cheaper diamanté furniture and mirrors hanging from the wall, all devoured by customers who cared nothing for the effects of the food on their health. Strangely, he felt like he was at home. In a safe place. Everyone here was a friend, an ally, united in their love of good food. It didn't matter what background they had, where they came from, or what they did for a living; here, all labels and prejudices were forgotten about.

Beside him was a family of three generations. The eldest was no older than fifty, and the youngest was no younger than ten. While Tomek tried to calculate the maths in his head, he was distracted by Morgana introducing herself for the fourth time.

'Can I get you another tea, darling?'

'Please,' he said, checking his watch.

She was late. Over an hour. But he wasn't ready to give up just yet.

'And what about food?'

Tomek considered for a moment. His stomach was growling. He'd waited this long. And he wasn't too precious about making himself look like an arse in front of her as he gorged on his bacon and eggs.

'Yes, please.'

She reached for the pocketbook in her apron and clicked her pen into action. 'What can I get for you?'

Tomek looked around the rest of the café. At the happy faces, at the knives and forks working overtime to slice their sausages open and tear apart the bacon, at the state of their napkins as they wiped the grease from their mouths.

'I'll have what everyone else is having, please,' he said. 'The heart-attack special.'

Morgana saw the funny side of it and laughed. 'Maybe we should call it that.'

'If you do, then I want at least a ten per cent commission on all sales.'

She smirked at him, flashing a set of teeth almost as bright as the reflection in the diamanté mirror. 'I'm sure we can work something out,' she said.

At first, Tomek hadn't picked up on the casual flirting, but as she placed the notebook back in her pocket and lingered a moment longer, he began to notice it.

'Where are you from?' he asked. 'I sense an accent.'

'You have good ears,' she replied. 'Estonia, but I've lived here almost all my life.'

'Likewise.'

Intrigued, she clicked her pen for a second time and placed it in her apron pocket beside the notebook. 'And you?'

'Born in Poland, moved here when I was five.'

'Very nice,' she replied. 'I wouldn't have known if you hadn't told me.'

He got that a lot. And so he should, he thought; over thirty-five years in the country, and he would have hoped by now that he was able to speak the language properly. Though, having said that, he'd been listening in to some of the conversations at the tables around him and he was confident that he could speak better English than at least half of them.

'You ever go back to Estonia?' he asked her.

But before she could answer, the door opened and in stepped the person he'd been waiting for. She had dyed her hair a darker shade of blonde since he'd last seen her. Either that or the depressing and encroaching darkness of winter had tinted it a deeper shade. She was dressed in a pair of patterned trousers and a black cotton jumper, with her hair fastened in a bun. Trailing behind her was a small wheeled briefcase, overflowing with documents.

'Sorry, I'm late,' she said, flustered.

'Just in time,' Tomek replied. 'You want food?'

She did. The same as him and everyone else. As she took Abigail's order, the smile on Morgana's face dwindled, and as she turned away from them it, and her interest in him, had all but gone.

'Hope you haven't been waiting long,' Abigail said, her voice calmer now that she'd sat down.

'You know I have. You were the one who told me to meet here an hour ago.'

'Sorry. Hectic morning.'

Tomek was sure it had been, but he wasn't interested in hearing it. Less than five minutes later, two plates complete with two eggs, two sausages, two bacon, two toast, two tomatoes, two mushrooms, two black puddings, and a smattering of baked beans, landed in front of them.

'Whatever you want more of, just ask,' Morgana said as she set the plates down.

Tomek thanked her and caught the faint outline of a smile on her lips.

'Stop flirting,' Abigail told him.

'I wasn't.'

'You were. You flirt with anything that breathes.'

'I don't flirt with you.'

'Because you've already been there, done that.'

Tomek rolled his eyes. He wondered how long it would take for her to bring up the drunken kiss that had happened between them one evening. It had been a mistake, on his behalf, particularly, but not for her. She still clung to the emotional turmoil of how he'd treated her afterwards.

'I asked you here to talk business, I'm afraid,' he replied.

'I know you did. I haven't got pictures of you on my walls at home, Tomek. I haven't got little love hearts next to your name on my phone. I haven't—'

'Prove it.'

She wouldn't. Instead, she ignored the request and tucked into her bottomless breakfast buffet. Tomek joined her, and he soon became one of the messy customers he'd been watching all morning. Grease over his fingers, a sliver of ketchup spilling down the front of his shirt, the grubby and soiled napkin that did little to wipe away the mess. But it was all worth it. The food, the wait, and the incipient heart attack were all worth it. Some of the tastiest food he'd had in a while.

'I need some help,' Tomek said after their plates had been taken away and another round of bacon and eggs were coming for him.

'Sounds important.'

'It is,' he replied.

'And what do I get in return?'

'That's still to be determined.'

Abigail knitted her fingers together and pursed her lips. 'Not very skilled in the art of negotiation, are you?'

Tomek sighed. 'What would *you* like in return?'

'To be lead reporter on whatever it is you need help with.'

That wasn't completely unreasonable, especially if she did already have experience on the case.

'Fine. But you only get a head start on what we'll be telling everyone else,' Tomek replied.

'We'll see about that.'

Tomek's relationships with the press were very much like his relationships with women. None of them had ever gone very well. And they'd always ended in heartache. He always expected too much and he hardly ever gave anything in return. But perhaps that was about to change.

Around them, customers continued to come and go, and as the time rolled past midday, the café became seriously busy, and a small queue had started to form outside. Tomek's second plate of food arrived shortly after, followed by another round of tea for both of them.

'A couple of years ago,' Tomek began, wiping the ketchup from his mouth, 'back when you were just a rookie reporter, feeding off whatever scraps your boss gave you I imagine, you worked on a piece about young schoolgirls in the area who'd been drugged at a series of concerts at the Cliffs.'

The case didn't ring any bells.

'They each had allergic reactions to chemicals inside the drugs,' he continued, trying to refresh her memory. 'And one of them died.'

Still nothing.

'Her name was Mandy Butler.'

To jog her memory, she reached into her small suitcase and pulled out her laptop. After logging in, she quickly found the article that she'd written.

'I remember now,' she said. 'Seventeen-year-old. Died at an Example concert.'

'That's the one.'

'But nothing was ever done with it.'

'Yep.'

Tomek reached out for the computer and took it from her. On the screen she had loaded the folder on her desktop that contained witness reports, the article itself, a folder titled "Photos" and another one listed as "Master". But Tomek wasn't interested in any of those. Instead, he wanted to see her screen saver. He minimised the windows until he found what he was looking for. It was a picture of the awards ceremony they'd attended together. A selfie of her and her colleagues. With Tomek in the background, talking to someone else.

A smile appeared on his face before he realised, and Abigail snatched the laptop from him before he could react.

'Don't say a word,' she said. 'It's an old photo. I've been meaning to change it.'

'Uh-huh.'

'Shut up. Now do you want my help or not?'

'Please,' Tomek said, bringing out the puppy-dog eyes. He massaged his arms and rested them against the table then lowered his voice and gestured for her to come a little closer. 'Yesterday a young girl's body was found. She'd died from an allergic reaction to latex. A condom and glove were discovered lodged down her throat.'

'That's horrible,' Abigail replied, though the emotion failed to make it to her expression. Like him, she had become desensitised to the extremities of the job. 'But what's it got to do with Mandy Butler?'

'I think they're related. The same way you must have thought all those girls getting drugged at concerts was related. I think there's a connection between the two deaths.'

Abigail tightened the knot in her hair. 'What do you need from me?'

Her demeanour had changed. No more funny, flirty Abigail. Instead, he was now sitting across from the serious, resolute Abigail.

'I need to speak with the individuals in your report. I need to know what they know, what they saw, who they spoke with, and if they've ever had any connection with Mandy Butler and Lily Monteith.'

'Lily Monteith,' Abigail repeated slowly. 'That's her name?'

Tomek nodded. Assigning a name to a body immediately made it more real.

'I'm worried something might happen again,' he continued. 'And if I'm right, I need evidence to take to the National Crime Agency.'

Abigail's eyes fell onto the mug of tea on the table, and she began gradually turning it, shifting it an inch at a time with her fingers. 'Let me see what I can do,' she said. 'I'm not giving you the names. Not yet. Let me reach out to them, speak with them, see if they're happy to be interviewed. Some of them were really young when they went through what they did, so it might be the last thing they want to discuss. But give me some time. I'll see what I can do.'

CHAPTER TWELVE

A bigail had been unable to put a timeframe on when she would contact him. It could be anywhere from the end of the day to the end of the week. But she had promised she would reach out to victims individually. She would make it her priority.

In the meantime, on the way back to the station, Tomek had found himself on the high street in search of a replacement shirt from M&S. The ketchup stain from Morgana's Café had been larger than he'd first thought, embarrassingly so, and he was in desperate need of a way to save his blushes when he returned to the office. As he sauntered along the high street towards the station, already wearing his new outfit, he surveyed the litany of shops and retail outlets. HMV, Waterstones, JD Sports, Sports Direct, River Island. None of the shops he'd ever seen Kasia visit or heard her mention. None of them he could pop into and find something for her for Christmas. The only exception was Boots, and even when he'd been in the shops with her, he'd always found himself so confused and nauseated by the dizzying amount of make-up and cleansing products that he'd neglected to pay attention. No, if he was going to get her anything, it would have to be from the list, the list that she still hadn't sent to him. And if she didn't send it anytime soon, then there was no guarantee that she would get what she wanted. This was their first Christmas together, their first of many, until she turned eighteen and disappeared off to university, or stayed with him until she was thirty when she realised the property market was a complete joke, and he wanted to make it memorable.

As Tomek passed the train station, he saw a man dressed in a high-visibility jacket, standing on the side of the high street, holding a bucket in his hands. Penny Picker Pete. A local legend of the Southend high street, Pete spent his days and evenings loitering outside the nightclubs and shops, picking up loose change from those ignorant enough to drop it. He was a local celebrity, and at night time, when the clubs opened up, partygoers and clubbers took photos with him. Tomek was certain he'd taken a photo with the man at some point in his life as well. Though he'd been sober and wearing a police vest at the time.

Upon his return to the office, Tomek spent the rest of the afternoon in meetings. It was 6 p.m. by the time he was finished for the day and he'd had little to show for it. No major breakthroughs, no word from Abigail, and no sign of the killer coming forward. All in all a shocking day. And it was made worse by the fact he'd managed to spill tea down his brand-new shirt from M&S at the dinner table.

'Bastard fucking thing,' he screamed, along with a few more choice words, as the liquid abseiled down his chest.

'Language!' Kasia said. 'You know, you shouldn't drink caffeine after midday anyway.'

'Really? Who said?'

'Science.'

Tomek rolled his eyes and wiped the front of his shirt down with a wet cloth in vain. 'Well, if science was any good then it would've come up with a way to get rid of this stain completely and for me to keep my whites white.'

'You *have* heard of washing up liquid and Vanish before, right?'

Tomek glowered at her and then removed his shirt. He threw it in the washing basket and then changed into a T-shirt. As he pulled the top over his head, Kasia called his name slowly, quietly.

'Dad...' Her voice was filled with hesitation.

'You're not going to ask me about Billy Turpin again, are you?

Because I've thought about it and I'd rather you didn't bring him here, or go to his, for that matter.'

When he opened his eyes, he saw her sitting with her legs and arms folded, a look of disapproval on her face. 'Why do you automatically think that's what I'm going to say? Why don't you let me finish before you start talking?'

'Because I'm the parent. It's what we do. You'll learn for yourself one day.'

'Can I finish?'

He hesitated longer than normal just to hammer home his point. 'Yes...'

'Fine.' She pulled a piece of hair away from her fringe and tucked it into her hairband. 'I was wondering if I could go out one time with Lucy and her friends.'

Lucy...

Lucy...

He ran the name through the Rolodex in his head but came up short.

'Who's Lucy?'

'Cleaves.'

Lucy Cleaves. Still nothing.

'Nick's daughter.'

'Nick's daughter?' Tomek repeated, his mind trailing behind a few seconds. 'As in, Nasty Nick? As in, Detective Chief Inspector Nick Cleaves? As in, my boss? You want to go out with his daughter?'

'Yeah.'

Well, Tomek could hardly argue with that. If Lucy Cleaves was anything like her father, then he knew that Kasia was in safe hands. Safer hands than a kid that wanted to beat up a tonne's worth of beef, anyway.

'What are you planning on doing with her?'

Kasia shrugged. And if he thought the gesture was noncommittal, her response was even more so. 'Just hang out...'

'Just hang out like a bunch of hoodlums.'

'No one says *hoodlums* anymore, Dad. I don't even know what it means.'

'Then it's best you and Sylvia don't just "hang out" with Lucy and her friends, otherwise, you'll soon learn the meaning.'

'It was just me,' Kasia replied defensively. 'I wasn't going to invite Sylvia along.'

Tomek raised an eyebrow. He could feel an important life lesson coming along. 'Why not? You're not ditching Sylvia for Lucy and her friends just because they're a year or two older?'

'Well...'

Tomek shook his head, wagging his finger as he did so. 'Nope. Not on, young girl. That's not flying. You can't just ditch the one friend who's been there for you ever since you joined that school. Take it from me, you need her more than you know, and you will regret the decision to leave her behind. Either you integrate her as well, or you don't go.'

He didn't care if this was a lesson she possibly needed to learn herself, he couldn't afford to risk her losing Sylvia as a friend. The young girl had been the only one to initiate contact with Kasia in school, and that told him she had a good heart, a kind heart. Lucy Cleaves could have been the nicest person in the school, but she would never be as nice as Sylvia. The same could be said for all the other girls in the school and in Lucy's friendship group. Otherwise, they would have been the ones to talk with her on the playground on her first day.

'Is that what you did with Saskia?' she retorted.

Saskia, Tomek's oldest and closest friend.

Saskia, the one he'd had a crush on for the longest time.

Saskia, the one he'd only recently reconnected with after thirteen years adrift.

'Yes,' he said. 'I did the same thing to her, and I regretted it for years.'

'Is that why you didn't speak to her for so long while she was in Scotland?'

'All right. Enough. Go to your room.'

'What! You're being totally unfair.'

'No, I'm not. It would be unfair of me to say you're grounded. Would you like me to say you're grounded? Say one more word and I can make that happen.'

He'd never grounded her before. Never had the balls to do it. But now she was about to test him. And he hoped she didn't call his bluff. He didn't want to be one of those parents, the same as *his* parents, where he prohibited her from doing everything. But she made it so impossible sometimes.

To calm himself down, he found Saskia's mobile number in his phone and asked if she was available for a drink.

'Another late-night drink at a bar?' she said coolly. 'People might start to wonder, Tomek.'

HE DIDN'T CARE what people thought.

All he cared about right now was a distraction. Something to take him away from Lily Monteith and Mandy Butler. Someone to take him away from Kasia and the similarities between her and the murder victims. Someone to take him away from the thought of her and Billy the Cow Fighter.

They met in what was fast becoming their usual hiding spot. A bar in the centre of Leigh Broadway called Moo-Moos, a name which was not lost on him.

'The usual?' asked the bartender as they made their way to the bar.

'Are we at that stage already?' replied Tomek, looking between the barman and Saskia.

'I think so,' she replied. 'We've only been here twice.'

'Must be the only ones keeping it in business,' Tomek whispered to her as the bartender made their drinks.

Once they'd received them, they found a space in the corner by the entrance. Tomek was sitting with his back to the window, while she watched everything take place behind him.

'Hope I haven't spoiled your evening,' he told her as he took a sip of his mojito. It was one of the nicest he'd ever tasted. He didn't know why he'd ordered one, and on a school night too; he was feeling adventurous.

'Just the usual. Sitting alone with a glass of white wine and illiterate children's homework in front of me.'

'I won't keep you too long,' he replied. 'Sounds like you need to get back to that asap.'

She laughed, and as she did so the whites of her eyes illuminated. They spent the next five minutes catching up. Filling in the gaps of the past few weeks since they'd last seen each other.

'What are your plans for Christmas?' he asked her after she'd finished explaining that her head teacher was on the cusp of leaving for a new role in a better-performing school.

'Nothing exciting. Going back home for the week. Visit Mum and Dad.'

'Nice.'

'You?'

'Kasia and I are celebrating together. Just us. She's got a whole itinerary planned. It's very strict as well. Presents in the morning. Then breakfast – scrambled eggs on toast, her choice. Then she wants to watch Disney's *Moana*. Then dinner, which will be enjoyed at the dining table without the television on in the background. Then we've got to play some games. Then we'll finish the evening by watching some romantic comedy film on Netflix or something, by which point I may end up falling asleep on the sofa.'

'Sounds like a wonderful day, to be honest. So why do you sound like you're not looking forward to it?'

'Because I haven't told her that we Poles celebrate Christmas on the twenty-fourth. I'm not sure what it's going to do to her plans. Might throw everything off balance and ruin them all.'

Saskia slowly took a sip from her glass of wine and eyed him studiously. 'Either way, it sounds like my idea of a good Christmas.'

'Mine too. I think we'll save visiting my parents for next year. She doesn't need to be subjected to that just yet. It's carnage of the highest order.'

At least, it had been the last time he'd gone.

Shortly after, the topic of conversation turned to school. And the conversation between Billy the Cattle Boxer and Kasia.

'What a stupid thing to say,' Saskia said. 'There's absolutely no way anyone can knock a cow out.'

Tomek rolled his eyes. That hadn't been the response he'd expected to hear. He'd hoped that she would tell him he was right to prevent his daughter from seeing Billy the Cattle Boxer, that she would affirm his parenting decision.

'The real question is whether you could *outrun* a cow.'

Tomek dropped his head into his hands. This was getting out of control. But as he sat there, staring into the gap between the table and his legs, he couldn't help imagining himself on the running track, pitted against a one-tonne bull.

'I only have to be faster than the slowest person,' he said.

'That's cliché. And shit. Don't ruin the fun of it.' She paused to take another sip. 'In a head-to-head. Who's winning? You or the cow?'

'What're we talking, Shetland or moo cow?'

'What's a moo cow?'

'One that goes *moo.*'

She shook her head derisively. 'It doesn't matter. Either. Just answer the question. Do you think you could outrun a cow?'

He considered a little longer. Imagined the scenario: himself, on a good day, fully equipped with the latest in high-tech aerodynamic sportswear, sprinting for his life in a race that was as fictional as it was ludicrous.

'Yes,' he answered unashamedly.

'Wrong,' came the voice of the bartender from behind the bar.

They hadn't realised it but in the heat of their discussion, they'd been raising their voices and were almost shouting at one another.

Over something fictional and ludicrous.

'Your average cow can run, on *average,* about forty kilometres an hour,' the bartender continued. 'Usain Bolt just about clocked forty-three kph when he broke the world record. Now, unless we're all as fast as the fastest man in the world, I don't think any of us have a chance.'

They thanked the man for his input and then he quietly slipped away back to his duties. As Saskia turned round to Tomek, she wore a smug, know-it-all look on her face.

'Oh, come on,' he replied. 'Like you knew the answer to that.'

'Of course I did. I'm a teacher. It's the first thing they teach you at teacher school.' She paused. 'Besides, we've had the same discussion in my class a couple of times before, though I'll have to bring up the topic of *fighting* one in my next class.'

'What is it with children and their fascination with cows? In our day we used to just tip them over for fun. We never thought we were bigger than cows. When did that whole mindset change?'

She shrugged. 'They're kids, Tomek. They say the stupidest shit. The other day someone told me that bald people are a conspiracy. One of them wrote "pigeons killed Bin Laden" on the whiteboard while I was out of the room. And someone told me they were going to buy me a Cameo for my birthday, and I don't even know what a Cameo is!'

'Unfortunately, I do. Kasia said it's something about celebrities charging extortionate amounts of money for a quick video of them saying happy birthday, or some other platitude.'

'What I'm saying is, at that age, they're just dumb thirteen-year-olds trying to be funny. They're full of hormones and they think the best way to impress each other is by injecting themselves with a potent combination of cocky and idiotic in equal measures every day. You've been there, I've been there, and I'm fairly sure you were exactly the same.'

'So what you're *really* saying is, I should cut this Billy Turpin kid some slack?'

'No. I'm saying you should stop being so uptight. It's not a good look for you. And you'll soon be looking like you're in your fifties by the time you're forty-one.'

Tomek didn't like the sound of that. He prided himself on the fact he looked ten years younger than he actually was. It boosted his narcissistic ego when the women he came across said that he was too young to have a thirteen-year-old daughter. He'd worked hard to look as youthful as he did. A considered and delicate daily routine of moisturisers, creams, and anti-ageing chemicals, with a little hair dye thrown in for his beard and hair now and then.

'I guess maybe you're right,' he said calmly. 'I probably used to think I could take on about five cows at once.'

'Double it, and that sounds like the Tomek I used to sit next to in science.'

Tomek chuckled and finished his drink. He'd needed this. A sounding board. Someone to talk to about the things he knew nothing about. Even though Saskia didn't have any children herself, she'd been around enough of them to know what they were like, and she was so much wiser than him in general, always had been, that he felt like he could ask her anything and she would have come up with a smart, logical and considered response.

When the topic of ordering another drink came up, Saskia thanked him but refused. Work. Early mornings. Nothing Tomek could argue with as he had the same in store as well. As they made to leave, they thanked the barman and told him jokingly that they'd see him again in a few weeks, in the new year.

As they headed back to their cars parked on the side of the road, Tomek heard his name being called. A shrill, high-pitched squeak.

He turned round to see Abigail Winters approaching from afar. She was dressed in a tight black dress with high heels and a mini bag under her arm.

'What are you doing here?' she asked.

He could have asked her the same thing.

'Out for a drink with an old friend,' he replied.

'Same. I was out for a few drinks with some of my old friends as well. Back from my early journalism days.'

He could tell. The smell of alcohol on her breath, and her slurred speech, suggested she'd had more than a few.

'Are you going home?' she asked, hope lacing her voice.

'Looks like it,' he replied.

'Don't fancy staying out for one more? My friends have called it a night but I reckon I could handle another glass or two.'

Tomek hesitated. Then became suddenly aware of Saskia watching their interaction.

'Not tonight,' he told her.

Then she approached, her high heels clacking on the pavement. 'Shame,' she said. 'I *was* going to tell you in private that I've spoken with the girls, but I guess I'll have to do it *now* instead.'

Tomek smirked awkwardly, finding the situation slightly uncomfortable. 'If you wouldn't mind,' he replied. 'What did they say?'

'I'm sorry, but they said they don't want to be contacted by you. They won't speak with you.'

'Did you ask why?'

She burped and covered her mouth with her hand. 'They don't want to relive the past. It's too painful for them all.'

'Did you tell them I'm a police officer?'

'Yes.'

'And it didn't make a difference?'

'No.'

Fuck.

'Fine,' he told her. 'We'll deal with this in the morning. Goodnight, Abigail.'

If she was offended by his abruptness, she didn't show it. When she left, she walked confidently away in her high heels, making sure that Tomek watched her as she went. Which he dutifully did. As her body swayed beneath her outfit, he was transported back to the night of their kiss.

And then he was brought back to the present by Saskia opening her car door. By the time he turned round to look at her, she was already slipping into her car, shooting him one of those glowering looks that she gave whenever she was unimpressed with him.

'What?' he called across to her. 'It's not what it looks like.'

'Which bit, the girls not wanting to talk to you or the one who conveniently found you in the middle of the high street at eleven o'clock on a Monday night and asked you to stay out for another drink?'

CHAPTER THIRTEEN

The yawn escaped his mouth before he could stop it.

'Boring you, am I?' DCI Cleaves asked.

Tomek shook his head.

'Good. As I was saying, are you sure you've covered all bases?'

'Yeah. The only problem is the victims don't want to speak with us.'

'Can any more pressure be applied?'

'I'm enquiring,' Tomek replied. 'But I'm more interested in why we're waiting so long to apply the pressure now.'

Nick's face scrunched. 'Excuse me?'

'I looked through the notes on Mandy Butler's death the other night and came across an email from Tony to yourself, sir, requesting more resources to investigate the attacks on the girls. His email didn't receive a reply. And no further resource was spared.'

Nick shook his head and slapped his palm against the desk. 'What the fuck is this? Is this some sort of interrogation? You working for the IOPC now or something? They got you looking into my mistakes?'

'No, sir,' Tomek said as calmly as he could manage.

'I made a mistake, all right? It was two years ago. About the time Robbie left for the army. I wasn't in a good headspace. We weren't in a good headspace as a family. It's as simple as that. I'll hold my hands up and say it was an oversight.' Nick lowered his head, the aggression and fight flooding out of him. 'But... but I'm going to make it up to those girls, trust me. That's why I wanted you to look after this. You're like a dog after a bone at times, and now you've got Kasia in your life, I think you'll have a renewed sense of determination to find whoever's responsible for this. I mean, *you* were the one to find the link.'

Tomek didn't know if that was supposed to massage his ego or offend him in some way, but he decided to stay quiet and let Nick continue.

'I... I...' He choked, then shook his head. 'You've got the meeting with the NCA in an hour. You need to prepare for that.'

Tomek slid out from beneath the desk and stopped halfway. 'Probably not the best time to mention it,' he began, 'but it seems our daughters are now in communication with one another. Where they got that idea from, I have no idea, and Lucy's invited Kasia and her friend to hang out some time.'

Surprise registered on Nick's face. 'Are you all right with it?' he asked. 'She's a couple of years older than Kasia.'

'Do you trust your daughter?'

'What?'

'If you trust her, then I trust her.'

'Of course I trust her.'

'Then that's fine. Settled. All okay with me. Your daughter and my daughter will be friends.'

'Don't think that means we have to do the same.'

Tomek stepped out of the chair. 'You know you love me really,' he said with a wink. 'Could you imagine if my daughter was a son and *then* they wanted to become friends? Now *that* would be interesting.'

'I'd rather sandpaper a tiger's arse in a phone booth than think about that particular prospect,' Nick replied. 'Now get out of here and do your job.'

His and Nick's relationship was a tricky one. Father-son on a good day, father-son on a bad day, just on opposite ends of the spectrum. Tomek had worked with the chief inspector for nearly fifteen years. He'd visited the family, spent evenings there, feasted on Nick's wife's delicious homemade meals. He'd even been invited to attend a few of their school assemblies when they'd been younger. Nick had three in total. Two girls and a boy. The girls were at school, separated by four years, while Robbie, the eldest, had upped and left school at sixteen to join the army. The decision had broken the family and was the result of a long-standing feud between the biological father and son. As a result, Nick had often come into morning meetings enraged at something, something he wouldn't explain to the team. Except for Tomek. Tomek was the only one who got to see, and hear, what happened behind closed doors.

As Tomek shut the door behind him, he realised that the man had been hurting hard at the time. That he'd taken Robbie's decision to leave the family harder than he'd let on. So much so that he'd been negligent in his work.

But that hadn't stopped him from defending Tomek whenever he'd needed it, whenever he'd put a foot out of line, made a mistake, pushed things too far. Nick had been the first to jump to his defence. And now it was Tomek's turn; as he let go of the handle, he decided that if anyone from the National Crime Agency wanted to know why the incidents involving the suspected drug overdoses hadn't been pursued further than a simple report and a few witness statements, then Tomek would defend, defend, defend.

Deny.

Deny.

Deny.

CHAPTER FOURTEEN

The meeting with the National Crime Agency hadn't gone as Tomek had hoped. The people whose job it was to notice and investigate the signposts of a serial killer had failed to comprehend the link Tomek had explained to them. They had ignored the evidence that a killer was targeting teenage girls based on their allergies.

'There's just too much of a leap,' Naomi Mackenzie had explained to him, the top half of her body visible on the screen. 'Even if there was a third victim, I still don't think it would meet the criteria.'

Tomek had baulked at that phrase.

The criteria.

The criteria that needed to be met so that an innocent person's murder could be investigated in a different way. The criteria that needed to be met to justify the extra resources and expense.

Tomek was ready to give her some criteria of his own, but had decided against it, and reminded himself that they were all on the same side. Even though, at times, it didn't always feel like it.

To calm himself down, and to further prove his point, Tomek left the office and made his way to speak with Elsie Rawcliffe. Friend of Mandy Butler. The one who had been with her on the night she'd died, the one who'd watched Mandy pay for the drugs that had killed her, watched her friend suffer and die right in front of her. Tomek had called into her college and asked to speak with her quietly and without attention. The head of the sixth form had been more than happy to oblige and had ensured that she would stay put while Tomek spoke with her but not before calling the parents to explain what was going on. At that point, Tomek had been forced to wait for Elsie's parents to leave work and get down to the school. They arrived nearly thirty minutes later, and in that time, Tomek had kept the discussion brief, generic – asking about her A Levels, college in general, life without Mandy Butler. The girl was visibly nervous, understandably so, and he could see her reliving the events of that night in her head, watching her friend die again and again before they'd even started the discussion.

'Take your time with everything,' he told her. 'You're not under arrest or anything, I just need to ask some questions about what happened to Mandy on the night that she died.'

'What's this about?' Elsie's mum, a woman who'd introduced herself as Doctor Rawcliffe, asked. She sat within a few inches of her daughter, ready and waiting to wrap her arm around her when things got too tough. Either that, or she was ready to pull her away the moment she decided that the conversation had become too difficult.

'The other day a young girl of similar age to Mandy when she died was found in John Burrows Park. She had died from anaphylaxis. We are currently investigating the two deaths to see if there's a connection between them,' Tomek told her. That was more than she needed to know. More than he'd wanted her to know, but he got the impression that Doctor Rawcliffe wasn't going to let him continue until she was satisfied with his answer.

'Very well,' the doctor replied, then turned to her daughter. 'If you want to stop this at any time, you can. You understand?'

Elsie nodded powerfully, maintaining Tomek's gaze.

'What do you want to know?' she asked him coolly, the steadiness of her breath evident as she breathed in and out in a controlled manner.

'Firstly, I'd like to know if you remember the face of the man that Mandy bought the drugs from. Was it even a man?'

'Yes,' Elsie replied.

Tomek had known it was a man, but it was better to play dumb; that way she would talk more, and the more she spoke, the more she might peel back the layers and remember a minor detail.

'Do you remember his face at all?'

'A... a little.'

'Could you perhaps describe him for me?'

'He... I mean, it was dark, there were so many people. And it was all over so quickly. He didn't exactly hang around.' She sucked in a huge breath, held it, then steadily allowed her body to deflate. 'He was medium height, I'd say. Shorter than you. Thick black hair. Maybe a beard.'

Tomek nodded, conjuring an image of the man in his mind. 'Would you be willing to give that description, and perhaps some more detail, to an artist so we can create an e-fit? Sometimes we find that helps jog your memory a little.'

Elsie paused and turned to her mum, who in turn nodded her approval. 'Okay,' she said quietly. 'I think that would be fine.'

'Excellent. I'll get one of my team to do that for you. They'll be in touch. At the time,' he continued, 'did you recognise the man or did he look like a complete stranger?'

Elsie shook her head. 'Mandy knew him. When he came over she gave him a hug and then she paid him for the drugs. I... I... I tried to stop her but she wouldn't listen. I don't know why she thought it was a good idea. She'd tried them before and I... I told her I didn't want anything to do with them, but she wouldn't listen.'

Tomek studied Elsie's face. The lines in her brow, the dilation of her pupils, the quivering in her voice, and determined that she was telling the truth. That she hadn't been tempted to try the drugs, that she wasn't just pinning all the blame on Mandy Butler to escape the wrath of her medically-trained mother.

'After the encounter,' Tomek began again. 'Did you ask Mandy to find out who the man was?'

'I tried, but she wouldn't tell me. Just told me it was someone she knew from school.'

'*This* school?'

Tomek turned to the head of sixth form sitting at the back of the room, as though expecting her to know the answer. The prospect that the killer had been someone from the same school that he was sitting in excited Tomek.

'Not this school, no,' Elsie replied, and a look of relief stretched across the headteacher's face. 'Mandy used to live in Manchester when she was younger. She moved here when she'd just started year ten, I think it was.'

'Yes. That's right,' the head of sixth added, though it was clear to see from the hesitation in her voice that she had no idea what she was talking about.

Tomek made a note. Manchester. Someone from a school in Manchester that she'd gone to.

'Do you know the name of the school?' Tomek asked.

Elsie shook her head again. 'She didn't talk about it. They only moved back down here because her mum was homesick. Her dad was from there originally.'

'And you mentioned that it hadn't been the first time Mandy had bought drugs,' Tomek started. 'Do you know how frequently she'd taken them?'

'I think only once or twice. Just weed... I think. She and a couple of the other people from our school went into the woods opposite and smoked it after school sometimes, but I never went near it. I was too afraid.'

So she'd upgraded her drug use from weed to ecstasy. A leap that had killed her. And become a poster girl for the dangers of drugs in the process.

Weed, the gateway drug that leads to death.

As he sat there, digesting the information, several things became clear to him. And he was ashamed to admit that it wasn't about Mandy Butler or Lily Monteith at all. Rather, it was about his own daughter.

That Mandy's and Lily's friends knew more about their friends than the parents did their own children. And that, if that was a universal truth, it was about time he started cosying up to Sylvia and her mum, Louise. Because the last thing he wanted was for history to repeat itself. And for Kasia to ditch her friend for someone cooler, break the rules, find herself involved in drugs, and then become another poster girl.

It didn't matter if she was only thirteen years old. The risks were still as prevalent as they were for anyone.

As he left the room, Tomek thanked Elsie for her time and took the family's details for the sketch artist to get in touch regarding the e-fit. Then he thanked the head of sixth, reminded her that he would be in touch, and started back to his car. Just as he was about to close the door behind him, his mobile phone rang.

Abigail.

Hopefully with good news.

'Three times in two days? This is more than I speak with my neighbour, and we see each other almost every day.'

'Would you like to make it four this evening?'

'Only if you've got something for me.'

'Why does it always have to be quid pro quo? Can't two friends go out for a drink and nothing be expected of either of them? You didn't seem to have a problem with it last night when I found you.'

'I thought you were too drunk to remember that.'

'Behave. I was tipsy. Nothing else. Now, what do you say? A drink tonight?'

Tomek paused a moment to check his imaginary calendar.

'I'll have to clear it with my daughter first, but I don't think it should be an issue.'

CHAPTER FIFTEEN

K asia's parting words to him before he'd left for Moo-Moos echoed in his mind as he stepped through the door.

'Doesn't look like you need any relationship advice at all,' she'd said. 'Two women in two nights. You're a busy man. Just no more brothers or sisters, please.'

The thought of that had made Tomek's stomach tighten. Not only was it at the idea of having a newborn in his forties, but it was also the fact that, only a day or two before, she'd shirked the talk of the birds and the bees. And now she was the one bringing it up. So what had changed? What had encouraged her to be so crass about it?

He didn't know, but he was both shocked and encouraged by her choice of words. When she'd first entered his home and been thrust into his life, she'd understandably been reserved and quiet, shy, timid. But now, now that she was feeling settled in her home and her school life (also now that the bullying had stopped), she was becoming more open, the bond of their relationship together becoming stronger. Not only were they father and daughter, but they were also fast becoming more and more like best friends as the days went by. They were discussing things like that – adulthood, friendships, relationships – far sooner than he'd expected. And he didn't want to get in the way of that. If she felt trusting enough to open up about those things with him, then he wasn't going to do anything to jeopardise that.

Perhaps allowing her to have Billy the Cow Fighter over for the evening wasn't such a terrible idea, after all.

As he made his way up to the bar, the man behind it began work on his order.

'Glass of wine as well for your company tonight?'

Tomek chuckled awkwardly. 'Not entirely sure, actually. I think she likes red.'

'Someone else, is it?'

Tomek knew where this was going. 'Just a friend.'

The bartender offered him a knowing look, handed him his drink, and told him he'd add it to the tab.

'I'll pay for it now, thanks,' he said. 'She can get her own when she gets here.'

'Wow,' the bartender replied. 'She *really* is just a friend.'

For now, at least.

Tomek couldn't deny the history, nor could he deny the chemistry and sexual tension between them. But right now he couldn't think about that. Didn't want to. Mandy and Lily were dead because a malicious and evil killer had murdered them, and he needed to find out who it was before he could even think about entering into a romantic relationship with anyone.

Tomek checked his watch repeatedly for the next ten minutes until she arrived. By the time she finally turned up, he had finished his beer in frustration, and in the end decided to pay for a second drink for himself and a glass of rosé for Abigail, ignoring the bartender's smirk as he'd tapped his card on the machine.

'This is nice,' she said as they sat down in the same seats that Tomek and Saskia had the night before. 'We should do this more often.'

'Maybe,' he replied. 'Don't think Sean would be too happy about that.'

'Sean won't mind,' she replied, instantly shooting him down. 'And you know it.'

Her relationship with the sergeant had been brief, an instant flash in the pan that had lasted only a couple of weeks, but Sean hadn't taken the break-up very well. He'd tried on several occasions to make it work but something had come between them. Something that had wedged itself into their relationship and caused a mighty divide: Tomek. All thanks to one drunken night, one drunken kiss.

But Tomek didn't want to go over old ground.

'What did you bring me here for, Abigail?' he asked.

'How did your meeting go with the NCA today?'

Tomek hesitated. How had she known about that? Did she have little recording devices on his desk? Had she planted one on him last night? Or was Sean still feeding her information? Either way, it unsettled him. And made one thing abundantly clear to him; she held all the power in the conversation, and she wasn't prepared to rush through it just to suit him.

'Not very well,' he told her. 'They didn't agree to look into it.'

'I'm sorry to hear that,' she replied, her tone laden with sincerity, which was one of the few times he'd noticed the inflexion in her voice.

'I need those girls to come forward and help in any way they can.'

'I know,' she said, running her finger over the edge of her glass. 'But I don't think they're going to budge on that.'

'Is there nothing more we can do?'

Frustration typically plagued cases involving young victims. The memories of what had happened to them kept them from trusting anyone, even the police, and so they kept quiet, which allowed their attackers to continue committing their crimes. But he had now come to accept that it was part of the job and that it was down to him to find new and innovative ways of circumventing the bottlenecks.

'I think I might have something that could be of interest to you.'

Tomek's eyes widened and his ears perked up.

'I'm listening.'

'I did some digging yesterday and today, spoke with a couple of contacts, met up with old friends.' She took a sip of wine, took her time, took the power away from him. 'And I think I found a similar case, involving a woman up in Manchester.'

'*Manchester?*'

Tomek could feel his palms beginning to sweat.

'Yeah. The place up north. I've never been, but I hear it's turned around recently.'

'What happened in Manchester? Who was it? When? Where?'

Tomek couldn't contain himself. His palms were now coated in a thin layer of sweat, his arse was on the end of his seat, and he was so far forward across the table it looked like he was about to kiss her.

'Five years ago,' she began, speaking slowly on purpose to antagonise him, 'a woman named Diana Greenock was found dead in her ground-floor apartment in Manchester. When her friend found her, they saw a cat sitting at the end of her bed. Diana Greenock was allergic to cats. She was also heavily asthmatic. The cat had been missing for a few days, and while Diana was sleeping one evening, the theory goes that the cat had climbed through the window in the middle of the night and killed her.'

'She was killed by a cat?' Tomek asked, dumbfounded.

'No. The post-mortem says that her allergy had reacted to the cat's presence, and that had set off her asthma, which was the thing that ended up killing her.'

'So a cat sneaks into her room, simply stands there, and then she dies.'

Abigail nodded. 'It's not quite how I'd word it, but then again, *I'm* the journalist.'

Tomek sipped on his beer slowly. If it hadn't been for the earlier discovery that Mandy Butler had once lived in Manchester, he wouldn't have picked up on the connection. But now he couldn't get it out of his head. That, if this was the same killer, then Diana Greenock could have been their first kill. That they'd taught Mandy Butler in some capacity at a school in Manchester. That they'd followed her and her family south. That he'd waited years to kill her.

The gaps between the killings concerned Tomek. Three years between Diana Greenock's and Mandy Butler's deaths, and now a two-year gap between Mandy Butler and Lily Monteith. Five years in total. From the little he knew about serial killers, which was now the correct term to use, if this really was the case, then he knew that whatever desire was driving them would soon become too much to bear and that the gaps between victims would become increasingly shorter. That he might have another victim come across his desk much sooner than anticipated.

'How old was Diana Greenock?' Tomek asked, after realising that he hadn't said anything for a while.

'I believe she was either twenty-eight or twenty-nine. I can't remember.'

That didn't seem to fit in with the pattern. Unless, of course, things had gone wrong with the first victim. That she hadn't died the way he'd wanted her to, and so he'd reduced the age of his victims to someone he could have more control over, more power over. And with the last two of his victims aged fifteen, he had found the sweet spot.

'Do you know what happened with the police investigation?' Tomek asked.

'As far as I understand it, the police interviewed the housemates in her block and left it at that. There was no sign of a break-in, and the cat had been missing for a couple of days prior, so it was assumed that it had just snuck in.'

'Or that's the way someone had made it look.'

CHAPTER SIXTEEN

Fern Clements lay there on the floor in the middle of the cold room. Naked, save her underwear. Beads of sweat dripping from her navel onto the smooth, solid surface, from her chin down to her neck, from her wrists down to her fingers, despite the cold, despite the chill that wrapped itself around the building and surrounding area. It was below freezing outside, not much warmer inside, and yet she was sweating profusely, her body working in overdrive to fight for survival.

He had been standing over her, watching her for the last twenty minutes, waiting for her to rouse from her slumber. When she had, she'd thrashed her arms about wildly, testing the bonds on her wrists and ankles for their durability. Each one had stood up to the task. Now, some minutes later, she continued to thrash and squirm, but her movements had become more of a wriggle, laboured, fatigued, her energy levels depleted. The alcohol she'd consumed in the past couple of hours had done little to help.

Her eyes were wild with fear, yet they still contained the murky fuzziness of alcoholism. And for someone her age, someone whose body hadn't built up the tolerance levels to withstand it, he assumed she would be like that for the next few hours. In a subdued, trancelike state.

Perfect.

She had done half the work for him.

As he stepped forward, emerging from the darkness of the room, he grinned from behind the mesh net in front of his face and moved towards her. As soon as she felt his touch on her forehead, the thrashing intensified. Her whole body this time, including her breasts.

He admired them for a moment, then continued.

This wasn't about anything sexual. It never had been and never would be. He had only removed her clothes because it was necessary. Because he wanted to see how *they* reacted. He would have done the same thing with Lily Monteith; placed her on the floor and taken his time with the latex, smothering the paste he'd bought specifically for her over her body. But the glove had worked much quicker than he'd anticipated, and so he'd been forced to cut their evening together short.

Tonight would be different.

Tonight he would have the time to savour it, to watch the events unfold in front of him.

To perfect the process.

'Shh,' he said as he stroked her hair slowly. The texture of it felt disjointed, distant beneath his fingers.

While the suit was for his own protection, he hated to admit it was ruining the experience of it all. Particularly the mesh net in front of his face that prohibited him from examining her body in as much detail as he would have liked.

The suit itself was exemplary. Sourced from a reputable supplier in Brazil. Elasticated at the feet, hands and waist. Made from the thickest poly cotton on the market. And it even had pockets on the thighs, in case he needed it.

He continued stroking her hair for a moment, hoping that it would settle her. But it wasn't having the desired effect. Instead, she continued to strain her muscles and worsen the abrasions forming around her wrists and ankles. Perhaps she thought that something was going to happen to her sexually. Perhaps she thought the suit was part of his fetish. But how could he tell her that the reality was going to be much worse without spoiling the surprise?

'Shh,' he continued. Still to little effect.

He couldn't promise her that everything would be okay, because it wouldn't. And he wasn't in the habit of lying or giving false hope. He liked to say things how they were.

With the obvious exception of keeping *this* a secret and saying absolutely nothing to anyone.

Realising that there was nothing more he could say or do (he had struggled to pull his eyes away from Fern's thin, slender, underage body as it was), he decided it was time to begin.

He gave her hair one last stroke, then turned and headed towards the exit. He returned a few moments later, object in hand.

At first, Fern didn't seem to recognise it. But as the intensity of the sound increased, she craned her neck and her eyes widened, her pupils focused and almost instantly it was as though she was sober again, the alcohol suddenly drained from her system.

She knew exactly what was coming.

He knew exactly what was coming.

Which meant it was time to begin the next stage in the process to rid the world of those weaker than himself, weaker than the general population.

One allergy at a time.

CHAPTER SEVENTEEN

Tomek yawned as he turned the fried eggs over. He needed to cook them thoroughly, Kasia had said. That had been a stipulation the first time he'd made breakfast for her. None of the soggy, uncooked bits at the top that looked like water. Her eggs needed to be cooked to almost within an inch of extinction. The same went for her toast and bacon, black on all sides.

'What lessons have you got today?' he asked as she entered the kitchen, her school uniform all askew.

'Nothing exciting,' she said. 'Maths. History. PE. English. And double science.'

'*Double* science?' Tomek asked. He could think of nothing worse.

'Yep,' she answered. 'Double the lesson. Double the boredom. But enough about me. I want to know how you got on last night.'

Tomek flipped the eggs over again, wincing at the yellow yoke that now resembled a spongy rubber ball.

'How I "got on"?'

'Yeah. Did you pull?'

Tomek chuckled. Decided to keep the farce going.

'None of your business.'

'That's a yes then.'

'No, it's not. It's an "it's got nothing to do with you, so keep your nose out of it" none of your business.'

'Did she look nice?'

Tomek hadn't thought about it. In fact, he couldn't recall what she'd been wearing.

'Erm, yeah. She looked nice.'

'What was she wearing?'

And then he remembered. A pair of white jeans, freshly washed and possibly ironed. A pair of white boat shoes that had faded in colour slightly. A black blazer sitting over a grey knitted shirt. An obvious effort had been made on her part and he'd been completely oblivious to it.

'Sounds like she got herself all dressed up.'

'Yes. Thanks, matchmaker.'

'When are you going to see her again?'

'In a professional capacity?'

'That's not what I asked,' Kasia replied, looking at him sternly. 'And you know it.'

'Nothing gets past you.'

Tomek finished with the eggs and placed her breakfast on the table. Kasia sat down excitedly on the chair.

'Have I met her?'

'No.'

'Can I?'

'No.'

'Why not?'

'Because she's a colleague. And there's nothing going on between us.'

'What about Saskia?' Kasia asked. 'Does Saskia know about Abigail?'

'How the f—' he began but then caught himself. He raised an eyebrow. 'How do you know her name?'

Kasia seemed to cower in her seat and busied herself with her breakfast, eating it quickly so she didn't have to answer the question.

'I have my ways,' she said carefully.

'Well, stop them. There's nothing going on with either Saskia or Abigail. Nor do I want there to be.'

'Why not?' The tone in her voice changed from eager and annoying to pensive and displaying genuine concern.

'Well...'

Careful here, Tomek.

'Because I've got you to look after, haven't I? And I've got work. Both take up—'

'Don't let *me* get in the way of your love life,' she told him as she finished the last of her breakfast. 'Not if it's going to stop you from being happy.'

'It won't. You won't. I...'

'I want you to be happy,' she said sincerely.

'And I want you to be happy too,' he replied in kind.

'Great. So is it all right if Billy comes over after school one night?'

And there it was. The ulterior motive. The reason she'd wanted to pry and interfere with his private life. The reason she'd wanted to build him up and make him unable to go back on his own words.

She had duped him.

Or so she thought.

'I've been thinking about that,' he started. 'I'd like to meet Billy. Maybe the three of us could go out for dinner so I could get to know him a bit better.'

'I... er...' The colour flushed from her face. 'I mean... I can ask. But, I don't think he'd be comfortable with that.'

Course he wouldn't. The boy was a joker in the classroom but a mouse outside it.

'So can he come round after school one evening?' she insisted when he didn't say anything.

He hesitated before responding. The word that filled him with fear came to mind.

Situationship.

All five syllables of it.

'What will you two be doing if he comes over?' Tomek asked. He placed his hands on the back of the dining room chair as he waited for a response.

Kasia had pushed the plate away from her and was in the middle of getting her school bag ready for the day. A lunchbox, her daily planner, notebooks, and a water bottle all made their way into the centre compartment.

'None of your business,' she replied eventually.

Tomek knew she was trying to be smart, trying to play him at his own game, but sadly for her, she'd just said the worst thing possible, and hadn't realised it.

Sit-u-a-tion-ship.

'You're too smart for your own good at times,' he said, 'but now you've just said that, there's no way I can let him come over. Not without adult supervision, at least.'

Kasia's face scrunched into a ball of fury, as though he'd just confiscated her phone from her – or something else just as life-threatening to a thirteen-year-old. But before she could reply, his phone rang, vibrating against his leg.

Weirdly, and yet also sadly, he knew what the call would be.

The intuition, the little alarm bells, were already ringing inside his head.

As he listened to DC Oscar Perez explain to him that another body of a teenage girl had been found, he knew that his next conversation with the National Crime Agency would go much better than the last.

CHAPTER EIGHTEEN

The crime scene was in complete contrast to Lily Monteith's.
The body had been left, half naked, undignified and
exposed to the elements and the unenviable stares of his colleagues
and the professionals that were working around her. Because there
were no clothes on her, save the underwear she'd put on before she'd
died, there was also no bag or form of identification.

The manner in which she had been discarded was different too.
This time she had been dropped onto the grass in the middle of
Belfairs Park, near Leigh-on-Sea, in anger, in frustration. Thrown
onto the ground like an empty crisp packet. Her arms were mangled
and disfigured, lying at awkward and unnatural angles; her legs had
been left the same way.

But that didn't stop them from seeing her injuries.

Oh, no.

Those had been left on show for the world to see.

The pinprick holes over her body. The oversized welts on her skin,
raised like tiny volcanoes. The mass of them on her face and chest.
The hives on the lips and cheeks. The stingers that still protruded
from the attack sites.

'*Jezus Maria*,' Tomek said as he approached the body. 'How
many are there?'

'One would have been enough to kill her,' replied Lorna, standing there with her hands in her forensic suit pockets. 'Assuming this is related to *your* killer.'

As though they were friends who kept in regular contact with one another.

Accompanying Tomek, however, were his *actual* friends. DS Campbell and DC Chey Carter, the team's youngest member.

Tomek tried to count the number of red dots on the girl's body. 'There's at least fifty stings. And that's on just one side.'

'So at least fifty bees,' Sean added.

'Yep. Good start.' His eyes scanned over the girl's underwear, at the area of flesh near her inner thigh. 'That one looks like it's still stuck in her.'

The tiny ball of black and yellow listed to one side, gently swaying in the wind. It was a miracle it had survived for so long. Tomek bent down for a closer look.

'Careful!' shouted Chey, thrusting a hand in front of Tomek's face. 'Don't touch it otherwise, it might become a zom-*bee*!'

For a moment Tomek didn't say anything. Not because he didn't know what to say (he knew the exact words that would come out of his mouth long before Chey heard them), but because he was so taken aback by the comment it took his brain a few seconds to work out whether the constable had actually said it.

Eventually, Tomek turned round to face the young detective and scowled at him, menace on his face. 'You're a fucking disgrace, mate. You should be ashamed of yourself. Have some fucking respect.'

The inexcusability of his comment quickly made its way onto Chey's face, and he apologised profusely. Tomek accepted it and then welcomed him to what he called The Punishment Team: a small unit that currently consisted of just Chey, who would now be doing all the long hours, the overtime, and the boring and monotonous tasks that nobody else wanted to do. If anyone in the team needed someone to fetch something from exhibits, Chey was the man. If they needed someone to attend a post-mortem on their behalf, Chey would be the first name in everyone's mind.

Tomek didn't want to lead with such an iron fist, but it was necessary. There was a time and place for comments like that and staring right at the body that had only been cold for a few hours was certainly neither the time nor the place.

'Too far, man,' Sean said, shaking his head as Chey cowered behind them both in an attempt to stay out of sight. 'Too far.'

'Like you haven't said any worse,' Chey whispered beneath his breath.

Tomek heard every last word. Saw it too. The fog on his breath was the biggest giveaway. 'Oh, we've been there, done that,' he replied. 'But we've learnt when and where. It's the same for you. Rite of passage.'

'Either way, I still think it's disgusting what he said.'

All three men turned to see the last of the fog leaving Lorna's mouth.

'Well, on behalf of young Mr Carter over here,' Tomek began, 'I apologise.'

'It's only disgusting because I didn't think of it first.'

Oh, great, Tomek thought. *Two inappropriate comedians in the team.*

Add that number to himself and Sean, and they were already well over his preferred limit.

Turning his thoughts to the matter at hand, Tomek pointed to the bee that was sticking out of the girl's thigh. To Chey, he ordered, 'Find a SOCO. Get them to *carefully* remove the insect and add it to the exhibits list. After you've done that, I want you to find out what type of bee it is and where it came from.'

Chey opened his mouth to speak but Tomek immediately cut him off.

'Don't you dare fucking say it came from a beehive, otherwise I will slap you off this team.'

Chey left the conversation with a wry smile on his face.

'Kids nowadays,' Sean said, rolling his eyes for sarcastic effect.

'Little gobshites, aren't they? *Gówniaki* we call them back home.

Roughly translates to *shitlings*. But Chey's one of the good guys, even if he doesn't know how to behave properly yet.'

'He's a bit like an untrained dog. Pissing and shitting all over the place.'

Tomek looked up to his friend, all six foot four of him, and slapped him on the back playfully. 'I've already got a pissing and shitting thing back home. She's not little, granted, and she's well housetrained, but she still pisses and shits. Don't suppose you want to take that one under your wing?' Tomek nodded in Chey's direction. The young man was nervously addressing a faceless figure in a white forensics suit.

Sean's face contorted as a gust of wind blew in carrying Lorna's words with it.

'What the fuck is wrong with you guys?' she asked. 'I thought *I* was the weird one. But you lot are something else. It's a fucking miracle any of you get any work done.'

'It's a miracle we get *anything* done,' Sean replied. The wind had started to pick up and was flapping the sides of his forensic suit in his face.

As he said it, a stray leaf slapped him on the cheek. Tomek was just about to laugh when he saw a pile of them, sodden and the colour of rust, hurtling towards them. His first thought was to protect the body. But the SOCO team were in the middle of retrieving the tent from their van and were battling with the wind themselves. Tomek crouched down beside the girl and began removing whatever leaves and other detritus had blown over her in the assault.

Mercifully, there were only a handful, and only a few of those had landed on any of the numerous bee stings marking her body.

'We need to get her covered as soon as possible,' he noted to no one in particular.

'They're working on it,' Chey said as he returned.

With him was a Scenes of Crime Officer holding a plastic bag in her hand. She bent down, removed a thin plastic tube from inside the bag and pressed it against the girl's thigh. Then, with delicate precision, she pinched the bee from the wound with a pair of tweezers and dropped it into the tube.

Tomek thanked her. She ignored him and advised Chey that someone in the team would be in touch with the exhibits officer regarding the exhibit number. And with that, she left.

'Do you know her?' Tomek asked.

'Who?'

'Her.'

'Who?'

'Are you a fucking owl? The young lady who just came over and thinks you're more senior than me.'

'Oh, *her*.' Chey's cheeks flushed red. Either it was the cold having a sudden impact on the blood flow to his face, or he'd just been caught out and he knew it. 'Noooo... never met her before in my life.'

Tomek folded his arms across his chest. 'Of course you haven't.'

'Is it one of those situationships?' Sean asked Chey, looking directly at Tomek.

'Fuck off,' he replied. 'Let's drop the entire conversation and move on. First thing I want to know is who this girl is. Then I want to know what she was doing here, where she'd been, who she was with, and what happened to her. Then I'm going to send Chey down for the post-mortem and victim identification. And, Sean, if you'd like to join him, then keep making silly comments about my thirteen-year-old daughter's social life.'

CHAPTER NINETEEN

B y the time they returned to the office, Rachel had finished setting up the major incident room, and everyone in the team was beginning to filter into it. Standing together at the head of the room, like they were two army generals about to give a final message before sending the troops to war, were DCI Cleaves and DI Orange, arms behind their backs, spines straight. Tomek approached them.

'What's all this about?' he asked. 'Looking like Thelma and Louise over here.'

Nick lowered his voice and spoke bluntly. 'I've moved the case over to Victoria's remit. She's in charge of it now.'

The words felt like a slap to the face, a punch in the stomach and a kick to the balls. All at once. Victoria. In charge. Nick had gone against his word and had chucked Tomek off the case. It was now no longer his to manage, his to oversee, his to prove himself.

'Given the complexity of the case,' Nick continued, 'I wanted someone with a little more experience to take care of it from here.'

Tomek couldn't focus on anything else, not the chatter behind him, not the sound of feet shuffling on carpet, not the noise of the door closing. All he could focus on was Nick's choice of words.

Someone with a little more experience.

Little being the operative word. Victoria had fast-tracked her way to inspector level, which didn't always mean she had the experience to go with it. As Nick had just proved.

Someone with a little more experience.

Tomek suppressed the rage beginning to burn within him. He had nothing to say.

'It's nothing personal, Tomek. I just want to get a handle on this before things get too out of hand. I've called a press conference for this afternoon. I want to know where we are by then.'

That explained why he'd seen a handful of cloaked figures hovering underneath umbrellas outside the front entrance to the station. As members of staff, they typically used the back entrance as it was quieter and drew less attention to themselves. And they were less likely to be accosted by a desperate journalist asking for comment.

'Cool,' Tomek said, hoping the sour taste in his voice was evident.

'Like I said. Nothing personal.'

'Do you need me for anything right now? I have a call I need to make.'

Nick and Victoria looked at one another. Nick sighed as he replied. 'We kind of need you here.'

'Why?'

'Well, because you've been the one running this investigation so far. You're the one who knows everything there is to know.'

'Interesting.'

Nick sighed again. This time deeper, longer. 'Don't make this more difficult than it is. And don't make it all about you.'

'I'm not.'

'You are. From where I'm standing you're coming across as a petulant child right now. Who do you need to speak with?'

'The National Crime Agency. I figured they might like to hear about our Jane Doe.'

'Can you call them after?'

He shrugged. 'Maybe.'

'Well, how long is it going to take?'

A lot less if you stop talking to me and let me go now.

Another shrug. 'As long as it takes.'

'Fine. Make the call. But come back.'

Like he would go anywhere else.

THE CALL to the NCA had gone better than he'd been expecting. He'd explained to his contact, Naomi Mackenzie, that a fourth body had been found. And when she'd questioned where the third body had come from, Tomek had described to her the events surrounding Diana Greenock's death in Manchester, and the link between her and Mandy Butler; the slight but significant link that was becoming more tenable as the days wore on. After hearing that, Naomi advised him that she and her team would look into the details of the case. All he had to do was send the information across and await their call.

It wasn't a flat-out no. It was a consideration. A welcome improvement.

Sadly, the same couldn't be said for his mood. He was still livid when he returned to the incident room. What annoyed him most wasn't the fact that he'd been replaced by someone only marginally senior with a marginally greater amount of experience; it was the fact Nick didn't trust him enough to do the job himself. Tomek liked to think he'd proven himself up to that point, that he'd unearthed two further potential victims, that he'd made the initial connection, with the help of Martin's thoroughness and analysis, between Lily Monteith and Mandy Butler. Without his intuition, there would be no press conference, there would be no serial killer, and there would be no justice for Diana Greenock and Mandy Butler.

So why the sudden change in leadership?

He knew he would drive himself crazy thinking about it, so he resolved to think about something else. To channel his aggression in a different direction. Instead, he chose to think about the next steps, the next steps *he* would take to find the killer.

But before he could think about it properly, he was called by Nick and Victoria to the head of the room to explain everything he knew. As he stood there, looking down at the eager faces of his colleagues, he pushed Victoria and Nick to the back of his mind, imagined they weren't there, and took a snapshot of his team when they looked their freshest, because he knew that in a few weeks, those wild and excited eyes would become tired and drained, exhausted from all the late nights and overtime, time they'd spend away from their families over the festive period. This would be the last time they looked like this, and he wanted to make sure it lasted for as long as possible.

'Five years ago,' Tomek began, turning his attention to the white-board. He cleaned it with the cuff of his sleeve and split the board into four sections. At the top of each section were the names of the four victims in chronological order. Diana Greenock, Mandy Butler, Lily Monteith, and now their latest unidentified victim, their Jane Doe. 'Five years ago,' Tomek started again, scribbling as he spoke, 'twenty-eight-year-old Diana Greenock was found dead inside her ground-floor apartment in Manchester. She was severely allergic to cats and cat hair and had asthma to top it off. She was discovered by a friend who had come over to visit her after she hadn't turned up for work. The friend quickly called it in but by the time she tried to resuscitate her, she was already gone. Post-mortem results indicate that she had died from an asthma attack *induced* by the cat that was found in her room.'

Tomek pointed to Mandy Butler's name and began writing the details of her death below it.

'Two years ago, so a gap of three years between Diana's and Mandy's deaths, seventeen-year-old Mandy Butler was killed in a concert at the Cliffs Pavilion. Suspected drug overdose. During the concert, a man who purportedly knew Mandy approached her and her friend and offered them drugs. Mandy took him up on the offer, subsequently took the drugs, and then died as a result. The drugs in question were ecstasy, but they just so happened to be laced with large quantities of ibuprofen and paracetamol, chemicals which Mandy was allergic to. She died on the dance floor, surrounded by hundreds of people, and was trampled over. Post-mortem determined the cause of death was the ecstasy, but her parents thought differently. And so do I.'

Tomek dragged his fingers across to the third name on the list.

'Lily Monteith. Died only a few days ago. Found in John Burrows Park in the early morning, fully clothed and without any indication as to what had happened to her. Turns out that, according to the post-mortem, a condom and latex glove had been shoved down her throat. Latex, a substance which she was fatally allergic to.

'Then here we have our Jane Doe, our latest victim. Found half naked in Belfairs Park, covered in nearly a hundred of what look to be bee stings. We have no name for this poor girl, as no identification was left at the scene.'

Tomek finished scribbling on the whiteboard and turned to address the team: *his* team.

'What we appear to have is four seemingly random and unrelated deaths. Except for one thing, one thing they all shared in common. A weakness that has been exploited and abused by a malicious and evil killer. Their allergies.' Tomek paused a moment to let the information sink in and for himself to catch his breath. He looked out at the wall of studious and attentive faces. It was clear to see they were all capti-vated and intrigued, that they all seemed to think this was his investi-gation. 'As far as I've been able to tell, none of the victims knew each other. However, that may change during our collective investigations. There is, however, something that links our first two victims.' Tomek wagged the whiteboard marker between Diana Greenock and Mandy Butler. 'Manchester... Diana Greenock lived and died in Manchester, and at one point Mandy Butler lived there too, before moving to Essex with her family a little over three years ago. That means she had been living in the area for over a year before she was killed. And, it is my suspicion that our killer seems to have followed her here. I spoke with her friend yesterday morning, and she confirmed that the man who sold her drugs knew Mandy from her time in Manchester.

'It is also my suspicion that we're looking for someone who knew them all. Someone who would have taken the time to get to know the girls before killing them and to find out what their *weaknesses* were before finding a way to exploit them. He would have needed time to prepare and time to plan what happened to them. The first kill happened five years ago, and the gap between Diana Greenock's murder and Mandy Butler's is three years. The gap between Mandy Butler's and Lily Monteith's is two years. And now the distance between Lily Monteith's and our Jane Doe is a matter of days. You can see where I'm going with this. The time between kills is getting rapidly shorter, which concerns me as there may be more to come. And we need to make sure we can find him before we find our next body.'

Tomek paused again to open the floor up to any questions. They came at him thick and fast – 'How old were the rest of the girls?', 'Was there any evidence of sexual assault?', 'Why was one of them half naked and the others weren't?' – but before he was able to respond to them, Victoria stepped in and ushered him to the side.

'Thanks for that, Tomek,' she said, smiling at him facetiously. 'I can take it from here.'

'Excuse me?'

The questions stopped and silence fell on the room.

'Thank you for that explanation, but I can take it from here.' She turned her attention to the audience before allowing him a chance to respond. 'These are all questions we're going to need to find the answers to. As Tomek said, we are looking for someone who is potentially close with the girls, or someone who has access to them. Someone in their lives that they all share. We need to find that person.'

Unknowingly, Tomek stepped to the side of the room, as though he was being moved by an unstoppable force. Until he eventually found a spare seat on the outskirts of the group. He slumped into the chair and listened to the words fall out of Victoria's mouth. He had little intention of doing what she asked of him. In his mind, this was his investigation, his plan, and the strategy inside his head was the right one.

At the head of the room, Victoria turned to the whiteboard and drew a horizontal line across all four names, splitting the table in two. Then, in giant letters, she wrote "Next Steps" with no care shown for crossing the vertical lines. Within each column, she began writing the next steps for each victim and started assigning tasks and roles to each team member.

'The best way to combat this is if we divide and conquer,' she began, scribbling as she did so. 'Nadia and Sean, I want you both to find out who lived in the block of flats with Diana Greenock. Work closely with Chey and Martin, who will be investigating Mandy Butler's death. I need you to find a link between the two of them. Anna and Oscar will look into the events surrounding Lily Monteith's death, while Tomek and Rachel will uncover the identity of our Jane Doe.'

Tomek sensed Rachel's head flick towards him in a gesture of unity, but he ignored it and continued to stare at Victoria writing on the board, still enraged that it wasn't him up there instead.

'In the next few hours we have a press conference scheduled,' Nick said, stepping to the front of the room. In the past few minutes, his body had tensed; his shoulders were pushed back, his wrists were flexed and his fists clenched. 'I will be attending on my own, however, if you find some information, I would appreciate someone else being there with me to whisper anything in my ear. That same person will need to apprise me of the facts before I go up.'

Nick's head automatically turned to DC Anna Kaczmarek, or Triple Word Score, as she was affectionately known. As media liaison officer (as well as her role as family liaison officer), it was her duty to prepare the information that was fed to the journalists. A part of Tomek had been expecting Nick to look at him, but when it hadn't come, he breathed a sigh of relief.

The relief was short-lived, however.

'Tomek could do it.'

The suggestion had come from Victoria. As soon as he heard it he clamped down on his jaw and ground his teeth against one another.

'I...' Nick hesitated.

'I'm busy,' Tomek replied. 'This isn't my investigation anymore. I have my own tasks to do.'

'Not unless I tell you to,' Nick replied, more assertive this time.

Tomek chose not to say anything further. He could see the small hole that he'd already dug for himself and decided he didn't want to sink any further. He'd been there and done that before, and having Nick tower over him while he pissed into the hole wasn't something he wanted to relive again.

'I think that's everything for now,' Nick said. 'You can all go.'

At once, everyone lifted themselves out of their chairs and made for the exit. Everyone except Tomek. As soon as the door closed behind the last person, Nick placed his hands on the back of a chair and sighed heavily. His trademark.

'You wanna cut this petty bullshit out?'

'What petty bullshit?'

'*That*. That immature shit where you pretend to be angry.'

'But I *am* angry.'

Nick sighed again. With each one they got progressively louder and longer.

'You understand why I had to change leadership, right?'

'To save face.'

'You what?'

'Because you feel guilty about the way you handled Mandy Butler's investigation and you don't want to be seen as making the same mistake by having a sergeant as SIO.'

This time there was no sigh. Just one long, continuous inhalation that he held there for a long time. For a moment Tomek wondered whether he was still breathing.

'You better watch your fucking tone, Tomek. Otherwise, I'll take you off this team and this fucking investigation.'

Tomek smirked smugly and placed his hand on the door. 'You've already made one promise you couldn't keep, guv. So I think I'll take my chances.'

CHAPTER TWENTY

The beauty of his almost father-son relationship with Nasty Nick was that they were able to fight and argue as much as they wanted, but they always kissed and made up shortly afterwards. There was very little love lost between them at the end of every disagreement – usually. Tomek had been pushing Nick's proverbial buttons for as long as he could remember, and nothing had come between them that seemed like that would change. Except for now. As Tomek departed the incident room, he had the sense that their relationship might take some time to heal following their falling out. That Tomek's comments had been out of line. That they'd been a personal attack on Nick and his ability to lead and fulfil his duties as a chief inspector. That was correct, of course, but Tomek was just as much a stubborn arsehole as Nick was, and so it would be a while before he apologised for his comments. Equally, he expected an apology for being promised the role of senior investigating officer and having that role pulled out from beneath him. And if that wasn't forthcoming, then he didn't know where their relationship went from there.

'You all right there, sarge?' Rachel asked.

'Never better,' he lied.

'Well, do you want to start the car? Only, I'm freezing and could do with the heating on.'

Tomek hadn't realised it, but he'd been sitting in the car for at least a minute without having done anything.

It took a few minutes for the car to warm up and for them to stop shivering. The drive to Fern Clements' house was a little over twenty minutes away in Hockley.

Shortly after Nick had called an end to the meeting, a call had come into the office from the switchboard notifying them of a missing person that matched the description of their Jane Doe. Now they were on their way to the Clements' household to confirm the girl's identity.

'What if it is her?' Rachel asked as Tomek drove along the arterial road.

'Then it's regrettable, but it'll save us a lot of legwork,' he replied. 'But either way, a family's about to be heartbroken.'

'Have you got the image?'

He had. But wished he didn't. The image that had been taken of the Jane Doe's face. The side that had the smallest number of welts on it. The side that would cause the least amount of distress to her family.

The side that, as it turned out, confirmed their suspicions.

Kelly Clements had only been able to look at the picture for a few seconds before nodding her head through tear-filled eyes. She had then disappeared to the bathroom, leaving her husband Ralph alone to absorb the information that their daughter was dead. The two of them lived in a nice four-bedroom detached house, with high ceilings and spacious rooms. The view from the patio doors at the back of the living room looked out onto a perfectly manicured garden that seemed to glow despite the bleakness of the wintry weather outside. A house that had just got a lot quieter, a lot emptier.

Tomek waited patiently for Kelly to return. She did so a minute later, armed with a handful of tissues in her arms, some spilling out from beneath her armpits.

'And... and you're certain she's gone?' Kelly asked as she sat down. 'You're certain it's her?'

Tomek admired Kelly's burning desire to cling to impossibilities.

That the girl in the picture wasn't her daughter, couldn't possibly be. That the girl in the picture was just playing with them, that the bee stings hadn't sucked the life out of her. Christ, he knew he would have behaved the same if he'd been in her place.

'Your daughter was found this morning in Belfairs Park. This photo only shows her head, however, the rest of her is covered in the same lesions,' Tomek explained.

'We suspect they're bee stings,' Rachel continued. Her voice was much softer and gentler than his and elicited a calmer reaction from Fern Clements' parents. 'Is your daughter by any chance allergic to them?'

Eyes wild, Kelly and Ralph Clements nodded slowly.

'But,' Ralph began but choked on the catch in his throat. 'Why would someone do this to her? *Who* would do this to her?'

'That's what we intend to find out,' Rachel continued. Tomek was more than happy for her to take control of this one, and for himself to step in only when necessary. *If* necessary. 'Before we move on to questions regarding the events surrounding your daughter's death, we think it's pertinent to inform you that, within the next couple of hours, our boss, Detective Chief Inspector Nick Cleaves, will be appearing on television regarding your daughter's death. Now, at the moment she will not be named, as we were not expecting to uncover her identity so soon, but we can change that if you wish. The only reason we are going to be giving away information and appealing for witnesses is because we believe Fern's murder is connected to three other murders. Now, we can't go into too much detail, but we are able to share everything that will be in the press conference. Do you have any questions about anything I've just said? I appreciate it's a lot to take in, and it's a lot of information to process, so take your time.'

They didn't have any questions. But Tomek did: teach me, Rachel. In all his years, that was perhaps the most eloquent and soothing way he'd ever witnessed a death message. His were usually straight to the point, matter of fact, almost emotionless. Rachel's had been the opposite. It wasn't exactly rocket science, granted, but Tomek thought he could learn a thing or two from her, which was something he had neglected to do in the four months she'd been a part of the team since transferring from the Metropolitan Police.

'We have a family liaison officer who will be your main port of call,' Rachel began, and then she continued to explain Anna's role to the family, and how she'd become like a third member. (Though she neglected to mention that she might be a sort of distant cousin, thanks to all the families she was having to add to her roster.)

'I would also like to add, before we continue, that I'm truly sorry for your loss, and that we will do everything we can to find out who did this to your daughter,' she finished.

A nice touch. And it seemed to work too.

'We... we appreciate that, thank you,' Ralph said, more courageous this time. 'I think... I feel... I feel confident and more comfortable knowing you're on the case, thank you.'

Rachel offered them a squeeze of the hand each then focused her attention on the details of their daughter's life.

'How old is your daughter?'

'Fifteen.'

'Where was she last night?'

'Out drinking with some friends,' Kelly Clements replied.

'They were having a little house party. Just a few of the girls, we were told.'

'Can I get the name of the girl hosting and the names of the others attending?'

Kelly told her to the best of her recollection.

'Do you know her plans for after the house party? Was she meant to be staying round a friend's, coming back here, or staying overnight?'

Kelly and Ralph looked at one another, as if asking the other for confirmation. 'She was supposed to be staying overnight. They all were. But, if she was found outside then she must have left the house for whatever reason. She must have tried walking home or something. Maybe she'd got into an argument with some of the other girls. I never really liked that Kirsty girl. But why wouldn't she call us if she was on her way back? Why didn't she ask anyone for help?'

Tomek could see what was happening. Kelly was at the beginning of a downward spiral of hypothetical and unhelpful thoughts but before he could put a stop to it, Rachel beat him to it.

'We will do everything we can to answer those questions,' she said, raising a hand then lowering it to subconsciously instruct Kelly to calm down. 'We will incorporate all of that into our investigations, don't worry. Next, I must ask about Fern's allergies. Who else knew about it?'

'Well, there was her school. All the teachers had to be made aware, and the pastoral care team looked after her a couple of times. Then there are her friends, they all know about it. It's... it's funny. She was always telling us how they used to jump on her to protect her whenever they saw a bee in the playground or the field nearby.'

The smile dropped from Kelly's face as her head fell into her lap. Her husband placed a consolatory hand on her back but it was too late. She had already gone back down the spiral, except this time she wasn't vocalising any of it.

Tomek stepped in. 'Were there, to the best of your knowledge, any boys or girls in Fern's life that she was involved with romantically? Was she in a... a situationship with any of them?'

Kelly lifted her face, a look of confusion etched into every pore of her skin.

'Situationship?' she repeated.

'Never mind. Was she involved with anyone, romantically speaking?'

Both parents looked at one another again, testing to see who Fern might have confided in. Then they turned back to him and shook their heads. To the best of their knowledge, Fern didn't have either a boyfriend or a girlfriend. But as he had already learnt several times so far throughout this investigation, it was sometimes the friends who knew more about the victims than their parents.

Which reminded him. He still needed to reach out to Sylvia and her mum. Later. At another, less inconvenient point.

Tomek thanked them both for their time, informed them that they would be in touch if they needed anything, but that Anna would be their main point of contact, and then left, making their apologies and offering their condolences as they did so. As they headed back to the car, Tomek received an email notification on his phone. Intrigued by the preview on the screen, he opened the app and read the rest of the message.

'Don't let them see that smile on your face,' Rachel said as he rounded the other side of the car. 'Otherwise, they'll think you're happy their daughter's dead.'

'What a weird thing to say.'

'Then *why* are you smiling?'

'Because I just got an email from the NCA. They're going to be joining us from now on with some guidance on our serial killer friend.'

CHAPTER TWENTY-ONE

Tomek was sitting in the room with his least favourite person and his new favourite person.

The least favourite person was the one who thought she was in charge of everything, including this discussion. Whereas his new favourite person was the actual one in charge and the one who took control of the conversation every time his least favourite person hijacked it.

'I'm the expert,' Tracy Pickard retorted. 'Do you want to hear what I have to say or not?'

Tomek liked her the moment she came in through the door, and even more so after that comment. She had already sussed out Victoria and it was clear to see she wasn't the type of woman to take things lying down. She was confident, forthright, and she had a job to do. And she was going to do it regardless of what people thought.

Tracy was one of the National Crime Agency's most trusted and experienced forensic psychologists. She had extensively reviewed the case notes that Martin had sent across earlier, and it had been her opinion that had convinced Naomi Mackenzie to give it the green light.

'No. Of course. Please, go ahead,' said Victoria, wobbling.

'Great, thank you.' Tracy brushed herself down before she spoke.

In front of her on the table was her laptop with a notepad beside it. She scribbled as she spoke. 'From what I've been able to review, it appears that the killer is almost certainly known to all the victims. This means that he's comfortable and confident around women, young women in particular. But it's also important to remember that they're comfortable around him. I believe that these people are voluntarily going with him or getting with him to these locations, rather than there being any coercion. This means it's someone that the victims trust, that the girls know and respect. As a result, the killer will come across as personable and friendly to them. I would also say that he might be slightly effeminate, or at the very least displaying signs of it. For the majority, girls of that age are taught to be wary of older men, regardless of their profession or role in society. Now it's possible that these girls are different and they like the older man, which would certainly fit with the theory that he likes to have power over them, but more on that later.

'I think he will be slightly effeminate, approachable, trustworthy and perhaps someone who reminds them a little bit of their father, or any other male role models they have in their lives, in terms of looks, dress sense and mannerisms. However, with four different victims, I would imagine it's difficult to find a man who matches all four fathers, even more so when one of them has sadly passed away.

'On the other hand, the individual could be someone in a position of power and authority. Someone largely attractive as well. Someone who is capable of dismantling his victims' barriers and someone who's not afraid to talk to them inside or outside school. Someone they might perhaps tell their friends about if they ever had a chance encounter with him. He possibly flatters them, but not in a cringeworthy way. And he might even be someone that his victims don't tell their parents or friends about. If that's the case then he's going to be quite manipulative and forceful, however, his victims are young and impressionable so it would not take much for them to believe anything he says.'

Tracy reached across the desk for her plastic water bottle. On it were markings for different times throughout the day to signify when she needed to drink; she had just reached her 2 p.m. water alarm.

'Next, we need to consider the killer's motivations. *Why* is he killing these victims via their allergies, and why this age group? And then we will move on to the how.' She screwed the cap on tightly and set the bottle back down beside her laptop. 'Firstly, I would argue the victims' age group is predominantly down to accessibility and power. He can have control over a teenager much easier than he can a fully grown woman. Obviously, there are some instances where that might not be the case, but our killer is intelligent enough to know which battles to pick and make a choice. I don't believe the sex of the victims has anything to do with it because there has been no evidence of sexual assault. There is no sexual motivator behind his actions, behind his killings, and I don't expect that to change in the future. These are almost his test subjects.' As she said it her eyes illuminated, as though she had just come up with the idea at that particular moment. 'He is playing with them, testing out different allergies and their reactions to them. First the cat, then the drugs, then the latex and now the bee stings. He perfects the method of killing per allergy and then moves on to the next. With Diana Greenock, if she really was his first victim, she died from her cat allergy. That was done and dusted so he moved on to the next. Ibuprofen. Now, as you know, this wasn't very successful because he tried it a handful of times with the other victims.'

'Did he?' asked Victoria, who looked as surprised as she sounded.

Tracy turned to Tomek, then bounced back to Victoria. 'Tomek sent me the newspaper article,' she explained. And that was that on the matter. Victoria would have to catch up in her own time. Then Tracy continued, eager to move on and get all the thoughts out of her head while they were still lucid. 'Once Mandy Butler had been successfully killed thanks to her reaction to the ibuprofen in her system, he moved on to Lily Monteith. Latex. That was an instant success and so he moved on to Fern Clements, our latest victim. With each successful kill, with each successful *experiment,* he finds a new victim.'

'What do you think about the times between the killings?' Tomek asked. So far he'd been transfixed with what she was saying. He didn't necessarily agree with it all, and at times struggled to see why she was as celebrated as she was, but he was enamoured with what she was saying, nonetheless.

'I did consider that, and I think that now that he's got a process down, he's going to be carrying out killings much faster. He may already have a roster of potential victims that he can target, a list he may have been putting together over the course of the past five years, and now he's ready to use it. These may have been girls that he's known since they were younger, and he's been waiting until they're a particular age before he wants to try it.'

'Why?' Tomek asked. 'Why's he waiting? Why not just try it when they're much younger?'

And then the answer became obvious to him. The latest three victims – Mandy Butler, Lily Monteith and Fern Clements – had all been out socialising in one form or another. They'd been away from their parents, alone, and the attacks had happened in isolation and in darkness (with the exception of Mandy Butler).

'He's chosen that age because they're starting to go out more. Fewer eyes watching them. They're more vulnerable.'

'Exactly,' Tracy said forcefully. 'He's intelligent, calculated. He takes a lot of pride in his plans and there's a lot of attention to detail.'

'What about other motivations?' Victoria asked. 'Forget about the girls for a minute. Why is he doing this in the first place?'

Now that was the million-dollar question. And Tomek was intrigued to hear whether Tracy had an answer to it.

She considered thoughtfully for a moment, seemingly aware that this was her moment to prove her worth.

'I wouldn't like to say for certain or stake my career on it, however, I would imagine it's because he views allergies as some sort of weakness. He is someone who will be of typically good health and he will laugh at the fact that something as small or minor as cat hair and latex can kill a person. He will draw pleasure from that thought. He may have some sort of God complex where he thinks he is better than everyone else, and so he is ridding the world of those weaker than him. He considers it his duty.'

Tomek nodded and was in full agreement on that point. A dangerous and evil ego was running the show. One that would take some stopping.

'Have you considered the possibility that this might be more than one killer? A duo of like-minded individuals or a *folie à deux*,' Victoria asked. She was referring of course to the past case that they had worked on together, the disappearance and murder of two young girls on Canvey Island, who had been abducted and killed by an estranged couple seeking revenge.

'If that's what you suspect of being the case, then there's no point my being here.'

'Just covering all angles,' Victoria replied with an unimpressed grin.

The conversation concluded and they both thanked Tracy for her time. Then Tomek led her out of the room and over to the small space that had been set up for her next to Anna in the office. When she'd asked for a space of her own, Tomek had chuckled and reminded her that she wasn't in London anymore. Shortly after, he reluctantly headed back to the room where Victoria was sitting waiting. Just the two of them. Alone. Left to discuss. Where he would do all the talking and she would take all the credit.

'What did you think?' Tomek asked, getting in early.

'I think it's a good starting point. I think it's given us a lot of food for thought and clarified a lot of uncertainties I was having. I think it'll be good to have her on the team.'

That sounded like interview-speak to Tomek. Telling him what he wanted to hear.

Sadly, he didn't feel the same way.

'Answer me this. Are we looking for an effeminate man who reminds them of their father, or a confident, attractive authoritative figure?'

To that, she didn't have an answer.

As Tomek expected.

Tracy's psychological profile of the killer had been contradictory at times, as Tomek had just pointed out, but there were still good nuggets of information that he thought relevant. Things that he didn't feel comfortable sharing with Victoria. For those, he would approach Nick directly.

'Anything you'd like to add?' Victoria asked.

Tomek hesitated. 'Yes,' he started as he made to leave. 'Do you think you could *outrun* a cow?'

CHAPTER TWENTY-TWO

Kasia waited all lunchtime to speak with him. Until the bell sounded and the area emptied. While everyone was worried about getting a detention, she grabbed him from the other side of the playground.

But she didn't care. She had something to ask him. Something important.

'Do you want to come over tonight?'

Billy's mouth opened and closed several times like a fish.

'Are you... erm, have you checked... is it all right with your dad?'

She sighed and folded her arms across her chest. 'Why are you so obsessed with him?'

Billy leant closer and whispered out the side of his mouth. 'Because he's a fucking fed.'

'Yeah. And? He said it's okay.'

Billy seemed dubious. Still didn't answer the question.

'He's not even going to be home. Look.'

She reached for the pocket inside her blazer and showed him her phone. On the screen was the text message from her dad that she'd received only a few minutes before, notifying her that he was going to be late, and wishing her good luck with her Polish lesson tonight.

'See! He won't even be there.'

Billy read the message through several times.

'How do I know you didn't just send that from another phone?'

'Why would I do that? Do you not trust me? Do you not love me?'

He placed his hands on her arms. 'Of course I do. I just... I dunno. What if he finds us?'

'I've already told you that he's fine with it. And I told you, I don't want to do *that*.'

The expression on Billy's face just dropped. Had she just given him another reason not to come?

'I was gonna go to the park after school,' he said.

In the pitch black? she thought but chose not to say anything.

'That's all right,' she replied. 'I've got my tutor coming over tonight so you can come after that. Say, seven?'

Billy hesitated for a moment, lost deep in thought as he weighed the decision in his mind. It was a simple yes or no answer, but he was making it much more difficult than it needed to be. She understood his hesitation. Her dad *was* a police officer. She could see how that would be intimidating, but why didn't he trust her, why didn't he listen to her? Even if Tomek hadn't said outright that Billy could come over, how would he know if he was going to be late? From experience, she knew that "late" meant anywhere between nine and ten, and that was on a good day. Some nights it was as late as eleven or midnight, and Tomek would find her still awake in her bedroom watching Netflix on her laptop. On a school night. But what he didn't know was that she sometimes stayed awake until even later just scrolling on her phone, watching videos on TikTok and Instagram. That was why she always felt tired but would never complain about it because she knew what he would say.

Go to bed earlier.

Stop scrolling on that phone of yours otherwise, I'll have to confiscate it.

All the boring dad things that she'd already heard so many times.

Well, tonight would be different. Tonight, by the time Tomek came home, Billy would have been and gone and she would be fast asleep.

The only problem was food. Getting something for dinner.

'Do you have any money?' she asked him.

'Yeah, course,' he replied with a proud nod.

'Can you buy a pizza or something and then we can eat it when you get to mine?'

Before Billy could answer, Mr Healy, the head of Year Nine, came out onto the playground. His stomach bulged out of his shirt and his tie was skew-whiff.

'Get to class!' His deep Scottish voice rolled across the playground. 'This is your last warning. Otherwise detention for both of you!'

Without saying anything, Billy went one way, while Kasia went the other. As she headed into the small building where her history classes were, she stopped in the doorway and watched Billy sprint across the playground.

'Seven o'clock,' he yelled, voice breaking halfway through the sentence. 'And I'll bring the pizza!'

CHAPTER TWENTY-THREE

Tomek was grateful he hadn't been forced into attending the press conference along with Nick. From what he'd been able to hear, which was all of it thanks to the *Live* video feature on *Southend Echo*'s website, it had been a car crash.

Nick had started fluently, eloquently, all very well. Explaining the situation, that two girls of similar age from different schools had been found dead in two separate fields, and that their deaths were being treated as suspicious and connected with one another. But then, as he'd begun to answer questions from the hungry wolf pack in front of him, he'd started to crumble, to babble.

It had been relentless. Word, thanks to Abigail Winters no doubt, had spread that Mandy Butler's death was inextricably linked and that there was a whole cohort of girls similarly aged who had experienced something similar. That a request for further investigation had been made and that nothing had been done about it. Naturally, the press had begun to question Nick's credibility and professionalism by this point. But it had all come crashing down as soon as mention of Diana Greenock had been made, also from Abigail Winters. (Tomek had to give it to her, she was a tenacious little bitch, and she wasn't afraid of who she went after in the process).

Two murders were bad enough.

Three murders with a host of related victims was serious.

But four murders, all related, was a step too far.

Two lives could have been saved if Nick had investigated more thoroughly into Mandy Butler's death.

'What are you going to do differently?' a voice asked off-screen, though he recognised it as Abigail's.

Again.

Relentless. A trait he didn't think he'd ever not admire about her, so long as she wasn't hassling *him* for information.

'Well,' Nick began, sighing heavily. He looked weathered and broken, ready for the conference to end. 'This time we have a team of some of our... of our finest men and women working on the case. We will also have the support of the National Crime Agency in helping us determine the profile of our killer.' Then he turned to the camera and addressed the viewer directly, his eyes piercing, gaze intoxicating. 'If anyone has any information related to the deaths of these four individuals, please come forward. We are appealing for as much information as you can give us. Thank you.'

'Why wasn't this done before?'

'How much do you really know?'

'Why are you still in charge?'

'Why do you think you're fit to run this investigation?'

The onslaught of questions that followed him out of the room was brutal, and a part of Tomek felt slightly guilty for the man. But only slightly.

'That sounded intense,' Rachel said beside him as he placed the phone in his pocket.

'At least he ended on a positive note. Maybe. Or at least he left with *some* dignity.'

'For what it's worth, I think you should have remained as SIO on this case, but I know my opinion doesn't count for much.'

'Thanks,' Tomek said. That meant a lot to him and he appreciated it, but like a typical man he didn't say any of that, rather he left it to internalise. 'A part of me wants to see her crash and burn. While the other part of me recognises the fact that four women are now dead, several more scarred for life, and the killer's still out there.'

'Ah, the classic Catch-22 situation of worrying about your ego or letting a killer kill more victims. Tough one to choose.'

She made the sarcasm in her voice well-known as she rolled her eyes and turned to look through the passenger window.

Her words gave him something to think about. Perhaps he was letting his ego get in the way. It was running the investigation for him so far, and if he let it get out of control then more young girls might die. And then he might find himself having abuse hurled at him from the other side of a microphone in ten years' time.

None of that sounded appealing to him.

Next on the agenda was an appointment with the only registered beekeeper in the Southend area.

Timothy Warren owned and lived on his farm in the middle of Great Wakering, a small village sandwiched between the Essex Marshes to the east and farmland to the west. He was a man well into his late thirties, a few years shy of Tomek, with greying hair and a thick gingery beard. His face was as you'd expect from a farmer: tired, weather beaten, and sporting an annoyingly good tan despite being six months out of date. And his body was in better shape. But Tomek liked to think his would have been as good if not better had he been lugging hay and farming equipment around all day every day.

'We keep the sheep on that side of the farm over there,' the farmer explained as he pointed to a large stretch of flat green earth. 'The chickens in that pen over there. Cows on the other side of that row of hedges. And a couple of horses in the stables beyond the house.'

'You're doing all right for yourself then,' commented Tomek.

'It ain't what it used to be. Brexit's a big fucker for us. We're being out-priced and out-sold everywhere. But what can we do? I was one of them ones who voted for it, so I've only got myself to blame.'

Yes, Tomek thought. *Yes, you do.*

'And then this is where we keep the bees.'

Timothy had led them through a small gap in a row of hedges and into another expanse of flat, green land. Over a hundred metres away were rows of small, white boxes. Surrounding the boxes was a field of flowers that had long since died in the winter. A narrow path, made by intricately placed wooden planks, had been laid down, leading all the way up to the apiaries. A low, monotonous hum that sounded like an electric toothbrush vibrated in the air. To Tomek's right, a short distance away, was a small manufacturing plant.

Timothy gestured them towards it, and Tomek felt himself relax the farther he got away from the electric humming.

The manufacturing plant was deceptively big inside and was separated into two compartments. On the left was the production line, where the honeycomb and produce were turned into honey products. And the section on the right was the end product. Rows of different-flavoured honey jars sat proudly on shelves along the back wall. Pumpkin spiced, turmeric, lemon zest, cinnamon. Alongside, on separate shelving, were rows of honey mustard, beeswax candles, and propolis lip balm, all with Timothy's bee farm branding plastered over it.

Hanging from the walls was a series of beekeeping suits at various stages of production. One was simply a hat with a net. Another was a hat and the top of the suit that stopped at the waistline. The final one was the suit in its entirety, complete with hat, net, and full body suit. The highest layer of protection available.

'As you can see, this is where I keep all the delicious goodness,' Timothy said.

Tomek wasn't sure anyone had said delicious goodness since the eighties, but he chose not to mention it. Instead, he let Rachel take the lead.

'How many bees do you have?' she asked.

'We don't work with numbers like that. It's difficult to keep track of that sort of figure. I could tell you how many colonies I have, if you'd like?'

'Yes. Obviously.'

'One hundred and seventy-two.'

'And how many bees in each colony?'

'Between a hundred and two hundred.'

'So you could have given us an estimate then?'

'If I had to put a number on it.'

Jesus, this bloke was painful.

'How long have you been farming them for?'

'Nearly ten years.'

'And you're the only one?'

'As far as the Bee Farmers' Association is concerned, yes. There are other people who try to farm them, but they don't have much success, and the majority of people who keep bees are just beekeepers and hobbyists. They do it for the love of it or a bit of money on the side.'

'But you're in it to make millions?'

Timothy shrugged. 'If you want to be crass about it. Are you here to dig into my finances? Because I pay all of my taxes and I donate a large chunk of my profits to the charities I'm a part of.'

'No,' Rachel said bluntly. 'That's not why we're here.'

'Then do you mind my asking why you're asking about my bees?'

Rachel hesitated, swallowed. 'In a minute. There are just a few more questions we'd like to ask, if we may.'

'Would you like a taste?'

Before either of them could respond, Timothy hurried over to the other side of the production plant. He reached for a jar of honey and handed it across to Tomek, who politely accepted it.

'Some of the best honey you'll ever taste, that is.'

Is that what you said to Fern Clements before you killed her?

Tomek opened the jar and dipped his finger. Timothy was right, it was delicious goodness. And he made the noise to prove it.

'I knew you'd like it,' Timothy continued. 'And some for you, miss?'

Before she could respond, Timothy took the jar from Tomek and held it in front of Rachel, who hesitantly dipped her pinkie finger up to her fingernail and licked it clean.

'Mmm. Delicious.' Her expression belied her statement.

'It's one of our best sellers.'

'Between that and meat?' Tomek asked.

'Yeah. And don't forget the milk. Would you like to come and see some of the bees?'

Tomek and Rachel cast a quick glance at one another. They'd both known it was coming, but neither were particularly excited about the opportunity.

'Only if you can tell us more about this,' Rachel said, reaching into the breast pocket of her blazer. A moment later she removed the exhibit that Tomek had signed out of storage. A small glass beaker, sealed in a plastic bag, with an exhibit number and log sheet attached to it. Inside the beaker was the small bee they'd extracted from Fern Clements' body.

Rachel didn't need to hold the beaker very high for Timothy to become interested. He was on her in a flash, seeking permission to hold it for himself.

'I know this!' he excitedly. 'But where did *you* get it? And what do you have it for?'

Rachel avoided the question with a disarming smile. 'We'd be grateful if you could identify it for us please, Timothy.'

At the mention of his name, Timothy's cheeks flushed red. 'Of course. Yes. Absolutely. It's... Well, it's an Africanised Honey Bee. They're one of the most aggressive bees in the world. Most commonly found in Brazil, and most stings are severely painful, but some can be fatal, especially if you're allergic.'

Tomek's ears perked up.

'You can't get them from this country,' Timothy continued. 'Well, you *can*. You can buy anything if you know where to look, but you just have to be so careful with them. They've been known to chase their victims for up to a mile once aggravated. A mile! Imagine that.'

Tomek preferred not to.

'Where can you get insects like these?' he asked.

'You'd struggle to find someone in the UK with them. Most of the time people bring them over from abroad by mistake or they end up here on shipments.'

'How many would you need to kill a person?' Tomek asked.

The childish excitement on Timothy's face dropped. '*Kill*?'

'Well, they are called killer bees, no?'

'Yes, but...'

'How many might you need to kill a young girl aged fifteen?'

'Young g—? Aged fif—?'

'How many stings before the Africanised Honey Bee dies? One? Or hundreds?'

'Hun—?' Timothy's mouth opened and closed as he struggled to get the words out.

Tomek took a step closer to the man. 'Does the name Fern Clements mean anything to you?'

The gasp from Timothy was audible. His eyes bounced between Rachel's and Tomek's. 'What *is* this?' he asked, accusatory. 'What are you here for? Why are you asking me about this? I've never heard the name Fern Clements in my life.'

'Where were you last night during the early hours of the morning?'

Timothy looked around the shed as though it would answer the question. 'I was here. At home. I'd had a hard day on the farm and needed to sleep.' He snapped his fingers, recalling something. 'Yes. I'd had an early night. I was knackered. I'd just finished watching *Holby City*.'

Tomek paused before he said anything else. To let the man sweat, to let him stew it over. He had no further questions, so gave Rachel the nod and let her finish the meeting.

'How many of these might kill a person?' she repeated.

'It depends,' he said, his breathing slowing down gradually. 'A couple would suffice.'

'And they die after each sting?'

'Just like normal bees, yes.'

So whatever had killed Fern Clements had been in the hundreds.

'And who might have large quantities of these bees?'

'I... I... I can't imagine any bee farmers would. Not anyone in the association, at least. They take over colonies if there are enough of them, and that's bad for business. But, maybe a hobbyist wouldn't mind so much about that. Maybe someone in the Beekeepers Association might have them.'

'There's another association?'

'For hobbyists, yes.'

'Where might we find them?'

'Same place you found me,' Timothy explained. 'Online. There are over a hundred and forty in Essex alone, and they're only the ones that are registered. You could be looking for someone who's just kept some in their back garden without being a member.'

'Is it possible for them to have cultivated a colony on their own?'

Timothy scratched a red chafe mark on his neck. 'I guess. But they'd need a couple to start with. Including a queen.'

Tomek absorbed everything he'd heard.

Realised that they could be looking for a needle in a haystack of a hundred and forty other registered beekeepers, or they could be looking for a needle in the middle of the world's oceans, someone who wasn't registered at all and had stumbled upon the bees somehow.

But at least they had a starting point.

'Thanks for everything you've told us,' Rachel began, sensing the conversation was over. 'You've been a great help. Here are my details if you need anything or have anything else you'd like to add. Likewise, we'll be in touch if we have any further questions for you.'

Tomek stopped and turned in the doorway. 'Perhaps we could see the bees some other time, Timothy. Enjoy the rest of your afternoon.'

CHAPTER TWENTY-FOUR

S he had been checking the clock constantly, her eyes flitting towards the tiny digits on the bottom of Phillip's screen, fighting the urge to tap her phone and look at the larger, visible letters just to make sure it was accurate – 19:01.

They were overrunning. Thanks, in no small part, to her attention floating off elsewhere, to thoughts of Billy and the impending intruder, her father. They should have finished nearly half an hour ago. That would have given her plenty of time to prepare the flat for his visit, tidy her bedroom, spray her lavender mist on the cushions, fluff the pillows and prepare the candles. But now she would have no time for that. No time for anything.

'Repeat after me,' Phillip began.

Kasia rolled her eyes internally and fidgeted uncomfortably in her chair.

'*W weekend idę do parku z przyjaciółmi.*'

'At the weekend I'm going to the park with my friends,' Kasia said slowly, trying her hardest to sound as disinterested and disengaged as possible.

'Very good for understanding. But maybe try saying it in Polish, like I asked.'

Kasia did but butchered her pronunciation. On purpose.

'No. You're missing the *prz* sound at the beginning of *przyjaciółmi*.'

'No, I'm not. I said it perfectly.'

'If that was the case, then I wouldn't be here thirty minutes after I'm supposed to be.' He checked his watch after looking at the time on the screen. 'In fact, I need to leave for work.'

As she was about to respond, her belly grumbled. Loudly. And for a split second, she panicked and almost thought she'd farted. After hearing the sound, however, Phillip didn't become weirded out by it. Instead, he took that as his cue to leave.

'It's dinner time. I'll let you cook whatever you're having. I should probably get something for myself too.'

'What you gonna have?'

He shrugged. 'Probably something really unhealthy and really bad for me. *Jedzenie na wynos*.'

'Eh?'

'Takeaway.'

Now it made sense.

Shortly after, Phillip grabbed his things and made to leave. He filed away the documents and printouts he'd brought for her inside his compartmentalised briefcase, then carefully inserted his laptop into the padded section. As he chucked on his coat, Kasia quickly checked her phone.

Still nothing from Billy.

Nothing to say he was on his way. Nothing to say he was running late. She was starting to think he wasn't coming at all. That he'd lied to her. Probably told all his mates that he was going over there and wanted to ditch her and leave her hanging for a laugh. Because they thought it was funny.

Phillip waved his hand in front of her face. It was a while before she noticed it.

'See you in two days?'

'Yeah,' she replied, trying not to sound too disheartened.

She followed him to the bottom of the stairs.

'No homework tonight,' he said as he placed a hand on the front door. 'But I won't be so lenient at the weekend.'

'Ha ha. Okay.'

He pulled the door open. '*Do widzenia.*'

'*Do wid*—'

She saw him before she could finish her sentence. Her heart leapt into her mouth and she froze, staring down at him. Standing in the doorway was Billy Turpin, holding two medium-sized pizza boxes in his hand. Staring up at Phillip. A look of unpleasant surprise on his face.

'Friend of yours?' Phillip asked Kasia.

'Er. Kinda. Yes. But, please don't—'

'Can I have a slice?'

A moment of apprehension passed between Billy and Kasia, neither knowing what to do. Kasia wanted more than anything to get rid of Phillip. And if a slice of pizza was the way to do that, then—

He helped himself to one before she could respond and chewed on it loudly as he lowered the lid.

'You've inspired me to get my own for dinner,' he said, licking his lips. 'Thanks, both. *Do widzenia*, Kasia.'

'*Do widzenia!*'

Without saying anything else, Phillip wandered off back to the car. As soon as he stepped off the front step, Kasia grabbed Billy by the arm and pulled him inside the building, shutting the front door behind him.

He'd gone! And he hadn't said anything about Billy or her dad!

Before the door had even closed properly, she leapt onto Billy and kissed him. She was so excited she didn't know what had come over her. His lips were dry, and she was sure she got a bit of teeth in there as well. And as far as first kisses went, it hadn't lived up to her expectations; her admittedly reasonably low expectations.

'What... what was all that about?' The smile on Billy's face told her that he was as pleased about the kiss as she was.

She shrugged. But before she could reply, her tongue swelled in her mouth. She chewed on it but within a few seconds, it had already ballooned to the size of a chocolate bar. And then her throat started to swell and constrict like a snake coiling itself around her oesophagus, tightening her breath.

'Kasia? Kasia!'

Billy placed his hands on her for stability but it wasn't what she needed right now.

Right now she needed her EpiPen. Her life support.

Failing that, Phillip.

She whispered the man's name and, mercifully, Billy understood what she'd meant. A second later, he was out of the door screaming after her Polish tutor. In the time that he'd been gone, she had collapsed to the floor, wheezing and clinging to whatever air she could get.

Just before she felt the enveloping embrace of unconsciousness wrap its tentacles over her, she heard the sound of two voices coming towards her.

CHAPTER TWENTY-FIVE

When Tomek received the call, he was sitting at his desk. Typing up his report on Timothy Warren, the bee farmer.

'She's where?' he'd yelled into the phone, and then hurried out of the office without saying anything to anyone.

Fortunately, the drive from the station to Southend Hospital was a short one. Two miles. Ten minutes. Typically. And in his haste, he completed the journey in seven. Jumping a couple of red lights, overtaking on a single carriageway, jumping in front of people at junctions, cutting them up at roundabouts. The sound of the horns blasting from the cars behind him continued to play in his ears as he dashed through the hospital corridors in search of Kasia's room.

He found it on the third floor.

But not before he found Phillip and a scrawny little boy standing beside him in the corridor.

'What the fuck's going on?' Tomek asked Phillip.

The hyperpolyglot stepped forward to meet Tomek, protecting the boy a little.

'Paramedics said she was having an allergic reaction,' Phillip said calmly and slowly. 'Fortunately, I was there to help her.'

Allergic reaction.

How?

After all the sacrifices he'd made to cut out peanuts, and any other form of nuts, from his diet completely, she'd still fallen victim to an allergic reaction. In his own home.

'How?' Tomek asked, finding the courage in his voice to vocalise the thought.

Phillip turned to the young boy. 'Billy here brought some pizza over, and—'

'Billy?' Tomek repeated, his body beginning to vibrate with anger. 'Billy? As in, Billy the kid who thinks he can fight a fucking cow? The same Billy that my daughter's been asking me to have over one evening, and after I've repeatedly said no, decided to come over anyway? Is that you, Billy?'

Before, while he'd been hiding behind Phillip, Billy had stood with his back straight and his chin held high. Cocky, brave. But now, after the beginning of Tomek's torrent, he dropped his head and cowered into himself, giving him the appearance of someone at least five years his junior.

'Answer me, Billy!'

Tomek's voice echoed up and down the corridor. Phillip stepped forward and placed an arm across Tomek's chest to hold him back.

'What were you doing at my home, Billy? Why did you give my daughter peanuts?'

Billy didn't answer. In fact, he didn't do anything. Frozen, rooted to the spot from the fear of a man twice his size and over three times his age shouting in his face. Tomek was well aware of the fact that he couldn't hit a thirteen-year-old kid, even though he deserved it (and no matter how much he wanted to), but that wouldn't stop him from making the little kid shit himself.

The little *gówniacki*.

Kasia could have died from his ineptitude; it was the least he deserved.

'What were you doing with peanuts around Kasia, Billy?' Tomek continued. 'What made you think that was a fucking good idea, huh? Did your mum and dad drop you on your head as a kid? Did they slap you about a bit?'

'Hey, hey, hey!' This time Phillip had squared up to Tomek completely, and the man's small, slender, skinny frame was the only thing he could see. '*Przestań*, Tomek! *Ja pierdolę*! Watch what you're saying. He's just a thirteen-year-old kid, for fuck's sake.'

Tomek stared into the man's eyes for a brief moment. 'I know how fucking old he is. He's trying to get in bed with my daughter. And now he's fucking nearly tried to kill her. If you hadn't been there she would have been thirteen forever and he would have grown up to live the rest of his shitty fucking stupid life!'

Tomek's chest rose and fell at a rate of knots. His body continued to tremble with a heady combination of adrenaline, fear and guilt. A concoction he was all too familiar with.

'I get all that,' Phillip continued, his voice softer than before. 'I really do. And I can only imagine what sort of emotions you're feeling right now, but taking it out on a little kid isn't going to make any difference. What's done is done. It was a simple mistake. He came over with some pizza, and then a moment after I left he came to find me. He told me he'd been eating peanuts with his mates at the park earlier.'

'Did he know about her allergies? I bet he fucking—'

'Well if he didn't before, he definitely does now.'

Phillip took a step back from Tomek and allowed him some breathing space. Whether it was inside his head or whether Phillip's presence had been that oppressive, Tomek didn't notice the difference. He inhaled a large gulp of air and swallowed it down before turning to the side, towards the hospital door.

'Can I see her?' he asked.

'Think so. Nurses said something about them taking some more test results in about half an hour, but that was almost twenty minutes ago.'

I'll go now then, Tomek thought, and headed for the doors.

He lost his breath as he entered the room. Kasia was lying there on the bed, tucked in up to her chest, eyes closed, resting peacefully, chest rising and falling softly.

Slowly, tentatively, he made his way towards the bed and grabbed her hand in his. As soon as he felt her touch, his body warmed. It was the first time in their three-month-long father-daughter relationship that they'd had such a physical touch. For some reason, he was transported thirteen years ago to this same room. The room, the furniture, the view outside the window, all stayed the same. The only change was that the young girl lying in front of him wasn't so big and grown up. Instead, he imagined she was a baby, a newborn, a brand-new addition to the world, and that he gripped her tiny hands and she wrapped the whole thing around his finger. The scene was entirely imaginary, of course, he hadn't known about her birth or her very existence until only a few months prior, but he liked to think that was what it would have been like to witness the birth, to have held her hand from such an early age. To hold something so weak and dependent on him. To hold something that relied on him for everything: food, clothes, shelter, protection. That was what it was like now. The same feelings, and the same requirements as a father. Just with a thirteen-year-old instead of a newborn.

And he'd failed. He hadn't been there to protect her, hadn't been there to rescue her from her allergies.

As he shuffled himself closer on the chair, he began to understand how Diana Greenock's parents had felt, how Mandy Butler's had felt, how Lily Monteith's had felt, how Fern Clements' had felt.

Now he added himself to that list. He just considered himself, *them both,* lucky that it hadn't ended in disaster.

IT WAS ten the following morning by the time Kasia had been discharged from the hospital. The nurses and doctors had wanted to keep her in overnight for observation, but it hadn't been necessary. She'd spent the entire night asleep, resting and recuperating from her ordeal. And when they finally got home, after being caught in the late-morning rush hour, Kasia was feeling ninety per cent.

'I'm sorry,' she said as Tomek chucked his house keys in the pot on the dining room table.

Scrap that. Maybe she was at fifty per cent, still under the effects of the painkillers and medication they'd given her; Tomek hadn't heard her apologise for something in a very long time.

'So long as you're okay,' he said. 'That's the main thing.'

He slipped into the kitchen and switched the kettle on. He was in desperate need of some caffeine. He'd lain beside her bed all night and the sleep had been terrible, uncomfortable.

'We will have to talk about you lying to me and inviting Billy over specifically when I'd said not to though.'

'I know. I... I thought it would be okay.'

You thought wrong.

Tomek made himself a coffee, and a tea for Kasia, and the two of them spent the next hour or so in silence, watching the television.

'Don't you have to go to work?' Kasia asked. She was lying on her back, scrolling on her phone, when the thought occurred to her.

'No,' Tomek replied. 'Nick's given me the day off.'

Much to his surprise.

'So it's just you and me today, kiddo.' He slapped her knee several times playfully. 'I've told the school and they're fine with it. So you just need to focus on resting up. And for one day only, anything you want, I'm the one to ask.'

Tomek later regretted that decision. It had been an onslaught of needy requests. A deluge of snacks – chocolate, crisps, all the good stuff – followed by drinks of Coke and refills of tea and glasses of water. He had even given her complete control of the television remote and was forced to sit through re-runs of the reality TV show, *Made in Chelsea*. A show that had made him want to pull his eyes out.

Still, at least it hadn't been *The Only Way Is Essex*; then he would have gone one step farther and raided the exhibits lock-up at work in search of a firearm.

Later that evening, as he made them both dinner – his favourite, paella – he reflected on what had happened to her. And how grateful he was that Phillip had been there to help her. A sensible adult who knew what to do in that sort of situation. And how he had completely forgotten to thank the man before he'd left for his shift.

Tomek was in the middle of sprinkling paprika on the dish when Kasia entered the kitchen. She dropped her can of Coke in the bin and went to the fridge for another. In the background, Moby was playing on the small speaker he'd purchased the other week.

'Wanna talk about it?' Tomek asked. Now that he'd had the whole day to process it, he hoped she had too.

'Not particularly.'

'I think we should.'

Kasia hovered in the fridge, holding the door open with one hand, a can of Coke in the other.

'So you kissed him, eh?' Tomek began.

'Dad... please...'

'How else did you come into contact with the peanuts?'

Kasia sighed heavily until it was almost a grunt. 'All right. Fine. Yes, I kissed him. Happy now?'

'Was that your first kiss?'

'Yes.'

'Ever?'

'Yes. Now, are we done?'

'Maybe.'

'What more do you want to talk about?'

'How many times has he been over without me knowing?'

'Just the once. That was the only time.'

'Promise?'

Kasia held out her pinkie finger. Tomek set the wooden spoon on the counter and wrapped his in hers.

'Pinkie promise,' she said.

'Pinkie promise,' he replied.

A sacred bond between the two of them.

'Have you spoken to Sylvia about going out with Nick's daughter yet?'

As the song changed to the Red Hot Chili Peppers, Kasia's face contorted in confusion.

'You mean I can still go?' Her voice was filled with hope.

'Yes. I'm not going to lock you indoors for the rest of your life.'

As much as I'd like to.

And as much as you probably deserve it.

'But I'm not going to let you see Billy anytime soon. And, to be honest, I don't think he'll be too keen on seeing you either. I think I might have scared him off at the hospital.' Then, under his breath, he added, 'Put the fear of living God into the little shitling, with any luck.'

CHAPTER TWENTY-SIX

Tomek had tried to switch off while he'd spent the day looking after Kasia. Not because he wanted to be totally present for her while she recovered, but because the similarities between the victims' deaths and Kasia's incident were too profound. The more he thought about the injuries that Mandy Butler, Lily Monteith and Fern Clements had sustained, the more he thought about Kasia following suit.

For the most part, it had been a success. He'd been able to switch off and largely think about the shitty television they were watching, and Kasia certainly kept him busy with her constant requests and demands.

But there was one thought that he was unable to shake. One thought that concerned him more than any.

Billy.

Billy the Cow Fighter.

Billy the Cow Fighting fuckwit who had almost killed his daughter.

He questioned whether it had been an intentional attack on her, whether it had been his attempt to kill her.

Yes, it sounded ludicrous. But it was sometimes the ludicrous ideas, the way-out-there ideas, that were always the ones to stick.

After briefly discussing it with her, he'd learnt that Billy had indeed known about her allergies. That it was, in fact, one of the first things she'd told him when they'd first had lunch together in the school canteen.

Which begged the obvious question: if Billy had known about her nut allergy, then why on earth had he gone round to her home moments after eating a bag of peanuts with his friends? Had he done it intentionally? Had he gone there knowingly, trying to attack her or put her life in danger?

Was a thirteen-year-old capable of that?

Then, as he'd lain there in bed at night, the thoughts had started to spiral out of control.

From the little he knew about the boy, based on the little that Kasia had told him and the little research he'd done into the boy's social media, he knew that Billy was an avid football fan and not a terrible player either. As a member of the Dagenham & Redbridge FC U14s youth academy, his Instagram feed was a kaleidoscope of skills videos and crossbar challenges. And, Tomek was forced to admit, the kid was capable of doing things on the ball that Tomek had only dreamt of doing at that age. He was talented, all right, but he was also a member of a large group of boys. The same boys that he'd been out with the night before, playing in the park. Tomek recognised the faces on several of Billy's Instagram photos. And he wondered: had the boys told him to eat the peanuts? Had they all agreed on it, that it was a funny thing to do? And then he'd wondered if they'd had connections to Fern Clements or Mandy Butler. Whether it was possible for a group of teenagers, a group of boys and men from the Dagenham & Redbridge football club, to target young women with allergies.

Ludicrous, yes. But not beyond the realms of possibility.

Something for him to think on, something for him to investigate in his own time, perhaps.

Sadly, however, as soon as he stepped into the office the morning after his time looking after Kasia, he realised there was no time for anything. The office was full, and everyone in the team was at their desk, talking loudly and typing furiously on their keyboard. All systems go. And he already felt like he was playing catch-up.

'Ah, Tomek, you're here!'

The cry came from Victoria, who was already out of her seat and pacing towards him as he entered. By the time he turned to face her, she was standing in the doorway to her office, gesturing for him to enter.

'I trust everything's well with Kasia,' she began, then gestured for him to sit down.

Tomek pulled the chair from beneath the desk and did as he was told.

'She's much better thanks. The school's looking after her.'

'Excellent. Well, while you were off yesterday, we had a senior meeting. Myself, Nick, and Sean were in attendance, and we discussed our strategy going forward.'

'Excuse me?'

That sensation of being slapped in the face, punched in the stomach and kicked in the balls all at the same time came back to him. Again.

'We thought it was important to align our hypotheses before we made any further progress.'

'And was it a conscious decision not to involve me in that discussion?'

Victoria shifted uncomfortably in her seat. 'We didn't want to disturb you on your day off.'

'It wasn't a day off. I was looking after my daughter after she'd been in hospital. They're completely different.'

'Of course. Sorry.'

'I still have a phone. I still have a laptop. I could have joined via either of those things.'

Tomek dug his fingernails into the palm of his hand.

'Like I said, Nick didn't want to disturb you.'

So it was Nick's decision then. Either that, or she was passing the blame onto him. Neither made him feel any better about the situation.

'You didn't even ask,' he said, trying to keep his cool. 'I would've been more than happy to help.'

'I understand. Well, perhaps next time, if there ever is—'

'I hope my daughter never nearly dies again, thank you very much,' he interrupted. 'So hopefully we won't need to have this conversation again.'

What a fucking stupid thing to say.

'Of course.'

'Well, go on then.' Tomek gestured with his hands for her to continue. 'What did you decide?'

More shifting uncomfortably. More of the dreaded sense that he wasn't going to like the words that were about to come out of her mouth.

'Well, *collectively*,' she began. He noticed the emphasis on the word; another chance to pass the buck as someone else's idea. 'Collectively, we agreed that we're going to cast our net wide. We're going to draft a list of all the male teachers who have taught any of our victims. If there are any common denominators, we'll find them. We're also going to speak with all the ticket holders who attended the concert during Mandy Butler's death. Lastly, Chey and Martin are going to be looking into the victims' social media profiles, see if they've been messaging an older gentleman, or if they've received any untoward or threatening or suspicious messages from our killer, anything that can give us an insight into who this person is.'

Or people, he thought. But kept his mouth shut. The idea that had been brewing inside his head was just a baby animal, a wounded one at that. One that required the right amount of nourishment and care before it was introduced into the world. For now, he would keep it within the confines of his mind until it was ready to be announced.

'That doesn't sound like you're veering away from what we've already discussed,' Tomek started.

And then it hit him.

A list of all the male teachers that have taught any of our victims.

Teachers.

A list that only catered to three of the four murder victims.

'What about Diana Greenock?' Tomek asked, the level of concern in his voice rising.

'We're taking a step back from Diana,' Victoria replied, her voice shaky despite the obvious effort to try to hold it together.

'Why?'

'Because, after several discussions and with the help of Tracy, we've decided that the link is tenuous. And that the circumstances surrounding her death are even more so. There was never any evidence to suggest a break-in, and the plausibility of someone climbing into her room and planting a cat in there is also hard to swallow. Both Nick and Sean were in agreement with that.' Tomek opened his mouth to speak but she continued, determined to finish before she was forced to field any of his questions. 'Besides, we don't have a lot of resources and it's a long way for us to have any sort of impact into that side of the investigation...' She hesitated, as though there was something else she wanted to say. Tomek waited to hear it. Eventually, she continued, 'You should also know that we will be phasing out Mandy Butler's murder from our investigations as well.'

'What's that supposed to mean?'

'Given the limited resources and budgets I have just mentioned, something which I was not made aware of until yesterday, we will be dedicating approximately ten per cent to Mandy Butler's case, while the remainder will be split evenly between Lily Monteith and Fern Clements.'

Tomek was in disbelief. Sheer and utter disbelief. He couldn't believe a word of what he was hearing. His hard work, his dedication, his intuition. All of it had been shat on by his seniors. Those with supposedly more experience than him (though he struggled to see how Sean had found himself in that fold).

'Do you not think each victim requires an adequate amount of time for us to investigate? And for us to not even dedicate ten per cent to both Diana Greenock and Mandy Butler *at least* is disgusting.'

'Tomek, I can see—'

'My focus, before this announcement, was on Fern Clements. Does that change?'

'Well, of course it doesn't, but—'

'And how do you—?'

Before he was able to finish his question, a knock came at the door. Silence instantly fell in the room. Tomek kept his eyes rooted on Victoria, as she quickly considered her response.

'Yes, come in,' she called.

It was Nick, looking surprisingly happy for a change.

'Morning, both,' he said, shutting the door behind him. He placed a firm hand on Tomek's shoulder and gave it a squeeze. 'Sorry to hear about Kasia. How's she doing?'

'Fine. Thanks.'

Nick rounded the desk and stood between them like the referee in a tennis match. Little did Nick know, Tomek was about to bring him into the game.

'What's going on?'

'I could ask you the same thing, sir. What the fuck?'

The chief inspector's face tightened, along with his grip on the edge of Victoria's desk.

'Do you want to ask me that again, Tomek?'

'All right,' he replied with a shrug. 'What the fuck's going on with this new strategy, *sir*? What about Diana Greenock? Mandy Butler? After what happened last time, sir, I'd've thought you'd be all—'

'Watch what you're about to fucking say there, mate,' Nick hissed. There was nothing pally about the way he said it. 'I really don't think you want to be taking that tone with me.'

'Are you going to answer the question or just keep running from it?'

'I don't have to stand here and listen to this.' Nick gestured towards the exit with his thumb. 'Get back out there and do your job. Or I can get HR to come down and give you another day off if you'd like some more time to cool the fuck down? Because you're behaving like a fucking arsehole and I will not stand for it.'

Tomek quickly left the meeting room without saying another word. The threat of another meeting with someone from HR was enough to get him out of there as fast as humanly possible. He still wanted an answer though. And he knew the person who could give it to him.

Sean.

But just as he was about to make his way over, his phone vibrated.

Abigail Winters was calling.

CHAPTER TWENTY-SEVEN

Thirteen minutes later, Tomek found himself in Morgana's Café. With the same thick, greasy, clammy air, the same beautiful, aromatic smell of bacon and eggs the same punters who looked as though they'd never left or were renting out almost the same seats.

Abigail had told him to meet in the same place as last time. And, just like last time, she was late.

Thirty minutes instead of sixty, mind, but late was late.

And in his current mood, her lack of punctuality didn't help much.

As thirty minutes turned into thirty-one, Morgana reached across his face and set a cup of tea down in front of him. He looked up at her and thanked her warmly. She looked prettier than the last time he'd seen her, though he couldn't determine why. Perhaps it was her hair that had been curled and bobbed, or perhaps it was the thin layer of make-up that had thickened a little, in particular under the eyes and eyelashes, accentuating the blue behind them, or perhaps it was her outfit – smarter, understated, almost presidential.

For a moment he thought about flirting with her again, but then he was reminded of what had happened last time. As soon as he'd started, Abigail had entered, as though she'd been watching him from outside and had done it on purpose. Tomek pondered on the decision for a moment longer: flirt with Morgana and immediately summon Abigail, or delay the flirting and continue catching each other's eye while he waited.

Sadly, this time, the decision was made for him.

The next person to walk through the door was Abigail. Except this time, she wasn't carrying the suitcase behind her that made her look like a primary school teacher.

'Hello, you,' she said. 'Looking nice today.'

Tomek looked down at the blazer he'd worn for almost three weeks straight without a wash and at the white shirt he'd owned for a year that had started to fade into a titanium colour.

'Thanks,' he replied awkwardly. 'You know, if my daughter sees us here, she's going to start asking me questions, on top of the ones she's *already* asking.'

'Good questions, I hope?'

Tomek took a sip of water by way of response. 'What was so important you couldn't tell me over the phone?'

At the prospect of declaring her news to him, Abigail's face and hair illuminated a lighter shade of blonde beneath the lights.

'Firstly, I wanted to give you fair warning about an article I'm preparing.'

'Right. Does the article involve me?'

'No.'

'Then you have my blessing.'

'It's about your chief inspector.'

That gave Tomek cause to pause a moment.

'Nick? What about him?'

'I'm researching his failings in the Mandy Butler case.'

You're going to love what I've just discovered then.

But perhaps it was best to tell her in two years and then she could slam Victoria's career as well.

'I don't... I don't think that's going to be a problem. I mean, how below the belt is it?'

Abigail ran her finger up and down a groove on the table. 'I

155

haven't figured that out yet. It's not off the scale, but some might argue it's close enough.'

'Just enough to be published though, right?'

She grinned. 'Exactly.'

Right now, neither Nick nor Victoria were his favourite people on the planet, so he didn't much care about what Abigail was planning on publishing. If they'd kept him on as the SIO of the investigation then his thought processes might not have been so destructive, but as they were, he wondered if there was anyone else he could chuck into the fire.

'The other reason I asked you here,' Abigail began, distracting him from his thoughts, 'is that I have a visitor for you.'

'Not another daughter I didn't know anything about,' he said slowly with a shake of the head. 'One's enough for me. I don't think I can handle the stress of another—'

'Shut up, you dingus. It's not *that*...'

As she trailed off, Abigail turned in her seat and gestured to a pair in the opposite corner of the restaurant. A mother and daughter, sitting beside one another, staring at them. Tomek hadn't seen them come in, and judging by the empty plates of food in front of them, they had been sitting there far longer than he had.

Abigail gave them a wave. They shuffled over. Tentative, cautious. As though he was a man with an incurable disease. The daughter, who had young features that reminded him of Kasia, was taller than her mother. She wore a thin hoodie that hung off one shoulder, and she wrapped one arm across the front of her body, anchoring it in place by gripping the inside of her elbow on the other side. Beside her was her mother who, had it not been for the grey diluting the brown of her hair, he would have mistaken for a sister.

They sat opposite him in silence. Three against one.

'Tomek, this is Nisha and Avena Kumar. Avena was one of the—'

'I recognise the name,' he said, nodding excitedly. 'From the article.'

He extended his hand across the table. Avena took it with the confidence of a seventeen-year-old, weak and desperate to get it over with quickly.

'Thank you for coming here,' he started. 'I don't think the importance of this can be overstated. Anything you're happy to tell me today is, of course, going to be treated in the strictest confidence, I assure you. Though...' He turned to look around him. At the bustling conversations. At the constant merry-go-round of customers coming in and out of the door. 'Would you not prefer to go somewhere a little more private?'

Abigail shook her head. 'This was their choice, funnily enough. And I said lunch was on you.'

Tomek shot her a facetious yet smiley grin that said, "Of course you did. Thanks very much."

And then, as though it had been rehearsed, Morgana arrived at the table with a bill in her hand. Tomek instinctively took it, he was used to doing it so frequently on dates and meals with Kasia that it was now a part of his muscle memory, and pulled out his debit card.

'I assume the bill for this table is still to come?' he asked as he entered his PIN.

'Yep.'

'Hear that, girls? Order up!' Abigail reached across the table and yanked a menu from the stand. 'It is Christmas, after all. Someone's gotta get in the holiday spirit, even if *he* won't.'

The Kumars had no idea what she was referring to, but it didn't seem to faze them; they perused the menu and chose an order of Diet Coke for Nisha and a banana milkshake for Avena. Morgana hurried away before Tomek was able to order another tea for himself.

The four of them sat in almost complete silence as they waited for their drinks. Tomek had decided that it was better to begin their discussion without the threat of interruption coming every two minutes to ask if they wanted any more refreshments. And as soon as the drinks had arrived, and Tomek had fronted the bill for it, shortly thereafter, they were able to begin.

'What would you like to know?' Avena asked. She spoke with the softness and charisma of a cabin crew member.

'Everything you can tell me. Everything you can remember from that night. Everything you've remembered since.'

Avena looked to her mother for support, who offered it with a soft hand on her forearm. Tomek pleaded gently with his eyes for her to remain firm and strong. He didn't want it to be a wasted trip for them all. Most notably his bank account.

'Well, there was a group of six of us. Me, Nala, Dein, Harrison, Priti and Prav. We was going to see Catfish and the Bottlemen at the Cliffs. It was a sold-out show and we was right near the front. We tried to stay together as much as possible but people needed to go to the toilet and kept ending up going to get more drinks and stuff. So, we eventually got split up. I was left with Harrison and Priti, while the others were on their own somewhere, I never found out where.'

She took a sip from her milkshake and set it on the table with extreme care, as though doing so harder would cause it to break.

'We was dancing, enjoying ourselves, screaming the lyrics to the songs in each other's faces, when suddenly this guy just turns up in front of us. He was about your height, maybe. A little shorter. Thick black hair. Wearing sunglasses. At first, I thought he was looking for his mates. But when he didn't move and just continued to stand there I thought he was looking for a fight. I dunno why, but it felt like he was looking me dead in the eye. As though he wanted to fight *me*.'

Sadly the truth wasn't much further away.

'Just as I was about to ask him if he was all right, Harrison prodded him in the arm and embraced him. They knew each other from somewhere.'

'Do you know where?' Tomek asked, pressing down hard on the end of his pen until the ink began to seep through the page.

'I think he said it was football. Something about playing together at Dagenham.'

Tomek's interest was piqued.

'Did they play together?' he asked.

Avena shook her head. 'This guy was a few years older at least, so I think he must have played a few teams above, or maybe in the first team.'

'And this is the man you bought the ecstasy pills from?' Tomek asked.

It was a while before she responded. As she did so, with a slight dip of the head, keeping her eyes closed, the door opened and another group of customers walked through. Lunchtime was in full swing, and the place was heating up. Tomek removed his blazer and placed it on the back of his chair, over his coat.

'Harrison was the one who paid for them. He made it seem like he'd done it before, the way he handed over the money. I almost didn't see it. And then he just dished them out, like they were sweets. By the time I looked up at it, the man was gone.'

'But you remember what he looked like?'

She nodded. And then Tomek advised that he would book her in for a meeting with their artist to put together an e-fit portrait of the man.

'Did either Harrison or Priti force you to take the pills?'

Avena's gaze dropped to her drink and she began spinning it distractedly on the table.

'Harrison said he'd done it before, that it was one of the best experiences of his life, but he didn't *force* me.'

Because his words were enough. She had been in the company of someone she'd trusted, someone she'd perhaps known and respected for a long time. So why wouldn't it be safe to try them?

'I only took a half though,' she said as an afterthought.

'Half a tab of ecstasy?'

'Yeah. It was my first time and I was scared.'

'So that's why...' he started, then caught himself.

'Why what?' asked Nisha, her mother.

'That...' He paused. 'Forgive my frankness, but that's the reason you're alive. The girl who sadly passed away from an experience similar to yours is dead because she took the whole thing.'

'And because Priti had Avena's EpiPen with her, and she *knew* what to do with it.'

Tomek's face fell flat. 'Well. Yes. Of course. That too.'

'Did that poor girl not have her EpiPen with her?'

159

Tomek wasn't so sure. He hadn't thought to ask Elsie Rawcliffe when he'd spoken to her. And, as someone with an anaphylactic daughter, he knew that it wasn't such an obvious and easy remedy to administer. If you didn't know how to use it in the first place, there was little more you could do.

Tomek was able to put the rest of the story together himself. Anaphylactic reaction in the middle of the dance floor, followed by unconsciousness, surrounded by hundreds of people, followed by an emergency trip to the hospital.

Not a night to remember for anyone.

After concluding the meeting and thanking them several times for their trust and bravery for sharing the story with him, Tomek handed over to Abigail, who explained that all communication would be dealt with by her and that Avena's name could be kept out of things if that was what they wanted.

All four of them left at the same time. Outside, Tomek and Abigail waved goodbye and watched them head off.

'Get anything you wanted?' she asked.

Tomek nodded.

He had.

Because now the football net had just got smaller, the gap between the goalposts narrower. He just hoped that he might be able to score the winning goal at some point soon.

CHAPTER TWENTY-EIGHT

During his "day off" – which he was rapidly becoming annoyed at everyone calling a "day off" – DC Rachel Hamilton had completed a large chunk of their collective to-do list relating to the investigation into Fern Clements' death.

Something which she didn't have any trouble reminding him of.

'It wasn't a fucking day off, all right? My daughter was in hospital.'

She held her hands up in surrender. 'Didn't know that, mate. Sorry. Message was that you were having a day off. No real explanation.'

'Who gave you that impression?'

'One-Third Jaffa Cake,' Rachel replied. 'She told us you were off. Not gonna lie, I was slightly pissed, but I guess now I have no right to be.'

'No. You don't.'

And now he would have no right to have a go at Sean for not sharing with him information about the strategy meeting the day before either. If Sean had been under the same misapprehension as the rest of the office, then he had no reason to be mad with his friend.

'What did you accomplish yesterday?' Tomek asked without

trying to sound too patronising. He realised it probably hadn't worked as well as he'd hoped.

'More than you're probably giving me credit for up there.' She prodded the side of her head.

'That's not true. You know I rate you highly.'

'Uh-huh. Tell that to my performance review.'

Tomek chuckled. Despite the gap in seniority, Tomek respected Rachel and saw her as an equal. She was experienced, had been in the job a few years less than him, and had all the hallmarks of someone who could progress further through the ranks if only she had the belief that she could do it. In the time that he'd been "managing" the detective constables (even though he hated the term), she was perhaps the one who showed the most drive and commitment, an eagerness to learn and grow and develop; essentially all the sort of stuff you put on a CV and hope nobody calls you out on. Not to mention she was a kind and wonderful person. She had only been in his life as long as Kasia, but she'd settled within the team after a few days and, now that she'd moved closer to the station, she was more available for drinks and social nights at the end of a long day.

To answer his question, she loaded up an Excel document on her screen. On the first tab was a series of four tables, filled with names and addresses. Above each table was the name of each of the four victims, emboldened and centred. And, on the far right column of each table was a series of Ys and Ns.

Tomek looked at the first table. Fern Clements. Their section of work. The list contained the names of everyone who had attended the gathering on the night she died. All the cells within that column had been marked with a Y – except one.

'You spoke with four different people from the party yesterday?'

'Five, technically.' She pointed to two names on the sheet. 'These two are twins. So I count that as one. And I'm glad they were otherwise I would've been working till midnight.'

Tomek knew her well enough to know that she'd been speaking literally, not figuratively.

'Well,' he started. 'Thanks for your hard work and effort. I really do appreciate it. As a thank you, I'll take the last one off your hands so you can put your feet up. How about that?'

She glowered at him. And not in the usual flirty way that he'd been so used to with other women. This was a hard, piercing stare that, admittedly, scared him a little.

'And who said chivalry was dead?' she said sardonically.

'That's not chivalry. Chivalry would be me asking if you got home safely last night. *Did* you get home safely?'

'Well. Yes.'

'Great. That's chivalry. Whereas me offering to speak with a teenage girl so you don't have to is my way of being a gentleman.'

Rachel looked at him blankly for a long moment. 'I think you misunderstand the concept of both those words.'

'And I think you misunderstand the fact that you're misunderstanding what I'm saying.'

'What?'

'Exactly. You tell me.'

'The fuck are you talking about, Tomek?'

'I don't know. Sorry. Honestly lost it there for a moment.'

'Sounds like you've got issues.'

He prodded the screen. 'Then add me to the list.'

CHAPTER TWENTY-NINE

Claudia Lowther was the last on the list of guests who'd attended the house party on the night of Fern Clements' death, and as far as Tomek and Rachel understood it, she was Fern's closest friend. Rachel, quite rightly, had made the decision to speak with the rest of the attendees before speaking with Claudia. She had wanted to hear all the wild allegations and untruths before eventually narrowing her field of vision and listening to the one version of events, the one version of Fern Clements' life that was probably the most accurate.

They were all sitting in a small room in one of the corridors in the science block. It was quiet, secluded and had been disguised as a chemical equipment cupboard so there were no chances of being interrupted, unless a teacher, looking for somewhere to have a cry, as he suspected the room might have been purpose-built for, stumbled in and distracted them. With them in the room was the head of pastoral care for Year Ten, Linda Vickers, a short woman with a bobbed haircut, glasses that spanned the width of her face, and an even bigger smile that seemed to reach her ears. She was soft-spoken, polite and gentle. And that smile; disarming, warming, and settling. It was clear to see why she'd been in the role for nearly fifteen years as she'd explained.

'I've got kids of my own, and I think it's important they see a smile every day, even if it is from their own mum,' she had said. 'The world could do with a little bit more happiness.'

That had been too deep for Tomek for a post-lunch proverb, but that was just the cynic in him. She was right, of course. The world could do with a lot more happiness. The only problem was, in his world, in his life dealing with death, crime, and the destruction of countless lives on a daily basis, it certainly wasn't the place to find it.

Once Claudia had settled from the initial shock of being called out of class by a police officer, Tomek explained who he was and what he was there for.

'I understand you were offered some time off from school to get your head around what happened,' Tomek began. 'How come all your friends have but you haven't?'

'Can't,' she said with a shake of the head. 'Need to keep myself busy. Otherwise, I'll go mad just thinking about it.'

'That's very conscientious of you,' he said, more as a note for himself on her character than for her benefit.

And then he began the interview in earnest. At first, he started by asking simple questions, touching lightly on Fern and their relationship, broaching the subject in a controlled and thoughtful manner. He asked about school, her grades, GCSEs, which classes she was taking, and which ones were her favourite (Spanish and French, same as Fern). All the bits that were designed to put her at ease. And she had reacted in kind: carefully and thoughtfully, gently and warmly.

Until he'd started to turn the screw a fraction.

'What happened on the night that Fern died?' Tomek asked.

'What do you mean?'

'Well, what happened to her?'

'I don't know who killed her.'

'That's not what I'm asking.'

'But you're making it sound like it though.'

Sensing that tensions were rising, Linda reached between them and placed a hand on Claudia's.

'The detective isn't assuming anything. He just wants to know what happened. That's all.'

Immediately, the girl settled.

And Tomek felt himself following suit as well.

'There was,' she began, but then caught herself. It took her a few moments to regain composure, and after a few deep swallows and even deeper breaths, she continued. 'There was a disagreement. We was all supposed to stay overnight at Bianca's, but Fern was a bit tipsy, and she'd spent the whole night messaging her boyfriend.'

'Boyfriend?'

'Well, not really her *boyfriend*. More a...'

'Situationship?'

'Yeah. A situationship. But she always used to call it a shituation-ship because he used to fuck her ab—'

Claudia suddenly realised what she was saying and then stopped, her eyes pleading for forgiveness from Linda.

'Please,' Tomek said, 'continue.'

'Right. Well. We'd all been drinking, just a few sips of WKD and some glasses of wine, nothing major. But Fern wasn't handling it very well, and she started talking loudly and talking over everyone. So we all had a go at her. And she didn't like it and started getting a bit aggressive. Then she said that she was going to meet up with Darren.'

'And Darren's the one she's having the situationship with?'

Claudia looked to Linda for approval. The head of pastoral care nodded at Claudia, who then nodded at Tomek, as though the message was being passed through the chain telepathically.

'Do you know if she ever met up with Darren?'

This time Claudia shook her head, a message that didn't need to go through all three of them.

'Does Darren go to this school?'

'No. He's older. He's about seventeen.'

'But doesn't go to school?'

More shaking of the head. 'No. She mentioned something about him getting a football scholarship to some team in Dagenham I think it was. Dunno why anyone would wanna play there – they're shit.'

'Language,' Linda reminded her. 'That one was a little bit unnec-essary, wasn't it?'

'Sorry, miss.'

While she was apologising, Tomek's mind drifted off. To thoughts of Darren and the shituationship. Darren the footballer. Darren the seventeen-year-old who played for some team in Dagenham. Darren the young man who had gone to meet Fern Clements on the night that she'd died.

It couldn't have all been connected, could it?'

'I haven't said something I shouldn't'a done, have I?'

Claudia's sharp voice brought him back to the room. He shook his head. 'No,' he replied. 'You've been a great help. Thank you.'

CHAPTER THIRTY

There were only a few people in the office that Tomek fully entrusted with listening to the thoughts inside his head. Especially something as far-fetched and left-field as this.

'You've got me on tenterhooks now,' Sean told him as Tomek left the table and headed to the bar in the Fork and Spoon.

Standing behind the bar was Jim, who had owned the place for as long as they'd been going there.

'Usual?'

'Please, pal.'

As Jim shuffled off to the other side of the bar, Tomek's eyes drifted towards the vending machine in the corner of the pub that was almost as bright as a set of floodlights on top of a cruise liner. Jim had implemented the extra source of income as part of his diversification strategy. He was charging the owner of the machine a flat, monthly fee for the space in the corner, and was then taking home ten per cent of the monthly earnings. It all sounded too good to be true. But that was only if the machine was being used, and as far as Tomek was aware, it wasn't; every time he'd been in there it was still fully stocked and looked as though nobody had ventured anywhere near it.

'How's that working out for you?' Tomek asked as the man returned with two drinks filled to the brim.

'Fucking shite!' Jim remarked. 'I wanna get rid of it. The little deadbeat's sold me a fucking dream. Conned me out of a thousand quid, he has.'

'A thousand quid?!' Tomek's voice hit an octave he hadn't reached for nearly thirty years.

'Well, I had to pay a deposit, didn't I?'

'For what?'

'The machine. In case it gets broken.'

'But I thought he was paying you for the space?'

'Well, if he is, I ain't seen none of it.'

Tomek reached into his wallet. 'He's well and truly bent you over there.'

Jim grunted at the sight of Tomek's wallet and held his hand out, ready for the cash that was about to fall nicely into it.

'That'll be fifteen quid please, pal.'

Tomek baulked and almost choked on his saliva.

'Fifteen quid. For two pints? Since when was this place located in the middle of Shoreditch?'

Jim shrugged. 'Well, I gotta pass those costs on somehow, 'nt I?' he explained as he thumbed in the direction of the vending machine.

'Why do I feel like I'm the one being bent over now?'

'Shit rolls downhill I'm afraid, mate.'

'Yeah. And it's always us blue-collar workers who've gotta bear the brunt of it.'

Jim had nothing to say to that. And so Tomek handed the cash over, *reluctantly*, and headed back to the booth where Sean was sitting.

'Can you believe that?' Tomek began, raging.

'Believe what?'

'Fifteen quid for two pints. All because he's realised that his savvy business decision wasn't so savvy after all.'

Sean took the pint from the middle of the table and sipped from it. As he lowered the glass to the beer mat, he left behind a thin foamy moustache. 'I kicked off last time I came.'

'The last time you came?' Tomek tried to hide the hurt in his voice but was unsuccessful.

'Yeah. Came a couple of weeks ago with Chey.'

Tomek nodded, unable to meet his friend's gaze, this time trying to hide the hurt in his face.

'We would've asked you if you wanted to come, but we figured you'd be busy with Kasia. And I'm fairly sure it was the same night you said she was starting her Polish lessons and that you wanted to get back for them.'

A silence drifted between them. Uncomfortable and tangible. Tomek filled it by taking a sip and gradually meeting his friend's gaze. Sean filled it by moving the conversation along as soon as he possibly could.

'How's she getting on with her lessons?'

'Yeah, good.'

'Seen much of an improvement?'

'Yeah, I guess. She won't be ordering *dos cervezas* in Polish any time soon, but she's getting there.'

'What did you say her tutor was?'

'Well, he's a tutor.'

'No, I'm sure there was a particular name for it.'

'Oh, a polyglot.'

Sean snapped his thick fingers. 'That's the one!'

'Technically, he's a *hyper*polyglot, but since he's not here I don't think he'll mind if we save ourselves the extra syllables.'

Sean chuckled awkwardly, and the conversation suddenly turned strange. The atmosphere had dropped, and it was as though they had run out of things to say, run out of things to talk about with one another. Something they'd never had to endure. Not like this.

They had been friends for nearly fifteen years and had spent most of that time talking about everything and anything, getting to know each other on almost every level, so now it was a strange situation for them to be in. Uncomfortable and unfamiliar. Things hadn't been the same since Kasia had come into his life, he was the first to admit that. She had become the priority, and through no fault of her own, had pulled him away from his old life that had been filled with drinking, socialising, having fun, getting to know women on a weekly basis, and thrust him into a life that was significantly more boring. Perhaps it was for the best and he just hadn't realised it yet. He *was* forty, after all. Perhaps he was too old to be sleeping around and warding off the fear of commitment for as long as was physically possible. Perhaps it was time that he settled down and found someone he could have a future with.

Which reminded him...

'I've been seeing Abigail, recently...' he started, then caught himself.

'You've been *seeing* her?'

Tomek waved his hands in the air. 'No, no, no. Not like that. Not in a situationship type of thing. In a *professional* sense. She's been giving me information about the girls who were spiked at the Cliffs. She's the one who helped me with the link between the murders, including Diana Greenock's in Manchester.'

'Nice.'

This time it was Sean's turn to unsuccessfully hide the hurt and pain in both his expression and voice. The pain and hurt of his and Abigail's fresh relationship which had ended only a few weeks before.

'I met with her this afternoon actually,' Tomek continued. 'She brought along a girl called Avena Kumar who was one of the killer's victims. She and a couple of her friends were at the concert together, seeing Catfish and the Bottlemen. But what she told me got me intrigued.'

'Abigail or the girl?'

'The girl.'

'Right.'

Then Tomek told him about his theory. That they had it all wrong. That they weren't looking for one killer at all. They were looking for a group of them, all united by one common element of their lives: football. And in particular, one football club. Dagenham & Redbridge FC. That they were all working together, as friends and accomplices, plotting to kill a group of girls via their allergies.

The words felt strange for Tomek to hear, but as soon as he'd finished saying them, he felt a weight lift. Sean was the only man he could trust with this type of thing, but he soon began to feel like he shouldn't.

'So, you think a group of fifteen- and seventeen-year-old boys, all of whom would have been fifteen at the time, were smart and intelligent enough to either befriend or get into relationships with girls who had allergies, and then proceed to find ways of killing them based on their allergies? You think a group of fifteen- and seventeen-year-old boys have got the technical dexterity to pull something like that off?'

Tomek fell silent. 'Well, when you put it like that.'

'I just think it's highly improbable.'

'But not *impossible*,' Tomek said, feeling a slight ray of light burst through the black canvas Sean had created with his negativity. 'I didn't think it would be probable for the first woman I've loved in a long time to crush my heart and turn out to be a serial killer. I didn't think it would be probable for a dad to fake his death and kill his daughter because he didn't think she was his... But that all happened.'

And in the space of the past few months, as well.

Sean scratched the side of his head, massaging the visible veins on his temples.

'I see what you're saying but, come on.' There was a genuine plea in his voice. 'Three murder victims—'

'Two of whom have boyfriends or people in their lives who play football.'

Not including Billy the Cow Fighter, who wasn't related to the murders in any way.

'And what about Diana Greenock?' Sean asked.

'Thought you didn't consider her a relevant matter in this investigation?' Tomek hit back in such a way that let Sean know he was pissed off.

'Listen, about that,' he began. 'I wanted to call you. I wanted you there, but Victoria said to just leave it.'

'Hmm.'

'We've only parked Diana Greenock for now. We've not forgotten about her entirely.'

'You might as well have, with the amount of resources you're dedicating to her murder, and Mandy Butler's.'

Sean rolled his eyes and breathed in heavily. His giant chest ballooned to almost double the size. Then he let it all out slowly.

'Your theory doesn't fit with the forensic psychologist's profile.'

'You mean the same one I had to listen to her make up on the spot not that long ago? Come on. You have heard it, right? It's more convoluted than the instructions to a waffle maker, way more confusing than they need to be. Tracy gave descriptions for two completely different men so that she could cover all bases. You think that's a solid profile to go by?'

'It's all we have.'

'Then it's like the blind leading the fucking blind out there.'

Tomek was in need of another sip. But when he looked down at his drink he realised that there was nothing left.

'*Your* round next,' he said to Sean.

'Same again?'

'Please.'

And then Sean shuffled out of the side of the chair and made his way to the bar. While he waited, Tomek checked his phone. No missed calls, just a message to say that Kasia had got there safely. A moment later Sean returned with drinks in hand.

'Cost twenty quid this time.'

'You what?'

As Sean returned to his seat, he waved two packs of crisps in front of Tomek. Walkers ready salted and cheese and onion. From the vending machine.

'Should've asked Jim to subtract the amount from the total,' Tomek replied.

'Maybe next time.'

Another awkward moment passed. A second in such quick succession. It concerned Tomek.

'Why don't we stop talking about work,' Sean began. 'It's boring and not something I want to spend all day thinking about.'

'Okay. Fair enough.'

'What are you doing for Christmas?'

'It's just the two of us. I wanted our first one to be just us two, alone, without the chaos of being at my mum's. We can save that for next year. You?'

'The opposite,' Sean replied. 'Sister and I are going round my mum's.'

Same as every year. Same story for as long as Tomek had known him. Sean was, in his own words, a mummy's boy. While Sean was young, his dad had died at an early age, a heart attack while confronting Sean's school bully's father, and so Sean had been forced to step into the role early on. He had helped provide for his mum and younger sister by selling sweets and drinks at school and earning himself a reputation as most likely to be an entrepreneur later in life. And then he'd joined the police when he still lived at home and continued to put food on the table while protecting his family from their tough neighbourhood with his even more impressive and intimidating reputation.

And each year there was the typical invite for Tomek to join. On a few occasions, he'd accompanied them, spending the evening indulging in Sean's mum's jollof rice and malva pudding for dessert, before heading home to his empty flat for an evening of shitty television and falling asleep on the sofa. A lot of the time he'd gone to work and spent the day with people he worked with daily. But it was different. For one day of the year, it felt as though the stress of the job had lifted and all the burdens that came with it.

'First Christmas together,' Sean murmured. 'Must be exciting.'

'She's looking forward to it. I, on the other hand, don't think much of it all, as you know. Though I am pleased to say she's bringing some of that festivity back into me. The reams of tinsel and Christmas decorations we've got around the house will do that to anyone.'

'Where is she tonight?'

'Who?'

'Kasia. Obviously.'

Tomek's eyes widened. 'Get this. She's gone out for a girls' Christmas meal with Nick's daughter.'

'The infamous Nick Cleaves who doesn't let his daughter do anything unless it's gone through several rounds of approval and is requested at least six months in advance?'

'The very same. So I've got the evening off.'

Sean pointed to the drink. 'Hence the drink.'

'Hence the drink.'

Another moment drifted between them. But this time it wasn't awkward. Well, it *was* awkward but only a little. A four out of ten on the awkward scale, as both men realised that this was the way it would be from now on, catching up in a social environment when Tomek had been afforded the night off from parent duties. A fact that they would both have to accept.

'Just make sure you don't turn out like Nick as a parent,' Sean said.

'What do you mean?'

'I imagine he's got his interview questions prepared ready for when she gets back. And he's probably got a tab on his iPad of her current position in the world.'

'Doesn't that come with the territory of the job?'

'Depends how far you take it.'

'Cool. Any more words of wisdom?'

'Yeah. Don't buy these crisps ever again – they're stale as fuck. In fact, don't buy anything from that vending machine, it's probably all outta date.' Tomek chucked the half-eaten packet of cheese and onion crisps onto the table and grimaced, showing the morsels of food in his mouth. Both men laughed.

'Oh, and for what it's worth, mate,' Sean started, easing himself into the back of his chair. 'If you *were* worried about having my blessing before anything happened between you and Abigail, and don't be like that, I know what she's like, and I know what she wants, then you don't need to wait. You can do whatever you want. She and I are long gone.'

CHAPTER THIRTY-ONE

The feeling of the sand in her feet, melting between her toes. The sound of the crashing waves in the distance and the noise of their voices quickly being drowned out by it. The sensation of the bitter cold that managed to bite through the fabric of her Zara jeans and top. And the other sensation in her body that numbed her to the feeling of it all a little.

Just a sip. A sip of the vodka in Lucy's bag. That was all she'd had. The girls wouldn't let her have much more, because they said that they were responsible and it was their job to look after her and Sylvia and make sure nothing happened. And not to mention it wasn't good for her. But the sip had been enough to go to her head and impair her reaction times.

So when they called her name, she didn't hear it. She was too busy staring out at the water, at the shimmering blackness of the Thames Estuary before her.

'Kash, are you coming or gonna just stand there like a lemon?' asked Lucy Cleaves, Nick's daughter, from the other side of the beach.

Kasia didn't like lemons, but she also didn't think there was anything wrong with being one.

Pushing that bizarre, and possibly vodka-induced, thought to the back of her mind, she bent down to pick up her shoes and then hurried across to the others. The rest of the group, Sylvia included, were situated a few feet from the water's edge. The smell of salt and dried seaweed was heavy on this part of the beach, so thick that it clung to the back of her throat. The beach was a small stretch of sand in Old Leigh called Bell Wharf, completely deserted now, but typically heaving during summertime, or as soon as the sun made an appearance, with hordes of beachgoers cramming themselves into every available space. On the other side of the Thames Estuary were the dampened, sparkling lights of Kent, only a few miles away. Above, shining through a thin layer of cloud, was the moon, bright and full of splendour, the glow bright enough to illuminate her new friends' faces.

Kathy, Vicky, Fiona, Yasmin and Lucy. And of course Sylvia.

They were all older than her (with the exception of Sylvia, who was only a few months younger) and she thought they were the best. They were funny, they were more experienced in life, in school and with boys, they were braver, they weren't afraid to say what they thought, they were intelligent, they were beautiful. All of them. From head to toe. Each in their own way.

And they were more sophisticated too. Some of the girls she knew from her own year group were fascinated with boys and TikTok and the latest trends, but she wasn't that interested in all of that. While, yes, she spent an abnormally long time on TikTok and all the other various social media platforms, she only did it because it helped fill the time, silence the anxiety. But she never made any videos herself, never thought about filming herself pulling off some stupid dance moves in front of a camera with only half her clothes on. Some of the girls in class were even talking about trying to become TikTok famous. Kasia couldn't believe that. It sounded stupid.

But it was the lack of boy chat that Kasia really enjoyed and appreciated. She'd had enough of Billy and didn't want to speak to him anymore. Especially after what he'd done to her. He'd known about her peanut allergy but had still brought traces of them to her. He'd known that she couldn't be anywhere near them, but had still tried to contaminate her with them. For that, he'd lost all her trust and respect.

And to think she'd kissed him!

What a massive regret that was. Never again. No, she would wait until it was someone she could properly trust, someone who respected her and didn't try to kill her, whether inadvertently or intentionally. Someone she fell in love with.

Or perhaps she would never kiss anyone ever again.

That seemed like the right way to do it for now.

'Did you hear about what happened in maths the other day with Mr Higham?' Yasmin asked. The whites of her eyes sparkled under the moonlight, and the shadows from her face and breasts only seemed to accentuate her nice figure.

The girls replied that they hadn't heard. Kasia and Sylvia sat in silence, waiting for the story to continue.

'Well, it was the funniest thing, right? Dexter Walker walked in late, right, and as soon as sir noticed him, he asked him what the answer was to the question on the board. And Dexter got it just like that!' She snapped her fingers and the sound punctuated the air and echoed through the street beyond. 'But the funniest thing was everyone's reactions afterwards. Sir's face just dropped, like someone had just flashed him. And then we all dossed about for twenty minutes. He couldn't control us after that. He's so smart.'

'I don't like Dexter,' Vicky replied. 'He's a bit of an arsehole. Don't you think he's a bit arrogant, like? Thinks he's the fittest one in the year.'

'I said he was smart,' Yasmin replied. 'That doesn't mean I think he's fit.'

Kasia was grateful that kind of conversation was brought to an abrupt stop. She hoped there would be no talk of boys and boyfriends and relationships and situationships at all tonight because she knew that if the topic came up they would be inclined to ask about her trip to the hospital and she didn't want to deal with the embarrassment of explaining it. Sylvia was the only one who knew, and right now she wanted to keep it that way.

Except for maybe Yasmin.

Yasmin seemed like the type of girl who could keep that sort of thing a secret, the same way Sylvia had. She got a suspicious feeling from the rest of them. That wasn't to say that they were bad or that they would go out of their way to hurt her, it was just that she didn't fully trust them. That was all.

She'd seen enough *Mean Girls* and teenage drama films to know what these types of girls were like.

Especially Lucy. She was the ringleader of the group, the Regina George. She was the one who'd brought the vodka, stolen it from her mum and dad's kitchen cupboard and replaced the missing liquid with water in the hope that they'd never find out. She was the one passing it around to the rest of them.

'Nah, I'm all right, thanks,' Yasmin replied quite sternly, forceful enough to get her point across but not enough to upset anyone. 'Think it's gone to my head already.'

'Lightweight,' Lucy said as she passed it round to the other girls.

Kasia watched them all take the glass bottle from Nick's daughter, put it to their lips, hesitate as they did so, and then grimace as though they'd just sucked on a lemon afterwards.

'Fucking disgusting,' Vicky said as she passed it on to the next. 'Yuck.'

'Why do people drink this for fun?'

'I don't know how my dad drinks so much of it.'

It was unanimous. The vodka was bad, tasted like shite, yet they continued to drink it anyway. Until there was nothing left, nothing but a small droplet that none of them were able to tease from the bottle.

'Give it 'ere,' Lucy said, reaching across to Fiona on the other side of the circle they'd formed in the sand.

'Why? You ain't gonna give it back to your dad, are ya?'

'Course not. I just... I just wanna put it in the bin. That's all.'

'Conscientious about the planet now, are we? But when I wanted to dispose of that BBQ we lit in the forest the other day, you said it would biodegrade.'

'Because that's what it said on the box!'

'Yeah, yeah.'

Kasia didn't know what was happening, and judging by the awkward and blank expressions on the rest of the girls' faces, neither did anyone else, but she sensed an argument looming. An argument about fucking littering, no less.

Tomek would be proud.

Not about the underage drinking or loitering on a beach late at night, but the littering; he always reminded her to put her rubbish in the bin whenever she was finished with something, otherwise he threatened to fine her.

For some reason though, she didn't think that her choice of sustainability-conscious friends would detract from the fact she'd drunk alcohol tonight.

But with any luck he would never find out.

'Can I have it then?' Nick's daughter asked for a second time.

'Go on then. If you must.'

Lucy snatched the bottle from Fiona and clambered to her feet, kicking hooves of sand into the air like a horse prancing on the dirty earth. For a brief moment, Kasia watched her disappear towards the bin on the esplanade but quickly lost attention when she heard Yasmin talking again.

'Did any of you see—?'

Before she could finish, an ear-piercing shriek perforated the silence and split the air in two. The sound was so loud it made Kasia physically jump with fear. Her body flushed cold and she held her breath for a fraction before she eventually turned in the direction of the sound. Even though the alcohol had distorted her echolocation abilities, she knew that it had been Lucy screaming.

Everyone knew it was Lucy screaming.

The only problem was, who was brave enough to find out why?

To her own surprise, she was already a few steps into her sprint along the beach before she realised what she was doing. Exactly that. Sprinting. Towards the danger. Towards the darkness. But also towards her friend who needed help.

The scream had been a singular, solitary, piercing sound, followed by a dull *thud*. And then silence.

Kasia didn't know what that meant. Hadn't prepared herself for what she might find.

At the end of the beach, at the foot of the steps, she found out. There, collapsed on the concrete promenade like a rag doll, was Nick's daughter, and standing over her was a small, heavyset man wearing a battered and torn coat. Blood trickled along the cement, impeded on its journey by the sand and washed-up seaweed.

At first, the man didn't acknowledge her – the smell of alcohol on him reached her from a few feet away – but as soon as she screamed Lucy's name, he drunkenly spun on the spot, his movements slow and laboured. And then she leapt onto him.

She didn't know what had come over her – rage, anger, stupidity – but it worked. After her first attempt, she knocked the man to the ground, and by the time she jumped on him, the rest of the girls had arrived. Screams erupted in the air at the sight of the blood and Lucy's body lying on the ground.

'Help me!' Kasia yelled. 'Jump on him so he can't move!'

It didn't take long for the girls to snap out of their inertia and assist her. Soon after, all five of them were on the man, pinning him to the ground. With the rest of her friends occupied, Kasia took the opportunity to clamber off him and hurry over to Nick's daughter. She found her collapsed on the ground, perfectly still. For a moment, Kasia feared the worst, that she had succumbed to a fatal blow to the head, that she had been murdered. But as soon as she noticed the gentle rise and fall of Lucy's chest, she jumped into action. The first thing she thought to do, before anything else, was call her dad.

He would know what to do.

And not just because he was a police officer, either. But because he was brave, intelligent, and able to think logically and clearly in times like these. He would be the hero she needed, they all needed, to save them from this nightmare.

CHAPTER THIRTY-TWO

Within minutes of Tomek arriving at the beach, the whole area had been secured. Keeping the attacker pinned to the ground, and tied up to a metal barrier using a set of cable ties Tomek kept in the back of his car, he and Sean had instructed the girls to protect the area. Kasia and Sylvia, the only two he knew and therefore trusted, had been instructed to remain by Lucy's side, along with Sean, who was gently moving her into the recovery position while trying to keep her body as straight as possible. The blood leaking from her head like a puncture in a bottle of water continued ominously, and a thick river of red gradually trickled down to the edge of the promenade and onto the sand, forming a dense puddle below. Meanwhile, two of the friends – he would find out their names later – were at the top of the bridge that led down to the beach. The final two friends – again, names weren't important right now – had sprinted to the other side of Old Leigh, the only entrance accessible for the emergency vehicles by road.

Tomek had called an ambulance and police support within seconds of his arrival. Mercifully, they had shown up two minutes sooner than their estimation. Brilliant blue and white lights flashed rhythmically on the restaurants and seawall surrounding them, almost blinding him in the darkness. One ambulance, two paramedics. And three police constables.

And then Tomek had made the call to Nick.

'What're you talking about?' he'd asked frantically. 'What happened? Where? Where is she? What happened to her?'

Tomek had struggled to answer any of his questions over the volume of Nick's voice, but as soon as the chief inspector paused to catch his breath, Tomek explained that he needed to get himself to Southend Hospital. That he should wait there for her to arrive. But it wasn't looking good. One of the paramedics had explained to him that the gouge in her head was substantial and that she needed immediate surgery to staunch the blood flow and stop the brain from drowning.

Once the ambulance had left and headed back in the direction it had come from, Tomek then turned his attention to the man who was being thrown into the back of the police car.

'Sean, can you go with him?'

'Yeah, of course. But why?' Fog misted in front of Sean's breath as he breathed rapidly in the cool night.

'Because someone needs to fucking deal with this cunt straight away. And I need to make sure the girls get home safely.'

He turned to face them all. Their haggard, shocked and frightened faces stared back at him blankly, almost as though he was staring at a group of zombies. Now it was time to find out their names, and while they waited for their respective parents to pick them up, Tomek led them through the town towards the train station. As they walked along the marina, a train blasted past them, one of the last of the night. The repetitive *da-dum da-dum* of the wheels over the tracks seemed to settle the girls, as though it had hypnotised them.

On their saunter to the station, Tomek asked them for one interesting fact about themselves. They needed to take their minds off what had just happened, and this was the only way he could think of.

Kathy could play the violin to a reasonable level.

Vicky's grandparents were originally from France, but she couldn't speak any of the language.

Fiona was gluten intolerant.

Yasmin's favourite film was *Die Hard*.

Sylvia didn't see what all the fuss was about when it came to vaping and cigarettes.

And Kasia admitted that she'd had a few sips of alcohol that night.

As soon as the words had left her lips, the group fell silent, and he could sense their stares burning holes into his daughter for grassing them all up to a police officer.

'Where...?' he began, unsure how to approach the topic. Dealing with one underage drinker was enough, but five of them. 'Where did you get the alcohol from?'

'Lucy,' Kathy replied quietly, as though she didn't want to be associated with saying the words aloud. 'She borrowed some from her dad.'

'Borrowed? You planning on giving any of it back?' He tried to sound like one of them, amicable, friendly, someone they could trust by dampening the anger in his voice.

The comment elicited a laugh from the girls and put them a little more at ease.

'You won't tell our parents, will you?'

Now that was the million-dollar question. They had all gone through a harrowing experience, their nerves were jangled, adrenaline was through the roof, anxiety even higher, fear stratospheric. The last thing they needed was a bollocking from each of their parents as soon as they got home.

'The doctors will find the alcohol in her blood and they'll tell the police when they come to get their report. Once they have that, they'll probably tell your parents. But that won't be until the morning. So you're safe for now.'

He gave them all a wink and a smile. At least he wouldn't be the bad guy, and they could all relax a little more now.

Nearly twenty minutes later, all the girls were gone except for Sylvia, picked up by panicked parents who briefly interacted with him, thanked him for looking out for their daughters, then headed home. Before they all disappeared, Tomek reminded them that police officers would be round in the morning to take witness statements.

'Remind me of your address, Sylvia,' Tomek said as he started the car.

Sylvia gave it to him and they arrived ten minutes later. When Louise, Sylvia's mum, opened the door, fear immediately flashed across her face.

'What's going on? What's happened?'

'She's fine,' Tomek said. 'Just a little shaken up. Do you mind if we come in?'

Kasia and Sylvia disappeared up to Sylvia's room while he and Louise moved into the kitchen. This wasn't the type of event to discuss in the living room.

'Do I need to be standing up for this?'

'Sitting down might be preferable, but I've got good reactions, so if you do decide to pass out on me I should be able to catch you.'

'Should?'

He shrugged and smirked at her. 'I said "good", not "great".'

'Filling me with confidence there, Tomek. Now tell me, what happened?'

And so he explained to her his second-hand understanding of the events. That, while they had all been sitting on the beach, chatting and talking (he neglected to mention the drinking for now), they'd heard a scream, followed by seeing a figure tower over Lucy Cleaves.

'Oh my God,' Louise replied, holding her hand to her mouth. 'How awful. Do you know the extent of her injuries?'

'No, but it didn't look good. She was bleeding from the head.'

'But aren't head wounds always worse than they appear? I got knocked on the head once, a tiny little cut, but there was blood for days.'

'Literally?' Tomek asked sarcastically.

'Literally for days, yes. Miracle I survived, to be honest.'

'Good thing you did, otherwise I would be none the wiser about the dangers of small cuts.'

185

Louise saw the funny side of it and offered him a tea. He refused. 'Beer and tea don't really mix very well.'

'You mean to say you've been drinking and driving my daughter home?'

Tomek looked to the floor and hesitated.

'What is it?' she asked, her maternal instinct immediately suspecting something was wrong.

'You should probably know, but apparently, the girls were drinking tonight. Lucy stole some vodka from her dad's cupboard.'

'Vodka!' Louise's cheeks flushed red with rage. 'Fucking drinking vodka at thirteen!'

'I know.'

'You seem oddly calm about this whole thing,' she said.

Tomek chuckled. 'Trust me, I'm not. But I've dealt with a lot of this type of thing in my life, so I guess I'm used to it by now. I don't like the idea of Kasia drinking at any age let alone at thirteen, so I will be having strong words with her about that, in any case. But they're shaken up, they're scared about Lucy, so shouting my head off isn't going to accomplish anything. If anything, it'll probably make her want to do it again.'

'Unless she's so scarred by tonight she never touches a drop of alcohol again.'

Tomek crossed his fingers in both hands and raised them.

When it was time for him to leave, he called Kasia down from upstairs and waited for her by the bottom of the steps.

'Thanks again for bringing her home,' Louise said, coming up to his side. 'I can't remember if I said it before.'

'You didn't. But that's okay. We can't all wear capes.'

She placed a hand on his arm and embraced him. Her body was warm, and a nice respite from the cold that still clung to him from the outside. 'Thank you,' she said again. 'It was a good thing you were as close as you were.'

A moment wedged itself between them. A moment where they paused, where everything seemed to freeze, and he seemed to be locked in a battle with her gaze. Neither unrelenting. Pulses pounding. Blood rushing.

Louise was an attractive, single woman. She was of similar age, slightly younger by a few years, and she was everything he looked for in a woman. Resilient, determined, brave, strong, charismatic. Everything he—

'Dad?'

Kasia's voice jolted him out of his reverie, and he snapped his neck towards her in the middle of the stairs. Behind her was Sylvia.

'Ah. There you are.'

'What's going on?'

Tomek pushed himself away from Louise gently, without meaning to cause any offence, and brushed himself down. Caught in the act. Like a pair of teenagers.

'You ready to go?' he asked, making sure to avoid her question as much as possible. 'I was just saying goodbye. Everything all right?'

Kasia's and Sylvia's faces brightened with glee, while Tomek's and Louise's flushed with embarrassment.

'You can wipe that smile off your face, Sylvia,' Louise said beside him. 'You and I need to have a chat in the morning. But for now, straight to bed after you've said goodbye.'

And Tomek and Kasia took that as their cue to leave.

CHAPTER THIRTY-THREE

Christmas Eve's eve. The day before the day before. And a solemn mood had settled in the flat. When Tomek had awoken the next morning, opening the curtains to a grey and drizzly sky, the weight of what had happened the night before felt like it had finally settled on *him*. Nick's daughter was in hospital. Nick's daughter had been attacked. The thought that it could have been any one of the girls, that it could have been his own daughter, finally began to play on his mind.

And when Kasia stumbled out of her bedroom, wrapped tightly in her hoodie as if relying on it for protection, it was clear to see the same thought had kept her awake all night as well.

'Sleep okay?' he asked as he made her a cup of tea.

'No. Couldn't sleep.'

'Me neither. Do you want to talk about it?'

'What's there to talk about?'

'You can tell me how you're feeling.'

'Scared.'

'Right. What about in particular?'

'Scared for Lucy. Have you heard anything?'

Tomek checked his phone and shook his head. He hadn't received any update from Nick or Sean. He was being kept in an information blackout.

'Can I go and see her?' Kasia asked.

Tomek had wondered the same thing as soon as he'd woken up. He wanted to pay them a visit. Not only for Lucy but also for Nick and his wife. He couldn't begin to imagine how they were feeling, how terrified they were. The angst and anguish they must have felt as they sat there in the hospital, awaiting an update from the doctors and nurses. Tomek had witnessed it first-hand with other families on cases that he'd worked. In those instances he'd always been an outsider, watching from the perimeter. But now that it was someone he knew, someone he cared for and respected going through the same Catherine wheel of emotions, he began to truly appreciate what it was like. Even if he was still one step removed.

Unlocking his mobile phone again, Tomek scrolled through his address book until he found Nick's mobile number. He gave his boss a call and waited for him to answer.

'Hi.'

'Hi, Nick. Can you talk?'

'Yeah.'

'How's she doing?'

'Not good. It's touch and go. Her skull's been crushed. A massive dent in her head. She's in a coma. Doctors reckon it could go either way. Possible permanent brain damage. Bleed on the brain. She might never wake up. Everything.'

'Fucking hell, mate. I'm so sorry.'

If he thought he was having a bad morning, it was nothing compared to what Nick and his wife were experiencing.

'How's Maggie holding up?'

'Worse. Daniela's fine, she's asleep, she doesn't know what's going on, but Maggie's beside herself with worry.'

'I can only imagine...' Tomek paused, swallowed and turned to Kasia. 'When the time's right, we wondered if we could come down. Perhaps take your mind off it.'

'Yeah, that'd be nice, mate. But it won't be for a while. I'll have a word with the doctors and let you know.'

Tomek had never heard his boss, his friend, sound so despondent, so defeated, so broken. It was as though he'd had his soul (whatever was left of it, anyway) ripped out of him.

He explained to Kasia that Nick would get back to them.

'You'll let me know as soon as he does?' Kasia asked, as though she was the one in charge.

'Of course I will,' Tomek said with a grin. He checked his watch – 8:48 am. 'I've gotta go to work. Find out what's happening with the arrest. I'll try and get someone to keep you company for the day.'

'I'm not five.'

'No, but you will want someone to talk to, and it'll make a nice change for it to be someone else for once. Besides, it's Christmas, I thought it was all about—'

'This is the worst Christmas ever,' Kasia said as she pulled her hood over her head and slumped onto the sofa.

Our Christmas is nothing compared to what Nick and his family are going through right now, Tomek thought as he began preparing breakfast for them both. Something salty. Something fatty. Something feel-good. When he was finished, and all the scraps were thrown in the bin, he began ringing round to see who could come over to keep Kasia company for the day. His first port of call was Saskia Albright, his longest-standing friend, but she was already in Scotland with her parents for the festive break. Next, he'd considered calling Abigail but knew that would only add fuel to the fire of Kasia's insatiable desire to wind him up and get involved in his love life. Besides, he didn't want to give Abigail any wrong impressions. Then he tried Louise and Sylvia, but they were visiting family in Colchester that afternoon. Which left the only other people he could think to call. The bottom of his list.

His parents.

CHAPTER THIRTY-FOUR

P erry and Izabela Bowen had been more than happy to look after Kasia for as long as he needed them to. Some bonding time, they'd told him. Long overdue. Private, without Tomek snooping and censoring everything they talked about. He wasn't too sure he felt comfortable with the idea of the two of them grilling her about boyfriends, school, *him*, and life in general, all over a packet of *paluski* and an extra-strong coffee, but he didn't have a choice. Perhaps he was being too cautious, too paranoid. They were Kasia's grandparents, after all. And he had told them very little about her and her life, so it was only reasonable that they were curious.

'She's in good hands,' Izabela Bowen had told him with a wry smile on her face before he'd left.

Tomek wasn't convinced, but he'd tried to push those thoughts to the back of his mind as he'd made his way into the station. And he soon found out that the nearer he got, the easier that became, because instead of thinking about Kasia and Perry and Izabela, his thoughts became plagued with images of Nick's daughter on the concrete, head caved in, bleeding. And then the images of her lying in the hospital bed with her parents by her side.

The images finally began to dissipate as soon as he laid eyes on his colleagues. And they all but disappeared as he saw the face of the man who'd attacked Lucy Cleaves on the TV screen. A live link had been fed into the back of the unit inside the incident room, and the team were watching him in the middle of the interview. Opposite the attacker were Sean and Chey, grilling him.

Now that he could see his face clearly, Tomek recognised the man immediately. Paddy Battersby. A paranoid schizophrenic known to the police for years. Previously arrested for assault, disorderly behaviour, vandalism, and a whole rap sheet of minor offences. For the most part, he'd been a broken man in desperate need of a fix; harmless, until last night, of course.

The faces that looked up at Tomek were bleary-eyed and swollen. They had pulled an all-nighter, and interviews had taken place throughout the night. With no let-up. Legally, Paddy was allowed eight hours' rest within the first twenty-four hours of being held in custody, but it was clear to see the team were going to make him wait as long as possible for that. It was the least he deserved.

In the incident room was a skeleton team of four. Victoria, Martin, and Oscar. It was Christmas, and a large portion of the people on the team were on leave, celebrating the festive period with their loved ones. And as a result the rest of them, Tomek included, would be expected to pull longer hours.

As soon as she'd spotted him, Inspector Orange pulled him into her office for an update.

'We've charged him with GBH,' she said, keeping her voice low. 'But now we're asking if he knows anything about Fern Clements and Lily Monteith.'

'Seriously?'

'What?'

Tomek pointed in the direction of the TV in the incident room. 'Him? Paddy Battersby? Paddy the Panda, the man who couldn't hurt a fly?'

'Well, he can clearly do a lot more than that.'

Tomek placed his hands in his pockets and slouched backwards slightly. 'You don't know him like we do. He's troubled. He's schizophrenic.'

'That doesn't excuse him putting Nick's daughter in hospital.'

'I'm not saying it does.' Tomek inhaled deeply to control himself. 'What's he saying happened?'

'His version of events is that he wanted to ask her if she had a tin of spam. When she saw him she panicked and lashed out, which made him panic. And as he tried to get away, he barged into her and knocked her over, smashing her head onto a pole.'

That must have been some force to cave her head in, Tomek considered.

'So it was an accident?' he asked.

'Accident or not, she's still in hospital. We'll see how his version of events stands up against the girls'.'

Tomek knew that it would be Paddy's word against theirs. All six of them. And in that case, it wouldn't make a difference whether it was an accident or not. Paddy Battersby's fate had been sealed.

'Has he admitted to killing Lily Monteith and Fern Clements yet?'

'No,' she said bluntly. 'His solicitor and responsible adult are telling him to stay quiet on that front.'

'So naturally you're more suspicious of him.'

'Yes,' she said.

But Tomek wasn't. What had happened to Lucy Cleaves had been a freak accident, one of those one-in-a-million stories, but nothing more. While tragic, yes, Tomek didn't think it was enough to unleash the witch trials and burn Paddy Battersby at the stake.

'How long's he looking at?' Tomek asked.

'After he's charged with their murders?'

'No. Because you haven't got any evidence against him for those yet. How long's he looking at for last night? The GBH?'

'Five years,' Victoria replied, her expression and voice flat.

'Wow.'

Poor bloke. But even poorer Lucy. Tomek couldn't have too much sympathy for him in that regard, not when she was currently fighting for her life.

'There's something else I wanted to discuss with you,' Victoria began.

Tomek placed his hand on the back of a chair. 'Do I need to sit for this?'

'You can sit if you want. That way you'll make me look taller and feel taller.'

Tomek reckoned she needed a lot of that right now. She'd made a few oversights recently, including in the double murder of two girls who had been abducted and strangled by a swing in a playground on Canvey. And as a result, he found it difficult to feel sorry for her.

'It's about your role in this team.'

He held his breath.

'Nick's going to be signed off for the next few weeks I imagine while he looks after his daughter. So that will put me temporarily in charge, and I'm going to need a number two.'

'Okay,' Tomek said, looking up at her, beady-eyed. 'Do you need me to tell you where the toilets are?'

To his surprise, Victoria hadn't seen that one coming. Fortunately, she *had* seen the funny side of it, and placed a delicate hand on her chest as she laughed, to show it.

'You don't ever stop with the immature humour, do you?'

'Where's the fun in growing up? I've had to do enough of it these past two months, I don't want to do any more. I need *some* immaturities, at least.'

'Some, but not all. Aside from that, aren't you going to say anything?'

'About what?' Tomek didn't realise it, but he was looking up at her the way a dog looks up at its owner: obediently and eager to find out what was happening next.

'*You're my second-in-command*. While Nick's on leave.'

'Well, well, how the tables turn.'

This was good. Very good. Because now, as second-in-command, he would have more say over which direction the investigation took. More control over the aspects he couldn't control by himself.

This was good. Very good.

CHAPTER THIRTY-FIVE

The first task on his list for the day had been easy: invite Kasia into the station for a witness statement. Throughout the day the girls would be interviewed individually for their take on what had happened to Nick's daughter. Their stories would then be cross-referenced with one another for veracity and then considered against Paddy Battersby's version of events. Tomek held a sneaky suspicion that they wouldn't differ too much, if at all. It was clear to him that Paddy would be charged with what happened to Lucy, the coffin had already been ordered and the funeral service paid for, but Tomek was willing to do anything he could to make sure that he didn't go down for the murders he had no involvement in. Wrongfully convicting someone of murder or rape or any other form of serious offence, was fortunately something he'd never fallen victim to. But he had heard the stories, seen the newspaper reports. Twenty years of a prison sentence served, only for the technological and scientific advances to rush in like a hero in the night to alter the outcome of a case and exonerate you. Twenty years of your life gone. Twenty years bought and paid for by the government by way of a settlement. There was no amount of money that could account for that many years of your life, so he was a firm believer in getting the right conviction at the right time. And if that meant taking longer than necessary or exhausting all the options and budget, then so be it.

It was Kasia's first time visiting his place of work, and he felt incredibly nervous. Mixed with a small amount of excitement. And with a sprinkle of sombre thrown into the mix as well. He was wary of what she would think of the place, what she would say about his colleagues. He would have liked to have given her a tour and properly introduce her to them (after all, they'd heard so much about her, and she so little about them), but that hadn't been possible. It was just a shame that the circumstances of her visit had been to give a witness statement.

A witness statement which had been conducted by Rachel, as calmly and politely as she could, the best in the job. The whole ordeal had taken her over an hour to complete, and by the end of it her eyes were red and her make-up had run. To cheer Kasia up, Tomek had offered to take her to the shops quickly to buy some of her favourite sweets.

'We can take out another payday loan and get some more Freddos if you like?'

'You don't have any chocolate here?'

Tomek had looked around at the bland and bleak office. It had no semblance of festivity about it and looked as though all joy and excitement for the holiday season fell into a black hole as soon as you walked in.

'Nadia usually does the chocolate,' he replied. 'But since her pregnancy, she's gone off it quite a lot.'

'Oh.'

'Yeah. Her new favourite thing though, if you're interested, is biltong.'

'Biltong?'

'It's some South African dried meat stuff. Weird. No one likes it which is good for her because, trust me, you don't want to go near her when she's eating her biltong, she protects it far better than the animals that are killed to make it protect their cubs. Plus no one wants to go near it because it stinks.'

Kasia looked around the office floor. 'Where is she?'

'At home. Probably making her own biltong for when all the shops are shut over Christmas.'

Kasia chuckled. It was only small, brief, a little snigger, but it was a step in the right direction. Right now she needed nothing more than some laughter and relief, a break from what had happened. But just as Tomek was about to take her to the shops, the relief was brought to a sudden end. Nick called to inform him that they could visit. And without wasting any time, and quickly clearing it with Victoria, they headed to the hospital.

They found Nick, his wife, Maggie, and their youngest daughter, Daniela, waiting for them outside the hospital room. Even though it had only been fourteen hours since the incident, both parents looked as though they hadn't slept in fourteen days. Broken, beaten, downtrodden. Whereas Daniela hadn't fully come to terms with what had happened to her older sister and looked like she was there to support her parents, rather than the other way round.

'Good to see you,' Nick said, the vigour stolen from his voice. 'Thank you for coming.'

'Of course. Anything. How... how is she doing?'

To answer that, Nick led them both into the room without preparing them for what they were about to see: a pale figure lost amidst the white sheets protecting her. Several tubes were hooked up to her wrists like something out of a horror film. And at the top of the bed was Lucy's head, encased in a metal bracket.

'Doctor said the dent in her skull is about as large as a golf ball,' Nick said, standing in the doorway while everyone else shuffled towards the patient, as though he was unable to bring himself any closer. 'They've put her into a medically induced coma.'

Kasia tugged at Tomek's arm and whispered into his ear. 'What's that?'

Tomek quickly told her before Nick continued.

'They still don't know when she'll wake up, or if.'

'Nick,' replied his wife. 'The doctors also told us to stay positive.'

'No, they didn't. They said that we should keep our spirits up, which is as good as saying we should pray for the best.'

'She can hear you, you know,' added Maggie scornfully, shooting him a look to match.

'Can she?' asked Kasia.

'Yes, sweetheart,' Maggie said. She rounded the other side of the bed and placed a hand on her shoulder. 'The doctors have said she can hear every word we're saying. Would you like to talk to her?'

Immediately the tension in the room dissipated.

Carefully, tentatively, Kasia stepped up to her friend's side, placed a hand on her shoulder the way her mother had, and whispered into her ear.

'Hey, it's Kasia, I... I don't really know what to... Everyone's worried about you. We've all been talking on the group chat and everyone wants to know how you're doing... I'll... I'll tell them that you're doing well... And that you'll be... be out of here in no time, all right? Because we're all missing you and we want to see you at school again. You make lunchtimes bearable, all right? So you have to get better.'

Kasia finished her monologue in a room of stunned silence. Tomek looked around and saw tear-filled eyes, both himself and Nick's family. Blubbering messes, unable to control themselves. Tomek was moved. That a little speech from a thirteen-year-old girl could have had such an effect on them.

After five minutes, the tears stopped, and Nick pulled Tomek out of the room and into the privacy of the hallway.

'You spoken to Victoria yet?' he asked, the vigour and work-speak coming back into his voice.

'Yeah.'

Instead of responding, Nick pursed his lips to stop them quivering, but it had little effect. As tears began to form in his eyes, he placed a firm hand on Tomek's shoulder and said, 'Keep her steady for me, will you?'

'Of course,' Tomek replied as he placed an equally comforting hand on Nick's back.

It was possibly the second time Tomek had seen any form of

emotion from his manager, from his *friend,* in all the thirteen years he'd known him. The last time had been when his son, Robbie, had fled the family to join the army.

'They're charging the bloke who did this with GBH,' Tomek said. 'It was Paddy Battersby.'

'Paddy? Really?' Nick sighed and rolled his eyes. 'The silly fucker.'

'DI Orange also thinks he's got something to do with our allergy killer.'

'Then she's thicker than I thought,' Nick replied.

'I've tried convincing her otherwise, but she's not budging.'

'Well, I'm gonna have to leave you to deal with it. With all due respect, it's the last thing I wanna fucking worry about right now.'

'Understood, captain,' Tomek said, feigning a salute.

As the two men made their way back into the hospital room, Tomek's phone began to vibrate in his pocket. He held a finger up to Nick, signifying that he would be through in a minute, then answered the call.

'Is it important?' he asked into the microphone.

'That's not very nice.'

'Just answer the question.'

'No, it's just about my article.'

Tomek sighed and looked at the door that led into the hospital room.

'Right.'

'I was wondering if you had anything else for me?'

Tomek tapped his feet. Fought with the decision.

'No,' he replied. 'I don't.'

'Come on, Tomek. You must have *something*. You owe me, remember.'

'I owe you nothing. Now leave it alone. And I think you should lay off Nick for a while. And don't print that article. Right now it'll only do more harm than good.'

'I can't believe I'm hearing this. You've changed your tune.'

'Yeah, well, some things are bigger than hitting your word count, Abigail.'

CHAPTER THIRTY-SIX

They stayed for no longer than an hour, not wishing to outstay their welcome any more than Tomek already thought they had. The family needed time to be together, to grieve, to process, and they certainly didn't need Tomek and Kasia there, hovering over their shoulders, listening intently every time the doctors or nurses interrupted to give the family an update.

Instead, Tomek swapped one family for another. His own.

By the time Kasia and Tomek arrived home that evening, after grabbing a McDonald's on the way (to lift Kasia's mood somewhat), the lights in the flat were still on and there were two shadows dancing in the windows. Tomek pulled up to the building and leant forward.

'Did your gran and grandad mention anything about staying the evening to you?' he asked.

'She might've said something about dinner,' Kasia replied slowly, looking down at the food on her lap.

'And you think to tell me this now?'

She shrugged. 'I wasn't going to say no to a McDonald's.'

Of course she wasn't. It seemed like her generation lived on the stuff. And with access to it so readily available, sometimes at the click of a few buttons, it was no surprise. Every time he wandered past the McDonald's near the high street on the way to get his Sainsbury's meal deal or, if he was treating himself to a Subway, the place was usually filled with teenagers her age with their fancy trainers, Adidas and Nike tracksuits and manbags. He couldn't think of anything more off-putting. Other than the thought of the amount of processing the food went through. That was enough to put some people off for life.

'You can be the one to let her down then,' Tomek said as they made their way to the front door. Then he handed Kasia the empty McDonald's bag.

'Because she can't shout at *you*.' Tomek inserted the key into the door. 'And watch, I bet you any money she'll still find a way to blame this on me.'

'Any money?' A hint of excitement flashed in Kasia's voice; maybe that was the way to make her feel better, shower her with money.

'No,' Tomek replied sternly. 'It's a figure of speech. Not everyone you ever talk to is going to give you money because you ask for it, Kash.'

'A sugar daddy would,' she whispered under her breath, but Tomek heard every last syllable of it.

He stopped on the stairs that led to the flat and scowled at her. 'What did you just say? How do you know about those things?'

'TV. There was a programme on Channel 4 the other day. Don't have a go at me.'

No. He couldn't, could he? Not when it was almost impossible to. With everything being even more readily available on streaming apps on mobile and desktop, keeping an eye on the sort of stuff she watched was becoming increasingly difficult to monitor. But, he considered, in the grand scheme of things, learning about sugar daddies in a documentary was tame compared to the other sorts of things she could be watching. So long as she wasn't watching beheadings or people setting themselves on fire, she was okay.

'You're home!' were the words that greeted them as soon as they stepped through the door at the top of the steps. Followed quickly by, 'And you've already eaten.'

Izabela stopped in her tracks and lowered the arms that she had raised to embrace them both.

'What are you doing with that?' she asked as she pointed at the bag of McDonald's in Kasia's hand. 'We made you dinner. I thought we could have a nice meal together.'

'She wanted it,' Tomek said, passing the blame across.

His mum raced up to him and prodded him forcefully in the chest. 'Yeah, but *you're* the one who bought it for her.'

Tomek caught a smug glance from Kasia that said, "I'm coming for that money whether you like it or not."

'What did you make?' Tomek asked, keen to move the conversation away from his bad parenting decision.

He sniffed the air and found out the answer himself. *Pierogi.* Dumplings. A Polish staple. The dinner he and his brothers lived off almost every day when they first moved to the country.

'Your favourite,' his dad said.

Tomek poked around the kitchen door and saw his old man standing over two large saucepans, stirring the contents slowly.

'At least it's an easy meal for you to cook,' Tomek replied.

'Are you saying I didn't put any love or soul into that meal? I cooked that dinner for you for weeks at a time when you were younger.'

'I thought that was just because we were poor.'

'No, it's because you and your brothers loved it. And I always had to make sure I gave the three of you the same amount of dumplings. Any more or any less for any of you, and I was at risk of being blamed for favouritism.'

If that had been the case, Tomek knew where he would have been on the favourite scale: Michał first, Dawid second, followed by himself sitting pretty at the bottom.

'To be fair, now and then I did give Michał an extra one after you and Dawid had left the table,' Izabela continued.

And if there was ever any doubt in Tomek's mind about his place on the ladder, it was dismantled with that final comment.

After getting themselves settled in, and quickly discarding the

McDonald's evidence, they seated themselves at the table and ate what they could of the *pierogi*. Tomek was able to stomach five of the meat-filled dumplings, while Kasia could only handle two. The conversation around the table avoided Nick's daughter and the incident as much as possible. It was Christmas, they said. It wasn't the time to talk about such matters.

'Speaking of which,' Izabela said with a beaming smile on her face, 'Dawid and the boys are coming over for Christmas tomorrow. Are you sure you both don't want to come? There's still plenty of room around the table.'

'And there'll be plenty of food,' Perry Bowen added.

'The leftover dumplings from tonight, you mean?' Tomek muttered, then looked to Kaisa, who was in the middle of pushing her food around her plate. 'I think we're fine here, thanks. Just the two of us. It's our first Christmas together and I want it to stay that way. Maybe next year. But I hope you have a nice time, and send Dawid and the boys our love.'

THE WHOLE THING had been a shitshow, and a complete waste of time, exactly the way Tomek felt about every Christmas. The joy and excitement of what was supposed to be the most wonderful time of the year had been sucked out of it by the events of that night. Kasia spent the next two days with her head down, sleeping, lying in bed, curled up beneath the duvet, either playing on her phone or messaging Sylvia. The decorations that she'd spent hours putting up earlier in the month, the ones that had sparkled and glistened for the past three weeks, had lost their shine and shimmer, and she'd even turned the fairy lights off in her room. The Christmas tree looked barren as Kasia consumed all the chocolates on it in the space of an afternoon. The tinsel was knocked off and left to dangle loosely and on the floor; not to mention the presents beneath the tree were sparse.

In the end, Tomek had gone for a handful of make-up and self-care products that he'd found on the shelves of Boots and Superdrug, along with the promise of going on a shopping spree in the near future.

'You get a hundred pounds to spend,' he'd told her.

'That's all right,' she said despondently as she set a box of powder on the sofa. 'You don't have to.'

'I know I don't have to, but I want to.'

And then they'd had the food. A traditional British feast: turkey, roast potatoes, Yorkshire puddings and a smattering of vegetables, drowned in an unhealthy amount of gravy. In truth, the food had been the only highlight of the day, and even that had been a disaster. As it was his first time cooking such a big meal for such a big occasion, he had little to no idea what he was doing, and he spent several hours in the kitchen like a bull in a China shop. Knocking things off the counter, dropping food onto the floor, smashing a few glasses in the sink. In the end, the turkey came out burnt, the roasties were almost raw, and the vegetables looked more like mashed potatoes than anything else; a very colourful and nutritious pile of mashed potatoes.

'I had big expectations for this dinner,' he admitted as he whacked a dollop of carrots onto his plate. 'But I can't help thinking a McDonald's Happy Meal might be more appetising.'

'Yeah,' Kasia said. 'You're probably right.'

Throughout the rest of the afternoon, and into the evening, Kasia's solemnity and despondency continued. Despite his original misgivings about Christmas, he found himself trying to cheer her up with board games and card games. To his surprise, he'd found an old version of Essex Monopoly sitting at the bottom of his wardrobe; somehow it hadn't been lost in the move a few weeks back.

'This was my favourite game as a kid,' he said as he unboxed it and began placing the tokens on the board. 'Though we didn't have an Essex version when we were growing up.'

'Cool.'

'You ever played?'

Kasia slowly tore her eyes away from her phone and looked at the box, as though she needed reminding of what it was. 'No. Don't think so.'

'Whaaattt?' he said, putting on his best American voice. 'You've never played Monopoly?'

'Didn't think people played board games anymore.'

'Pfft. Back in the olden days, we did. Before all these mobile phones and tablets.'

'Mum and I didn't have either. Think the only thing we had was a deck of cards.'

Tomek raised his eyebrow. 'I thought you said you played loads of card and board games at your mum's for Christmas?'

She dropped her head a fraction. 'I lied,' she said. 'We didn't do all those things. We didn't have the money to. And Mum was usually out trying to score. We didn't have decorations, nice food, a tree – any of it. That was why I was so excited for this one, it was going to be my first real, proper Christmas.'

'Oh, Kash.'

Tomek felt horrible. He'd had no idea. And now he felt incredibly guilty for having put on such a lacklustre display.

'Well, we're going to enjoy what's left of it!'

'By playing Monopoly?'

'Oh, yes. You just wait. You're going to be hooked.'

And so, after explaining the rules to her several times, they set about the board, purchasing local tourist attractions and locations, and building houses and hotels on them. Throughout, he noticed Kasia's mood lifting. And even more so when he let her win at the end.

'Ha! Suck on that!' she screamed, waving her money in front of his face with the first smile she'd worn all day.

Tomek rolled his eyes and began collecting the playing pieces. 'Beginner's luck,' he told her.

WHEN BOXING DAY finally came around, Tomek was forced to trade the board game for the game their little serial killer was playing with them. By now, weeks had passed since Lily Monteith's death and years, if you included Diana Greenock in the list (which he of course did) and they were still no closer to finding the killer. Tomek was due the day off but had decided he needed to go in. In his mind the Christmas period was over (Boxing Day was just an excuse to go shopping and contribute to the consumerism and capitalism inspired by their board game the night before), and there was only so much sitting around he could do while he mulled the thoughts over in his mind, and while Kasia sat on the sofa doing the same, both thinking similar, equally depressing thoughts. And so they both needed cheering up. Tomek knew how to do that for himself – work – but when it came to Kasia, things became a little tricky. He toyed with the idea of forcing her to spend Boxing Day with his parents, but if he wasn't willing to do the same then it wasn't fair on her. And then he'd thought about letting her go over to the hospital to see Lucy Cleaves, but then he quickly realised that was equally, if not more, depressing. In the end, he settled on the one thing he knew made her happy.

Sylvia.

Sylvia and her mum, Louise.

Tomek pulled up outside their two-bedroom semi-detached house in Daws Heath and followed Kasia to the doorway. The young girl walked with a marked spring in her step and bounced on the balls of her feet as she waited for her friend to open the door. As soon as Sylvia greeted them, Kasia waved him goodbye and then shot upstairs, leaving him to stand in the doorway. Looking and feeling like a lemon.

Eventually, several long moments later, Louise appeared, dressed in the same Christmas pyjama set as her daughter, green Christmas trees against a backdrop of red on the bottom half, and a candy cane T-shirt on the top. As soon she recognised him, she panicked and reached for a thicker, blander jumper from the nearby banister.

'Sorry about that,' she started, unable to look him in the eye. 'It was Sylvia's idea. I–'

'You don't have to apologise. Although if Kasia comes home with the brilliant suggestion that we need to wear matching pyjama sets for New Year's, then I know who to blame.'

'Oh, I can see that looking quite good on you.'

Tomek looked down at her trousers. 'I've always thought green was my colour.'

'Really brings out your beard.'

Tomek chuckled. The other night was the first time he'd picked up on her flirting. At first, he'd thought it was born out of emotion and the stress of what had happened. Now he wasn't so sure but after already being scared away from flirting with Kasia's teacher for obvious reasons, he wasn't sure if the same rules applied to her school friend's mum as well. Perhaps he would have to find out.

'How was your Christmas?' she asked as she hugged herself against the cold.

'Different,' he replied. 'Difficult. A first for both of us.'

Louise was no stranger to their situation. In fact, she was one of the only few who knew. And so he felt like he could be open and honest with her about his relationship with Kasia. He didn't know the ins and outs of her divorce, but every time they'd spoken to one another, he'd got the impression that she understood. That she understood more about their situation than he did, and he was the one in it. He supposed that a part of it was fed down the food chain from Kasia to Sylvia, and from Sylvia to Louise, so that every nugget of advice and wisdom was coming from Kasia by proxy. That her real thoughts and feelings were being meted out by a game of Chinese whispers.

'How was yours?' Tomek asked, feeling obligated to ask the same question.

'Oh, you know. Six hours cooking, twenty minutes eating, followed by another six hours feeling as though you can't move. Topped off by another couple of hours of washing up.'

Tomek nodded politely. 'Ours went a little something like that. In the end, we swapped the washing up for a game of Monopoly.'

'Who won?'

'Kasia. Obviously.'

'Because she's better than you or because you let her?'

'Isn't it obvious?'

'Right. Because she was better. That's a tough one to take, but there comes a time when they soon become better at everything than you. Your ego takes a real dent..'

'Says the one wearing a matching pyjama set.'

Louise threw her hand to her mouth, feigning offence. 'This was actually a Christmas present from my daughter, I'll have you know. Not sure how she bought it, but she used someone else's money to pay for it.'

Tomek was reminded of the time Kasia had stolen fifty pounds from an emergency stash he'd hidden inside a paperback. He wondered whether Kasia had bought him a Christmas present with more money she'd stolen from him. And if she had, he'd like to see it soon.

He took a step closer and lowered his voice. As he spoke, he glanced up the stairwell and flicked his eyebrows. 'How's she been getting on after everything?'

'Rough. She's trying to process it but I think she's been finding it hard. They're only young, and for them to have seen something like that, it's a lot for them to go through. And dredging it all up again in the police station didn't help.'

'I know, but it's all part of—'

'No, no, no. I wasn't having a go. I don't want you to think I was making a dig.' She placed a hand on his shoulder and left it there. 'It'll just take them time to get over it.'

Was this one of Kasia's Chinese whispers messages that had trickled down the tree? Or was this sage wisdom coming from Louise herself? Either way, if there was one thing he'd learnt from having a daughter he knew nothing about, it was that a lot of things took time.

Time for her to get used to her new school.

Time for her to get used to being around him and having to listen to him.

Time for her to get used to life in a new area, with new friends, a new *family*.

And now this. Time for her to get used to the images and nightmares of what had happened to Lucy.

The same way Tomek had been forced to get used to the nightmares that had plagued him after his brother's death.

208

CHAPTER THIRTY-SEVEN

The first thing Tomek noticed when he walked into the Major Incident Room was the sound. Music, belting out of the radio. Discussion, filtering through the corridors and out of the meeting rooms. The second thing Tomek noticed about the MIR was the room's brightness. As though someone or something had turned the lights up a few notches, painted everything a more luminous and prosperous colour, and changed the filter that had fallen on the building in the past few days.

The whole place was a far cry from the state he'd left it in.

And then he found out why.

DC Nadia Chakrabarti. The life and soul of the office. Without doubt one of the happiest and most bubbly people he'd ever had the fortune of meeting. She always wore a smile on her face, even when she was having a bad day, and she was always there to pick the team up when they needed it. And there was no greater need for it than now.

The team still wore the fear and fatigue of the allergy killer. And they all wore the dread of Lucy Cleaves' incident in their expressions. Enter Nadia. Cheerful, joyful. Exactly what the team needed. And as Tomek entered the room, she harangued him with a cup of tea thrust in his face.

'Welcome back, sarge,' she said, smiling ebulliently. 'Saw you pulling in so got this ready for you just in case. You look like you could do with one.'

'Right. Thanks.' Tomek took the cup from her and had a drink. Perfect. Made to order. 'Not sure if I should be offended or flattered.'

'Both.'

'Thanks, Nadia,' Tomek responded. 'You're a good egg.'

'I try my best.'

Tomek was sure that was the case. In almost all aspects of her job, she applied herself. As the constable in charge of arranging the action points via HOLMES 2, she was in charge of cracking the whip and ensuring all the necessary follow-ups and relevant criteria were being met. As a result, she and Tomek worked quite closely with one another on occasion. Except for the past few weeks when he'd neglected to give her the time that she needed and deserved.

As Tomek made his way to his desk, he surveyed the rest of the team's faces. It would be a lie to think that they were all well-rested, that was a false economy in this job, but they looked a little less uptight, a little more relaxed. In the background, the radio played some offensive and poorly-tasted rap song that upset him. For two reasons. One that the melody had been sampled from a classic pop song from the nineties. And two, the lyrics were trash. There were no good songs on the radio anymore. None of it was original. None of it was tasteful. None of it was enjoyable.

He recalled a simpler time when Blue and Five were at the height of their careers and he would sit on Southend Pier listening to them on his Walkman, or blasting Take That and NSYNC from the speaker in his friend's flat. Simpler, happier times. With much less to worry about.

'This *your* choice of music, Chey?' Tomek asked across the office.

'You'd think, but no. I'm much more into the nineties stuff, me,' the young constable replied. 'Mum and Dad got me into it. Oasis, Blur. All the classics. Though I think that's probably because they were off their faces at raves and gigs at the time.'

'Yeah, they were all the rave then.' When no one laughed at his joke, Tomek tried for another. 'I hear drugs are making a comeback though. Or should that be come*down*?'

Tumbleweed.

Tomek was almost sure he could see some floating across the carpet, and the sound of crickets. Even the music had stopped in protest against his shite jokes. But when he swivelled on the spot, he found out why. Victoria, standing in the doorway to the MIR.

'Interrupting, am I?'

'I think you need to call a doctor,' Tomek answered. 'Everyone's lost their sense of humour.'

'Or perhaps it's just you. Getting a bit boring in your old age.'

Tomek felt a slap on the back, followed by the sight of the person who'd done it. Sean, with his ginormous frame, sauntered past him, a ginormous smirk on his face, and made his way into the MIR. Everyone else shortly followed suit and seated themselves around the whiteboard at the head of the room. Before entering, Victoria pulled Tomek to the side and informed him that he would be the one leading it while she maintained the bureaucracy.

Tomek felt a slight tingle abseil down his spine as he heard those words. The moment he'd been campaigning for since the responsibility had been snatched away from him and passed across to Victoria.

He was back, baby!

But within the space of a few minutes of standing at the head of the room, he wished that he wasn't.

Rather, he wished that he'd been left in charge of the investigation from the outset.

'I want an update,' he said. 'I want to know as much as you do about everything. For the next few minutes I'm going to be a sponge, I'm going to absorb everything you tell me.'

'Sounds like you've been training your entire life for this,' Rachel noted sarcastically from the front row.

'Absolutely. My entire adult life, concentrated in this one moment.'

And all the others leading up to it.

On the whiteboards and noticeboards around the perimeter of

the room were their victims' names and faces, with the vital pieces of information detailed below each. Tomek moved over to Fern Clements' name and asked for an update on the young girl's death, as that was the freshest. As Rachel had been looking after it, with his tentative supervision, she would know the ins and outs, the day-to-day.

'Well, the good news,' she started, 'is that she's still dead—'

'What?'

'I... Er... I was just trying to make a joke. You know, banter. Like you just tried to do. It seemed like the sort of thing you might say.'

Tomek placed a hand on his chest. 'I would *never* be glad someone's dead.'

Though he could think of a few names where that wasn't the case.

'No,' she started. 'Not you. Just in general. *Someone.*'

She was flapping, embarrassingly so, and Tomek decided to pull her from the hole that she'd just dug for herself and place her on solid ground.

'Continue. Quickly, please.'

'Right. Yes, sarge. Fern Clements. As you know, she died from bee stings. Forensics have combed through the field where she was murdered but haven't found any DNA or trace evidence in the surrounding area. They have however found black fibres on her underwear inconsistent with her own. Now, given that she was at her friend's house, I need to take samples of everyone she came into contact with on that night.'

Tomek nodded thoughtfully.

'And what about Timothy Warren, our bee farmer?'

'Clean.'

'I thought he looked quite dirty when we saw him, but whatever you're into.'

Rachel rolled her eyes at him and shot him a look that said, You arsehole, that was the type of joke I was going for.

'I've checked him out and he's clean. Nothing there. He doesn't know anything about Fern. And he's got solid alibis, he works all hours of the day so it's hardly a surprise.'

'What about our list from the Beekeeper Association?'

'Still making my way through it, sarge.'

'And?'

'About twenty people in. Got another hundred and twenty to go.'

'Busy week for you then. And don't forget to ask if any of them have been to South America recently.'

Rachel confirmed that she would.

'And, lastly, what about her boyfriend-not-boyfriend, Darren?'

Rachel consulted her notes. 'Spoke with him on Christmas Eve. Ruined his and his parents' whole year I think, the way they behaved. But he never met up with Fern. After the party, they'd agreed to meet outside, but she wasn't there when he got there, and he tried calling her dozens of times. He showed me the messages and call history to prove it. I also checked his and Fern's telemetry data, and her phone was switched off before he got anywhere near the house party. She was gone before he turned up. Possibly dead before then as well.'

Tomek absorbed what he'd heard and nodded, masking the disappointment he felt after receiving the first blow in his football theory. Then he turned the conversation to Lily Monteith, and Anna and Oscar who had been looking into her death.

'Nothing new, sarge,' Martin began, tightening the man bun on his head. 'I did have the genius idea of calling up all the grocery stores and pharmacies to see if anyone had come in to purchase any condoms or disposable gloves around the time of Lily's death. But then I realised that wasn't so genius after all. And that in the grand scheme of things it was pretty fucking stupid.'

'Not entirely,' Tomek replied. 'I think there's something there. Have we got anything on a possible medical connection, GPs, nurses, doctors? Do they all share the same one, for example?'

'Not sure,' Martin replied. 'But we can absolutely look into it.'

'Good. Let me know what you find.'

'Of course.' He cleared his throat, letting Tomek know there was more to come. 'We also checked Lily Monteith's telemetry data on the night that she died and her phone was switched off right outside the park.'

'So he abducts them and the first thing he does is switch their phones off?' Tomek asked, more for his own benefit than anyone else's.

'Must do. Not surprising really, considering the girls are probably stuck to them and it's the first thing they unlock when getting into his car.'

Tomek nodded and checked a mark against Lily's name in his head before moving on to Mandy Butler.

'I've spoken with a contact in the ticketing office for the Cliffs Pavilion,' DC Chey Carter said. 'And I've requested all the ticket holder information for those that attended the events we've been looking at.'

'Do you know when you might get them?'

'Already have.' The young man smirked. Tomek wanted to beat it out of him. Ever since Chey had come into the team, Tomek had been purposely hard on him. Not because he wanted to be an arsehole (which he was anyway, but he wasn't a spiteful arsehole), but because he saw sprinkles of himself in Chey. The cheeky chappy, full of bravado and confidence, who thought he could get away with everything. When he'd been that age, Tomek had had Nick to guide and supervise him. Now it was his turn.

'I checked through the lists of all the events involving the victims found in Abigail Winters' report. Five in total. And in all of those lists, I found four names who had bought tickets to all five events.'

Tomek's ears perked up. Four names. Four individuals. He hoped they were connected in some way to the boys at the football club.

'Have you spoken with them yet?' Tomek asked.

Chey shook his head. 'It's on my list of things to do. But, I've gotta be honest, sir, I'm not too hopeful. I've been to the Cliffs plenty of times, and each time I've been there are always some cocks standing outside the front trying to sell last-minute tickets to desperate fans for an extortionate price. It's stupid and an absolute con.'

'It's only stupid if it doesn't work,' Tomek replied. 'I know what you're talking about, though, and you'd be surprised how successful they are. But I'm not worried about how much money they've made from it. I want to know if any of them have a connection with Mandy Butler and the rest of the victims. It's very possible they sold the tickets to our killer, whether knowingly or unknowingly, and we need to find out. And if one of those ticket resellers sold five tickets to the same guy, sometimes for the *same* show, then they're bound to remember. Alarm bells must have been ringing.'

'Unless they were just a *massive* fan.'

'I'm a massive fan of pizza, but you don't see me eating a Domino's five days in a row.'

'You would if you could though, wouldn't you?'

'What are you talking about?'

'Eating pizza for five days straight.'

'I mean, I *could*. Anyone *could*. Doesn't mean I'm going to.'

'No, but what I mean is if they were healthy, if they weren't as bad as everyone makes them out to be.'

'Then I wouldn't want to. Anyway, we're getting off-topic.' Tomek clapped his hands to get the discussion back on track. 'I want to discuss Diana Greenock. Where are we with her?'

Silence. Nobody answered. And they all turned away from him as they shirked responsibility.

'That hasn't been part of our focus, mate,' Sean said, the only one who could get away with saying it as Tomek's closest ally and friend.

'I know. But I was expecting *something*. We must have the list of Diana's flatmates, at least? A list of people we can speak to? We seem to be so good at making lists of people for all our other victims, but not this one?'

More silence. By now everyone had rotated their head so much that it looked like they were doing their best impression of *The Exorcist*.

'Right. If that's the case then I want someone to get me a fucking list. I don't care who. I just fucking—'

Tomek caught himself as soon as he realised he sounded like Nick. The aggression, the expletives.

'Sorry,' he said, calmer this time. 'Don't know where that came from. The list of her flatmates, her work colleagues. If someone could get that to me.'

'Already got it,' replied Nadia, typing away on her keyboard. Then added, 'Sir.'

'Thanks,' Tomek replied sheepishly. He cleared his throat and brushed himself down, unable to shake the feeling of a dad who'd just shouted unnecessarily at his children and now they were all staring up at him, afraid.

And it was all going so well.

A few more uncomfortable seconds passed until he summoned the courage to speak.

'I...' he began. 'I was wondering if I could run something by you all. I have a hypothesis that's been bothering me.'

CHAPTER THIRTY-EIGHT

D agenham & Redbridge FC had been stuck in the National League, the fifth division of football, for what was now their seventh season. The highest they'd ever reached on the football pyramid was League One. It was a story not too dissimilar from their neighbours on the opposite side of the Essex/London divide, Southend FC. The highest-ranked Essex football team was Colchester United, occupying a semi-permanent spot in League Two for the better part of eight years.

For a county that was so big on football, supporters had very little to get excited about locally. There had been no trophy parade in Essex since the seventies and the only source of elite contribution to the sport was West Ham, the local "big" team, the one with the most recent success, most notably the team's run in the Europa League where they lifted the trophy. That was why it was Tomek's local team. Even though he'd grown up and lived closer to Roots Hall, home to the Mighty Shrimpers, he still considered Upton Park (and later the London Stadium) to be his second home. It was a generational thing. His father before him and his father before him had all supported the Hammers. Until 1965, the team, and the area as a whole, had been considered a part of Essex, so Tomek had heard stories of his grandfather attending games in the mid-sixties with his parents and friends, watching the inimitable Geoff Hurst and Bobby Moore battle it out on the pitch in the claret and blue jersey. Generations of ardent football fans had flocked to the London Stadium every week just to see their hearts broken. It was a funny old sport.

But there was nothing funny about his hypothesis regarding Dagenham & Redbridge FC.

Tomek had been told to wait in the reception area for what felt like half an hour. In that time he'd been left with a small paper cup and a half-functioning water fountain that looked as though the water had started to develop bacteria and new forms of life. He'd taken one sip, tasted the metallic tang from the fountain's head, and left it. Fortunately, as Tomek had chucked the cup into the bin, Lance Hull, the chairman and owner of the club, had pulled him into his office.

'Sorry about the wait.'

No, you're not.

'That's all right,' Tomek replied. 'I can appreciate you're a busy man.'

'Especially after Boxing Day.'

'How'd you get on?'

'Drew two-two.'

Tomek smiled politely and seated himself opposite the man. Lance Hull was everything he'd come to expect from a football club owner: a well-pressed suit, almost immaculately placed hair, had it not been for the small strand that stood erect on the top of his head, and the well-kept stomach that suggested he liked to eat on the finer side of the table but was reminded of it every waking moment in the gym with his personal trainer. By Tomek's estimation, he was on the wrong side of fifty but was doing everything he could to keep that number as low as possible.

'I don't mean to sound rude,' Lance began, 'but I have another meeting in twenty minutes, so if we could get this done as soon as possible, that would be great.'

It was comments like that that really got Tomek's back up. Now he didn't want to move along so quickly. Instead, he wanted to waste as much of the man's time as possible, make him regret the decision to hurry him.

'After you hear what I have to say,' Tomek replied, 'you might want to cancel your meeting.'

Lance's Adam's apple convulsed up and down as he swallowed deeply. Then he shifted uncomfortably in his seat. Here was a man who wasn't afraid of difficult conversations, they were almost a daily occurrence in football, having to release players, suspend, and withdraw their contracts, but having a police officer sit opposite him and tell him something was wrong was clearly a more difficult conversation than he'd bargained for the day after Boxing Day.

'I'm sure you've heard the news recently about the deaths of the two teenage girls in Hadleigh and Leigh-on-Sea. Well, during our investigations, the names of two of the boys in your academy have come up.'

'Come up how?'

'I can't tell you that.'

'Well you need to. I need to know what my players are being accused of.'

'They're not being accused of anything. Their names have simply come up in conversation. How often do the boys train here?'

'You need to tell me their names first.'

Tomek was reluctant to release that information. As he was only there on a hunch, a *feeling,* he was hesitant to name-drop the two individuals in case nothing came of it and he was responsible for dragging two boys through the dirt. But then he thought of the victims, Lily Monteith and Fern Clements, and how they had been left in the *actual* dirt.

'The first boy's name is Harrison Rossiter and the second boy is called Darren Edgerton, a member of your under seventeen squad. You also have a Billy Turpin who plays for your under fourteens.'

Lance nodded thoughtfully as he made a note of the boys' names. Then he turned his attention to his computer screen and entered their names into his system.

'Yep. Got them. What do you need to know?'

'How frequently do the boys train together?'

'Well, they don't.'

'What do you mean?'

'Harrison Rossiter recently got scouted in the summer by a French Ligue 1 team, Toulouse FC, and is now playing for their academy.'

'In France?'

'That's where they play football, yes. His family moved country to support him. They were all very excited about the opportunity. We even helped him settle in with school, the language, friends, the team. He was probably one of our best players, but the prospect of playing in the French league was better than playing with us. Who were we to say no to him?'

Very noble, Tomek thought.

'What about before he left?' Tomek asked as he tried to keep track of the thoughts rattling around his brain. He hadn't expected this. If Harrison Rossiter was living in France, then interviewing him would prove to be more difficult. But it also begged the question: was there another reason, footballing prospects aside, that he had chosen to move country?

'What about it?' Lance asked.

'Did they train together?'

'It's possible Darren and Harrison would have trained together on the weekends. Same with Billy Turpin. From our under elevens all the way up to the under seventeens. Not in the same field, as there'd be no space for them. But, yes. On the weekends they would have trained together.'

'And what about with the first team?'

Tomek was reminded of Avena's words: This guy was a few years older at least, so I think he must have played a few teams above, or maybe in the first team.

'Not typically. The men's team trains during the week and plays the majority of their games on the weekends.'

'But they would have come into contact with one another?'

'Depending on how sociable they are, yes. They don't all sit there in silence. You've seen a football team before, right?' Tomek nodded. 'So you'll know that they're all pally, that there's a camaraderie between them. It's the same here. We try to create an ethos of inclusion. We don't want anyone to be left behind.' Lance placed his hands in his lap and began threading his thumbs together. His demeanour had changed. Now he'd become stiff, sterner. Less willing to give Tomek the answers he was looking for. 'Are you going to tell me what these boys have got to do with those two girls' deaths?'

'No,' Tomek replied bluntly, then crossed one leg over the other. 'Would it be possible to get a list of the players' names from the first team all the way down to under elevens? I'd also like a name for the managers, the backroom staff and everyone else behind the scenes you've employed in this place in the last two years.'

'I... Some of that information might be hard to come by.'

'Why's that?'

'Because it might be. It's a breach of our data protection.'

'Not when the police are involved, it's not.'

Now Lance was just trying to be purposely difficult. Tomek checked the time and saw that fifteen minutes had somehow passed. Which left five to go.

'I wouldn't want to come back here with a search warrant and shut the place down while we get the information we need. Doesn't look very good from a brand perspective. And that's the last thing you'd need. How much does the club turn over? Not too much, I'm sure. At least, not in comparison to some of the other teams in the leagues above. So I'd hate for the funding to stop, for the fans to stop coming.'

Although, if Tomek's theory was right, then the arrest of two of their players, possibly three, would have a detrimental effect on the club's assets anyway.

Lance Hull thought long and hard about the decision, though his expression gave nothing away. Instead, he just sat there, staring at Tomek, and Tomek stared back.

'I can get you the information you need. When do you want it?'

'Now.' Then he remembered to add, 'Please.'

'Great. I'll pass you on to Alicia in HR. She'll be able to handle all of that for you.'

As Lance lifted himself out of his chair, already buttoning up his blazer to signify the end of the meeting and subtly say, Get the fuck out of my office, a knock came at the door. Standing there, poking his head through the gap was a man with greying hair wearing a tracksuit.

'Detective,' Lance began, 'this is Alexandre Lefebvre, our first team coach.'

Tomek extended his hand. 'Good to meet you.'

'Alex here is going to help us reach League One, aren't you, Alex?'

'*Oui*. Yes, sir. I'll try my best,' Alex replied joyfully, his accent thick. Though from the strained look on his face, he knew it wouldn't be as easy as Lance expected it to be.

Tomek surveyed the Frenchman scrupulously before following Lance through the building to the HR department, which consisted of a team of two individuals. Both women were in their fifties, sitting beside one another in a small portion of the building.

'Alicia,' Lance began. 'I've got a gentleman here who needs some access to our records.'

'Why?'

'He's with the police. So whatever he asks for, make sure he gets it.'

CHAPTER THIRTY-NINE

'Abso-fucking-lutely not,' was the response he'd been expecting from Victoria after he'd finished explaining that he needed to travel to France.

'Why not, ma'am?'

'For obvious reasons,' Victoria replied.

Tomek pursed his lips and shrugged his shoulders. 'You might need to explain those to me.'

'Budget, for starters. With all the DNA evidence we're testing and retesting, and with all the interviews and overtime I've had to approve, there's very little of it left for you to have a holiday in the South of France.'

'Nobody said anything about the South of France, ma'am. I think the actual region is called...' Tomek looked through the notes he'd made in the HR department. 'Toulouse. Shit.'

'See?'

'Well, yes, it *is* in the South of France, but it's not *the* South of France you're thinking of. I'm not planning a weekend stay on the Côte d'Azur.'

'Hmm.' Victoria folded her arms across her chest and eased backwards in her seat.

'You know, you're not much fun now that you're *la jefa*.'

223

'Did you just call me a fucking elephant?'

'No, no, no!' Tomek waved his hands, desperately clawing for a surface to pull himself out of the hole he'd just inadvertently dug for himself. 'It's Spanish! It means "boss" in Spanish.'

'Look at you go, you little linguist.'

'The term's polyglot actually, ma'am. But that's not important right now. What's important is that I speak to Harrison Rossiter and find out his connections to Darren Edgerton and Billy Turpin, and the murders of Mandy Butler, Diana Greenock, Lily Monteith and Fern Clements.'

Victoria scratched the underside of her chin. 'So you're saying that a seventeen-year-old footballer is going around killing young girls?'

'No.'

'Then explain it to me. Tell me *exactly* what you told the team because they all seem to be rallying behind you.' As she said it, her impervious stare narrowed in on him, and he sensed her channelling her inner *jefa*.

Tomek swallowed deeply before responding. He didn't know why, but he suddenly felt pressure to perform. As though he needed to pull out his A-game to convince Victoria of the veracity of his hypothesis, something he'd never felt whenever he'd worked under Nick.

'The way I see it,' Tomek began, already realising he'd started terribly, 'is that these two boys, Darren Edgerton and Harrison Rossiter, have been working together, with the help of Billy Turpin, to plot to kill these girls.'

'Right.'

'It first occurred to me when Kasia was admitted to hospital. Her boyfriend, no, not boyfriend, her boy... *friend,* put her in hospital because of her nut allergy. Afterwards, I checked his social media, you know, as paranoid and protective parents do, and found that he played for Dagenham & Redbridge under fourteens. Later, when I spoke with Avena Kumar, one of the girls who was drugged at the Catfish and the Bottlemen concert in the Cliffs Pavilion, she said that one of the boys she was with knew the guy who sold them the drugs, Harrison Rossiter, the one who's now moved to the South of France. She said that it was an adult who worked at the club, either as a member of the coaching staff, backroom staff or in one of the men's teams. Selling drugs to supplement some of their income. These low-league teams aren't paid the exorbitant amounts that Premiership teams are. Anyway, that was two years ago. And, as luck would have it, Billy Turpin joined the under elevens at the same age. So for the past two years to eighteen months, both boys have got to know one another. In addition, Darren Edgerton, who plays in the under fifteens, is the boyfriend of Fern Clements.'

'But I thought Rachel spoke with him and he had a solid alibi?'

'Yeah, she did. And yeah, he did. But I still think there's something there.'

'That they're a cabal of teenage footballers who are killing young girls via their allergies?'

'Yes. But not them.'

'Not them?'

'The drug dealer that Harrison knew from the concert.'

'And you think this all makes perfect sense?'

'Well, it makes perfect sense to me. And the rest of the team all seem to be behind it as well.'

'So what are the next steps, aside from going to the South of France?'

Tomek removed the printout that had been given to him by Alicia in HR. 'This is a list of everyone who's been employed by Dagenham & Redbridge FC in any capacity in the last two years.' He held it in the air and prodded it sharply with his finger, almost putting a hole in it. 'I believe our killer's name is somewhere in this list.'

'How many names are on there?'

'Over a hundred.'

'Busy afternoon.'

'Or I could cross-reference it with the names in all the other fucking lists we seem to have.'

Victoria shook her head. 'I don't think so. If what you're

suggesting is true, then this only accounts for Mandy Butler's death. What happened to your daughter is irrelevant, forgive me for saying, but I don't see how it bears any similarity. It still doesn't explain what happened to Fern Clements or Lily Monteith.'

Or Diana Greenock, Tomek thought but decided not to open that wound again.

'I'll get Rachel to dig into Darren Edgerton again, but it's still possible they're all working together,' Tomek answered.

'So you're suggesting it *is* a cabal of teenage footballers, with the help of one adult, going around killing these girls?'

As strange as it sounded, and when it was put to him like that it did sound strange, yes, that was exactly what he was thinking. He didn't know why, but he had been unable to shake the idea ever since the seed had first been planted while scrolling through Billy the Cow Fighter's Instagram.

'I think you're barking up the wrong tree, in all honesty, Tomek,' Victoria added.

In all honesty, he thought the same about her. That her misman-agement of this case had led them to the position they were currently in; that they were several weeks into the investigation without any concrete leads, just a few hundred names on a sheet and two more dead bodies.

'Let me speak with Tracy, let me pitch the idea to her and see what she says.' Victoria continued, 'It might not agree with her forensic profile.'

'I'd rather do that myself, ma'am. Considering I was the one who brought the NCA into this in the first place. Plus it is *my* hypothesis, I'll be able to explain it better.'

'That's what I'm worried about. I'm afraid you'll convince her to let us chase our tails and head farther down the rabbit hole.'

Tomek scratched the side of his head. 'Forgive me, ma'am. But you're making it seem like you don't want us to catch this killer – or killers.'

Victoria tutted. 'Of course I fucking do. What a stupid thing to insinuate. But without Nick here to help oversee things, I'm feeling pretty fucking stretched as it is. So I need us to both be aligned on this one. Otherwise, we're not going to get anywhere.'

'And for that to happen you need me to follow *your* hypothesis?'

'Yes. I'm SIO.'

As though that settled the argument. As though that settled all arguments for now and eternity.

'Is that how it worked up in Colchester? Dictate what others should think or do, suppress them if they have any original thoughts of their own?'

In response, Victoria bridled at his tone, then turned her attention to the open folder on her desk. Keeping her head down, ignoring his presence, she said, 'Pleasure talking with you, Tomek. I've arranged for you to attend a press conference in a little over an hour. If you could speak with Anna to prepare what you're going to say, I'd greatly appreciate it. And you can shut the door on your way out.'

CHAPTER FORTY

A light rainfall had started, just light enough for Tomek to use the windscreen wipers on the first setting but not heavy enough for the second. The heating was on inside the car, but it made little difference. In the short time that it had been sitting there, while he'd discussed the case with Victoria and conducted the press conference, the late winter's chill had wrapped its fingers around the vehicle and numbed everything inside. It was so cold that a cloud of vapour appeared in front of his face every time he breathed. Even more so when he exited the car and made his way to Billy the Cow Fighter's front door. It was a little after 4 p.m., and Tomek hoped the boy was home.

He pounded his fist on the door, the sound rolling up and down the street in Chalkwell. The little boy opened it a few seconds later.

'Jesus Christ, mate—' he started, then caught himself as he locked eyes with Tomek.

'Not disturbing you, am I?' Tomek asked.

At once, Billy's face turned red. And not because of the cold that flooded into the house.

'I... What are you...? If this is about the other day, I'm sorry, all right!'

'It's not about that, although I would like to discuss it.'

'You ain't coming in.'

'Why not?'

'Because my mum and dad told me I ain't s'posed to talk to strangers.'

'I'm not a stranger. I'm the police.'

'Yeah. And my dad says you're just as bad as strangers. Sometimes worse.'

Dads. Dads and their fucking opinions. They always had them.

'It's raining,' Tomek said quietly, hoping the gentle plea would work with the young man.

It didn't.

'Ain't my fault you didn't bring a coat.'

Tomek took a moment to survey Billy's outfit. He was dressed in his full Dagenham & Redbridge tracksuit, complete with red and blue trousers and a black raincoat that had the team's crest emblazoned on the breast.

'I like that,' Tomek began, pointing to it. 'Did you get that from the merch stand at the stadium?'

Billy blew air through pursed teeth. 'Did I fuck. I play for them. Under fourteens. Been playing for them for 'bout two years.'

'Wow. Impressive.'

'Yeah.' Billy's face inflated with smugness.

'What position do you play?'

'Striker.'

'So you're fast?'

The smugness continued until his face ballooned.

'One of the fastest.'

'You ever won any trophies?'

'Nah. But we came close once. I've got a runners-up medal on my wall.'

'Can I see it?'

Billy stopped himself for a moment as he considered. And slowly the ego continued to grow to an exorbitant size.

'Don't see why not,' Billy said, completely forgetting who Tomek was and what he was there for.

A few seconds later, Tomek was safely inside the house, with his shoes off, being led through the hallway. As soon as Billy started to climb the stairs, Tomek stopped.

'You gotta go up them to see it,' Billy remarked.

'No, I'm all right thanks. Changed my mind. What I'd *really* like is for us to discuss your relationship with Harrison Rossiter and Darren Edgerton.'

At the mention of the other academy players' names, the ego and smugness that had been shining through every pore in the young man's face drained away in an instant.

'Harrison Rossiter?'

'Yeah.'

'Darren Edgerton?'

'That's what I said. I know you know them, so don't play dumb.'

'What do...?' Billy moved down a step tentatively, eyeing Tomek with every movement. 'What do you wanna know?'

'Why don't we take this into the living room or kitchen?' Tomek responded.

So they did. Into Billy Turpin's kitchen. It was one of the brightest kitchens he'd ever seen. With immaculate marble worktops, white floor tiles, and brilliant silver lights dangling from the ceiling over the central island, bathing the entire room in a different type of money. He could imagine himself and Kasia cooking in there, hosting gatherings or parties, maybe even inviting Louise and Sylvia over for dinner and drinks one night. Shame they would all have to put up with their tiny little affair in the meantime.

'How much contact have you had with either Harrison or Darren?' Tomek asked as he approached a bar stool in the centre of the room.

'Not much.'

'Did you ever talk to them, exchange numbers?'

'Maybe. I got a load of numbers from school so might be difficult to check.'

Of course it would be. The egotistical little prick probably thought he was the most popular bloke in the building.

'You ever discuss a girl called Mandy Butler?'

Billy paused a moment while he ran the name through his head. 'Can't say I ever heard that name before. Don't ring no bells.'

'You sure? Think again.'

Billy thought again. But this time for much shorter, a fraction of a second.

'Nope. Don't remember it. Soz.'

The last word made Tomek cringe. Writing it in a text message or social media post was bad enough, but actually verbalising it, that was criminal.

'What about Fern Clements?'

Billy pursed his lips and shook his head. He stood tall, back straight, as though he was ten years his senior.

'What about drugs?'

But that seemed to bring him back down to size.

'What about them?'

'You ever seen any? Been offered any?'

'Only time I've ever seen drugs was the other day in the hospital with—'

Billy had just inadvertently taken the conversation down an alleyway from which there was no return. And Tomek was pleased to note it hadn't been a part of his own engineering.

'Tell me about what happened,' Tomek said.

'But I thought we were talking about drugs. I want to go back to talking about drugs.'

'Kasia. Tell me about Kasia. Now. What happened?'

And then Billy told him. About how they'd discussed him going over while in the playground on the same day. About how he'd turned up after playing a round of football in the park with his mates in the dark. About how she'd told him to come late because Tomek had been at work and she had a Polish lesson to get out of the way. And then Billy had told him that he'd brought pizza along with him (funded by his pocket money), and as soon as the door had closed and they'd shared a kiss, Kasia had started to have an allergic reaction to the packet of M&M peanuts he'd eaten with his mates in the park.

In the end, Billy's story matched that of his daughter's and Phillip Balham's version of events.

It had all been one terrible and almost tragic accident. And by the end of it, Tomek started to wonder whether he'd got it all wrong. That his desire for retribution and retaliation on a thirteen-year-old boy was over the top, uncontested and wrong. That he'd fabricated a witch hunt on a group of teenagers who'd had nothing to do with any of the girls' deaths and that their connection to the girls, Harrison Rossiter's in particular, was nothing more than a coincidence.

But then again, he'd been in the job long enough to know that coincidences didn't exist. That things happened for a reason. Always a reason. Christ, if he hadn't put the connection together between Mandy Butler's and Lily Monteith's deaths, if they'd been put down as "coincidences", then he wouldn't be here right now, he wouldn't currently be hunting down another serial killer.

'What do you know about the staff at Dagenham?' Tomek asked, deciding it was worth continuing with the reason for his visit. Billy wasn't getting away with anything that easily.

'I only really speak to my coach and the other members of the coaching staff. Don't see much of anyone else. They always ask how I'm doing, but I don't stand around and chat.'

Of course he didn't. The egotistical little twat probably thought he was bigger than all of them when the reality was the opposite, he was small and skinny, more Wayne Rooney than Peter Crouch.

'And no one's ever tried to offer you drugs, or you've never seen them being exchanged around the grounds at all?'

'What? Mate, I don't even know what drugs look like. I don't even know which ones there are.'

Tomek wasn't so sure that was true. He was fairly confident that, by the age of thirteen, he knew all about the different classes and what they looked like. Especially weed. Kids were smoking it and selling it in his classes by that age. Perhaps it had been a different time then, when the rules were a lot more relaxed, or the kids were just smarter about it.

'Let me ask you again,' he said, speaking slowly, enunciating every word. 'Have you ever seen drugs exchanged on the football pitch or in the locker rooms amongst any of the adults, whether in the first team or backroom staff, since you've been a member of the academy?'

Billy sensed the severity in Tomek's voice and this time thought harder about the question. But before he was able to answer, the front door opened.

The woman who entered was, Tomek presumed, Billy's mother. A woman dressed in a Prada coat with a Prada handbag hanging off her arm, and dozens of bracelets dangling off her wrist. She screamed wealth and money, but as was all too often the case, it didn't mean that she necessarily had either. That it was all for show.

'Who're you?' she asked, her Essex twang thick.

'Detective Sergeant Tomek Bowen.' He flashed his warrant card in front of her. 'You must be Billy's mother.'

'Yeah, I am. What's he done? This about that incident with the girl the other day? What's her name?'

She looked to Billy for the answer but Tomek beat her to it.

'Kasia... My daughter...'

'Oh. So it *is* about that then. Are you even allowed to be here on personal matters?'

'I never said I—'

'He's not harassing you, is he?' she interrupted.

For a moment Tomek thought the question was aimed at him. Then he realised the woman had been addressing her son.

'You do know that was an accident, right?' she continued, now focusing her attention on him. 'He hasn't done nothing wrong about that. I'm glad your daughter's okay and everything, but there ain't much else he needs to do. He's already apologised, so I thought it was all done with. I thought we was moving on.'

Had little Billy the Cow Fighter apologised? It was the first he'd heard of it. Unless he'd done it to Kasia via text message or Snapchat or some other platform they typically communicated on.

'Like I said, Mrs Turpin. This isn't about my daughter's hospitalisation as a result of your son's ineptitude. It's about—'

'What did you call him?'

Tomek sighed. This was going about as well as a mountain climber ascending a mountain wearing flip-flops.

'My son isn't inept.'

'No.'

'Then why did you say it?'

'I—'

'Apologise to him. Apologise to him like he apologised to your daughter.'

'I'm not so sure I received the apology myself, Mrs Turpin.'

They were at an impasse, neither willing to stand down.

In the end, Billy's mum ran out of patience and moved the conversation along.

'Why are you even here again?'

'He's asking me about drugs at football,' Billy the sanctimonious little bastard said.

'That's not strictly—'

'Drugs?' she hissed, then hurried over to Billy and placed an arm around her son's shoulders. 'Drugs? He's thirteen! What does he know about drugs?'

Tomek was quickly losing his grip on the conversation (if he hadn't already lost it) and was also losing his grip on his sanity. If he stayed there much longer he might start thinking he could fight a cow.

'Listen,' he said, raising his hands in a futile attempt to salvage the discussion. 'Your son, and two other members of his football team, have come up in our investigations into a handful of murders recently. It's our belief that someone within the club, at what level we don't know yet, has been selling drugs outside the club. We want to speak with this individual in connection with the investigation.'

Tomek had quickly realised that the only way to shut her up and make her understand was to tell her more than he probably should have.

It seemed to work, as she turned to her son. 'Is it Mitchell?'

'What?'

'I always thought there was something wrong with him. Was it Mitchell? Do I need to speak with his parents? Or was it Lawrence?'

'Mum, what're you talking about it? It wasn't no one.'

'I knew it. I knew we shouldn't have rejected Ipswich Town. I knew it.'

'Mum, you dunno what you're talking about. It's got nothing to do with anyone in my team. Has it?' he asked Tomek.

Tomek shook his head, grateful he didn't have to say anything. And as he stood there, watching the incipient domestic ensue, Tomek wondered whether Billy's original question about fighting cows was, in fact, a euphemism for punching his mum.

He guessed the operative word "cow" made sense.

'Is that your final answer?' Tomek asked, preparing to leave. 'You don't know anything about who might be selling drugs or who might have sold some at a concert?'

'No. Sorry,' Billy said with a hint of desperation in his voice. Desperation at wanting to be saved from his mum. Funny, in the space of a few minutes, Billy had gone from a smug, belligerent, laughing arsehole to a small, desperate little boy.

Funny how things quickly changed when you were that age.

One minute you're cock of the walk, next you're flat on the concrete. Besides, if Tomek was wrong about the cabal of footballing teenagers, and his investigations didn't jeopardise Billy's playing career, then it looked like this discussion would.

And his mum was going to do it for him.

Either way, Tomek would have the last laugh.

Justice for putting his daughter in hospital would be served.

CHAPTER FORTY-ONE

The information coming into the investigation room had stagnated while the team were out of the office continuing their inquests. Oscar, with the help of Martin and Chey, was interviewing the individuals behind the ticket reselling. Meanwhile, Rachel, Anna and Sean were the brave souls making their way through the list of the remaining hundred and twenty beekeepers in the Southend area.

So while the team were out doing all the hard work, Tomek got a taste of the inspector lifestyle. And it consisted of one thing and one thing only: paperwork, paperwork and paperwork. With a little more paperwork thrown in.

Reviewing the reports the team sent to him. Approving their overtime. Estimating budgets. Processing all the information for the many cases that they were simultaneously working on. While some required more of their time than others, the team's focus was unfortunately split. It was at times like this, when they were understaffed and missing their lead figurehead in Nick, that he was grateful for the support of the police constables and other uniformed officers as well as the civilian support staff who helped the ship stay afloat. Without them, and without everyone else involved in making sure Tomek and the team were able to do their job properly, he wasn't so sure he'd remember to breathe in.

Or breathe out.

He also wasn't so sure that the life of an inspector was what he wanted. Not if the past few days had been anything to go by. A baptism of fire, of sorts, with little hand-holding or direction from Victoria, who was getting her own baptism of fire as stand-in for Nick. Perhaps it was the bureaucracy he didn't like, or the mundanity of having to sit in the station while the rest of the team did the legwork. Because it was the legwork that he liked, and a lot of his colleagues liked it as well. Looking into the eyes of a murderer, sizing them up. It was what he had lived and breathed for the past ten years as a sergeant. All he'd known.

But, on the other hand, there was now the added consideration of Kasia to think about. A more sedentary life behind a desk might be the best thing. If anything happened to him while out in the field, she would have no one other than her grandparents. And nobody deserved that.

Perhaps that was the main driver for his desire to become an inspector: so that, if anything happened to him – if he died, became a vegetable, or even lost the use of one of his legs – he couldn't bear putting Kasia through five years of living with his parents, counting down the days until she turned eighteen and could legally do what she wanted. (Though, with his recent flat purchase, unless Tomek had a cool hundred thousand pounds he didn't know about to give her, she would be living at home for a long time.)

After lunch, a BLT from Subway, a nice little treat, Tomek called an impromptu meeting with Anna and Rachel while Sean was still out in the field, speaking with another bee enthusiast. Informal, just the three of them. Relaxed. His way. Something which he hoped was translating across to the rest of the team. He didn't like to lead with an iron fist like some of the other people he'd worked with. He also didn't want to be too relaxed. Instead, he wanted to find a happy medium.

He wanted to be the Goldilocks of management. Just right. Without the flagrant breaking and entering, theft and other criminal activity.

'Fancy seeing you two here,' Tomek said as he pulled a chair out from Chey's desk and slid it over to the space between the two women.

'We've been here all day. Where have *you* been?' Rachel asked.

'Hiding in my office. You won't catch me with your kind anymore.'

'Women, you mean?' Rachel responded. 'You're probably doing us all a favour.'

Tomek noted the hint of flirtation but chose not to act. Not with Anna watching him scornfully. As the team's media and family liaison officer, and the only other Polish person in the team, she was also the sternest, the most uptight, and didn't like conversation straying too far away from its original topic. Rachel, on the other hand, was the opposite. Transferred in from the Met, she was used to the banter in the office (though it had taken a while), and she was also good at her job, incredibly so. So much so that, if the position ever became available, Tomek would put her forward for promotion to sergeant. But that was a conversation for another time. Right now, they needed to focus on finding a serial killer.

'What have you got for me?' Tomek asked after a moment's silence.

'Not a lot,' Anna replied bluntly. 'Since yesterday, we've spoken with another thirty members of the Beekeepers Association. None of them recognised the Africanised Honey Bee, nor do they seem to have any. One of the people I spoke to is even doing it in a flat, which is the most stupid thing I've ever heard, but each to their own—'

'To each their own,' Rachel corrected.

'Right. Sorry. *To each their own,*' she said, with a slight hint of distaste in her voice. 'I think we need to keep in mind that we're no experts. These people are showing us their bees, and we have no idea what we're looking for. Yes, I've got the images from Google, but they can only go so far. The amount of times I've been stung these past few days.'

Just be grateful you're not allergic to them.

'What are you suggesting?'

'That we start to bring Timothy Warren along with us. Or someone from the Bee Farmers Association, or even the Beekeepers Association head office. An expert who's going to know what we're looking for.'

Tomek liked the idea of that. He liked the idea of that a lot. The only problem was it would be more time-consuming, and an extra week for them to revisit the hobbyists they'd already spoken to. But it was a necessary part of the investigation.

'Fine. Do it. Reach out to Timothy Warren and the heads of those organisations. One of them can fill in for the other if they can't make it. That should help expedite the process.'

'Of course, sarge. Thank you.'

The smile on Anna's face warmed him. That she was pleased and excited to be heard, to be listened to.

Leading the team the right way.

'Have any of the people you've already spoken with got any links to South America or Brazil?' he asked.

Both women looked at each other, as though silently determining who should be the one to answer. In the end, it was Rachel who took the reins.

'Nothing. They all want to go to Brazil on their holidays, and a couple of them have been, but *years* ago, but other than that, nothing that jumps out as suspicious.'

So that was proving to be a dead end.

In truth, he hadn't expected too much to come out of it; owning an Africanised Honey Bee was pretty unique, and not something a hobbyist or bee enthusiast would have typically taken up lightly, so it was a long shot. But even so, that didn't make it any less demoralising.

Setback after setback after setback.

And Tomek expected more of the same for the next part of his morning: speaking with Martin and Oscar about the Cliffs Pavilion ticket resellers.

'Let me guess,' Tomek said before either man had a chance to respond. 'Another dead end?'

'Actually, Tomek, I might have a surprise for you,' Oscar said, excitement lifting the sides of his face.

'A name?'

'I said a surprise, not a present.'

'Aren't they the same thing?' Tomek began, but then shut that avenue of conversation off straight away. Semantics weren't important right now; what was important were the words about to come out of Oscar's mouth.

'Now, there were four of these guys in total, right?' Oscar spoke slowly, as though Tomek was stupid. He should have been annoyed, but that was part of the captain's personality, the misguided belief that he was smarter than everyone else and knew it, that Tomek had slowly and painfully learnt to accept.

'You should've seen their faces as soon as we told them what we were there for. I think they all thought they were about to be arrested. Shame we couldn't, otherwise that would have been quite an enjoyable experience I reckon. Most of them were in their late fifties, early sixties. You could see that they were preying on the desperate. Apparently, they always sold out their tickets on big nights. Not every night was as successful, but when the big-name artists were in town, that's when they sold all of the tickets they'd bought under their own names.'

'And what about our killer?'

'One of them, Randy McGinn, had bought tickets to every single concert and performance that those five girls attended. And he sold a ticket to the same man on every one of those nights.'

'You mean this bloke sold five tickets to the same man?'

'Yes.'

'And he didn't think that was weird?'

'Yeah. Of course he did. But he wasn't going to question it. The killer was paying almost double the retail price of the tickets just to get in on the night. He's not gonna turn down a profit.'

Tomek felt excitement bubbling in his feet. Within a few minutes, he hoped it would be up to his stomach.

'Does he remember what the man looked like?' Tomek asked optimistically.

And then it fizzled out with a shake of the head.

'He can't remember the man "for toffee", unfortunately,' Oscar replied. 'It was so long ago and he's seen thousands of people since then. He'd love to help us out.'

'I want to bring him in to see our artist regardless. Something might jog his memory.'

Over the Christmas break, the two girls who had seen the killer had been brought in to speak with the artists, and together they had come up with the e-fits of their killer. Both were wildly different depictions of the same man, and neither held any further purpose.

'I'll speak with him,' Martin said, grateful to get a word in beside Oscar. 'I will try to convince him to stop in.'

'Excellent. Anything else you need to tell me?'

Oscar shook his head. And before Martin was able to do the same, the door to the incident room burst open.

Standing in the entrance, grinning like a Cheshire Cat, was Chey.

'We're gonna be best friends after this,' he told Tomek as he came in, brandishing a piece of paper.

'I've already filled up my available spots I'm afraid, mate.'

'Then you're going to need to open up a new one. Or knock someone off. Anna, get rid of her. Never liked her anyway.'

'I heard that!' Anna called from the other side of the office.

But Tomek was unable to focus on the banter. Instead, he was preoccupied with the bead of sweat forming on Chey's chin. The bead of sweat that looked as out of place as an oil tanker at a Green Peace convention.

'Have you just run here from your home?'

'No. Better. The storage room downstairs.'

'Right.'

'And I printed out this.'

Chey thrust the document in front of Tomek's face.

It took a while for him to register what he was looking at, but when it finally clicked, he stared blankly at the young constable. Perhaps this wasn't going to be a bad day after all.

'Is this what I think it is?' he asked.

'Yep.' The sides of Chey's mouth rose. 'Does that mean a spot's opened up?'

'No. You'll remain my colleague and friend. But not best friend. For now, though, I could fucking kiss you!'

CHAPTER FORTY-TWO

The tiny little dot on the piece of paper that Chey had given him denoted a small building in the east of Southend. The dot, near Great Wakering, was situated on the doorstep of MOD Shoeburyness, the estate which had been used for the past hundred and seventy years to test, maintain and evaluate military weapons used in the Armed Forces. It occupied a space of over nine thousand acres, a number that stretched to over forty thousand when the tide went out, and was home to over two hundred private residences, seven working farms, and a little over seven thousand acres. Access to it was strictly prohibited and controlled, with a number of the surrounding beaches cut off from civilian access. And if the thought of being arrested and prosecuted wasn't enough of a deterrent, then the narrow, winding roads to get to it certainly would be.

By the time Chey slammed on his brakes and pulled the car up to a stop outside the small building, Tomek felt sick. Like the contents of his breakfast and lunch might come up to greet him. On the drive down, the young constable had thrown the car left and right through the sharp bends and narrow turns, as though he'd stolen the bastard thing.

'This place is deserted,' he'd informed Tomek, as though the comment was supposed to put him at ease and make him withdraw his hands from the safety of his seat belt. 'Nobody's driving around here. Not unless the military are about. Don't worry. We won't crash.'

They hadn't. But that didn't mean Chey hadn't tried; there had been one corner, just as they'd left the bustle of Shoeburyness and headed into the flatlands of Great Wakering, where Chey had come face to face with a small duck and her family of ducklings. Upon seeing the four-tonne vehicle hurtling towards them, the mother duck stopped on the verge and retreated to a safer distance. Unfortunately, Chey had done the same on the opposite verge, and almost spun the car in the process, losing a game of chicken to a family of ducks.

As Tomek stepped out of the car, he placed a hand on his chest and felt his heart pounding beneath his ribcage, the adrenaline of the drive that had nearly killed him still coursing through his veins.

'You remember that spot on my friends list you were after?'

'Yeah.'

'Well, you can fucking forget it now. Friends don't try to kill their other friends while driving. Especially not best friends.'

Chey's beaming smile dropped, but Tomek paid him little heed as he waited for the rest of the entourage to arrive: Rachel, Sean, Anna and Martin were arriving in two separate cars, along with an ambulance, a liveried police vehicle, and a forensics van. All five remaining vehicles arrived at various points one after another as they too had struggled to traverse the narrow roads, in particular, the ambulance.

Once they were all there, and kitted in their white forensic suits, they turned their attention to the dot on the map.

The dot was nothing more than a small brick building that looked as though it hadn't been inhabited in fifty years. Moss, lichen and ivy had claimed the walls for their own, while weeds and overgrown grasses had taken control of the small unmade path that led to it.

Except for two tread marks.

Tomek estimated the small building, perched on the side of the road and with farmland behind it, would have been used in the war at some point. Probably some sort of watchtower, a lookout for advanced warnings of air raids and intrusion perhaps. It was not, however, the place to torture and murder teenage girls.

As he stood at the mouth of the path that led to the building, Tomek sensed an aura. Of evil, of malevolence, of sin. As they approached, the air temperature seemed to drop a few degrees, and the breath that escaped his face mask misted in front of his face. With each tentative step, Tomek tensed his body tighter and tighter. There was no knowing what was on the other side of that door.

The killer.

His latest victim.

Both...

Though he prepared himself for seeing *something*.

Gradually, they reduced the distance to the building.

Ten metres.

Five.

And then it came into view.

The reason for the black dot in the first place.

The Volvo X70 that had been used to abduct and kill Fern Clements and Lily Monteith. As part of their initial investigations into the girls' murders, Chey and the team had reviewed numerous amounts of home surveillance and security camera footage around John Burrows and Belfairs parks. The quality of the footage had been poor, so the make and model of the car was difficult to discern. But after reviewing footage of a potential route that the driver might have taken on the night of Fern Clements' death, Chey had discovered what they suspected was the killer's vehicle.

Its exact location had been discovered by the telemetry data in Fern Clements' phone. Chey had misread the original pieces of data and missed a small window where Fern's phone had been switched back on, shortly after she'd been kidnapped. It had only lasted for a few moments before being switched back off again, but it had been enough.

Tomek was first to the building's door. He placed a firm hand around the handle and, giving one last look to the team before he did it, opened the door.

The gust of wind that blew into the building disturbed and unsettled the dust by his feet. He let go and the door opened quickly to reveal a small space of nothing. Emptiness. There was nothing in there, and nobody in there either. With no risk of someone jumping out at them, Tomek stepped into the building. The walls had been constructed of brick, and the floor made out of concrete. The temperature inside was much cooler than outside, almost zero.

In the corner of the room, to Tomek's immediate left, was a small patch of disturbed earth and dust. *The place where Fern Clements had been abducted and imprisoned*. However, there were no signs of a struggle, no signs of blood on the floor. And nothing to suggest that she'd been tied up at all.

Tomek tried to imagine what it had been like for her.

Getting into the car, whether conscious or unconscious, knowingly or unknowingly, being transported to the arse end of nowhere in a place that nobody would think to look, then waking up in the middle of a dark and freezing box. Maybe not even waking up at all. But if she had, what would she have seen? What would she have felt? When would the bees have been brought out to kill her? How long would she have suffered for, crawling into a ball on the solid concrete floor in a futile attempt to protect herself, screaming, begging for help, while her words and effort fell on deaf ears? Until eventually the poison from the stings had had its desired effect and she'd lost all consciousness, left to the mercy of the bees.

And then what had happened?

Had the killer stood over her, watching, waiting? Or had he watched from afar? Or, more sordidly, had he waited outside, listening to the sounds of Fern Clements' screams with glee, counting down the seconds until they stopped and he was safe to return?

The thought gave Tomek the chills, as his mind wandered off and replaced the images of Fern Clements with Kasia.

'Is that what I think it is?' a voice asked.

Tomek hadn't realised; he'd been standing in the middle of the room, silent, for the past few moments, but by now the rest of the team, including the scenes of crime officers, had joined him, and were currently surveying the area.

The question had come from Chey, who was crouching in the

corner where Fern Clements had been kept. He waved a hand in the air and requested one of the SOCOs hurry over with a torch.

The small area of concrete was quickly illuminated, almost blinding them all.

There, pressed against a wedge in the brick wall, was a small yellow and black object.

'Unless it's a dirty sherbet lemon,' Tomek said, 'I think that's *exactly* what you think it is. And I think it's *exactly* what it looks like.'

'A dirty sherbet lemon?' Rachel asked playfully.

'I wouldn't recommend biting into either. Can we get that bagged and sealed up as evidence?' Tomek asked, and the SOCO nearest rushed over and picked the fuzzy little insect up with tweezers before putting it into an evidence bag.

'With any luck, this'll be the same as the one found in Fern Clements' leg,' Rachel said.

'Yeah, but where are the rest of them?' he whispered to himself.

Tomek looked about the room as though a hundred bees would magically manifest. When they didn't, he turned to the space in the corner of the room. Images of Fern Clements, cowered into a ball, knees tucked up to her chest, appeared, eyes wide open as her brain registered the sight and sound of the bees being set loose upon her. Knowing what was about to come.

'He's cleared this area and removed all the bees from the floor,' he started, continuing his monologue. Then he swivelled on the balls of his feet and looked at a mark in the dust. It was a long, thick line, which turned left at a right angle. Tomek followed the line with his finger until the bigger picture came into view. It was the outline of a bee box, similar to the ones that he had seen at Timothy Warren's bee farm.

Tomek took a moment to consider what this meant for the wider investigation. If the killer possessed an entire colony of Africanised Honey Bees, he must have got them from somewhere. Online, perhaps. The Dark Web. The black market of bee selling. Or if he hadn't bought them online, then he must have found another method of acquiring them, of importing them into the country.

He breathed a long, deep sigh as he looked out at the room around them.

His theory that a cabal of teenage footballers had anything to do with the girls' murders was rapidly crumbling in front of his eyes, dripping away like a honeycomb. It was almost impossible for Billy the Cow Fighter to know about this place, even less likely that he would have found it on his own. The same applied to Harrison Rossiter in France. But that didn't exonerate the man at the club who had sold the spiked drugs to Mandy Butler and all the other victims; he was still at the forefront of their investigations. The only other option was Darren Edgerton, Fern's boyfriend. Seventeen and old enough to drive. But could he have sourced the killer bees? Would he have known how to?

'The car,' Tomek said as the thought suddenly occurred to him. 'I want it swabbed and a deep forensics sweep undertaken. Our killer's DNA is going to be all over it. We might not find it in here, especially if he was wearing a bee suit to protect himself from the bees but the car is key. The car is the answer to all this. Good work, Chey.'

From behind the young man's face mask, Tomek recognised the lift of a smile.

'Now we just need to find out who owns it,' Rachel said.

'And find out why it's been left here.'

That point gave everyone reason to pause.

Whether the car had been left there because the killer was finished with his killings.

Or whether he was storing it for later, only to return for his next kill.

But before anyone could answer, a cry came from outside the building. Tomek and the team raced outside to find a SOCO holding onto the boot of the Volvo.

'It's unlocked, Sarge.'

'Have you opened it yet?' Tomek asked, moving closer to the man with his arms raised, feeling like he was in a war-torn country trying to defuse a bomb.

'Not yet,' the SOCO replied.

'Then I suggest you do so carefully, and, everyone, step back.'

The sound of feet shuffling across the earth echoed above the wind.

And above the sound coming from inside the car.

As soon as he heard it Tomek, knew exactly what it was. But it was too late. Before he could say anything, the SOCO lifted the boot, and immediately a dozen or so Africanised Honey Bees leapt out of the boot and started swarming around the SOCO, buzzing vehemently.

At the sight of them, everyone screamed, including Tomek, and they all raced back to their respective vehicles, seeking shelter in the confines of their cars.

But it was a futile endeavour. By the time Tomek had leapt into the car that he and Chey had driven in, one of the bastards had followed him into the vehicle and was aggressively buzzing in front of his face, a tiny black and yellow-striped insect intent on seeking vengeance.

Tomek screamed in the driver's seat, as he thrashed his arms wildly, his knuckles punching the window and steering column by accident. He was grateful that he was alone so that his colleagues couldn't hear his whimpering and screaming. But when he opened the car door to escape, he noticed the rest of the team had been caught by surprise as much as him: several bodies dressed in white forensics suits were running across the field, being chased by the crazed insects while Chey, who in his assault of the tiny insect had displaced his hood and face mask, was flailing his arms about, looking like a boxer trying to fight the air with his eyes closed.

The sight brought a thin smirk to Tomek's face, but it was gone as soon as the bee that had selected him as its victim returned and landed on his forehead.

Before he could even react, and before the scream was able to leave his lips for the fourth time, he felt a massive slap on the forehead. So hard that it knocked him off balance and tumbled him into the car.

'Gotcha, you little bastard!' yelled Sean, standing there with his arms flexed, grinning viciously like a rabid animal.

Tomek didn't care about the growing pain in his head, so long as the little *gówniaki* was dead.

'You got it?'

'Fucking bet I did! I got the reflexes of a cat,' yelled Sean triumphantly.

So much so that he single-handedly killed the remaining bees (the ones that hadn't already died by stinging his colleagues) with his fists and his heavy, size-fourteen feet. Once the area had been deemed a bee-free zone, Tomek tentatively made his way to the Volvo.

As far as he could tell, everyone was okay. Except for one of the SOCOs and paramedics who had been stung. But fortunately, nobody was allergic. So at least everyone would live.

As the injured men were taken to the paramedic where they received first aid, Tomek moved closer to the Volvo. Sitting there in the boot of the vehicle was the box that had been placed inside the building, and lying beside it was a pile of dead bees, the ones that had been let loose on Fern Clements.

'Vicious little bastards, aren't they?' Chey asked.

'Yeah,' Tomek remarked, staring at the graveyard of bees. 'And now I know that, if it ever came to it, I would much rather one hundred per cent prefer to fight a cow than one of them again.'

CHAPTER FORTY-THREE

That evening, when Tomek came home, his neighbour scared the living shit out of him and he almost tripped over.

As he'd locked the car and hurried to the door that led up to their first-floor flat, he saw her pale face pressed against the window, staring back at him like she was some sort of insidious spirit from a horror movie.

'*Kurwa mać!*' Tomek hissed beneath his breath as he almost had a heart attack.

In the short time that Tomek and Kasia had been living in their new place, Tomek had only seen his ground-floor neighbour a handful of times. In fact, less than that. Once or twice, perhaps. And if this was the way she wanted to greet him going forward, he would try to keep that number as low as possible.

By the time he made it into the stairwell that separated their flats, she was standing outside her own, waiting for him.

During their first interaction, Edith had told him that she was retired, had been a senior midwife at Southend Hospital all her life, and was now living on a pension that just about saw her get by. As soon as Tomek had explained his role in the police, she had felt a kinship for him, some sort of affinity. An unspoken and invisible bond between them. Both had seen some stuff in their time, and it was only something people like them were able to relate to.

'Evening, Edith,' Tomek said, trying to hide the fear and alarm in his voice. 'Is everything all right?'

'Sorry to startle you, Tomek,' she said as she took a step closer. 'I was watching outside.'

'Everything all right?'

Tomek made a half-turn.

'I think so. But I heard some noises.'

'What kind of noises?'

'Banging.'

'Close, as in right outside the building? Or outside, as in on the street?'

'Both.'

'Okay.' Tomek swallowed and inhaled deeply. 'Want me to check the area?'

She placed a delicate hand on his forearm. 'Oh, no, it's all right, dear. Probably nothing. Probably silly old me getting paranoid about things.'

Again. It wasn't the first time she'd come to him about noises and disturbances. Second time in as many weeks. Noises outside the house, followed by the sense of someone standing outside or going into their garden. Tomek couldn't blame her for not wanting to leave the house to find out what it was. And, as she was on the ground floor, she was more susceptible to theft, especially if the criminals knew she was older and less likely to defend herself the same as Tomek might.

The problem was it was hard for him to do anything about it. He didn't have the time to sit and stand guard outside the building or check the windows twenty-four seven. But he did have the funds to set up a communal front doorbell camera. That might help deter any unwanted intruders or visitors. Though he might have to turn off the notification sounds; there was nothing worse than sitting in the office or wandering around the high street hearing the same infuriating tune alerting the owner that someone was at their front door.

In the office, Nadia was the worst for it. Online shopping arrived at all times of the day from various companies, almost every day of the week. Purchasing bits for the baby, she said, because neither she nor her husband had the time to go out and do the shopping like normal people. But Tomek still held the suspicion she might have had a shopping addiction.

'I'll get some cameras put in for us,' Tomek explained.

'Are you sure?'

'Absolutely. It's not a problem. I'll order it online and set it up when I get a chance.'

By channelling his inner Nadia.

Tomek wished her a good evening then headed up the stairs to his flat. As he did so, he cast his mind back to a few moments ago. Whether he'd spotted anyone or anything out of the ordinary. Whether he'd seen someone loitering around the building recently.

Before they had moved into their new flat, there had been an incident with an individual who had been sent by a contact in prison. The contact, Charlotte Hanton, a former lover of Tomek's turned serial killer, had sent the individual to intimidate him. And he had moved flat as a result. He hadn't seen the man in a while, but that didn't mean to say he wasn't there tonight or hadn't been in the past few weeks.

Though how he'd found out their new address, if it was him, raised some obvious concerns. If they were being watched by Charlotte in her bid to monitor and keep tabs on Tomek out of some confused and warped definition of love, then he would have to do something about it.

'You're home,' a soft voice said as he stepped through to the living room. 'Are you all right?'

'Yeah.'

'Sure? Look like you've seen a ghost.'

Tomek thought of Edith's expression, and how the comparison would be slightly harsh though not entirely inaccurate.

'Not quite,' he replied. 'Just a lot going on up in the old computer system.'

Tomek tapped the side of his head.

'What are you talking about?'

'My brain. My computer.'

'Right.'

'Speaking of which, can you order a home security camera system for us, please? And get it delivered to downstairs.'

'Why?'

'Because I've asked you to and it's my job to ask the questions, not yours.'

CHAPTER FORTY-FOUR

The Volvo X70 found at the crime scene of Fern Clements' murder was registered to Ray Elliott, an eighty-three-year-old man who was currently residing in a care home in Grays, Greater London.

'I'd say he's more... *existing*, at this point. Breathing, that's about the bare minimum we're getting out of him. The Alzheimer's is pretty far advanced. Doctors don't reckon there's much more left in his tanks.'

Ray's only living relative was his grandson, James, the man currently sitting opposite Tomek and Sean. Before leaving the office to speak with him, Chey had run the thirty-eight-year-old's name through the PNC, but nothing had come up. No prior arrests or convictions.

As far as Tomek and the police were aware, James was a good egg.

'I'm sorry to hear about your grandfather,' Sean said gently.

'Thank you,' James replied. 'I appreciate it.'

The three of them were inside James's two-bedroom home. The house was modern, with panelling on the outside and a sleek white finish. The inside was extravagant and opulent. Ornate furniture, marble surfaces, large mirrors hanging from the walls, flashy decorations that wouldn't look out of place in a footballer's home. In fact, as

Tomek had surveyed the fixtures and furnishings, he was reminded of Billy the Cow Fighter's house, as it looked as though they'd had the same interior decorator. But inside James's living room was the centrepiece, the focal point of the entire room: a sixty-inch flat-screen television mounted onto the wall, sitting above an electric fireplace.

'Bet the game looks good on there,' Tomek remarked.

'Like you wouldn't believe. Especially the Championship and Prem, in all that masterful high-definition. But nothing beats the real thing, being pitch-side and getting to experience the atmosphere first-hand.'

Tomek and Sean lost James to a moment of reflection.

'Pitch-side?' Tomek repeated, for clarification.

James nodded. 'I work for Dagenham & Redbridge FC,' he said. 'So we get front-row seats to the best team in the county. It's not the same as going to the Emirates or the Etihad, mind, and we've got about a sixth of the capacity, but it's still a good atmosphere, and still better than watching it on a thirty-inch TV screen.'

'Or on a sixty-inch one, as the case may be for some,' Sean noted, on the half-turn towards the giant black mirror hanging from James's wall.

'Exactly. Yeah.'

But Tomek wasn't listening. Instead, he was replaying the few words that had sent the alarm bells ringing inside his head.

I work for Dagenham and Redbridge FC.

They grew louder and louder with every repetition like they were stuck inside a plastic cup.

'You work at Dagenham and Redbridge?' Tomek asked slowly.

'I'm the kit manager.'

'For the first team?'

'Yeah.'

'And that pays for this house?'

'Well.' James shifted uncomfortably in his seat. 'I have a loving wife who works all hours of the day and then comes home to look after our two kids. All while I'm out watching football. She's the real hero.'

Tomek grinned facetiously. 'Has anyone used that word to describe you then?'

James's back stiffened and he tilted his head to the side, the spidey senses coming out. He took a moment to respond.

'I'm sorry, gentlemen,' he said eventually. 'I don't believe you've told me the purpose of your visit.'

'That's because we haven't,' Tomek replied, then turned to Sean. He gave his colleague a nod, and then the sergeant explained.

As he waited, Tomek observed the man's reaction, searching for a hint of recognition or shock or, more worryingly, fear. There was none.

'Why's my grandad's car been found all the way over there?' James asked.

'We were wondering if you could tell us,' Sean said. 'We've checked DVLA and all the other relevant records, and they all say that the car is registered in his name. But if he can only, like you say, *exist* at the moment, then we want to know who has it and why the ownership hasn't been changed.'

More uncomfortable shifting. Then James looked to the carpet and reached down at his feet to scratch an itch.

'Can I get either of you two a drink?' he asked.

'Are we going to need it? Do you propose we'll be here a while?' Tomek asked.

James didn't answer the question. Instead, he left the room and headed to the kitchen. As they watched him go, Tomek and Sean looked at one another, and immediately Sean was on his feet, following the man out of the room. In the time that they were in the kitchen, Tomek took the opportunity to look around the living room. What for, he didn't know. But a sign, a clue. Anything that might indicate he had something to do with the murders.

A glove. A condom. A small jar of honey lying around the place.

But he found nothing. And by the time the two men returned, he was back in his original position, as though he hadn't moved at all.

'Gotta say,' James said as he handed the drink to Tomek. 'All this is quite disconcerting. I can promise you my grandad hasn't done anything wrong here.'

'That doesn't mean to say you haven't,' Tomek noted.

Once Sean returned to his seat, Tomek pulled out his screwdriver and began turning the screw. And with the way he was feeling, he felt like screwing it in so tightly that he splintered the wood around it.

'Who has control over your grandad's estate?' Tomek asked.

'Me.'

'So you would have had control over what happened with his car?'

'I... I guess.'

'The answer's yes, James. You *would* have had complete control over it, and you know it. And now we know it too. So you know exactly what happened to that car and why it might be there.'

'No, I don't. I don't know what's going on with it! I haven't got a clue. Honest.'

Tomek smirked. 'When people say "honest" after they've just made a statement of truth, we've typically found them to turn out rather dishonest. Wouldn't you say, Sean?'

'Absolutely, Tom.'

'So perhaps you should start by being honest with us. It'll go a long way.'

'How?'

Tomek hesitated. Nobody had ever come back with a response to that. He'd always found that the meaning was obvious and implied. Either James was incredibly thick, or he was stalling for time so he could come up with an alibi.

Tomek suspected the latter. So chose not to answer, and moved on.

'What did you do with your grandfather's car once you'd put him in the home?'

'I... I... I sold it to a mate.'

'Who?'

'I can't remember.'

'Bullshit,' Tomek said.

'Can't have been a very good mate then,' Sean added.

They gave James some time to stew on his words, consider the best way out of the hole he was about to dig for himself. And Tomek watched it all play out on the man's face. The quiet desperation, the bouncing of the eyes left and right, the missing eye contact. It was all there in the beautiful tapestry of James's expression.

'Who did you sell the car to, James?' Tomek asked.

Twisting, turning.

'It wasn't a mate. It was, it was just some randomer.'

'What does that mean? Someone came up to you in the middle of the street and offered you money for the car, and you took it?'

James dropped his head into his lap and pressed the sides of his nose with his thumbs. Tomek sensed the tears weren't far away. 'You don't get it. It was a really shitty time. I had a lot of stuff going on with work, with home, with other stuff, and to top it off I had to deal with him.'

Deal with him, Tomek thought, as though James's grandad had become a burden. The choice of words repulsed him.

'What did you have going on at work?' Sean asked, beating Tomek to it.

'Redundancies. There were loads of them about eighteen months, two years ago. There was no money coming into the football club. The owner had to make savings. It was a really stressful time for everyone. I had to fight for my job and prove my worth.'

'And they eventually came to their senses and realised the players couldn't be trusted to clean their kit on their own?' Tomek asked.

While he was turning the screw, he was happy to throw in a couple of right and left hooks now and then, just to wake James up a bit.

'My job is just as important as everyone else's in the team. All the backroom staff, all the physios, all the people behind the desks, everyone that helps the club function. Like a house of cards. If one of them falls, the rest of us do.'

Tomek nodded sarcastically and turned to Sean, giving him the silent go-ahead to continue with his line of questioning.

'Did the threat of redundancies have a knock-on effect on your marriage and home life?'

'Of course it did,' James replied. 'That's like asking if water's wet.'

Or if you reckon you could fight a cow.

And then the tears came. Almost as if on cue. James's body shuddered as he cried and then wiped the tears away. Neither Tomek nor Sean offered a hand or consolatory statement. They weren't there for that.

'Our marriage almost fell apart, and I almost lost custody of the girls,' James continued.

'And what about the other stuff that you had going on at the time?'

A look of confusion dried the tears from James's face. 'What other stuff?'

Tomek glanced down at his watch. 'About two minutes ago you said that you had a lot going on at the time your grandad was being put in a home. Work, home, your grandad. And you also said other stuff. Care to elaborate on that a little for us?'

James paused as he calculated a response. Tomek chose to ignore it, whatever it was. The man was hiding something from them, it was clear to see. And Tomek had quickly realised there was no amount of twisting and turning, prodding and probing that was going to unearth it. Not in the safe environment of his own home. Stick the man in an interview room with the possibility of looking at a lifetime of imprisonment, and Tomek was almost certain they'd get an answer then.

'There was no other stuff,' James replied bluntly. 'It was just a turn of phrase.'

'You clearly meant *something* by it,' Sean retorted.

James shrugged slowly. 'You know how it is. When things are in the shit and everything seems to come at once. Like some fucker up there' – he pointed skyward – 'is looking down at you and saying, "This is long overdue, fuckface. This is all that you deserve." I mean, sure, we also had some money issues going on at the time, but who doesn't?'

'Money problems how?'

'Gambling,' he replied candidly. 'I got myself into the casino game a few years ago. Spent a lot of nights there. Nearly lost everything we had.'

'And did the club find out?'

'No,' he said, dropping his head. 'My wife and I had a few arguments and she helped me see sense about it all, helped me kick the habit.'

Tomek noted the pun, then moved the topic of conversation on to Billy Turpin, Darren Edgerton and Harrison Rossiter.

'Do any of those names mean anything to you?'

'Of course they do. They play in our academy, well, except for Harrison, of course. I know all of the kids. Sometimes they come up to me and ask if they can have one of the first teams' shirts, but I tell them to go and ask the player instead. A lot of the time the players are happy to do it, but it's nice that they come to me first.'

'How well do you know the three boys?'

'Not very well, to be honest. I only speak to them a little bit in passing. And when Harrison was here, he was really shy. Not sure how he's getting on in France though.'

'*Très bien*, I hear,' Tomek said, even though he hadn't heard anything of the sort. Then he reached into his pocket and produced a printout of the list of names given to him by Human Resources at the club. 'How long have you been at the club, James?' he asked.

'Fifteen years. Same age as my girls.'

'And, in those fifteen years, have you ever known, or ever heard any rustlings, of someone selling drugs at the club?'

'Drugs?'

'Yes, they come in all sorts of shapes and sizes,' Sean commented.

'And, not to mention, with different levels of fatality,' Tomek added.

The two detectives allowed James a moment to cast his mind back through the years. By now the tears had completely stopped, and the only lasting evidence of them were his slightly rouged cheeks.

'Not that I can think of,' he said, much to Tomek's disappointment.

'Nothing about drugs laced with other drugs, or selling anything to any of the players?'

James shook his head. 'Sorry,' he said, then added, 'But what's all that got to do with my grandad's car?'

Tomek ignored the question and moved on. 'Do the names Mandy Butler, Avena Kumar, Klaudia Golec, Chanelle Pendrey, and Sonia Riggle mean anything to you? What about Lily Monteith and Fern Clements?'

The expression on James's face, as soon as he heard the names of the murder victims and those who'd been spiked at the Cliffs Pavilion, was as flat as the salt plains of Bolivia. 'I've heard of them – but only from the news. I saw the case the other day. Is that what this is about? Is that why you're here about my grandad's car?'

Tomek fell silent for a moment as he thought of a way out of the question. Then realised it was in his best interests to be honest.

'I'm going to be honest with you here, James, and I'd be grateful if you could do the same.' Tomek paused, licked his lip, inhaled. 'Yesterday, your grandfather's car was discovered, as my colleague said, beside an abandoned building in Shoeburyness. We have reason to believe the same vehicle was used in the abductions and murders of Fern Clements and Lily Monteith. Now, given that you were the last person to legally have ownership of the car, we'd love for you to help us out here. I'd hate for this to have the same impact as the threat of redundancy did on your family. Now, I'm going to ask again.' Tomek let all the air out of his lungs. 'Who did you sell the car to? Who's been killing these girls?'

James contemplated for what felt like forever, and after an even longer moment, he looked Tomek dead in the eye and said, 'I don't remember who I sold the car to. And I don't know who's killing those girls.'

CHAPTER FORTY-FIVE

James Elliott was lying to them, that much was obvious. Which put him right at the top of Tomek's suspects list.

A list that consisted of only one name for now.

The kit manager knew something, something that he wasn't telling them. Locked inside his head was the name of the individual he had sold the Volvo to. The name of the individual who had been killing the girls. James was hiding it for a reason, and Tomek intended to find out what that reason was. And so he had instructed the team to conduct an investigation into the man and enact a deep dive into his life: his financial records, his relationships, his work history, his entire background. And if there were any abnormalities and inconsistencies, any names that matched those of the massive list they'd garnered already, then they would pursue them. But until then, Tomek made his way to the Southend seafront. After returning to the station, he'd received a message from Nick that he wanted to meet on the sand.

Tomek found the chief inspector sitting on a bench overlooking the estuary with Kent in the background. A blistering wind whipped in from the shore and sent the flaps on Tomek's coat flying. The smell of salt and decaying seaweed, combined with the omnipresent smell of drugs, lingered in the air. And the sound of screaming and excitement coming from Adventure Island, Southend's premier hot spot for thrill-seekers and families, echoed in the distance.

'Never had you pegged as a Maritimer,' Tomek said as he lifted the tail of his coat before joining Nick on the bench.

Nick scoffed. 'There's a lot you don't know about me.'

'Well now's the time to get all your darkest confessions off your chest. I won't arrest you just yet. I promise.'

The start of a smile flashed across Nick's face and then immediately left.

In the few days since Tomek had last seen him, Nick had lost a worrying amount of weight. His eyes and the skin on his face were heavy, and he looked tired, broken, despondent. Even his bald head seemed to have lost some of its shine and vigour, the same shine and vigour that saw him get mocked relentlessly in the office as they'd referred to him as a cue ball.

'I hate seeing you like this,' Tomek said openly. 'When was the last time you slept?'

'The night before the incident. Properly, at least. The rest of it has just been one long... agonising... painful... day.'

Even his voice had lost all its essence. Before, there had been a vigour and shine to it (though this one received little to no mocking) and was responsible for keeping a room of fifteen individuals captivated during their meetings. Now it was flat, monotone, like talking with Andy Murray. Except without the accent.

'How's the investigation going?' Nick asked, much to Tomek's surprise.

'We don't need to talk about work if you don't want to.'

'I do. It's the only thing keeping my mind active. Distracts me from constantly thinking about Lucy. Poor Maggie, she doesn't have anything like this, and her work doesn't require her to think about anything else during her shift, so she's just sitting there stewing, thinking, overthinking.' Nick rotated his finger in the air like a pinwheel. 'Victoria's been keeping me up to date, by the way.'

This was news to him.

'I asked her to. Don't think she's been going behind your back.'

'What's she shared with you?'

'Everything. My brain needs it.' Nick paused and lifted his gaze to the water. 'So this football thing...'

Tomek suddenly felt embarrassed. 'Yeah.'

'Tell me about it.'

'No. I want to hear what you think about it first. If you've heard everything there is to know, then I want to know what you think. Am I completely mad, or do you think I've got something there?'

Nick looked at Tomek as though he'd been expecting the question, yet the rest of his expression gave nothing away.

'I don't think you're completely insane,' Nick said. 'I actually think you might be onto something. But I don't think a group of seventeen-year-old boys are behind this. I think your killer's someone at the club. Either in the first team or someone else on the staff. Or possibly even someone who used to work there.'

'Why?' Tomek asked, genuinely intrigued.

'The witness statement at the concerts. If one of the players from the academy saw the killer, *knew* the killer, rather, then that's key.'

'I asked to speak with the player, but he's in France. Victoria blocked the request.'

'I heard. Leave it with me.'

Maybe Nick really did know everything that was going on.

'You're like God, aren't you? Omnipresent.'

'I think you mean omniscient,' Nick corrected. 'But yes. I know everything about everything. It's what made me such a good dad. Every time Lucy came up to ask me a question, I knew the answer. And even if I didn't, I made it up and made it seem like I did. She never knew the difference.'

Tomek placed a hand on the man's back, sensing the tears were about to come.

'Nobody said you ever stopped being a good dad,' he added.

'Thanks.' And then the tears came. Only a few, but they were there, despite Nick trying his best to hide them. 'Sorry,' he said. 'It's the wind.'

'Tell me about it,' Tomek replied. 'The wind keeps getting to me as well.'

'What have you been crying over?'

'Oh no, not crying. *Farting*. For some reason, Kasia's been making us eat baked beans for breakfast.'

Nick rolled his eyes, then said: '*Beans, beans the musical fruit...*'

'*The more you eat...*'

But Nick chose not to finish the rhyme.

A moment of silence, of listening to the wind and the waves and the screams in the distance, passed between them. As he listened, Tomek closed his eyes and focused on his breathing. In. Out. In. Out. One of the many reasons he loved living by the sea was its ability to instantly calm and relax him. As though it was a little bubble where everything reset. Where there was a moment of calm, tranquillity, peace. And sometimes there was nothing the ear-shattering scream of a teenage mum yelling at their child could disturb.

'Did you hear about the car?' Tomek asked. Then realised. 'Of course you did. Well, we spoke with the owner. Kit manager for Dagenham and Redbridge.'

'More fuel for the fire,' Nick commented. 'Is he your man?'

Tomek grunted. 'Not sure. I'm not keen on the bloke, but he claims he sold the car to a mate, who he conveniently can't remember the name of. But it's all right, I've already got the team doing a deep dive, so if anything comes up we know where to find him.'

'Good man. Sounds like you've got a good grip on everything.'

Tomek smirked as his ego inflated a little. Then he fought it down. The case wasn't over yet, and there was still a long way to go. Even longer if you considered the trial and the application to the Crown Prosecution Service. They needed to make sure absolutely everything was air-tight, which was why, for now, James Elliott would have to remain outside an interview room. Until they were able to connect him with the crimes, he was an innocent man.

Innocent until proven guilty. The backbone of the entire judicial system. And the man was slapping them all in the face.

'Maybe we won't need you to come back after all,' Tomek said jokingly.

'You can fucking bet your arse I will be. And I'll be coming down hard on yours like nothing's changed.'

'Like nothing's changed,' Tomek echoed, grinning.

CHAPTER FORTY-SIX

The biggest problem the investigation faced was waiting.

Waiting, waiting, waiting. It was the bane of every investigation. In the past two days, Oscar and a team of scenes of crime officers had visited James Elliott's house to gather some DNA samples. They had collected them, but now it would be a week, if not more, until they found out whether James Elliott's DNA matched that taken from the brick building and Volvo X70. A combination of the busy Christmas period, annual leave and the backlog that was delaying a lot of other investigations from proceeding was getting in the way of this one. Until they had the proof that James Elliott was involved in the murder, they would have to wait. And find something else to occupy their time.

Oscar, or Captain Actually as he was called in the team, had come up with the idea of checking the land registry to find out who owned the small plot of land the building was situated on. The small spark of excitement and hope that the idea had inspired had lasted all of a few hours until a quick check had confirmed that the land belonged to the Ministry of Defence and that there were no private owners nearby that could have used the building. The team had spoken with several of the neighbours, and they had found nothing to suggest any concern.

The only small prospect of excitement had come in the form of a second set of tyre marks discovered at the scene, unearthed by a SOCO. But the excitement had lasted as long as the land registry idea had because they soon realised it would be difficult to trace the second vehicle the killer had used based solely on the tyre prints. It was great if they had the vehicle so they could compare the two tracks, but because they didn't even know what they were looking for, it was impossible to tell.

Tomek hated waiting. It infuriated him, upset him. And in a world where everything was instant almost all the time, he found himself growing increasingly frustrated with it. To combat his impatience, he made himself a coffee.

He was in the middle of boiling the kettle when his phone vibrated in his pocket.

'Yes?' he answered without checking caller ID.

'I've dropped the article about Nick.'

Abigail.

'Finally. Thank you. I appreciate it.'

'How much?'

'Excuse me?'

He sensed where this was going already, and as he stirred the coffee granules in his mug, he sighed internally.

'How much do you appreciate it?' Abigail asked.

'I don't have time for games, Abs. What do you want in return?'

'I have something that might be of interest.'

'Like what?'

'Like a German woman who—'

'I'm not looking to get into anything weird, thank you,' he said, but she didn't see the funny side of it.

'Shut up. Let me explain. After your press conference the other day, something the woman from the BBC said got me thinking.'

Tomek knew exactly what she was referring to: during his press conference, one of the faceless journalists hiding behind the glare of the spotlights had raised the possibility of whether the killer had ever killed abroad. At the time, Tomek had ignored it. But clearly, Abigail hadn't.

'Those lot over at the BBC are doing your job for you,' he said.

'I'm surprised. They're usually too busy getting themselves out of some sort of scandal,' Abigail said, resentment and disdain lacing her voice. Then she added, 'But it gave me an idea. I thought I'd check with some of my contacts from overseas publications to see whether they'd heard of anyone dying or almost dying from an allergic reaction.'

'I imagine they laughed at you.'

'Yes, but after I explained what was happening here, they suddenly shut up and listened.'

'And?'

'And, I think I've found a woman in Germany who almost died from an allergic reaction under suspicious circumstances.'

Tomek dropped the spoon onto the kitchen counter, oblivious to it skittering across the surface and onto the floor.

'What suspicious circumstances?'

'Exactly the same as Diana Greenock.'

Tomek held his breath.

'In what way?'

'Every single way. Ground-floor flat. Missing cat coming in through the window. And she's also severely asthmatic.'

Tomek nodded as he stared into the kitchen cabinet, his mind devoid of thought.

'He was practising,' he whispered to himself.

'What?'

'What distinguishes her from Diana Greenock? Why did *she* survive and not Diana?'

'Because this woman had someone staying over the night the cat came in. She had someone to call the emergency services and save her.'

'Who is she?'

'Martha Buhl.'

'Have you made contact with her?'

'Not yet. I wanted to run it by you first.'

Tomek nodded, his mind racing.

'Okay. Fine. Good. Great. You should make first contact, then explain what's happening over here, and then bring me into the picture.'

'So you think she might know who the killer is?'

Tomek didn't want to get ahead of himself. So far all he knew was that a woman had almost died under very similar, almost identical, circumstances to Diana Greenock. That was it. Nothing more, nothing less. It would be irrational and almost reckless for him to assume that there was anything more than coincidence to it. Not until they had proper, hard evidence.

The crimes were separated by hundreds of miles.

But then again, so were Diana Greenock's and Mandy Butler's.

'When did all this happen?' Tomek asked.

'Roughly ten years ago,' she said.

Tomek froze.

That fitted in with the timeframe.

Five-year gap between the German incident and Diana Greenock's murder.

Three years between her and Mandy Butler.

A further two years between Mandy and Lily.

And now a gap of two weeks between Lily's and Fern's deaths.

A killer slowly perfecting the art of killing.

A killing spree years in the making.

CHAPTER FORTY-SEVEN

Every year the team, hosted by none other than their resident Miss Party Organiser, Nadia, held an event for New Year's Eve. It was usually a veritable soup of alcohol, music, and a smattering of snacks and nibbles, with catering provided by the local Tesco Express on the high street, with a few sweets thrown in from the nearby Poundsaver. The evening was an opportunity for them to let loose, and to look back on the year and congratulate themselves for making it through to the end.

In previous years, Tomek had attended the event and found himself at the end of several bottles of beer, and on the odd occasion falling asleep at his desk. But that had been during the younger, carefree days of his late twenties and early thirties. This year, however, he was forced to miss out on it. Instead, he'd swapped a night of drinking, talking, music and fun, with exactly the same thing. The only difference was the location. And the company he'd be doing it with.

'So are you gonna make the move tonight?'

'What move?' Tomek asked.

'The one you see in all the films.'

'Sadly life isn't like that.'

'But are you gonna do it?'

Tomek wasn't quite sure when Kasia's fascination over his love life had begun, but it had intensified in recent weeks. To the point where he was considering involving her in every conversation he ever had with a member of the opposite sex. Ever. Perhaps she was like a drug sniffer dog and could smell the loneliness and desperation in him, and was desperate to help.

'I'm not going to *do* anything. We're just going over for New Year's Eve,' Tomek told her. 'There's no need to read into it.'

'Too late,' she said with a smile that illuminated her face.

After a few minutes more in the car, they arrived outside Louise and Sylvia's house. Like them, they too had removed the Christmas decorations from the window, and Tomek was grateful he now had an ally in the matter. Convincing Kasia that even having them up after New Year's Day was wrong had proven to be a difficult argument for him to win, but she had eventually conceded defeat. And to make her feel better about the decision, Tomek had suggested they head to Louise and Sylvia's for a night of fun, drinking, music, talking and maybe even a few board games.

'Good evening, you two,' Louise said delightfully as she opened the door for them. 'Just in time. We've just finished setting up.'

'Great,' Tomek replied, then nudged Kasia on the shoulder. 'At least that's saved us a job!'

'No matching pyjamas tonight?' Louise asked.

Tomek looked between him and Kasia. 'Sadly not. Though you've not made the effort either, so I don't feel quite as bad.'

For the evening, Tomek had bought a bottle of white wine – £11 from Sainsbury's – for himself and Louise, and a small four-pack of alcohol-free cider for the girls. As they entered the kitchen, Louise took the bottle from Tomek and observed it.

'Oyster Bay. My favourite. How did you know?'

'I'm a police officer. I have my sources and little informers around the place.' He pointed to Sylvia, who had just emerged from the living room, and Kasia, who was standing as close to her as possible. 'Namely, these two.'

'Well, that's very kind of you,' Louise said, then turned her attention to the ciders. 'And who are these for?'

'The informants.'

At that, the bright, ebullient smile on Louise's face, dissipated and changed a darker shade, as though a shadow had just settled over her.

Tomek felt the need to jump to his own defence.

'They're alcohol-free. After last time, I figured that this is a good taster for them. Get them used to the flavours from a young age and in a controlled environment with people who are going to look out for them. You don't have to if you don't want to. And if you don't want them here at all then we can chuck them in the bin.'

Louise picked up the package and surveyed them studiously. 'I guess you're right. No point preventing the inevitable, only delaying it.'

With that settled, Tomek and Louise poured the drinks while the girls headed off to the living room, where they were immediately lost in the wonders of TV and their smartphones.

'How's work?' Louise asked.

'Tough. Long. But I got a semi-promotion so that's quite nice.'

'How does a semi-promotion work?'

'It's one of those where they make you do all the extra work while someone's off sick or on leave for a few weeks.'

'So you're a stop-gap?'

'Absolutely.'

'Well, congratulations. A little bit of experience at a higher level is never a bad thing.'

It wasn't and Tomek was fully aware of that. Didn't make him any less bitter about having to deal with Veronica though.

'Thanks, by the way,' he started, as they made their way into the living room, drinks in hand.

'For what?'

'For taking down all your Christmas decorations. We had a few arguments about it earlier today.'

Louise rolled her eyes and exhaled deeply. 'Tell me about it. Sylvia was the same. But I told her if I had it my way they'd be down on Boxing Day.'

'Or not even up at all.'

She turned to face him and smiled. 'Now that's where I draw the line. I'm a big Christmas fan, don't get me wrong, but once it's over, it's over.'

Their conversation was brought to an end as they entered the living room. Resting atop a pouffe in the centre of the carpet was a large tray of treats, with another tray sitting on a coffee table. A delectable selection of light snacks and goodies: cheese savouries, Thai sweet chilli crisps, breadsticks, Lindt chocolates, a box of Celebrations, cheese, crackers, and a small punnet of grapes. But the real clincher, the thing that appealed, and surprised, Tomek the most, was the small glass of *paluski*. The narrow, salt-covered sticks protruded from the end of the glass like a mini forest. They were a staple of the Polish diet and were to be enjoyed on almost every occasion. Even then, you probably didn't need an occasion. They were salty, tasty and devilishly moreish.

'*Paluski*!' Tomek screamed excitedly. 'Where did you get those from?'

'I, too, have my sources and also my informants,' Louise said with a smile.

As he reached down for a stick of *paluski*, he caught her giving the girls a wink.

'At least we know the way to each other's hearts.'

The words had escaped his mouth without his realising. And now all three of them were staring back at him.

Quick. Quick. Think of something.

'And I guess the way to *your* hearts is Christmas.'

'Christmas!' the girls yelled, then turned to themselves and began nattering away about their decorations and how sad they were to pull them down.

Good save, Tomek thought.

They spent the next few hours sitting in front of the TV, but not really watching the crap that had been scheduled. Instead, they'd talked, laughed and then Tomek had the brilliant idea of playing board games. Fortunately, he had just the thing.

'Essex Monopoly? I didn't even know they did an Essex Monopoly.'

'Best believe it, baby,' he said as he opened the packaging. 'Now, do you all know how to play?'

Everyone confirmed they did.

'Great. Next question. Do you all have three working days for us to play this?'

Everyone confirmed they did.

'Right. Well I don't, so I'm going to have to beat you lot in a few hours!'

And it took him exactly that. Three hours of rolling, buying, charging, owning, building and strategically taking himself to first place. Once all the other players were officially bankrupt, Tomek counted his winnings in front of them.

'Go on then,' Louise said, as she held her third glass of wine in her hand. 'How much did you win by?'

'I lost count,' Tomek answered, when the truth was that the margin he'd won by was too large, and to save them from the embarrassment, he kept the information to himself.

Buoyed by his overwhelming victory, Tomek suggested the next game. Singstar on the PlayStation. A game that required two microphones and two willing karaoke enthusiasts. The aim of the game was simple: to sing along to a popular song as in tune as possible. At the start of the game, Tomek was under no illusion where he'd place in the rankings. But by the end of the first song, he'd realised that he could get away with humming in tune rather than singing the actual words and had ended up coming first, much to the chagrin of his opponents. For the rest of the session, he was forced to play the game "properly" by embarrassing himself with his God-awful singing talents. By the end of it, however, he finished a respectable third, narrowly beating Louise, with Kasia at the top.

'Does that make it two-nil to the Bowen family?' Tomek asked, smugly.

'You're our guests,' Louise replied. 'We have to let you win.'

'Or we were just better on the night. Sore loser.' Tomek gave her a wink then poured himself his last glass of wine. He'd only had one, and any more would put him over the limit. Not to mention it would set a terrible example to his daughter.

Shortly after, the four of them welcomed in the new year with an embrace, party poppers, and the sound of glasses clinking together. Much quieter and calmer than the furore of thirty people screaming in each other's faces with their alcohol breath, making their way arduously around the room to make sure they wished everyone a happy new year.

'Happy New Year, girls,' Louise said. 'What did you wish for?'

Sylvia and Kasia glanced at one another before responding.

'We wished for Lucy to get better.'

Pride swelled within Tomek. Of all the things she could have asked for – the Apple Watch he hadn't bought her for Christmas or the clothes and pairs of shoes she badgered him for on an almost weekly basis – she had instead chosen something deeper, something more meaningful and wholesome.

'Well, the good news is that she's getting better,' Tomek explained. 'I saw Nick the other day and he said she's still in her coma, but she's improving.'

'That *is* good news,' Louise stated.

'Have you found who did it yet?' Sylvia asked.

The question stumped Tomek. As far as he was aware, she had given a witness statement the day after the event.

'What do you mean, hon?' Louise asked.

'The... the other...' She swallowed deeply and avoided their gaze.

When she didn't continue, Tomek took it upon himself to press her, gently.

'Is there something you need to tell us, Sylvia? You can say it here. This is a safe environment.'

She paused, waited. Controlled herself.

'That night,' she began softly, staring into the carpet. 'That night, I saw another figure... a man. At least I *think* I saw him. It's been going round and round my head all this time. He was just... standing there, in the darkness, by the fish and chip shop, watching us.'

CHAPTER FORTY-EIGHT

'The killer was there on the night of Lucy's incident.'

'How can you be sure it was the killer?' Victoria asked.

'Intuition.'

'I don't want us to get ahead of ourselves, Tomek,' she said softly.

The two of them were locked inside her office, discussing the vital piece of information Sylvia had given them. News of the anonymous figure had spread through the rest of the team and they were currently investigating it.

'It might be nothing,' he said. 'But, on the other hand, it might be *something*. And if it is, then I want to make sure we use every available weapon in our arsenal to ensure we find out who it is.'

'Have you asked yourself why the killer might be there?' Victoria asked.

The thought hadn't occurred to him. Not that it needed to.

'Have you asked yourself why the killer's fucking killing people in the first place?' he asked in retaliation. 'Why's he doing any of this at all?'

To that, Victoria had no response. Sitting in her seat, she crossed her knees and rested her hands atop her kneecap. Then she yawned, deeply, stretching her mouth wide open, revealing her teeth. She rubbed her eyes as she fought off a second yawn.

'Heavy night last night, was it?' The disdain in Tomek's voice was abundant.

'A little,' she replied. 'A lot of us are nursing a few of the headache gremlins this morning.'

There was a time when Tomek would have regretted missing out on the annual New Year's Eve celebrations – a classic case of FOMO, the fear of missing out – but now he couldn't have given a shit how any of them were feeling. Yes, in previous years he would have felt the same way, tired, head pounding, sick to the stomach, and in desperate need of something fatty and acidic to combat the poison in his system, but he always managed to get on with his job. He always managed to see it through. And right now he was getting the impression from Victoria that she wanted the anonymous figure to wait another day, for Tomek to postpone it while she secretly napped in her office with the blinds shut and a pair of sunglasses over her eyes.

Well, he wouldn't stand for it.

Nick never had, so why should he?

As Tomek watched Victoria open a bottle of water as if she had Parkinson's, the door opened and Chey popped his head round the side. His face, thanks to the brilliance of youth, was able to mask the hangover he was clearly suffering from. Sadly, hints of it lingered in his voice, crackly and broken. Not to mention the smell of alcohol remaining on his breath from where he'd failed to brush his teeth properly.

'Sorry... sorry to bother you, sarge, *ma'am*.'

'It's fine,' Tomek snapped. 'What do you have?'

'CCTV footage from the fish and chip shop and a couple of the restaurants along the Old Leigh promenade.'

Tomek propelled himself off his chair and followed Chey to his desk, where he found Martin, Nadia and Rachel already hovering. All eagerly awaiting the news.

As he approached, he noticed the air around them was thick with perfume and aftershave, a smell that clung to the back of his throat. If their attempts to hide the alcohol currently seeping from their pores was meant to be discreet, it was anything but.

'Hello, everyone!' Tomek yelled, slamming his palms on the table repeatedly.

After the first bang, they all placed their hands to their heads, cupping their ears. All except Nadia who, thanks to the baby growing in her stomach, had stayed sober the entire night, and was enjoying watching her colleagues wallow in pity.

'The fuck you doing, you dick?' snapped Martin, who was the most hungover of them all.

Tomek slapped the man on the back and said, 'Just making sure you're all alive and fresh this morning.'

'You're lucky no one's thrown up,' Nadia said. 'It was... *messy.*'

Tomek took the seat at the front that had been left for him. A few moments later, the most lucid member of the team (aside from Tomek and Nadia), had loaded the video footage and pressed play.

On the constable's computer screen was darkness, the faint outline of shapes barely visible. In the centre of the footage was the beach, to the left, were Lucy Cleaves and Paddy Battersby, and down in the bottom, tucked just out of sight, was the anonymous figure, a silhouette of black, his features indiscernible.

As the footage progressed, and as all the girls reacted to the incident and jumped on Paddy, the figure moved. At first, his movements were slow, tentative, but then as he became more confident about the fact he wouldn't be seen – the girls were too focused on detaining Paddy and tending to their friend – he walked straight past them. At the end of the promenade, he jumped down onto the beach and disappeared into the distance, keeping a wide berth until he reached the end of the beach where he climbed back onto the promenade and continued into the darkness, in the direction of Southend-on-Sea.

'Where does he go after that?' Tomek asked.

'Well, there's no footage around there. It's just a narrow—'

'What about when it comes out at Chalkwell?'

'You didn't let me finish,' Chey snapped. Then he clicked a few more buttons and up popped a second screen of darkness. 'This is footage farther along the seafront between Chalkwell Beach and

Southend.' He pointed to a moving shadow on the beach. 'By my estimation, this is the same guy. Same height, same build, same outfit.'

'Where's he going?'

And then he found the answer in another piece of CCTV
footage. The figure, masked by a large coat and his proximity to the
cameras, was heading towards Grosvenor Casino.

'Go back to the first shot, on Bell Wharf.'

Chey did as he was told, and Tomek leant in for a closer view, his
eyes inches from the screen.

'What are you looking at, sarge?' Chey asked.

'I'm trying to work out who it is,' he said. And then added, 'I
think it's James Elliott.'

CHAPTER FORTY-NINE

The team's earlier search into James Elliott's financial records had shown just how unhealthy his past with the casino on the seafront and the various online platforms had been. An unhealthy past that had almost led to a divorce and putting himself out of a job. Over the course of two years, he had lost nearly thirty thousand pounds and had almost been at risk of losing his house over it.

Tomek had experienced something similar in his life. Two of his friends from school had both found themselves facing bankruptcy from their addictions. They had lied to their partners, lied to themselves, and got themselves killed in the end after getting in too deep with a loan shark they were unable to pay.

As for James Elliott, Tomek wasn't concerned the same thing was happening. Rather, he thought the opposite. That James Elliott was the one doing the killing.

'Where is your husband, Mrs Elliott?'

Amber Elliott, a woman who looked as tired as Rachel felt sitting beside him, dabbed at the heavy eyeliner with a tissue. She had been crying ever since their arrival, her mind already beginning to fear the worst. It was New Year's Day, one of the busiest days in the footballing calendar for the National League, and her husband was nowhere to be seen. He hadn't turned up to work in the morning for

Dagenham & Redbridge FC's three o'clock kick-off against Eastleigh. Nor had he come home from a late-night trip.

'I don't know where he is,' she replied, sniffling.

'When was the last time you saw him?' Rachel asked.

Tomek had asked her to join him, along with Anna, who was currently keeping the Elliotts' two daughters entertained in the kitchen.

'He went out last night,' she replied, her voice breaking halfway through.

'Do you know where?' Rachel continued.

Tomek was happy to take the backseat and let his colleague drive the conversation.

'He said he was going to a football event. They usually have a New Year's Eve party for the players and staff. A tame thing. Nothing too wild because they have a game the following day. The families are invited, but Lara wasn't feeling very well last night so we didn't go.'

'Is she feeling any better now?' Rachel asked as she shuffled across to the other side of the living room and perched herself beside Amber.

'Yes, she's fine now. Thank you.' Amber dabbed at her eyes again, folding the tissue over several times as she did so.

'When did you notice something was wrong?' Rachel continued.

'When I woke up this morning. He wasn't there. I tried his mobile, but he wasn't picking up. A part of me thought he'd stayed at the club and was just going to the match from there, as it's a couple of hours' drive away. But when I got a phone call from one of his mates at the club saying that he couldn't get hold of him either, that's when I knew something was wrong. That something might have happened to him.'

Or that he might have done something to someone else.

'Has your husband ever done anything like this before? Disappeared for a night at a time and not come home?'

Amber Elliott was unable to meet Tomek's eyes as she nodded her head, slowly, solemnly. 'Back when... back when things were really bad... with the money and the gambling,' she started, then coughed as she choked on the tears welling in her throat. 'Back when things were bad between us, there were times he would go out gambling and not come home until the following morning, having lost all our money.'

The concerns in Tomek's head continued to grow. If James Elliott was gone for nights at a time, there was no knowing what else he could have been doing. Gambling, yes. Attending concerts and killing innocent girls in the meantime? Possibly.

From the kitchen, playful screams and laughter echoed through the door. Amber lifted her head and turned to face the kitchen.

'Mrs Elliott,' Tomek said, pulling her attention back to him. 'Your children are fine. They're in good company. I'm going to show you some photos and I'm going to ask you some difficult questions now, okay? And I need you to think really hard for me. Okay?'

At that moment, Amber turned to Rachel for emotional support. The constable showed it to her by placing an arm over her shoulder and gently stroking her back. From her reaction, Tomek got the impression she knew what this was about.

'Where was your husband on the night of the nineteenth of December?'

The night of Fern Clements' death.

Fighting back the tears, Amber pulled out her phone from her jeans pocket and looked through her calendar. 'He was at an away fixture. They were playing Tranmere Rovers.'

'And three nights before that?'

The night Lily Monteith died.

'He... I can't remember. I think he was home.'

'But you can't be certain?'

'No. Sorry.'

As Tomek opened his mouth, he was about to ask her where her husband was two years ago, on the night of Mandy Butler's death, but then he realised it was unfair to expect her to know such a thing.

'Did your husband ever go to any concerts, Mrs Elliott?' Tomek asked.

'I... Why? What's that got to do with anything?'

'Just answer the question, please,' he replied firmly.

'I mean, he might have done. We've never been to any. Not in a long time, anyway. Only when we first started going out. That all changed when he got his job. He's always out, going to places, travelling around the country.'

'What about bees? Does your husband have an interest in them or has he ever mentioned bees in conversation?'

'I... I... I don't think so.'

Tomek nodded. 'How often do you see your husband, Mrs Elliott?'

'Not much.'

'How much?'

She threw her hand down onto her knee aggressively. 'Do you want me to put a number on it? Want me to give you a percentage?'

'Please,' Tomek said with a slight dip of his head.

Sighing, Amber replied, 'Twenty-five per cent of the time. Maybe more. He's hardly home. And I'm always busy at work as well, so the girls are left to fend for themselves most of the week. Fortunately, they're at an age where they can do that, but it wasn't always that easy.'

Tomek waited a moment before moving on to the next question. In the kitchen, the sound of excitement and playful laughter continued, putting Amber a little more at ease.

'I understand the two of you went through a rough patch two years ago.'

'Yes.'

'What happened?'

'That was when I first found out about the gambling. He denied it, as you'd expect, but I had proof. I saw his bank account and all the emails he was getting from the betting companies with offers and free bets. So I lost it. It nearly broke us up. The two months that we were apart really helped us mend our relationship. We wouldn't be together if it weren't for that.'

Tomek's ears perked up. The window of Mandy Butler's death appeared in his mind.

'You were separated?' Tomek asked for clarification.

'Yes.'

'Do you mind me asking when?'

She straightened her back at the question. 'Well you've asked about everything else, I don't see why I would have a problem with *that* question.'

Tomek didn't respond, and when she realised he wasn't going to, she continued, 'It was between March and July. Two years ago. I remember it because we got back together just before the school holidays and he treated us to a holiday to Florida. Bought and paid for with his winnings.'

Tomek took a moment to absorb the information. James and Amber's separation had happened at the same time as Mandy Butler's death. Which put him very much in the frame for her murder.

Which left one: Diana Greenock.

Was it possible for him to have killed her as well? Tomek wanted to believe it, but couldn't find a way for it to fit together. And then it struck him: Dagenham & Redbridge FC. The National League had two teams from the Manchester area: Rochdale and Oldham Athletic. Perhaps James had befriended her at some point, possibly at one of the matches. Perhaps they'd exchanged numbers and flirted via text message for weeks or months afterwards, counting the days until his next visit. And perhaps on that night, he had broken into her house to kill her.

It wasn't entirely impossible. But it would require some more digging for sure.

'Do the names Diana Greenock, Mandy Butler, Lily Monteith or Fern Clements mean anything to you, Amber?' Tomek asked, handing over a printout that Chey had produced. On it were recent photos of the four victims, with their names above their heads. 'Please, take your time.'

And she did. Two minutes, in fact. In that time, Tomek pulled out his phone and checked his emails, while Rachel disappeared to make a cup of tea for her and Amber and a glass of water for him.

By the time she returned, Amber had finished analysing the document.

Tomek hadn't noticed it at first, but when she looked up at him, he saw the tears forming in her eyes, and the two that she'd already lost control of were now abseiling down her cheeks.

'Does this mean what I think it does?' she asked, her voice wobbly.

'We don't know anything for certain, Mrs Elliott.'

'Do you think my husband did this?'

'We're currently looking at all lines of enquiry,' Tomek replied. 'Do any of those names mean anything to you?'

Slowly, tentatively, Amber Elliott pointed to a name on the sheet.

'Lily Monteith. She goes to the same school as the girls.'

The night Amber couldn't account for her husband's whereabouts.

CHAPTER FIFTY

'It needs to be more concrete,' Victoria said, dropping an Alka-Seltzer into a glass of water.

The bubbles hissed and fizzed like Tomek's frustration.

'How much more do we need?' he asked. 'Do you want us to be standing over him as he's abducting a girl and killing her by whatever method he's chosen next, just so we can be absolutely sure?'

Victoria shot him a look of derision. 'There's no need to be facetious, Tomek.'

'Sometimes I think there is. So far James Elliott is the only suspect we can say with a degree of certainty, no matter how big it is, that he's our killer.' Tomek reached into his blazer pocket and pulled out his notebook, then flicked through the pages close to the front. 'Tracy Pickard's forensic profile suggested that he was in a position of power and authority, someone largely attractive, someone that is capable of dismantling his victim's barriers. And I think Elliott fits the bill. While he might be just a kit manager, he's from a football club. Certain types of girl seem to love that, especially if he goes out wearing his tracksuit. When I spoke with him he came across as confident and slightly manipulative. And, I'm no expert, but I'd say he was quite handsome as well. Not to mention he knows of Lily Monteith, possibly from hanging around outside her school, and his wife can't account for his whereabouts on the night of her death. He travels up and down the country, so it's possible he's come into contact with Diana Greenock and Mandy Butler at some point in their lives. He's a part of the football club and has connections with Darren Edgerton and Harrison Rossiter, and his features are distinguishable in each of the e-fit illustrations our witnesses have done.'

'You're kidding, right?' Victoria asked as she took a massive gulp of the fizzy water. As she finished it, she winced and set the glass on the table, shaking the bubbles out of her skull. 'All of those illustrations have a white male with brown hair and a pointed nose. That looks like almost half the blokes in this town. One of them even looks a bit like *you*.'

Tomek silently agreed. One of them did look like him and while e-fits typically weren't supposed to be so heavily relied upon, they did have their uses and convincing his acting chief inspector of the validity of his claims was one of them.

'Answer me this,' Victoria began. 'What's his gambling got to do with anything?'

Now this was the part that had stumped Tomek as well. It didn't seem as obvious to him as the rest of it all, but he was sure there was a connection there somewhere. And sometimes the only way to find it was for him to start talking.

'I was thinking about that,' he started, 'and I think it has something to do with the car which is another thing we've got him on, right? The car's registered in his family's name, and he wouldn't tell us who he sold it to. I don't think he sold it to anyone.'

'The gambling, Tomek,' Victoria said sternly, seeing right through his façade despite her dampened reaction times. 'What's the connection with the gambling addiction? What motive does that give him to be killing these girls?'

'It's not related at all,' he said. 'The gambling addiction was just another one of his vices. The night that Lucy was attacked on the beach, he was there for something else. Maybe he was on his way to the casino anyway. He just happened to be at the wrong place at the wrong time. His wife explained to us that he sometimes disappears at night and that he's always out at the football. Perhaps he was fuelling his addiction that way and wanted to walk along the seafront in the darkness to hide his identity.'

Victoria rubbed her eyes and pondered a moment. Before she could respond, a knock came from the door to her office. Victoria bade them entry.

It was Oscar, all five foot four of him.

'How can we help, Captain?' Tomek asked.

'It's about James Elliott.'

'Someone's found him wedged into a kitbag?'

'No, but uniforms are patrolling the fields in the area for more victims like you asked, and we've got alerts out on any missing persons matching our murder victims' descriptions.'

Tomek nodded. 'Good man. What is it?'

'Actually, it's about what you just said, sarge.'

'They've found him in a kitbag?'

'Yes. And no. I just spoke with the head of HR, and they informed me that they let James Elliott go about two months ago. Sacked him because they found out about his gambling problem. They can't be seen to have someone doing that sort of thing in the club. Grounds for instant dismissal. He hasn't worked there for about eight weeks.'

Tomek turned to Victoria, then back to Oscar. 'So what the fuck's he been doing in that time?'

Then he looked down at the printout containing the victims' names and faces.

'So, he's been an unemployed gambling addict for the past few weeks who's been lying to his family,' Victoria said, acting as the infernal voice of reason. 'It still doesn't explain his connection to all of the girls. Have you checked the lists?'

The lists. The bastard lists of all the men who had ever come into the victims' lives. Over four hundred names across four different spreadsheets.

Tomek nodded. 'I ran a simple search function for each, yes.'

'And?'

'Nothing.'

'There you go then.'

'But the lists aren't to be taken as gospel,' he defended. 'I'd say they're about as useful as the e-fits.'

'What was the point in us putting them together then?'

Sensing that this was a discussion out of his league, Oscar slowly began retreating from the room. Tomek noticed him in his peripherals, and just as he was about to address the man, Sean appeared in the doorway, filling it entirely with his giant shoulders.

'What is this? A party in my office and everyone's invited?'

'No, ma'am. It's better than a party, not that you couldn't host a good party, I'm sure you could, it's just...' Sean eventually came to a gradual stop, staring deeply into Victoria's eyes. For a brief moment, Tomek thought he looked like a lost schoolboy, waiting for direction.

'What do you have to say, Sean?' Victoria asked gently.

'Someone's just called in a missing person for a teenage girl, aged fourteen. Last seen last night.'

Tomek flashed a quick look at the inspector. 'James Elliott and a teenage girl go missing on the same night. Coincidence?'

She couldn't argue with that one.

THE GIRL'S name was Remi Sane, which was one letter away from where her parents wanted her to be: safe.

'She went out last night round a friend's house and was supposed to come home but she never did,' explained Roger Sane, Remi's father. 'We've tried calling and calling, but she just won't pick up. We've seen all the things that's been going on in the news with the killings and the other girls that have died, and we're so worried that something might have happened to her.'

'What's her allergy?' Tomek asked crassly, without realising the offence he might have caused.

'Allergy? She... she doesn't have one.'

'Right.'

Just like that, their hopes of the missing girl being connected to Lily Monteith and the other victims flew straight out of the window.

'What difference does that make?' asked Phoebe Sane from her husband's side. 'She's still missing, whether or not she's got an allergy.'

It just means that she's a lot more likely to be alive, Tomek thought. Then decided it would be in everyone's interest if he didn't say anything else.

'Absolutely,' interjected Anna. 'We just wanted to rule your daughter out of our investigations into the murders you mentioned. The killer has a particular type of victim, and based on your description of your daughter, she doesn't match that. So you have nothing to worry about in that respect.'

'So what you're saying is she might be missing, you just don't think she's dead.'

And it had all been going so well. Tomek thought Anna had handled it professionally and diplomatically, but clearly not well enough for Remi's parents' liking.

'It's important for us to know who your daughter was with last night,' she continued, avoiding the allegation.

'Her friends.'

'Yes. Do you happen to know their names?'

As much as he hated to admit it, as soon as he discovered that Remi didn't have an allergy, Tomek began drifting off. If she wasn't related to the killings, then he was wasting his time when it could have been better spent finding James Elliott.

Tomek's mind had become warped with thoughts of the man who had been lying to them all. Lying to them about his job, lying to them about his addiction, lying to them about the car that had been found outside the building in Shoeburyness. The man had a large target over his head, and Tomek couldn't wait to get him in the middle of his crosshairs.

A few minutes passed of half-listening, nodding when he thought something important or sensitive had been said, and smiling when he thought he heard something uplifting. Meanwhile, his head was running away with itself. At over a hundred miles an hour.

Diana Greenock. Mandy Butler. Lily Monteith. Fern Clements. The Volvo. The building. Dagenham & Redbridge FC. Billy the fucking Cow Fighter.

But before he could think of them anymore, a sound came from the front door. Loud, abrupt. A banging sound. Not one of distress, but the desperation behind it was obvious.

'Remi!' Phoebe exclaimed as she leapt off the sofa and left her husband behind.

Roger shortly followed her out of the living room, with Tomek and Anna in tow. By the time the three of them made it into the hallway, Phoebe had her arms wrapped around her daughter, hugging her tightly, pressing her against her chest, cradling the back of her head, and kissing her forehead.

Keeping her close.

Remi Sane was now exactly as her parents wanted her to be.

Safe.

'Looks like you won't be needing us any more,' Anna said, as the two of them headed towards the exit.

CHAPTER FIFTY-ONE

Tomek had been sitting at his desk for hours, slowly driving himself insane, working himself into a hungover-like state, experiencing all the same symptoms. Headache, tiredness, depression, a sense of self-loathing, loss of dignity and regret.

A hangover of his own.

He had been staring at the same information for hours, trying to find ways to wedge the pieces into the puzzle, to find a way for it all to make sense. But in the end, he had become myopic, and everything had become a blur.

It wasn't until he felt a firm hand on his shoulders that he blinked. Or at least thought that he'd blinked. He couldn't exactly remember the last time he had.

'You look like you could do with some sleep,' Sean said as he sat beside him.

'Or a drink.'

'Cheeky New Year's Day pint down the Last Post later?'

Tomek shrugged. 'I would. But Kasia, She's been home all day. I don't wanna...'

'I get it. The new normal.'

'The new normal.'

Both men smirked at one another and shared a look that put Tomek at ease.

'We're gonna have to put something in the diary,' he said. 'Like women.'

'We could learn a thing or two from Nads. I think she's sent out next year's Halloween invites already.'

Tomek rolled his eyes and chuckled to himself. 'Think I'll put myself down as a "maybe" for that one. Not after this year's disaster.'

His ex-girlfriend had gate-crashed the event and broken up with him on the spot then gone on to kill a paedophile. He'd had more pleasant nights with the team, that was for sure.

'West Ham are at home at the end of the month, if you fancy going?'

'Would love to. I'm sure the wee bairn will be happy with it, she can just go over to her mate's or something.'

'And her mum can babysit them both.'

'Speaking of love interests,' Tomek began.

'Love interests?' Sean's eyes widened. 'We weren't on the topic of—'

'I'm asking about you,' Tomek replied frantically. Keen to turn the conversation back on Sean. '*Your* love interests. I want to know what's going on with you.'

'Me?' Sean surveyed the room and lowered his head. 'I don't have a love interest.'

'Then what was that fumbling earlier? In Victoria's office?'

'Oh, with Vicky? That was—'

'Vicky?' Now it was time for Tomek's eyes to widen. 'You're on a cutesy first-name basis now, are you?'

Sean flipped him the finger and told him to fuck off. Which Tomek had no intention of doing.

'You're the one who came over here,' he added. 'Now tell me everything.'

For only the second time since Tomek had known him, Sean looked embarrassed, adopting the same nervous schoolchild look he'd worn earlier in the inspector's office.

'We just went out for a couple of drinks one night. The rest of you had gone home, I think, so we thought fuck it and went to the pub. Then we just got talking. You know how it goes.'

'Ever the bachelor,' Tomek remarked. 'And things are... progressing in the right way?'

Sean nodded, his cheeks flushing a darker shade.

'Oh, boy. I can't wait for you to explain that one to Nick when he gets back.'

'No fucking way. I'm leaving that up to her.'

Tomek chuckled. 'Who said chivalry was dead? That must be what she sees in you, that undying need to put others before yourself. In this case, that's exactly what you'll be doing – feeding her to the wolf first.'

'I don't even know what she sees in me.'

'Well, at least we don't have to worry about you selling yourself short!'

Tomek couldn't stop the burst of laughter exploding from his lips. The sound echoed around the office, disturbing those closest to them. When he opened his eyes, he saw Sean clutching his stomach, also giggling along to the joke.

It was moments like that which reminded Tomek there was some light in the darkness. Their job was usually so depressing and devastating that they needed some brightness, no matter how small it was, to keep their spirits up.

'Now you need to tell me about *your* love interest,' Sean said to Tomek, suddenly bringing his laughter to a halt. 'Or should I say *interests*?'

'Me? Love interest? No. I have no idea what you're talking about.'

Before Sean could respond, Tomek's phone began vibrating loudly on the table.

'Saved by the bell.'

Until he saw who was calling.

Edith, his neighbour.

The fourth time in less than two days. Letting him know whether she'd seen anything strange or suspicious in the street. Clarifying when he was going to put up the home security system he'd bought for the building (answer: whenever he remembered and whenever he had the time, which seldom occurred at the same moment).

'Hey, Edith,' he said, rolling his eyes at Sean.

'Hi, Tomek. How are you doing today?'

'Fine, thanks. Is everything all right?'

'Just wanted to let you know that I've seen him again.'

'Who?'

'The man.'

'Oh, right.'

'Yeah. He's been there for about twenty minutes, I'd say. Did you not get the notification on your phone?'

'What notif—? Oh, right, *that*. Well, I haven't had the chance to put up the security camera yet, I'm afraid.'

'Oh. I see.'

'Sorry about that. Work's just been really busy at the moment. I would say you could get Kasia to do it but I think she'd be worse than useless.'

'That's all right. Some other time.'

'Did you want to go and see her?' Tomek asked. 'Might be worth seeing if she saw the man as well. She makes a good cup of tea if you fancy one?'

The sound of rustling echoed through the phone.

'I'll go and knock on the door now. See if she's seen anything.'

Tomek waited on the line as she did so. The noise of slow, steady feet shuffling up the stairs, – the same floorboards he tried to avoid every time he came home late but failed miserably – sounded in his ear.

Until... 'The door's open,' she said. 'Should the door be open?'

'No.' Tomek's voice began to crack.

Edith moved closer towards the door. He could almost see her placing her hand on the handle and gently pushing it.

'Kasia?' came the soft call through the mobile phone.

'Kasia?'

Nothing.

By now Tomek's breathing had stopped, his body had tensed, and his mind had faltered.

'Kasia?'

Still nothing.

Then... 'Are you sure she's supposed to be home, Tomek? Because she's not here.'

CHAPTER FIFTY-TWO

Tomek had never driven home so fast in his life.

In fact, he'd never driven anywhere so fast in his life.

Dangerously so. Swerving in and out of traffic, jumping the lights without easing his foot on the accelerator. All the other cars that had followed him had struggled to keep up. And as he'd pulled up to his home, Sean had called out to him, 'You fucking idiot! You're no good to Kasia if you're dead!'

That may have been true, but right now he didn't care. The most important thing to him was finding Kasia alive, and not dead in some field.

'I want all available units searching the fields in the area,' he ordered to no one in particular. 'Hadleigh. John Burrows. I want them all on high alert for James Elliott.'

There were no more than fifteen people in his tiny two-bedroom flat. Everyone from the team, except for Nadia who had been forced to stay behind and supervise the phone lines if anything came in. A four-person unit of uniformed officers and a two-person scenes of crime team had all ventured his way.

That was the extent of their army. Fifteen, highly-specialised and trained members of the police service versus one man.

So far they had turned the entire flat over, with Tomek doing the bulk of the work, and yet there was no sign of her.

No sign of forced entry. No sign of a struggle.

As he stood in the middle of her bedroom he forced himself to imagine how it must have happened. How the doorbell must have rung, how she must have opened it, expecting it to be him, and how she must have been overpowered. Forced into submission, beaten over the head, bound, tied, then carried back down to the killer's car.

Then his eyes fell on the small Amazon package on the floor beside Kasia's wardrobe.

The home fucking surveillance system.

Mocking him, laughing up at him, telling him *told you so*.

If only he'd put it up sooner. If only he'd done what had been asked of him countless times, he would have at least seen who had abducted her. He would have at least seen the killer in all his conniving glory.

Fury swelled within him, bubbling away like Victoria's Alka-Seltzer. Until eventually it boiled and spilled over the top. Tomek tensed his entire body, grabbed the box from the carpet and began tearing it apart on the bed. Cardboard, plastic, and the components of the device flew in the air as if trying to escape his furious clutches.

It wasn't until Sean yanked him by the shoulder that he stopped.

'The fuck are you doing?' he yelled in Tomek's face.

'I need to install it. Someone needs to install it.'

'They're not going to be able to if your big hands have broken the fucking thing.'

Tomek paused, surveying the carnage he'd made.

'Get someone to do it,' he ordered. 'It needs to be done. Now.'

'You got a drill? A screwdriver?'

Tomek looked at him, baffled.

'I'm going to need those things when I screw it in.'

His brain wasn't functioning properly. So much so that he couldn't answer Sean's question and walked out of the room, leaving the man to it. As he entered the living room, he pointed to Chey and said, 'Help Sean find a screwdriver or something. Didn't realise it took two people to install a fucking security camera.'

Chey nodded, uncertain of himself, then ran off into the bedroom.

As Tomek moved about his flat, he was oblivious to everything and everyone around him. They had blurred into the background, becoming a mirage of shapes and colours. Yet the lucid part of his brain realised that they were still objects and needed to be avoided.

He moved from place to place, pacing, not even thinking.

His mind was working overtime as panic had settled in. He now, finally, began to fully appreciate and understand the torment that all of the families impacted by the killer had gone through. How they must have driven themselves crazy with fear. Even though he was only at the first stage, immediate panic, he knew what else was coming.

Paranoia. Desperation. Dread.

Each with their own nuanced feelings and behaviours.

Lashing out at friends and family, the ones who cared about him.

Driving himself crazy with the thoughts hurtling around his mind like the Large Hadron Collider.

He just prayed that his situation wouldn't end up like all the others. With a dead teenager lying in a field.

A lump swelled in his throat at that thought.

It was gone as soon as he saw who had just walked through the door.

'I've spoken with your neighbour. She's given a witness statement to uniform. We've got her number if we need anything.'

'What are you doing here?' Tomek asked.

'What do you think? I'm back.'

'To help?'

Nick placed a firm, yet comforting hand – the hand of a father – on his shoulder. 'Lucy's not going anywhere, and I can feel myself getting skinnier just sitting around doing nothing. Plus I could do with the distraction.'

A faint flicker of a smile flashed on Tomek's lips. Nick the knight in shining armour. Coming in at the last minute to rescue him and save the day.

As Tomek was about to turn his attention to the next order of business, Chey and Sean exited the bedroom, security camera in hand, carrying it carefully as though the fate of the world rested on it.

'Good to have you back, guv,' Sean said first.

Then Chey. 'Nice to see you again, sir.'

'Gentlemen.'

'Have you got everything you need?' Tomek asked the two handymen.

'We found a screwdriver and drill in your room. Weird place for you to keep it, but I won't pry. Although now we're just missing a couple of batteries.'

CHAPTER FIFTY-THREE

The batteries had to be borrowed from a neighbour. Few of the people in the four houses that they had spoken to owned any. And the ones who did didn't have any that worked.

After several frustrating attempts, of drilling into the wall incorrectly or dropping it onto the floor every time they attempted it, Chey and Sean had finally installed the doorbell camera and it was now fully functional, with notifications coming through to his phone repeatedly.

Two uniformed officers, along with Martin, had remained at his home for the time being, and as they came and went, either for cigarette breaks or phone calls or just to check on the state of the street, Tomek's phone chimed constantly. The first few had been tolerable, manageable, but shortly after that, he'd made the decision to switch off the notifications. The sound was driving him crazy, and he could no longer force himself to listen to it. Besides, if there was an emergency or an update, they'd call.

It was nearly two in the morning, and he was one of a few members of the team left in the office. Sean, Rachel and Nick had remained, while the rest of the team had gone home, ready for an early start in the morning.

'I think you should do the same, mate,' Nick told him.

Shaking his head, Tomek replied, 'With all due respect, guv, no. Home is the last place I want to be. I'm one of the few people who can actually do something about what's happened to Kasia. The rest of these families that go through this are forced to sit there and think the worst. They're useless, they can't do anything to find their loved one. Whereas I can. I'm in the privileged position to be able to do so. I'm not going to throw that away.'

Nick chewed on his bottom lip. 'Admirable, I get it. But you need to sleep at some point.'

'There's a comfortable sofa in one of the interview rooms. Or I'll just spend a night in one of the holding cells.'

'So you can torture yourself even further?' Sean asked from a few metres away. 'Christ, man, never had you down as a masochist.'

Tomek flipped him the finger then turned his attention back to what he was doing.

It was the middle of the night, and so far none of the team of uniformed officers that were stationed in the many fields and parks of Hadleigh and Leigh had reported any sightings. Unfortunately, because the Castle Point borough was so large, with dozens of potential locations and not enough staff to cover them all, the teams were forced to drive around constantly, dipping into each one sporadically. It wasn't the ideal way to do things, but Tomek had quickly come to the realisation that if Kasia had been spotted in any of the fields in the area, then she was dead. A hard truth he had been forced to face in the toilets, while staring into the mirror, wiping his eyes of tears.

The only place they had any reasonable suspicion the killer might have taken her was the building in Shoeburyness. But Tomek wasn't too worried about that as an unmarked police vehicle had been stationed outside there since they'd found it, in the event the killer decided to return.

In the meantime, Tomek was forced to go back to his roots, back to the tasks he used to manage as a detective constable.

The telemetry data for Kasia's phone had been requested, but it turned out her phone had been switched off, the same as all the other victims.

House-to-house enquiries had been conducted along his street, though nobody had seen anything in particular, and those who had, hadn't seen anything important or worth following up on. Instead, he had been left to trawl through the homeowners' various bits of CCTV footage, searching for the killer in the smallest of images.

After twenty minutes of mindlessly staring at the screen, he saw a car pull up to the flat. But thanks to the traffic on the busy street and the angle of the camera, he was unable to discern its make, model or number plate. All he had to go on was the top of the vehicle, white and narrow, a small section of the side panel, and a set of headlights. Nothing else. Even the images of the figure exiting the car were grainy and completely useless.

'Waste of time,' Tomek hissed as he pushed the keyboard away in frustration.

'I know you are,' Sean started, 'but what am—'

Before he was able to finish the sentence, the telephone rang in the office, puncturing the silence. The sound was so loud it made Tomek jump.

'Fuck a duck!' he screamed. 'Who the fuck is calling n—?'

And then he realised. Kasia. Someone calling with information.

At once, Tomek leapt out of his chair and raced across the office to the nearest desk with a phone on it. He yanked the device off the handle and prodded the button that placed it on loudspeaker.

'DS Bowen Southend CID speaking,' he said.

'All right, sarge?' came the voice of a young man who sounded as though he'd just left puberty behind. 'Just a quick one. A car's just driven past the building we've been watching.'

The building where Fern Clements had been stung to death.

'Okay.'

'We think we saw it the night before as well.'

'When last night?'

'About midnight. Maybe the same time.'

Tomek checked the clock: 02:16. He couldn't imagine there were many cars on the road around that time of night unless they were there for one thing: killing, or plotting to kill.

'What do you want us to do, sarge?'

'What do you mean?' Tomek asked, confused.

'Do you want us to follow it?'

'What do you think? Course I fucking do. Get after it and don't call back until you find it.'

CHAPTER FIFTY-FOUR

S oftness.

A softness that felt as though it was protecting her.

That was the first thing she felt. The softness of the mattress. Beyond that, everything else was numb. Her legs, her hips. Even her hands and feet, thanks to the restraints keeping them bound together. The only part of her body that could *feel* was her upper back.

Then she opened her eyes and saw what looked like a bedroom. The only indicator that it was such a room was the mattress she was currently lying on and the wooden wardrobe in the corner. Aside from that, there was nothing else. The walls were bare, save for the holes where picture frames or other indicators of personal effects had hung. At the top of the walls, by the ceiling, the claggy wallpaper was beginning to peel and disintegrate.

The next of her senses to return was smell.

The smell of damp and mould and all the things she'd smelt when she used to live with her mum. Smells that transported her back to that horrible time, to that horrible home.

But this wasn't that home. This wasn't that horrible time.

This was much worse.

She knew what this was. Had read through all of her dad's case notes when he hadn't been looking, overheard him discuss things on his phone calls and heard him allude to them in their conversations with one another.

This was the serial killer who had been kidnapping girls her age and killing them with their allergies.

Well, if that was the case and she was in the killer's secret lair or his home, then she was fucked.

Even the thought of going near a bag of nuts was enough to make her go into anaphylactic shock.

She had no idea how she'd got there. All she remembered was opening the door to a man in a mask, wearing gloves; the same gloves her dad had thousands of pairs of.

Forensic gloves. The kind that stopped his DNA from showing up on any evidence.

What was he going to do with her? Was he going to kill her there and then? Or was he going to make her wait?

It was a long time before she found an answer to those questions.

It was still dark outside when she heard a noise from downstairs. The middle of the night. What time, exactly, she didn't know. But she had been falling in and out of sleep, dipping her toes in and out of the waters of unconsciousness, for the past hour or so. Pulling herself out of the water every time she heard a floorboard creak or a window pane move.

But this time she heard the sound for real. The sound of footsteps approaching. Closer, closer...

A pause, as the killer waited on the other side of the door. The noise of his breathing was audible from behind the wood.

Kasia held her breath so as not to disturb the silence.

Held it until her lungs were about to burst.

And then the figure turned away and headed back downstairs again. The sound of footsteps gently receded, until the whole house eventually fell silent.

It was at that point, once she determined she was as safe as she was ever going to be, that Kasia dipped her toes into the water of unconsciousness again. And within a few seconds, she dived right in.

CHAPTER FIFTY-FIVE

The post-pubescent constable never called back, which as Tomek was about to find out, meant they never caught up with the car.

Once light had finally broken over the horizon, Tomek had decided to pay a visit to the small building. There was little point in him venturing out there in the middle of the night, where his skills and expertise would have been less than useless in the dark. Now, however, with the sun's rays penetrating through the thick grey haze above, he hoped that would change.

A light rain, laced with the chill in the air, had been falling since the early morning, making the drive to the building in Shoeburyness arduous and more treacherous than it needed to be. The roads were narrow enough as it was, and it was made worse by the mud covering the tarmac and his unrelenting impatience to get there as soon as possible.

Waiting for him outside the building were the two constables who'd been watching the building overnight. They were both as young as Chey, if not younger. Early twenties. Very early twenties. And looked as though they had just graduated from college. They were almost identical in every way, height, build, hairstyle, and hair colour. They even had the same tanned skin – except for their noses. Cody, the constable who made the call, was the proud owner of a thin, narrow nose, while Flint, the other constable, had a larger, broken one that seemed to hang off his face.

'Morning, sarge,' Cody said, holding out his hand.

Tomek shook it and then extended the gesture to Flint. Both young men had strong grips for their age. He didn't need to wonder why.

'Tell me everything you know,' Tomek said.

Before Cody could start, the convoy arrived. Nick, Rachel, Sean and the scenes of crime team. Tomek had given himself a head start over them, breaking a few speeding laws on the way. Once they were all out of their respective cars and had completed the introductions, Cody began speaking.

He had the complete floor, all seven of them looking up at him, listening intently. And it was clear to see the nerves of the situation were getting to him. Before he'd even begun, his eyes widened and he started scratching the back of his head.

'Well, we first saw it the other night, didn't we?' he asked Flint. 'Not last night. But the other night. The night before.'

'Two nights in a row,' Tomek commented impatiently. 'Yeah, we get it. Continue.'

'Right. Well, the first time we didn't think nothing of it, you know? We just thought it was some resident who lives round here on the other side of the farms, but then when we saw it again last night, more the early hours of today, really, we thought something might've been up. Not that common for the same car to be driving around here two nights in a row at three o'clock in the morning. Know what I mean?'

Tomek sighed internally. While he realised the constable was still young, and gave him the benefit of inexperience and naïvety, he still found it infuriating to listen to him.

'How do you know it was the same car?'

'Because I recognised it,' Cody responded. 'Well, actually it was Flint who questioned it.'

'Okay,' Tomek said as he turned to the other constable. 'Flint, you sound like the switched-on one. What did you see?'

'Well, it was white.'

'Good start.'

'And that was about it.'

Tomek sighed heavily, this time externally. But as he did so, a gust of wind blew through the field, stopping everyone else from hearing him.

'So you saw a white car and thought to call us?'

'Yes, sarge.'

'Were there any distinguishing features on the car?' Rachel asked, stepping in. 'Did you get a read of the number plate? The make? Model?'

Flint considered for a moment. 'I mean... it was pitch black, and the headlights were switched off. But I think... I think it was a Cactus or something.'

'A what?' Tomek asked. 'We're not in the desert, kid.'

'*Tomek*,' Nick asserted sternly, then took a step forward. 'Do you mean the Citroën Cactus?'

Flint nodded. 'The one with that massive panel in the middle of the side of it that looks like a kid's just drawn a letterbox on it.'

Tomek didn't know what car they were referring to, but judging by the expressions on his colleagues' faces, they knew exactly which one they needed to look for. A white Citroën Cactus.

A white Citroën Cactus that had his daughter locked inside it. Tomek tried to think of James Elliott's cars; of the cars registered in his name, or those he'd had on the driveway. But given that he didn't know what the car looked like in the first place, he realised the endeavour was futile, and that the task was better suited to someone back in the office.

'Have you looked inside the building?' Nick asked.

Both constables shook their heads.

'We've been monitoring it all night. As far as we know, nobody's been inside.'

'Except for when you followed the car.'

Cody's cheeks flushed red. 'Well, yeah. Except for then.'

'So it wasn't all night then, was it?' Tomek said bluntly.

'No. I guess not.'

'Then don't say things that aren't true—'

'Sergeant!' Nick's voice cut through the wind like a scythe and immediately silenced Tomek and the rustling of leaves and trees around them. 'That's enough, thank you. Now, gentlemen, could you please show me to the building?'

The visit was pointless. It was exactly as Tomek had last seen it. Nothing had changed, nothing was out of place. And more importantly, he hadn't found Kasia in there. Which meant she was still out there somewhere, being kept in a secret location they knew nothing about.

Where? Tomek asked himself. But nothing came to mind. Throughout their entire investigation, this was the only building they had discovered. The only place that had a semblance of villainy and evil about it. And there was nothing to suggest that James Elliott had kept any of his victims in his house, or that he had another property he had been keeping them in.

Shortly after seeing the inside of the building, Nick advised that they head back to the station. Unable to turn in the road and head back the way they'd come, they were forced to drive the long way round. Tomek led the pack, with the convoy of cars in his mirror. By now the rain had let up and the clouds had started to break. On the radio, the latest pop song played loudly through the speakers. Kasia liked to listen to it loud, probably because her eardrums were already so destroyed by the volume in her headphones, and he didn't have the heart to turn it down.

As Tomek traversed the narrow, winding roads, avoiding the low-hanging trees and slippery tarmac, something caught his eye. Birds. Specifically, crows. Big, vicious crows, circling over a particular spot in a field to his right. Immediately above the spot was a small, thin cloud of black.

Tomek pulled over abruptly and slammed the handbrake on. The sound of tyres squealing to a stop sounded behind him, but he paid little heed as he exited the car. He didn't know why, but something was pulling him to the birds, to the spot. A magnetism, his intuition.

'What the fuck're you doing, Tomek?' Nick asked as he erupted out of his car. 'Where are you going?'

Tomek ignored them and continued. Skipping over mounds of wet earth, splashing into puddles, wading his way through the rows of vegetables that were growing there. The murder of crows was no farther than a few feet away, but Tomek had noticed the body long before then, thanks to the smell, rancid, putrid, picked up by the wind and carried over to his nostrils.

'Over here!' he screamed, his voice breaking. 'Quick! There's a body!'

Tomek approached with caution, surveying the ground for shoe prints or indentations where the body had been dragged along the surface. His stomach tightened and his body turned cold with fear.

A few feet separated him from potentially staring into the eyes of his dead daughter.

'Stay there!' Tomek called back. If this was Kasia lying face down on the ground, he didn't want anyone else there. He wanted a moment with her before the team came and did the rest. Before they abused and manoeuvred her.

He approached the body slowly, his legs shaking.

It gradually came into view.

And then he breathed a sigh of relief.

The shoes were different: men's. As were the jeans and the coat. And the hair was different too.

A man's. Definitely a man's.

As Tomek crouched down by the man's side, he realised who it was.

Staring into the ground, half his face submerged in the earth, was James Elliott.

CHAPTER FIFTY-SIX

Tomek felt a confusing mix of relief and despair.

Relief that Kasia wasn't dead, that her body hadn't been ditched in the middle of a field somewhere.

And despair that she was still missing, that there was still the chance her body could be ditched in the middle of a field at any point.

The only question remained where... and when.

But he tried not to think about it. Tried to think positively, optimistically. Glass half full, and all that.

A few hours had passed since the discovery of James Elliott's body. In that time, a forensics tent had been erected over him, and a large team of SOCOs were currently gathering evidence from the site. It would be a long time before they were finished and sent home. The cause of death was strangulation, and the working hypothesis was that he had been killed elsewhere, then transported to the farm, where his killer had pulled over on the side of the road, carried his body over to the site, and dropped him there. So far the team had failed to find any shoe prints in the mud, which suggested that his body had been dumped there when the soil had been dry. They had, however, managed to find a set of tyre marks on the side of the road which matched those discovered at the brick building earlier in the investigation. It still didn't confirm the make or model they were looking for, but at least it increased the likelihood that the car they were looking for was indeed a Citroën Cactus.

Based on James Elliott's state of decay, Lorna Dean had estimated that the kit manager had been there at least thirty-six hours, maybe forty-eight.

The first night Flint and Cody had spotted the Citroën Cactus.

New Year's Eve.

The night the car hadn't been followed by the two constables.

The night James Elliott had gone missing.

Which meant someone had abducted and killed him.

Silenced him.

For a particular reason. And Tomek intended to find out what that was. But in the meantime, there was something he needed to do, someone he needed to speak with.

Tomek knocked on the door and waited. The rain had started again, this time harder, carrying with it a vengeance, a dark premonition of things to come.

The door opened a few moments later. Standing in front of him was Mrs Turpin, Billy's mum, wearing a white dressing gown, looking as though she'd just been woken up.

'What are you doing here? I don't want you anywhere near my son. You have to leave otherwise I'm calling the police.'

Tomek chuckled to himself at that last comment. It always made him laugh. 'I am the police,' he retorted.

'This is harassment!' Mrs Turpin reached into the pocket of her dressing gown and pulled out her phone.

Tomek raised his hands in surrender and lowered his tone. 'Please,' he said. 'You don't understand. I need to speak to your son.'

'No!'

'It's about my daughter. She's... she's gone missing.'

That seemed to stop her in her tracks. Slowly, she lowered her phone to her side and loosened her grip on the front door. 'Oh, my God, is she okay? I mean, do you know if she's okay? If she's been hurt? How long's she been missing for?'

'Since last night. She was abducted from our home.'

Billy's mum hesitated a moment then tilted her head to the side. 'I'm so sorry,' she said. Then added, 'But what's this got to do with Billy?'

'I want to speak with him, see if he knows anything.'

'Of course he doesn't. Why would he know anything about your daughter going missing?'

'Because of the football club,' Tomek admitted. 'Someone from his football club is responsible for this and I need to know if anyone's reached out to him, messaged him about Kasia, or asked personal questions about her.'

Billy's mum hesitated, weighing the decision on whether to let him enter.

Eventually, she conceded and stepped aside. Tomek offered her a thankful nod as he entered.

Billy was in the living room, playing on a Nintendo Switch, legs crossed on a sofa so big it swallowed him whole.

'Billy, Kasia's dad is here to see you.'

'What? Why?'

His mum placed a hand on his shoulder. 'I'll let him explain.'

Then she passed the floor to Tomek, who lowered his gaze and met Billy's. The young boy's eyes were wild with fear and apprehension. As though he knew he'd done something bad and was waiting to find out what Tomek knew.

'Last night, Kasia was abducted from our home. I want to know if you know anything about it.'

'I... No...' Billy dropped the games console on the sofa and pressed his knees closer to his chest. 'Is she okay?'

'I don't know.'

'How did it happen?'

'I was hoping you might be able to tell me,' Tomek said. 'Has anyone from the football club been asking questions about Kasia? Anyone wanted to know her movements?'

Billy didn't need to think on it long; he shook his head profusely almost immediately.

'I have no idea. No one from football's messaged me or anything. I don't know why anyone would want to do this to her.'

Tomek did. Tomek had known instantly why she'd been taken. Her nut allergy. The one that Billy had forgotten about and put her in hospital with.

Now that he thought about it, he realised that the black figure had been at the beach for another reason. He had been there for Kasia, watching her. Waiting. If it hadn't been for her proactiveness on the night defending her friend and calling the police, Tomek wondered whether she would have been taken sooner. Whether she would be dead already.

That didn't bear thinking about.

Yet it remained at the forefront of his mind, haunting him, flashing in front of his eyes now and then. Tormenting him.

'So you don't know anything about what happened to her?'

Billy shook his head. 'I'm sorry. No, I don't know anything.'

Tomek looked down to the carpet, dropped his shoulders. 'If you think of anything, or if anyone reaches out to you, please give me a call.'

He reached into his pocket and produced a business card. Billy's mum took it gently from him and inspected it.

'Of course. We'll be in touch if we hear anything. I hope you find her. And I hope she's safe.'

So did Tomek. But if recent history was anything to go by, the window of opportunity to find her alive was closing.

And fast.

CHAPTER FIFTY-SEVEN

Tomek had been back in the station all of thirty seconds before Nick popped his head out of his office door and called him over.

No time to chat with anyone. No time for an update. No time for anything.

And something about the way Nick had called him over suggested the chief inspector wasn't about to tell him anything important either.

'Take a seat,' Nick ordered firmly.

Tomek did as he was told, as he had done so many times in the past.

'A couple of things have come to my attention,' Nick began, 'but first I want to ask how you're doing.'

How do you think I'm fucking doing? Tomek wanted to say but held it in. He remembered his conversation with Nick about Lucy and how Nick had responded to the same question: calmly, controlled, and respectfully, even though he more than likely had felt exactly the same way Tomek did now.

In the end, Tomek answered, 'I just want to find her. I just want to know that she's safe and that nothing's happened to her.'

'I get that. I really do. But I've witnessed the way you're

addressing people, the way you're ordering them around. You can't treat people like shit, Tomek. The way you spoke to Cody and Flint earlier, that was unacceptable, mate.'

Tomek bit his lip. Took his frustration out on his gums.

'And the way you've been ordering members of the team. We all want to find Kasia. Honestly, we do. But behaving like that isn't going to help, and it isn't going to make us work more effectively. You're under a *lot* of stress, I get that, *we* get that, but there are boundaries, mate. Christ knows what you must be going through. This is nothing like what happened to Lucy, but I think out of everyone I'm probably closest to it. And I had nothing to do with the arrest of Paddy Battersby, and I think that was a good thing. I think I needed to be distanced from that. Otherwise... fucking hell, I would have gone into that interview room and beaten the fuck out of him.' Nick ran his hand over his bald head as if polishing it with his sweat. 'Do you see what I'm saying?'

Of course he saw what Nick was saying. How couldn't he? It was as obvious and as blinding as the reflection on Nick's scalp.

'You want me to take a step back from the investigation into my own daughter's kidnapping?'

'I—'

'You must be joking, right? No. No way. I'm not gonna fucking sit back and put my feet up like some cunt.'

'No one's asking you to. You can still have an active role in finding your daughter. You just...'

'What?'

'...let us do all the talking.'

Tomek had had enough of grinding his teeth and instead clamped down on his tongue so hard he quickly began tasting metal in his mouth.

'Is that it?' he asked bluntly. 'My daughter's missing and you've just come to have a go at me and tell me off for overreacting and behaving the way I am.'

'Like nothing's changed... remember?'

Tomek was reminded of their conversation on the seafront.

'Like nothing's changed,' he said, expelling air through his nostrils and turning away from the chief inspector.

'Are you going to calm down before you go back out there?' Nick asked.

'Maybe. Why?'

'Because I need you to. I have a surprise for you.'

'Unless you've found my daughter, I wouldn't use that word around me if I were you.'

Nick shifted uncomfortably on his chair. 'Right. Yes. Apologies.'

'Well... Go on then, what is it?'

'*LEAVE IT WITH ME*,' Nick had told him on the seafront.

And so he had. But not because he trusted Nick to come through on his promise (that was a given already), but because he had completely forgotten. Harrison Rossiter had been forced to the back of his mind as trying to find James Elliott and his daughter came to the fore.

But now the young man was here. Arriving at the station in less than ten minutes. Flown in by Nick on a last-minute flight.

'How did you get him over here?' Tomek had asked.

'Well, I told him it was a police investigation, and if he didn't, then we'd send some of the French police round to his house. That put the fear of God into him, and now here he is.'

Ten minutes later, Harrison Rossiter, the Ligue 1 academy player, entered through the station doors and was welcomed by Anna and a civilian support officer. He was then led to one of the interview rooms and Tomek was notified.

As he headed to the room, Tomek began to sweat, and a smell seeped from his underarms. He was nervous. More than nervous. Shitting himself.

The young man, all six foot two of him, potentially knew the identity of the killer.

Knew the identity of his daughter's abductor.

The answer to where Kasia was being kept, and who was keeping her under his control.

Tomek braced himself as he placed his hand on the handle.

He opened the door.

Found Harrison Rossiter sitting at the table, back straight, hands knitted together, resting calmly on the surface. The complete opposite of Billy the Cow Fighter. He imagined the seventeen-year-old would have been slouched on the chair, legs spread wide open, maybe even one of his feet resting on the edge of the table. But not Harrison. The young adult had an air of decorum, respectability and manners about him. As though the French had drummed those attributes into him not just on the football field but also in the real world.

Because, as Tomek read so frequently, the chances of him ever making it professionally were astronomically small, so they had to prepare their academy players for the wider world of life.

Tomek just hoped he was as honest as he was respectful.

He reached out his hand. 'Pleasure to meet you, Harrison. Thank you for coming on such short notice.'

'That's... okay.'

'Do you know why you've been brought into the station today?'

As soon as the questions started, Harrison began playing with his fingers. 'The officer we spoke to, Chief Inspector Cleaves, said it was about a concert a few years ago.'

'Yes. That's about right. In particular, the concert you attended two years ago at the Cliffs Pavilion. Do you remember it?'

Harrison didn't think for long. 'Catfish were playing.'

'That's the one. What can you tell me about that night?'

Tomek fought every urge in his body to ask the kid outright who he'd bought the drugs from, but he suppressed it. Against his better judgement. It was wiser to settle the boy in, relax him, get him used to the questions and the types of questions, and then he would go in for the kill.

'It was Avena's idea to go. I wasn't much of a fan myself, but I'm always up for doing stuff with my mates, creating memories and that. So I left all the organising to them and just paid what I owed and turned up. From what I remember, we got there quite early so we could be near the front, but then throughout the night we all got split up as someone invariably ended up needing the toilet, so someone else would go with them, and then someone else realised they needed to go as well. So, I mean, before the accident, there was just me, Avena and Priti.'

'How far away were you from the stage?'

Harrison chuckled softly. 'Typically, because we all kept getting split up, we floated farther and farther away from the stage into the middle. There was nobody to secure our positions and, you know what it's like, everyone tries to push in as much as they can.'

'And at what point did someone offer you drugs?'

Then the conversation stopped. Harrison's body lost all posture, he stopped playing with his fingers, and the steady rise and fall of his chest quickened.

As his face contorted, deep in thought, his pupils began to dilate.

'You're not in trouble for it,' Tomek said. 'And nobody needs to tell your parents if that's what you're worried about. Kids take drugs all the time. Obviously, we don't like it at all. But what we really have a problem with, and what *I* really have a problem with, is when people lace those drugs with chemicals and poison. That's what happened to your friend Avena, isn't it?'

Harrison dropped his gaze into his lap, and nodded, unable to look Tomek in the eye.

'Fortunately, your friend was lucky. She was lucky she was sensible enough to only have half that pill, and she was lucky that you all reacted as fast as you did. But some other people haven't been so lucky. Do you understand what I mean?'

Another nod, this time lifting his head a fraction higher.

'The person who supplied you and your friends with drugs has done a lot worse since that night,' Tomek continued. 'And now we need to find out who he is and where he is.'

More nodding, more lifting.

'And when I spoke with Avena, she informed me that you seemed to know the person who sold you the drugs. Said you gave him a hug. Said you knew him from football. Is that right?'

'*Oui*,' Harrison said, then corrected himself. 'Yeah.'

'Great. Now, I just want to let you know, that by telling me his name, nothing's going to happen to you. We're not going to arrest you, and we will keep your name out of the investigation as much as possible, but I hope, like me, you want to put this guy where he belongs. Behind bars, right?'

'Right.'

'Great. Now, in your own time, I want you to tell me who sold you those drugs from the football club.'

CHAPTER FIFTY-EIGHT

Within seconds, the name that had come out of Harrison Rossiter's mouth was written at the top of the whiteboard in the incident room.

Within minutes, it was common knowledge, and everyone in the team, including the emergency response units that had been sent to his last known address, were made aware.

As part of their earlier discussion, Nick had requested Tomek stay behind, while the rest of the team went on the hunt. That way, if Tomek came across him, he wouldn't be tempted to bash the man's face in.

Not that he would, of course, because for the past thirty minutes, he'd been unable to process anything at all. He couldn't even think of his own name, so beating someone to within an inch of their life was beyond him.

While he didn't agree with the decision to be left behind, he realised that he could use the time to try to better understand the killer's role in each killing. To gather the evidence for each murder, so that when the case went to trial, the CPS would have everything they needed.

It was a rather logical, well thought through decision that surprised even himself.

At first, he started with the most recent case. Fern Clements. The fifteen-year-old girl from Hadleigh. He scanned through all the evidence the team had compiled over the weeks; the list of individuals at her school, her teachers, her family friends, anyone she'd spoken to online, and found the killer's name amongst it all.

Then he moved on to Lily Monteith's death. Surveyed the evidence that had been collected in her murder, similar evidence to that gathered for Fern Clements. Found the killer's name in there also.

And then, after an hour of investigating, he'd arrived at Mandy Butler's death. And all the other victims who had been spiked. Tomek found the killer's name amongst them all. Linked by one thing: their school. At each point, all five victims had gone to the same school but later found themselves in different institutions for one reason or another.

And then it came to Diana Greenock. And the list of tenants who had been living in the same building as her. The list that had been sitting on his desk for the past week. The one he'd been too busy to look through. The name that had been sitting on the fifth row of that list.

The name of the killer.

Lastly, Tomek checked the list given to him by the Human Resources administrator at Dagenham & Redbridge FC. On this particular list, he was unable to find the killer's name. But after a quick phone call, speaking with the same woman who originally gave him the list, Tomek received the confirmation he needed to prove that the killer had worked at the club in a limited capacity, and only for a brief time.

By the end of it all, he felt spent, almost bereft. His mind had only just finished processing it, and he didn't know what to think. Didn't know how to think.

He lifted his gaze to look at the killer's name on the whiteboard.

Felt his blood begin to boil.

And then his phone vibrated.

A notification from his home security camera, this time without the sound.

Someone was at his door.

Had arrived two minutes ago.

Tomek prodded the notification and waited for the biometrics of his face to unlock the device.

And then he saw it. The killer, Kasia's abductor, holding his daughter in his arms, carrying her into his home.

Using her key.

Then shutting the door behind them.

Tomek almost dropped the phone onto his desk.

The killer was there. The killer was in his home.

But more importantly, Kasia was alive.

For now.

CHAPTER FIFTY-NINE

S oftness.
    A softness that felt as though it was protecting her.

And this time it was.

Familiar. Friend not foe.

The softness of a mattress that was her own. The smell of her Persil washing detergent and body odour pressed into the fibres. The dip in the centre of her pillow, the grooves of her body from where she slept in the foetal position.

She was in her own bed, her own bedroom. Unless it was an eerily exact replica.

Then the lights switched on and she confirmed it.

Her bedroom, their flat.

But why? Why here?

Had he had a change of heart and wanted to give her back? Or was he going to kill her here to make it more symbolic?

The past few hours had been a blur. She had lain perfectly still for most of them, staring at the sunlight through the curtains, listening, waiting. Ignoring the sound of her stomach growling at her. She couldn't remember the last time she'd eaten, nor the last time she'd had water. And she was feeling weak, her body depleted of all its energy. If he came in and attacked her now, she didn't think she could defend herself. She didn't think she could do anything.

And then the door opened. And she saw her attacker for the first time. In all their previous interactions he'd been wearing a mask and rubber gloves. And now was no different. Except he had no face mask on, and in his arms, he held several giant bags of nuts, of different sorts. Peanuts. Cashews. Macadamia. Brazil. Pistachios.

All the types of nuts that could kill her if she didn't seek urgent medical attention.

The most bizarre and ridiculous murder weapon ever.

'Good evening, Kasia,' he said, his voice tempered, cold. 'Or should I say, *dzien dobry*?'

CHAPTER SIXTY

Tomek skidded to a stop in the middle of the road. Before the engine had completely shut off, he was already out of the car and racing towards the killer's vehicle.

The killer's Citroën Cactus.

The car that he had seen several times but had never noticed.

Before leaving the office, Tomek had grabbed a pair of scissors, more as a weapon of defence than attack, and as he skipped up to the kerb beside the Citroën, he stabbed the blades into the tyres, puncturing each one as he made his way around the car. That way there would be no quick and easy escape.

With the air hissing out of the rubber behind him, he hurried towards his home. The front door was closed, locked.

Bastard.

If he went in guns blazing, which was very much what he wanted to do; he wanted to kick the door down and rugby tackle the killer to the ground but then he would lose the element of surprise and might risk endangering Kasia's life. More so than it already was.

Instead, he was now forced to do it slowly.

Time ticked by as he quietly removed his house key from his pocket and inserted it into the lock.

Tick. Tock.

Images of Kasia lying in the flat somewhere – *dead* – flashed in his mind.

Tick. Tock.

And then the door unlocked. He was in.

At the bottom of the stairs, he stopped, waited, held his breath, listened.

The sounds of a struggle, of discomfort echoed through the flat. But not the sound of distress or screaming.

Had he started yet? Or was she in her last paroxysms, fighting the final throes of death as she suffered on the floor or the bed?

Tomek decided not to wait any longer. To fuck with the element of surprise.

Fuck it all.

He bounded up the stairs, leaping them two at a time, his heavy feet shaking the building. From the top of the stairs, he saw Kasia's bedroom light was on and headed towards it. He didn't wait at the door – immovable object met unstoppable force – and burst through.

The sight made him want to cry.

Lying there, in the centre of the bed, with her hands tied behind her back, was Kasia. His daughter, his lovely daughter. Surrounding her was a mountain of nuts and peanuts, covering every inch of her exposed flesh and her pastel-coloured duvet. She was cowered into a ball, gasping and wheezing as her body fought for the strength to survive.

He didn't know how long she had been like this, but he knew that she needed immediate medical attention.

And then he saw the killer. The man who had been haunting so many girls, ending their dreams and no doubt living in the nightmares of other girls like them.

The man who had come into his home several times.

The man who had witnessed Kasia's allergies first-hand. By accident, yes, but he had still witnessed them, nonetheless.

Phillip Balham.

Standing over her on the other side of the bed, sprinkling peanuts over his daughter's almost lifeless body.

'*Cześć*, Tomek,' Phillip said, the hint of a smile flashing behind his teeth.

'Fuck you!' Tomek spat and lunged towards Kasia's bedside table, where he grabbed one of her EpiPens. Then, crawling on his knees, he raced back to her side, swept a mound of nuts from Kasia's leg, and pulled down her jogging bottoms, exposing the top of her thigh. Without thinking, he tore open the packaging, and jammed the pen into her leg, slowly injecting the antidote into her bloodstream.

'Kasia!' he screamed, slapping her face gently. 'Kasia, can you hear me?'

But she couldn't. Her eyes were rolling in the back of her head.

He slapped her face again, harder this time. Shaking her. Willing her to come round, for her mind to return to the present, to the bedroom, to him.

'Kasia! No, no, no! Come on, stay with me. Don't you fucking dare do anything like this to me. I can't lose you.'

More slapping, more shaking.

Until, eventually, her eyes became more lucid, as though she was in full control of them now. And then she blinked. Repeatedly.

'Dad?'

It wasn't much, but it was enough to let him know that she was going to be all right. That she was going to live.

That he had saved her.

'I'm here, sweetheart,' he told her. 'You're going to be all right. I'm going to make sure of it. But first, there's something else I need to do.'

Tomek reached for one of her several pillows and lowered her head carefully onto it. Then he turned his attention to where Phillip Balham had been standing.

But the man was no longer there.

Phillip Balham, just as he had done throughout the entire investigation, had slipped out of Tomek's clutches.

CHAPTER SIXTY-ONE

Tomek didn't like the idea of leaving Kasia alone. But he liked the idea of letting Phillip Balham escape even less.

So he made the decision to leave Kasia in the bedroom. Alone. But as he made his way out of the building, he stopped at the flat below, beating his fists on her door.

'Edith! Edith! It's Tomek. Are you home? I need your help. Can you—'

The door opened, and standing in front of him was a tired and scared Edith, shielding herself behind the door.

'You're home,' Tomek said, gasping for air. 'I need your help. I need you to call an ambulance. It's an emergency. Kasia's going into anaphylactic shock. Tell them that she's had an EpiPen injection. Tell them who I am and get them to send the police. I need you to stay with her while you wait.'

'Is it safe up there?' she asked weakly.

'Yes. The man who did this has gone.'

'Where?'

Now that was the question.

'I don't know,' he said, turning towards the street. 'But I intend to find out.'

He set off before she could respond. At the end of the driveway, he came to a stop. The Citroën Cactus was still there, presumably left abandoned after Phillip had noticed the tyres. Which meant the man was escaping on foot.

But where? Which way? Left or right?

Tomek was reminded of a similar situation he had been in the month before when Kasia had run away. While he had been saying goodbye to her teacher, she had snuck out of the bedroom window and disappeared down to the beach at Old Leigh. Back then Tomek had asked Sean to put a trace on her mobile number. But there would be little time to do that now. Not with what he had planned for Phillip when he finally got his hands on him.

Think, Tomek, think.

If he was Phillip Balham, where would he be? Which way would he have gone?

He ran through the information he knew about the hyperpolyglot: the man lived somewhere in Southend, not Leigh, which suggested he might not know the area very well. But there was one particular area of Leigh-on-Sea Tomek knew for a fact that Phillip was familiar with.

And that was the same place Kasia had gone when she'd tried running away.

Bell Wharf Beach, Old Leigh.

The same place Lucy Cleaves had been attacked. Where, he now realised, Phillip, and not James Elliott, had been waiting, watching in the shadows, and then escaped along the seafront to the Grosvenor Casino: his place of work.

The journey to the seafront was a little under half a mile. A ten-minute walk on a good day. And Phillip already had a head start on him. On foot. Running.

Tomek didn't know much about the man's athletic ability, but he knew that he was in fairly good condition. Daily runs for the past twenty years had kept him in as good a shape as he could manage. However in recent weeks, since Kasia had come into his life, he had found the well that had once contained the time to run, and his willpower to do it, suddenly dried up. And as he made it to the end of the road, some two hundred metres from the house, he was seriously beginning to feel it. Panting heavily, blowing out of his arsehole.

It was as though his lungs now had the capacity of a sixty-year-old, and he was only a few more strides away from keeling over.

But so, too, was Phillip Balham.

Tomek spotted the murderer a few hundred feet in front of him, faltering, his pace slowing.

And then the man looked back. As soon as he saw Tomek bounding after him, he increased his pace and lengthened the gap between them.

A few minutes later, both gasping for breath, both wishing they had never run in the first place, they reached the steep steps that led down to Old Leigh. They were the metaphorical steps between new and old town centres, and Tomek had climbed them hundreds of times – on his own, on his runs, with friends – but none of those times was harder than this. By the time he reached them his legs were like jelly, and with each step, he felt like his body was going to give way. Fortunately, there was a handrail for him to hold on to and support his weight. Using it, he guided himself down the steps, happy to forgo his dignity for one evening.

At the bottom of the steps, he hobbled after Phillip, who was still a few strides ahead, running towards a small bridge that crossed the train line from London's Fenchurch Street to Shoeburyness. This time he was forced to climb the staircase, and he grunted with each step, his lungs and body screaming at him.

The distance between them gradually diminished.

Ten feet.

Nine.

Tomek could smell the man's desperation to escape.

And he could smell his own desire to stop him at all costs.

When the distance between them was only a few feet, Tomek launched himself at Phillip, rugby tackling the man to the floor at the apex of the bridge. The man's body felt soft as he placed all his weight on it. Years of rugby training both socially and playing for the force's team had taught him how to attack properly, safely, and without causing injury. It had also taught him how to tackle someone to the ground in the worst way possible, using his body weight against theirs to crush them and inflict as much pain as possible.

For Phillip Balham, Tomek had used the latter technique.

'Get off me!'

'Go fuck yourself! You're lucky I don't throw you off this fucking bridge!'

Using his left forearm, Tomek pinned Phillip's face to the concrete bridge, pressing his other arm into the small of the man's back.

He fought every urge in his body to lower his forearm onto the man's neck and hold it there.

'You're going to pay for what you've done,' he said.

'I think you arrived too late,' Phillip said, goading him. 'Too late to save your own daughter. What sort of a father are you?'

'One who's very close to taking the law into his own hands.'

Phillip's eyes flicked from the ground up to Tomek for a moment.

'Do it,' he said, as he chewed on dirt and spat it back out again. 'Do it. It won't bring her back. It won't bring any of them back.'

'I know it won't. But it'll stop you from taking any more victims.'

'Kasia was always going to be the last one,' Phillip said. 'I saved her for last.'

'Why?'

'Because she was the big finale. Death by touch. Death by peanuts. How can something so tiny and insignificant can have that effect on a human? I was doing everyone a favour. I was ridding the world of its weaknesses.'

'So you killed teenage girls using their allergies? Befriended them until they trusted you? Trusted you enough to get into your car at least?'

'Those girls didn't trust me,' Phillip gasped between breaths as Tomek increased the pressure he placed on his face. 'They just saw me a couple of times a week at school or when I came over to teach them their languages. They were stupid and dumb and saw that I had a car.

I was the friendly Polish, French, German and Spanish tutor; who would ever think to question me?'

Tomek hadn't. The man hadn't given him a reason to. Phillip had seemed normal to all intents and purposes. Just an ordinary bloke trying to make his way in the world and getting by with the money he earned from tutoring, teaching in schools, and working in the casino.

'Did you kill James Elliott as well?' Tomek asked as soon as the thought popped into his head.

Phillip didn't answer. Instead, he began maniacally laughing into the filth.

'James was a loose end that needed tying up,' he replied. 'He wanted to meet on New Year's Eve, so I obliged. He was getting worried about the questions you were asking regarding the car, so I took care of him. Couldn't have him opening his mouth and spilling my name out of it.'

Tomek struggled to suppress the rage from boiling within him. It increased every time Phillip spoke, every time the man flashed that smug grin at him. As though he was proud of his achievements, proud of all that he'd accomplished: ridding the world of five individuals who possessed a unique weakness. Tomek felt a wave of frustration flood through him and added more force to the man's face.

Continued pressing and pressing.

Pressing and pressing.

Thinking of Kasia... And the bed... And the peanuts... And the intrusion into his home.

Until...

'Tomek! Tomek!'

The voice, deep and hoarse, was succeeded by the heavy sound of footsteps stomping on concrete. A moment later, Nick appeared at the top of the bridge, gasping, panting, his stomach and man-boobs catching up with the rest of him a fraction of a second later.

'What're you doing here?' Tomek asked, still pressing his weight down on Phillip.

'I followed you,' he said. 'Just took me a while to catch up.' Nick came to a jolting halt a few feet from Tomek and placed his hands on his knees, bent double, gasping. 'Don't do anything stupid, Tomek. He's not worth it.'

Nick took a tentative step forward, raising his hands slowly.

'Get off him, Tomek. Let me take it from here.'

But Tomek couldn't hear him. Couldn't hear anything. By now the aggression and fury inside his head had muted all other sounds, and the only realisation he had that he was still crushing Phillip's face into the concrete was the writhing man himself.

As soon as Nick approached, he placed a hand on Tomek's shoulder, bringing him to.

'Get off him, mate,' Nick said gently. 'It's done. It's over. You got him.'

But Tomek didn't hear him. All he could think about was that it was done. That Phillip Balham would no longer be able to hurt anyone.

That Kasia would be safe.

CHAPTER SIXTY-TWO

Tomek awoke as soon as he felt the soft touch of her fingers on his hands. He opened his eyes drearily, groggily, and looked up to see Kaisa at the end of the hospital bed, hooked up to the machinery, her brown hair tied above her head.

At that moment, she looked so much like her mother. Beautiful, elegant, powerful, even though everything about the situation and her surroundings suggested the opposite.

'How long have you been here?' she asked.

'I never left,' he replied as he sat up straight. Then he squeezed her hand, feeling the tiny bones and cartilage flex underneath his strain. 'How are you feeling?'

'Like I've been hit by a bus.'

'Double-decker or single?'

Kasia rolled her eyes. 'Minibus, *actually*,' she said, with an "actually" that the Captain would be proud of.

Then she began laughing. But as soon as she started, she burst into a coughing fit. Within a few moments, the contents of her lungs were on her hands, and she wiped them on the bed.

'Doctor said that might be one of the side effects,' Tomek said.

'Coughing?'

'No. Having a dry sense of humour.'

'I think that's just a symptom of being your daughter.'

The thought made him smile.

Your daughter.

His daughter.

My daughter. Even the notion of it seemed strange to him still. So much had happened since she'd come into his life, a complete upheaval but he wouldn't have changed anything.

Well, not quite anything.

'That's the last time you take a Polish lesson. You want to learn the language, you can watch some Polish TV shows and pick it up that way. Or you can go to your grandma's and learn it in the comfort of her living room from her. Your choice.'

For a while, Kasia didn't answer. Her face contorted and she looked as though she was deep in thought.

'Not literally, by the way. You don't have to choose right now.'

'I know, I just...' She dropped her head. 'I wondered... What's happened to him? Did you... did you find him?'

'Yes,' Tomek said bluntly, straight to the point. He wanted to be transparent and honest with her and hoped that one day in the future she would be transparent and honest with him. 'You won't ever have to see Phillip Balham again.'

'Why not?'

'Because we took him into the police station and he's being charged with what he did to you.'

'Like Paddy,' Kasia repeated. 'The same as what happened to Lucy?'

'Yeah, like that.'

'Have you told Mum I'm here?' Kasia asked.

Not only did her voice take him by surprise and draw him from his thoughts but the content of her question startled him. Kasia hadn't spoken about her mother in weeks, almost to the point where Tomek had forgotten she existed, and where he'd been convinced that she'd forgotten about her as well.

But now she had chosen to mention her. Now of all moments.

He sighed and chewed his bottom lip.

'I haven't, no. Not yet. Would you like me to?'

'Yes.'

And then an idea popped into his head.

'How about we tell her in person, together?'

A scintilla of appreciation flashed across her face.

'Yes, please. But make it on a school day. I want an excuse not to go in,' she said, then lowered her head to the pillow again.

That was an argument Tomek couldn't refuse.

CHAPTER SIXTY-THREE

Everything about it had become familiar to him now. The sound of shouting, chatter and laughter over the noise of food frying. The smell of bacon and egg and all manner of delicious goodness wafting through the air, and sitting comfortably in his nostrils. The sight of the café's regular clientele.

And even the company he found himself in had become familiar to him now.

Abigail Winters had, as always, arranged the meeting last minute, expecting him to drop everything he had going on in his life for her. And, on this occasion, fortunately for her, he had nothing keeping him busy: Nick had forced him to take a backseat while he processed what had happened to Kasia. Meanwhile, Kasia had returned to school. So the flat was empty, and there was nothing for him to do.

The woman sitting beside Abigail, however, was not familiar to him.

Abigail had introduced her as Martha Buhl, the sixth and potentially first victim of Phillip Balham.

'You know, you should really be doing this with Sean or someone else in the team,' he told Abigail just as the waitress arrived with their servings of double egg, double bacon, and double toast. Tomek thanked her and then watched her go. And as she left, he noticed her looking back, catching his eye.

'I don't *want* to talk to anyone else in the team,' Abigail replied, pulling him back to the conversation. 'I want Martha to tell *you*.'

'Fine. Then tell me.' He turned to Martha, who had pushed her food to the side. 'What did Phillip Balham do to you in Germany?'

And then he found out.

Several years ago, ten, to be precise, Martha Buhl had been living in a block of flats in a quiet, secluded part of Frankfurt. She had first encountered Phillip just after he'd moved into the building, and the two of them had become friends. She had admired his bravery in moving to a country for a year just so he could learn the language. At the time, Martha had been working in a hospital, living in the ground-floor flat, working all hours of the day and night, and finding herself asleep at all parts of the day. Until, one evening, while her boyfriend at the time was staying over, a cat had come in through the window and caused her to have a severe allergic reaction. If it hadn't been for her boyfriend, the one Phillip knew nothing about, rescuing her with her EpiPen and a swift phone call to the emergency services, her allergies – the ones Phillip knew *everything* about – would have ended up killing her. Martha's first suspicions had begun as soon as Phillip had started to take a keen interest in her allergies and her dislike of cats. He had, according to her, adopted one during his stay in the building, treating it and feeding it as though it were his own. The same cat that had climbed in through her window in the night, sent to kill her, placed there by the vindictive killer, Phillip Balham.

As soon as she had been discharged from the hospital, Martha had taken the case to the police, only to be laughed at and sent away. And by the time she had returned to the block of flats, Phillip had moved out of the building and gone to another part of the country. For a short while she had shouted and fussed over the Internet, but in the end she had run out of steam and decided that he was never coming back to hurt her.

Until she had heard about the stories in the UK.

The one in Manchester which bore the same hallmarks, and the one that had been all but confirmed thanks to Phillip Balham's name turning up on the tenant list at the same time Diana Greenock had died.

'Abigail told me that Phillip has killed four other women?' Martha finished.

'Yes. He knew them from either working in their schools in a pastoral role, embedding himself heavily into the lives of those with allergies that way, or teaching them foreign languages, either in school or... from the comfort of their own homes. He targeted them based on their ages and their allergies. They were weaker, vulnerable, more susceptible to him.'

'He is despicable,' she hissed.

'That he is,' Tomek said. 'That he is.'

'How did he do it?'

'Well, his first victim in the UK was Diana Greenock from Manchester. A nurse, allergic to cats, living in a ground-floor flat, just like you. We believe he got to know her during his time at football games. A chance encounter that turned into a murder. And based on what you've told me, I would say what he did to you was the blueprint for what he did to her. At the time, he was teaching in the area, where he befriended Mandy Butler, his second victim. There, he taught her Spanish in her secondary school for her GCSEs. And after he found out about her moving down to Essex, he followed her. Only to stumble upon a wealth of opportunity in our schools. It was a while before he killed again, but in that time he was selecting them, working his way into his victims' lives one way or another. Teaching them, helping them, gaining their trust.' Tomek finished the last of his breakfast. 'But now he won't be able to hurt anyone again. Other than himself.'

'That would be a coward's way out for him,' Martha replied.

'Sadly, I think that's just the type of person he is.'

When the meeting had finally come to an end, Tomek paid the bill and then walked the two women to Abigail's car. Martha slipped into the passenger seat while Abigail rounded the front of the vehicle and came to a stop immediately in front of him.

'Told you I could get you a meeting with her,' she said triumphantly, eyeing him up and down.

'I'm impressed.'

She placed a hand on his arm and squeezed. 'I know you are. Don't forget,' she said as she opened the driver's door.

'Don't forget what?'

'You owe me.'

'No, I don't,' he replied.

'One date, Tomek Bowen. That's all I'm asking you for. It's not like I'm asking you to marry me.'

DEATH'S KISS

Tomek Bowen returns in...

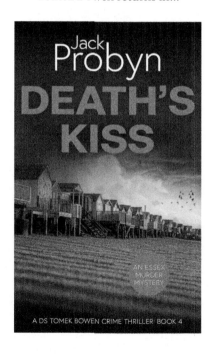

The darkest secrets never stay secret for long...
When the body of a homeless man is discovered on Southend
seafront, wedged between the beach huts of Thorpe Bay, the people
of Essex don't raise an eyebrow.

But when the post-mortem reveals the identity to be that of local MP,
Herbert Tucker, the town begins to sit up.

As the tide of political and media pressure begins to swell, DS Tomek
Bowen must navigate the turbulent waters of the MP's past to
determine who would want to stage such a dramatic end for him.

Although, with a history as colourful as Herbert's, it soon becomes
clear there's no shortage of suspects.

Read Now

ALSO BY JACK PROBYN

The DS Tomek Bowen Murder Mystery Series:

1) DEATH'S JUSTICE

Southend-on-Sea, Essex: Detective Sergeant Tomek Bowen — driven, dogged, and haunted by the death of his brother — is called to one of the most shocking crime scenes he has ever seen. A man has been ritualistically murdered and dumped in an allotment near the local airport. Early investigations indicate this was a man with a past. A past that earned him many enemies.

Download Death's Justice

2) DEATH'S GRIP

Annabelle Lake thought she recognised the Ford Fiesta waiting outside her school, and the driver in it. She was wrong. Her body is discovered some time later, dangling from a swing in a local playground on Canvey Island.

Download Death's Grip

3) DEATH'S TOUCH

When the fog clears one December morning in Essex, the body of a teenage girl is discovered lying face down in a field. But as soon as the investigation begins, Tomek discovers Lily's death may be linked to a killing spree that has lain dormant for many years — with no one ever being brought to justice for it.

Download Death's Touch

4) DEATH'S KISS

The body of a teenage girl is found face down in the middle of a field. The evidence surrounded her death is scant, until a vital clue uncovers a terrifying serial killer lying in wait...

Download Death's Kiss

The Jake Tanner Crime Thriller Series:

Full-length novels that combine police procedure, organised crime and police corruption.

TOE THE LINE:

A small jeweller's is raided in Guildford High Street and leaves police chasing their tails. Reports suggest that it's The Crimsons, an organised crime group the police have been hunting for years. When the shop owner is kidnapped and a spiked collar is attached to her neck, Jake learns one of his own is involved – a police officer. As Jake follows the group on a wild goose chase, he questions everything he knows about his team. Who can he trust? And is he prepared to find out?

Download Toe the Line

WALK THE LINE:

A couple with a nefarious secret are brutally murdered in their London art gallery. Their bodies cleaned. Their limbs dismembered. And the word LIAR inscribed on the woman's chest. For Jake Tanner it soon becomes apparent this is not a revenge killing. There's a serial killer loose on the streets of Stratford. And the only thing connecting the victims is their name: Jessica. Jake's pushed to his mental limits as he uncovers The Community, an online forum for singles and couples to meet. But there's just one problem: the killer's been waiting for him... and he's hungry for his next kill.

Download Walk the Line

UNDER THE LINE:

DC Jake Tanner thought he'd put the turmoil of the case that nearly killed him behind him. He was wrong. When Danny Cipriano's body is discovered buried in a concrete tomb, Jake's wounds are reopened. But one thing quickly becomes clear. The former leader of The Crimsons knew too much.

And somebody wanted him silenced. For good. The only problem is, Jake knows who.

Download Under the Line

CROSS THE LINE:

For years, Henry Matheson has been untouchable, running the drug trade in east London. Until the body of his nearest competitor is discovered burnt to a lamppost in his estate. Gang war gone wrong, or a calculated murder? Only one man is brave enough to stand up to him and find out. But, as Jake Tanner soon learns, Matheson plays dirty. And in the estate there are no rules.

Download Cross the Line

OVER THE LINE:

Months have passed since Henry Matheson was arrested and sent to prison. Months have passed since Henry Matheson, one of east London's most dangerous criminals, was arrested. Since then DC Jake Tanner and the team at Stratford CID have been making sure the case is watertight. But when a sudden and disastrous fraudulent attack decimates Jake's personal finances, he is propelled into the depths of a dark and dangerous underworld, where few resurface.

Download Over the Line

PAST THE LINE:

The Cabal is dead. The Cabal's dead. Or so Jake thought. But when Rupert Haversham, lawyer to the city's underworld, is found dead in his London home, Jake begins to think otherwise. The Cabal's back, and now they're silencing people who know too much. Jake included.

Download Past the Line

The Jake Tanner SO15 Files Series:

Novella length, lightning-quick reads that can be read anywhere. Follow Jake as he joins Counter Terrorism Command in the fight against the worst kind of evil.

THE WOLF:

A cinema under siege. A race to save everyone inside. An impatient detective. Join Jake as he steps into the darkness.

Download *The Wolf*

DARK CHRISTMAS:

The head of a terrorist cell is found dead outside his flat in the early hours of Christmas Eve. What was he doing outside? Why was a suicide vest strapped to his body? And what does the note in his sock have to do with his death?

Download *Dark Christmas*

THE EYE:

The discovery of a bomb factory leaves Jake and the team scrambling for answers. But can they find them in time?

Download *The Eye*

IN HEAVEN AND HELL:

An ominous — and deadly — warning ignites Jake and the team into action. An attack on one of London's landmarks is coming. But where? And when? Failure could be catastrophic.

Download *In Heaven And Hell*

BLACKOUT:

What happens when all the lights in London go out, and all the power switches off? What happens when a city is brought to its knees? Jake Tanner's about to find out. And he's right in the middle of it.

Download *Blackout*

EYE FOR AN EYE:

Revenge is sweet. But not when it's against you. Not when they use your family to get to you. Family is off-limits. And Jake Tanner will do anything to protect his.

Download *Eye For An Eye*

MILE 17:

Every year, thousands of runners and supporters flock to the streets of London to celebrate the London Marathon. Except this year, there won't be anything to ride home about.

Download *Mile 17*

THE LONG WALK:

The happiest day of your life, your wedding day. But when it's a royal wedding, the stakes are much higher. Especially when someone wants to kill the bride.

Download *The Long Walk*

THE ENDGAME:

Jake Tanner hasn't been to a football match in years. But when a terrorist cell attacks his favourite football stadium, killing dozens and injuring hundreds more, Jake is both relieved and appalled — only the day before was he in the same crowds, experiencing the same atmosphere. But now he must put that behind him and focus on finding the people responsible. And fast. Because another attack's coming.

Download *The Endgame*

The Jake Tanner Terror Thriller Series:

Full-length novels, following Jake through Counter-Terrorism Command, where the stakes have never been higher.

STANDSTILL:

The summer of 2017. Jake Tanner's working for SO15, The Metropolitan Police Service's counter terrorism unit. And a duo of terrorists seize three airport-bound trains. On board are hundreds of kilos of explosives, and thousands of lives. Jake quickly finds himself caught in a cat and mouse race against time to stop the trains from detonating. But what he discovers along the way will change everything.

Download Standstill

FLOOR 68:

1,000 feet in the air, your worst nightmares come true. Charlie Paxman is going to change the world with a deadly virus. His mode of distribution: the top floor of London's tallest landmark, The Shard. But only one man can stop. Jake Tanner. Caught in the wrong place at the wrong time. Trapped inside a tower, Jake finds himself up against an army of steps and an unhinged scientist that threatens to decimate humanity. But can he stop it from happening?

Download Floor 68

JOIN THE VIP CLUB

Your FREE book is waiting for you

Available when you join the VIP Club below

Get your FREE copy of the prequel to the DS Tomek Bowen series now at jackprobynbooks.com when you join my VIP email club.

ABOUT THE AUTHOR

Jack Probyn is a British crime writer and the author of the Jake Tanner crime thriller series, set in London.

He currently lives in Surrey with his partner and cat, and is working on a new murder mystery series set in his hometown of Essex.

Don't want to sign up to yet another mailing list? Then you can keep up to date with Jack's new releases by following one of the below accounts. You'll get notified when I've got a new book coming out, without the hassle of having to join my mailing list.

Amazon Author Page "Follow":
    1. Click the link here: https://geni.us/AuthorProfile
    2. Beneath my profile picture is a button that says "Follow"
    3. Click that, and then Amazon will email you with new releases and promos.

BookBub Author Page "Follow":
    1. Similar to the Amazon one above, click the link here: https://www.bookbub.com/authors/jack-probyn
    2. Beside my profile picture is a button that says "Follow"
    3. Click that, and then BookBub will notify you when I have a new release

If you want more up to date information regarding new releases, my writing process, and everything else in between, the best place to be in the know is my Facebook Page. We've got a little community growing over there. Why not be a part of it?

Facebook: https://www.facebook.co.uk/jackprobynbooks

Printed in Great Britain
by Amazon